PRAISE FOR

Every Woman Deserves An Adventure

'Provocative and entertaining . . . bawdy, delightfully funny
novel by a friendly (to men) feminist with some serious
points to make about the changed life of a woman now that
she no longer needs marriage as the sole path to security
and respectability'
Daily Express

'A thoughtful and witty first novel'
Daily Telegraph

'Both an entertaining satire on contemporary sexual
mores . . . and a touching portrait of a woman's search
for self-respect'
Vogue

'Yvonne Roberts is a natural. She's wonderful; the wittiest,
most inventive novelette writer in ages'
Image Magazine

'A spirited caper'
Options

'Funny, topical and sexy . . . A first novel which has the
smell of success'
Publishing News

'An amusing look at life after monogamy'
Company

Yvonne Roberts

The Trouble With Single Women

MACMILLAN

First published 1997 by Macmillan
an imprint of Macmillan Publishers Ltd
25 Eccleston Place, London SW1W 9NF
and Basingstoke

Associated companies throughout the world

ISBN 0 333 66936 3

1 3 5 7 9 8 6 4 2

A CIP catalogue record for this book is available from
the British Library.

Typeset by SetSystems Ltd, Saffron Walden
Printed and bound in Great Britain by
Mackays of Chatham plc, Chatham, Kent

To Meg and Rob Evans, Valerie, Margaret and Gaynor

ACKNOWLEDGEMENTS

My thanks to Jacqueline Korn for her continued support and guidance; to Ania Corless for her hard work; to Ian Chapman and my editors, Suzanne Baboneau and Arabella Stein, whose enthusiasm and professional skills are much appreciated.

It is always incomprehensible to a man that a woman should ever refuse an offer of marriage.

Jane Austen

'I can't explain myself, I'm afraid sir, because I am not myself, you see.'

Lewis Carroll,
Alice in Wonderland

Chapter One

ADAM WILLIAMS'S sock drawer told Fiona Travers all she needed to know about her possible future.

It would offer no wicked little deviations, no sudden bursts of romantic whimsy or clashes of passion; just the unremitting certainty that as it was today, so it would be tomorrow; safe and orderly and unsurprising.

Still, Fee told herself, shouldn't that hold its own attractions for an unattached woman of thirty-seven like herself?

Adam pulled his drawer open a little further, hunting for the small box he had hidden earlier. Fee's gaze continued to take in thirty-one pairs of identical dark-blue socks, lying in rows, each pair folded into an identical ball, each a giant navy marble.

'No odd socks?' Fee asked, knowing the answer.

'If you lost a sock now and then,' Adam replied, smiling in a way that frankly, turned Fee's stomach, 'I wouldn't mind at all.

'So, how about it then?' he pushed. 'I think you'd agree we tick along nicely. And it's all right, isn't it? You know . . .' he glanced towards the bed.

Fee nodded vigorously in agreement. 'All right' was exactly the right assessment; no more, no less.

Intercourse with Adam was the equivalent of a Janet and John book; simple, with a lot of repetition. Just like his socks.

In the several months since they had first met, only once had Fee attempted to inject a little variation in bed.

'Are you trying to tell me something?' Adam had immediately

1

asked. At least give him marks for astuteness, Fee had thought to herself. He had then, disconcertingly, rummaged under the bed and produced a spiral-bound notebook and pencil.

'Start talking,' he had instructed, pencil poised.

'Let me read what the others have said first,' Fee teased.

'If you can't say it, draw it,' Adam demanded, his engineering background coming to the fore. He had shoved the notebook into her hands.

Fee stared at the page. Draw it? How do you draw subtlety, sensuousness, sensitivity? Come to that, how do you draw disappointment and boredom? And how do you sketch the unease at realizing that while virtually everyone else of your years is married with two children and a mortgage you are hurtling towards middle age, *on your own*.

Some people assumed that Fee's solitary state was the consequence of rejection: an unwanted woman. In truth, it wasn't so much rejection that had been the pattern of her love life so far – as mismatch.

Those who fancied Fee Travers she actively despised (not least for their poor taste). Those for whom she yearned treated her . . . Fee searched for the appropriate word. It didn't require much thought.

'Shabbily' probably summed it up, she told herself cheerfully. And still she came back for more.

The notebook that Adam had given her was already decorated with a frieze of his doodles. A series of boxes, each identical. Box after box after empty box.

It was at this point, surrounded by navy-blue socks and courted by a man who was too eager to please, that Fee finally acknowledged what she had been trying to avoid for several months: the time had finally come to grow up.

'So, what do you say?' Adam had closed the sock drawer, and now held something clenched in his left fist. At the same time, he was using his right hand to pat strands of Fee's hair back into place. He preferred his women reasonably tidy.

He continued, 'We could make an announcement on your birthday. It's soon, isn't it? We've still got time to get it into the paper.'

'Why on earth would we want to make an announcement?' Fee thought to herself. Who would give a damn? Apart, of course, from her mother. And, of course, Claire.

Claire was nearly forty – not the ideal age to be abandoned to bob about on a sea of circumstance, waiting for someone, anyone, to throw the lifebelt of love.

Didn't she and Claire rely on each other? Single, together?

How would Claire react? Fee already knew the answer. She would smile, say congratulations, wonderful, so happy for you. All the words you're supposed to shower on a best friend in such a moment of triumph. Then, out would come the truth.

'How could you do this to me, Fee? How could you be so selfish? So unthinking? So *treacherous*? Don't you think of anyone apart from yourself?'

Fee smiled.

'Why are you smiling?' Adam asked seriously. 'Is it my socks?'

Adam had pale-brown hair, hazel eyes, a slightly bulging fore-head and very good teeth. In fact, it was Helen, Fee's mother, who had pointed out the state of his teeth. Probably because she couldn't think of much else to say about him. Adam was not as attractive as he imagined.

He was thirty-seven. He had his own house, car and a well-paid job as an executive in an oil company. He could cook, sew, clean. He wanted a wife now, Fee suspected, not to make his life complete but to prove to himself that he was no longer a little boy; not so much romance as rites of passage.

On their second meeting, Adam had announced to Fee that he was ready for Commitment. He had made it sound as attractive as an indefinite stay in Broadmoor. Since then, Fee had found Adam's quirks increasingly difficult to overlook.

For instance, he placed little muslin caps over his open jam and honey jars and became quite cross if Fee forgot to do likewise. The surfaces in his kitchen had to be bare; no knick-knacks, milk bottles or stray cornflakes packets allowed. All his boxer shorts were folded in the same manner by the woman who cleaned and ironed. And Adam occasionally had a certain way of talking to Fee that irritated her profoundly.

'I can see my little girl is getting tired,' Adam had been known to remark in company. 'It's time to take her home.'

Fee would take him to one side and point out that she was not 'his'; she was not 'little', she was not tired and she was certainly not going home.

Adam would then apologize profusely and that to her shame made her feel even more – well, she had to admit, even more *contemptuous*.

Adam's problem was that he made himself too available. He was too decent, too *willing*. Fee preferred more of a challenge.

Still, she was fond of him. Fond enough to keep seeing him; fond enough to remain vigilant in case her heart might suddenly leap or her skin might register an electric shock or she might receive some other signal that Adam Williams had miraculously become The One.

So far, love had proved elusive. And just before Adam's proposal, Fee had begun to wonder whether the fondness she felt for him was not, in fact, desperation – heavily disguised, of course.

'So what's it to be?' Adam demanded again, agitated, peering into Fee's face. During the most intimate moments, he frequently talked as if he was propped up in the pub. ('Fancy another?' he'd occasionally ask after a brief raid on Fee's anatomy.)

'Marriage? Yes or no?'

Fee said nothing but reopened the drawer and scooped up an armful of socks. She threw them in the air and, as they fell like confetti, she whooped loudly.

Adam, unsettled by the sudden disorder, nevertheless smiled, relieved.

'So I take it that's a yes?' he asked.

'You know something?' he continued, now on his hands and knees, crawling around anxiously in search of wayward socks, 'I only want what's best for you . . . And I'm sure I can make you happy. Can't I?' he added, unnerved by Fee's continuing silence.

He stopped sock-hunting and looked at Fee. She was now sitting on the bed, smiling distractedly into the distance. He told himself there was still time to back out. He reappraised the situation. Fee wasn't pretty but she had well, *something*, in a quiet, quite classy kind of way. Something that wouldn't date too rapidly.

But why hadn't she spoken? Why hadn't she shrieked, thrown her arms around his neck and said yes, Adam, yes and thank you, thank you, thank you? Perhaps relief and gratitude had sent her into a state of shock?

The previous three women he had taken out had been *voracious* to marry him – and they hadn't even hit thirty. Quite honestly, Adam told himself, even if he hadn't been eligible, which he clearly was, could Fee afford to bloody well play about like this?

Choice, after all, is a young woman's game – always has been, always will be.

'See here,' Adam said, pointedly looking at his watch and trying a different tack. 'Can we get this over? I'm a bit pushed for time—'

Fee smiled on as if, well, as if she could see something on that bloody blank wall. Adam took a long second look at his intended wife. Perhaps he'd been too hasty after all. Perhaps she was a little bit, well, unstable? A little bit too career-minded, for his taste. Even, at times, a touch too opinionated?

'Dreaming of a white wedding?' Adam asked, nervousness making his voice a good deal higher than usual.

Fee examined the man who had suggested that they spend the rest of their lives together. Or, at least, a respectable length of time.

Her mother would love him as a son-in-law. To be frank, she would love anyone as a son-in-law for Fee, this late in the day.

Fee's sisters had already remarked on Adam's finer virtues. And Fee? She knew Adam could probably grow on her. She knew that it probably made sense to say yes.

The man under surveillance cleared his throat, nervously. 'Perhaps, there's something you haven't told me?'

'Not in the way that you mean,' Fee answered obliquely.

'Is there someone else? Someone I know?' Adam persisted, unsettled by her continuing evasiveness.

He mentally cursed the fact that he would have to begin the hunt for a companion all over again – unless, of course, he could revive interest in that midwife with the red hair and legs that felt like a baby's woollen blanket?

Fee belatedly noticed the small jeweller's box in Adam's hand.

'Tell me,' Fee asked cryptically. 'Have you ever come across the man they call The Lone Ranger?'

'Of course I have,' Adam replied crossly. 'But what's he got to do with us?'

'A lot more than you might imagine,' Fee replied, giving to Adam what appeared to be a very odd smile. 'A whole lot more.'

'You lived in Manchester, didn't you, Fee?' interrogated Gill Booth, sitting at the top of her dining-room table, two nights later.

The walls were avocado green and decorated with menus of restaurants that Gill and her husband, Simon, had visited during the course of their ten-year marriage. As the anniversaries passed, and children arrived, so the venues had become noticeably less exotic. A menu from the Pizza Express was the latest addition.

Gill turned to Philip Cross, a pixie of a man sitting on her left. An excess of energy made him constantly fidget as if he had a hotplate fitted to his chair.

Philip was also clearly the kind of man who charmed with his personality since his features looked as if they had been ordered at random from several different mail-order catalogues; nothing quite fitted or matched.

Fee had known at 8.15 p.m., as soon as she met Philip, that even if she had been looking, *it was not going to happen*. Gill always said Fee ought to suspend this 'instant-judgement lark'.

'At your age, you have to start giving the six-out-of-ten men a chance,' Gill constantly warned. 'Or you'll pay the price.'

'Look at Simon and me,' Gill would say by means of encouragement. 'Nobody thought we would get on—'

Fee was too considerate to point out that 'Nobody' had increasingly been proven right.

In Fee's view, attraction for another human being was as irrational as looking for a house to buy. As soon as you crossed the threshold, you knew: this wasn't the one. So why bother to examine the plumbing, the wiring and the knocked through lounge?

'You know Manchester, don't you, Fee?' Gill continued, determined to spoonfeed conversation to her guests.

'Well,' Fee replied equably, 'I ought to. As you know, I was born there—'

On the phone earlier, Gill had sworn that this time she wasn't trying to fix Fee up. It just so happened that Simon had wanted Philip to come to supper as they'd just begun to work together. It was pure coincidence that it was the same Tuesday that Gill had organized with Fee.

'By chance,' Gill had discovered that Philip was forty-four, divorced for three years, he had one adopted teenage son and he was solvent. But, according to Simon, only just.

He had no anti-social diseases, perversions or latent tendencies of which Gill knew. She wasn't entirely sure because this had come secondhand from Simon and, 'Men don't discuss the nitty-gritty about themselves, do they?'

*

'Well now,' Gill continued doggedly, as she passed around bread rolls, 'Fee lived in Manchester for a long time, and you, Philip, lived in Dumfries, so *haven't* you got a lot in common?'

'Such as what?' asked Fee, smiling. Gill looked surprised. Normally, Fee played the game.

'What have we got in common?' Fee repeated mildly.

'Well,' said Gill, drawing a map in the air with her soup spoon. 'Well, you've got the North for a start. I mean, you both lived in the North . . . And Simon tells me you adore cooking, Philip? Fee loves it too – '

'No, I don't,' Fee smiled again.

What *was* wrong with the woman, Gill thought crossly.

When Fee was living with Bill, Gill had been relatively content. The couple split up after five years, and from that moment, Gill had found herself increasingly obsessed with 'getting Fee sorted'.

Two years on, the woman needed to be tied up, or down, for everybody's peace of mind. Especially Gill's.

Gill read the *Daily Mail*. She knew what happened when you invited single career women to sup at your table. They stole your husband.

Although, to be fair, Fee had always appeared extremely reluctant to spend any time with Simon at all, let alone run off with him.

Gill fluctuated between concern as to precisely why Fee didn't fancy her husband – was there something wrong with him? And a conviction that all this indifference was a cover for some torrid affair between the two that she had so far failed to expose. A third possibility, of course, was that there was something seriously amiss with Fee.

Over nearly fifteen years of close observation, since Gill and Fee and Claire had first shared a flat, Gill had yet to uncover in Fee any trace of the sexual abuse, frigidity, shyness, lesbianism or physical abnormalities that might explain why Fee had always been so damned, well, *contrary* when it came to men. Or why – infuriatingly – Gill always seemed compelled to weigh up her own lot in life by what was happening to Fee.

They couldn't be more different, for God's sake.

Gill had always found Fee unsettling.

'You lack direction,' Gill would instruct her friend sternly. 'Decide what you want and go for it.'

'Why?' Fee would ask mildly. 'Why not let things happen?'

'Because it will all pass you by,' Gill would say. And that's exactly what had occurred, Gill told herself with some satisfaction.

Fee had a good job, a car, probably a bit in the bank, but she didn't have A. N. Other. Or children. Or family life. She wasn't *wanted*.

When Fee, Gill and Claire had first met, Fee, then a teacher, was the drifter. Claire was a junior headhunter who fully expected that, at some point, she would take delivery of a husband, two children, a (preferably dead) mother-in-law, a Volvo, a comfortable house, a pension and a couple of labradors.

Gill, in contrast, neither drifted nor placed her faith in fate handing out the right cards. She plotted.

At twenty-one, Gill had a blueprint. She had a rolling five-year plan for life.

On cue, at twenty-two, she became a junior tax adviser to a chain of banks. At twenty-three, she bought her own flat and Claire and Fee became her lodgers. At twenty-four, she met Simon and, at twenty-five, she married him. He was an architect who was five years older.

At thirty, right on schedule, Persephone arrived. A boy was again due at thirty-three, but twins, Ivo and Euan, arrived 3 years later, the only hiccough in her plan so far. Now, at thirty-nine, Gill was aware that something she had never experienced in her life before had begun to trouble her. Gill was having Doubts.

Doubts, for instance, about Simon. Had she married the wrong man? She'd spotted him as a high-flyer but recently there'd been a couple of alarming crash landings, workwise.

Gill had doubts too about the wisdom of having children. Or, to put it more bluntly, Gill wondered how she had managed to produce offspring with whom she had so little in common?

People had trial marriages these days: why, for God's sake, couldn't they have trial children? She would have returned her three within the first fourteen days.

Gill had assumed that she would 'do' full-time motherhood as efficiently as she had tackled her career. So why this incandescent almost uncontrollable rage whenever she encountered a childfree woman?

She didn't resent men at all, with or without children; but *women* without children, well it was just so unfair . . . Nobody had prepared her for quite *how* unfair. They didn't know what it was like to face the sleepless nights, the demands on times, the agony of constrained ambitions and a dying social life.

'Mummy—' Persephone yelled from upstairs, 'Muuu-uuuummy—'

'Simon,' Gill said tartly. 'Percy wants you—'

'Like a hand, dear?' Simon asked mildly as he returned to the table a few minutes later. Gill was dunking the soup ladle into the tureen with all the force of a lifeboat hitting the sea in a Force Eight gale. Simon wiped a few drops of soup from his face.

'Of course I want a hand,' Gill responded waspishly. 'I need several bloody hands.'

Gill realized her guests were inspecting her with voyeuristic interest – could this be the making of a marital row? So she quickly added, for their reassurance, 'Ha, ha, ha.'

Gill glanced at Fee. She had dark brown hair, cut in a bob and shining. Well, it ought to shine. Fee could wash it seven times a day if she so chose. Gill's hair never shone – not since the birth of the twins.

Fee was slimmish. She had an olive complexion, almond eyes

and no broken veins. Gill had two which left a thin red trace along the side of her nose, a baby's autograph – the scars of a marathon first labour.

When Gill and Fee were in their twenties, Gill had always said that Fee failed to make the most of herself. She wore little make-up, preferred jeans and hated jewellery.

Fee still believed less was best and Gill had to concede that it gave her a clean, uncluttered look. Gill, in contrast, had always regarded herself as 'an accessories person'. Now she felt more like a jumble sale waiting to happen. Fee wasn't drop-dead stunning, but, Gill conceded generously, you could watch her without wincing.

'Still,' she reminded herself, savagely splashing soup down the front of her long, flowing, purple and black, Monsoon dress, bought for her second pregnancy.

'*I* am the fortunate one—'

Tonight, in addition to Philip Cross and Fee, Gill and Simon had invited Adrian and Moira Padstow. Adrian was a vet with his own practice. He had always dreamt that he would limit his family to two children, so he could retire early and live on a mountaintop in Spain. Once Moira had discovered she was, in her opinion, a natural mother, the family had stopped only at her fifth pregnancy.

Moira was now into phrase two of her life. After being 'a vocational wife' for far too long, she was into space.

'Space for aerobics, massage, facials, walking in Tibet, that kind of thing—'

Her husband, overflowing from his chair with exhaustion and self-neglect, rubbed his eyes as if in weary disbelief that he had managed to ensnare himself in such marital feudalism: he slaved, while his wife flowered.

'I don't suppose you bother to cook much, do you?' Moira addressed herself to Fee. 'I mean, who bothers if they're on their own?'

The woman's speckled salt 'n' pepper hair, cut very short, stuck

11

up like a cockatoo's crest. She wore a long black Lycra dress and so many silver bangles on each arm that each time she gesticulated it sounded as if the cutlery drawer had been thrown across the room.

'Me, I'd be hopeless living alone, far too neurotic,' Moira gave a little shudder. 'Don't get me wrong, being in a couple isn't easy. We certainly have our ups and downs. Don't we, Adrian?'

Her husband raised his eyebrows in a neutral response.

Moira continued, assuming affirmation. 'We have our ups and downs but at least we do it *à deux*. Life matters so much more when you're one of a pair . . . *together*—'

She elongated the word as if to cover her entire marriage in protective tarpaulin. 'I think I'm just one of those people God never intended to be single,' she added smugly.

Fee was not unfamiliar with this line of conversation. She'd heard it from her mother, Helen, for decades. Helen believed that marriage meant the end of a woman's hopes, health and happiness. But for a woman not to be married was infinitely worse.

'We compromise a great deal. I mean, what marriage isn't based on compromise? Isn't that right, Adrian?' Moira clanged as she waved her right arm in the direction of her husband.

'If you say so, darling,' Adrian wiped his eye – a tear? Or a drop of soup?

Moira beamed at Fee. 'Don't you ever worry about becoming just a tad selfish, set in your ways, you know the kind of thing I mean?' she asked. 'And what about children?'

'Cow,' Fee thought. 'Why don't I tell her I had to have a hysterectomy at twenty and then see how she sweats her way out of that?'

Moira pressed on. '*Everybody* wants children. They can be horrible little blighters but they make one's life. Don't they, Adrian, Philip, Simon . . . Gill?'

Moira looked around the table. Gill was missing. Having despatched Simon to the kitchen for more wine, she had reluctantly left the table to deal with Percy upstairs.

'I mean, otherwise what's it all for . . .?' Moira looked around again for confirmation. 'And I expect you've got that biological clock ticking merrily away, eh?' She leaned across the table and patted Fee's hand; barbed wire disguised as comfort.

'No, there's nothing quite like a strong union of two,' Moira pronounced, as Gill returned to the table. 'Don't you think so, Gill?'

Gill smiled absent-mindedly by way of reply and shouted over her shoulder in the direction of the kitchen, 'Simon, I asked you to open another bottle of wine, not drink the bloody thing out there—'

Then, just in case her guests might acquire the wrong idea, she added, 'Darling.'

'I mean it take years to build up harmony and understanding,' Moira was now addressing Philip. He ignored her and stared intently into his soup bowl filled with transparent beige liquid.

Moira raised her voice several decibels. 'What I say is, if—'

Her words were interrupted by Philip Cross jiggling excitedly on his chair and waving his soup spoon triumphantly in the air.

'I've got it! I've got it! I know what it is,' he almost shouted. 'It's onion, isn't it? I'm damn sure it's onion . . . See, there's a bit . . .'

Gill stared at Philip nonplussed. Was he trying to be funny? Or plain rude? This was always a problem when you invited unknowns to your table: you never knew how they should be *read*. Unexpectedly, something large and juicy within Gill suddenly burst.

She leapt up from the table and pointed an accusing finger at her husband.

'You told me he liked soup,' she barked. 'You didn't ask him, did you? Christ, it's not too much to ask is it? All you had to say was, "Philip, how do you feel about soup?"'

'More to the point, "how do you feel about onion bloody soup?"'

'Well?' Gill bellowed at Simon while the rest of the group fell silent. 'Did you ask him? Well . . .?'

Each guest turned simultaneously to observe their host.

'God, Gill,' Simon Booth said quietly. 'Give me a break.'

Philip broke the tension.

'So you lot feel fulfilled, do you?' he queried, looking amiably around the table as Gill began to slam empty soup bowls together.

'I'm surprised,' he added mildly. 'I lived with someone for seventeen years and for much of the time, I felt stifled, irritated, trapped, depressed, frustrated, put down, ignored, taken for granted, cuckolded, but I don't recall being fulfilled. No, that must have passed me by.'

Adrian smiled broadly. Moira's bangles jingled a small protest.

'I agree with Philip,' Fee found herself saying. 'I used to live with someone too – and it was quite nice a lot of the time . . . but I don't think I felt fulfilled either. If anything, when I was with Bill, I sort of felt . . . half there . . . if you know what I mean?'

Fee turned to Philip, who was nodding his head vigorously in agreement.

Triumph swept over Gill's face. She beamed at them both, her previous mood forgotten.

'So you two *do* have something in common, after all,' she said, smiling broadly. 'See, what did I tell you, Simon? I *knew* Philip and Fee would find a little spark—'

The evening ended early. Fee made the first move, followed by Philip. As they both waited for their coats in the hall, he suggested casually, 'Why don't I take your number?'

Automatically, Fee began to rummage for a pen in her bag and then stopped. *She didn't have to do this any more.*

No more waiting; waiting for a man to extend the first invitation; waiting for Mr Right to appear; waiting for life to suddenly change gear; waiting for the promised phone call; forcing herself to give no-hopers, the six-out-of-ten men, the benefit of the doubt. *No more waiting.*

In terms of compatibility, Philip was, in truth, probably a two-out-of-ten man. But now it no longer mattered. *She didn't have to bother.*

'Take my number? I don't think so,' Fee smiled sweetly. 'I'm thinking of starting afresh. A new beginning – well, kind of a new beginning.'

'Emigrating? You're not joining the great exodus to South Africa, are you? Everyone's going there now it's kosher.' For the first time, Philip appeared genuinely interested.

'A new beginning . . .?' Gill let out a shriek and wrapped her arms around Fee.

'Ooooh, Fee! Why didn't you say? It's Adam, isn't it? He's proposed. Oh how marvellous!' Gill pushed Fee back into the sitting room.

'Did you hear that, Simon? Oh, Fee, you should have said. Well, it's taken you long enough – but welcome to the club. Oh, I'm so relieved . . . for you, I mean.'

'What did I always tell you, Simon? I always said Fee would settle down one day, didn't I? At heart, she's just an old-fashioned girl. Nothing wrong in that, eh? Well done, Fee.' Gill was dribbling in her enthusiasm. 'Sooner or later, a girl's gotta do what a girl's gotta do, isn't that right, everybody?'

Fee stared at the semi-circle of expectant faces, hitched for too long to hijacked hopes. Then, very faintly, she heard the distant thunder of hoofs.

'You're right, Gill,' Fee smiled. 'A girl's gotta do what a girl's gotta do.'

Chapter Two

F EE STOPPED outside Adam's unlit terraced house.
  She hadn't intended to make this detour but, after leaving
Gill's and Simon's, she'd decided that starting afresh can go stale if
delayed too long. And the poor man deserved an answer.

A second car, a pale lemon MG, was parked next to Adam's
BMW in the drive. It had an immaculate interior; no sweet papers,
parking tickets, money-off coupons, empty Coke cans, old newspapers or broken umbrellas. It did have two matching white teddies,
one with a pink bow, one with a blue bow, sitting in the rear
window.

'Now, *this* is more his type,' Fee thought. Then she recalled
that Adam had told her that his cousin was coming for a couple of
days.

If she rang the doorbell, Fee knew she would be expected to
stay. She ripped a piece of paper out of her address book, wrote a
short note and dropped it through the door.

'Well, that's all straightened out as tidily as Adam would like,'
Fee told herself as she drove off. 'And not much self-inflicted harm
done. For once.'

At 5 a.m., Fee was woken by the slamming of doors, running feet
and the sound of breaking glass.

She went into the sitting room and opened the French windows
which led on to the balcony of her second-floor flat. The flat was

one of five in a large, converted, Victorian nursing home. The street below was deserted.

A spider's web of fractured glass filled the windscreen of her Fiat. The right wing blistered and bubbled, the paint peeling away like some grotesque half-completed facial.

Adam?

'God,' she said to herself. 'Perhaps he's more interesting than I realized. Come to that, perhaps I'm more interesting than I realized.'

Then she thought again. Adam saw passion as European and highly suspicious. It couldn't be him.

His former girlfriend? Gill paranoid, as ever, about Simon? The cousin in the lemon MG?

'Fee? Fee? Are you in there, Fee?'

Someone was banging on the door and Fee recognized the voice. Will Evans lived in the flat above hers.

She and Will had met when they were both teaching. Will later moved into advertising and married. He and his wife, Lucy, had split up two years ago when both were thirty-six because she had wanted children and Will emphatically didn't.

Fee had helped him to get a job in the company for whom she worked. He, in turn, had suggested to her that she look at the flat below his when it became vacant just after she split up with Bill. Now, when both were without partners, they'd spend time together platonically.

Except that Will was rarely without a partner. Having experienced years as part of a monogamous couple, he was now a born-again boyfriend, changing women with increasing rapidity.

'Fee?' Will asked again, as if he was in doubt that it was really her. He was standing at the door, barefoot, in his dressing-gown and looking seriously disturbed. His normal demeanour was relaxed. So much so that some mistook his casualness for superficiality. Fee liked to believe she knew better.

Will had a long, red, livid graze down one side of his face. In his hands was an empty can of something that smelt strongly of acid.

'I'm so sorry,' he apologized.

'Touching up your scratches?' Fee enquired, indicating the can.

Even as she spoke, a figure in a long dark coat charged up the stairs behind Will. Screaming, it leapt on his back. Will toppled forward, falling heavily on Fee. Three bodies, entwined in a shambolic human knot toppled into her hall.

Will and the figure disentangled themselves but Fee lay winded. As she did so, she observed a disturbing sight. Her giant copper urn, allegedly once employed by Tibetans to hold the ashes of the dead, but now used as a door stop, had begun to wobble.

Now, Fee watched, unable to move, as the urn gracefully, gradually, descended upon her head.

An hour later, Fee came to. She was lying on her sitting-room sofa. Will was by her side, his face now decorated with a second, deeper scratch. She had a phenomenal headache and a cold flannel on her forehead.

'I know now what they mean by hard-urn'd sleep,' she smiled feebly.

'What can I say?' Will shrugged his shoulders. He often affected an 'I can never quite get the hang of his Life thing' attitude, which added to his appeal for some women.

'You can say, "I'll make you a cup of tea, Fee, and pay for the car, Fee, and promise not to play leapfrog with my girlfriends in your hall again, Fee. And I'll take that bloody urn away, Fee." That would do for a start.'

'She's not my girlfriend,' he replied.

Fee tried to raise one eyebrow. It was a surprisingly painful exercise.

'She's somebody I once knew—' he added. 'Well, at least now she's somebody I once knew—'

'Yeh, yeh—' she waved his excuses away – not for the first time.

Later, Fee sat at the table, while Will made tea and toast in her kitchen. He was tall and thin with short, curly black hair, bony wrists and beautiful hands. Even in his dotage he would probably look like an overgrown schoolboy. Friends found him attractive, but to Fee he had been part of her life for so long he was just Will.

Ironically, now he worked with her, they saw less of each other. Fee had been at F. P. & Daughters for two years. It specialized in identifying future consumer trends and conceiving new products.

The F. P. stood for 'Future Perfect', the '& Daughters' was a marketing ploy, a tribute to the commpany's conviction that 'The Future is Female' – although, in the here and now, apart from Fee and her younger colleague, Diana Woods, females didn't figure at all at a senior level at F. P. & D.

Fee had recently been promoted to Projects Director. If, for instance, a chain of stores with a staid image decided that it needed to attract a younger age group to survive, F. P. & D. would carry out market research. It would also draw on its own resource centre, which tracked current tastes and possible future changes via two dozen categories of consumers.

Fee, for instance, was a MUSIC – mature unattached single; intelligent with a conscience. You didn't have to be very old to be mature – thirty was the threshold. And you didn't have to do very much to be classed as having a conscience – paying your parking fines would do.

F. P. & D. would then construct for the chain an entirely new image, an advertising campaign and a five-year sales plan. Fee would be in overall charge. Will was responsible for turning the research into something visual.

He had recently helped Fee to retarget a line of soups whose customers had been in two categories – dead or dying. On that occasion, F. P. & D. had labelled every tin 'earth-friendly' and sold it via a hi-tech television commercial that advocated that everybody should 'get canned'.

Soup drinking amongst fifteen to twenty-five olds had risen by 21 per cent. The only hiccup was a tendency by graffiti artists to change the 'a' in the slogan on hoardings to 'o'. Increasingly, Fee had found herself in sympathy with this sentiment.

Now, Fee watched Will as he meticulously buttered the toast, cutting the bread tidily into two triangles. She was more inclined to stick a dollop of butter in the centre of the slice, fold the bread in half and leave the dry bits uneaten. Will had patience, she didn't. According to Will, they had other differences too, fundamental differences.

'You want love,' he'd tease her. 'All single women past thirty seek love. Me? I want sex. And no babies. It's the male genes. I can't help myself. I'm a hunter. You're a nurturer.'

'But I don't want babies,' Fee would protest.

'Oh yes, you do,' Will would correct her firmly. 'You just won't allow yourself to say it.'

Will's view was that he'd been faithful to his wife for nine years – now it was time to play the field, run free from commitment. Fee had also been faithful to her former partner, Bill Summers, for the shorter time of five years. According to Will, what she now required was more of the same: another long-term relationship to replicate what had gone before.

'But why?' she would ask, puzzled.

'Because you're a woman – and that's what women are like. Except they won't admit it.' Will would duck even as he spoke to avoid whatever missile had come to Fee's hand.

*

'If I was to ask you what you looked for in a woman, what would you say?' she asked Will now, accepting a plate of neatly arranged toast.

'Easy,' he replied. 'I'd say, "Size 10. Age twenty-two. No emotional baggage."'

'That's ridiculous,' Fee protested mildly, abandoning her attempt to chew on the toast. The effort made her head ache even more.

'No, it isn't,' Will replied. 'What's wrong with being straight about your needs? I want beauty, no demands, no hang-ups. And definitely no assumptions that a relationship has a future.'

'Did the woman who took it out on my car assume a future?' Fee asked.

'I'm really sorry about your car,' Will replied. 'She thought it was mine. Mind you, the fact that she thought I'd choose anything as naff as a Fiat confirms my worst fears about her,' he smiled.

'Well,' Fee asked again, 'did she assume a future?'

'I know what she didn't want,' Will offered evasively. 'She didn't want the truth. Not many of you women do when—'

'Bullshit.'

'Look,' said Will. 'I want to be honest. I want to say to someone "You're really wonderful but I don't think there's much point in us meeting any more." I want to say that, but have you any idea what happens if I do?'

He rolled his eyes up to the ceiling. 'I'll tell you what happens, I'm called an emotional coward, immature, I'm told I don't know what I want, on and on and on. And all because I *do* know what I want, and it isn't her. Not sounding too brutal, am I?' he asked lightly.

'Yes,' Fee replied. She was never quite sure when Will was being truthful and when he was simply trying to provoke her. It was a tactic she recognized since she was fond of using it herself – particularly on her mother.

Will continued, 'Emotional mayhem is avoided if I lie. All I have to say is, "I'll give you a call," and everything is hunky-dory. Her pride is saved, I'm off the hook, no post-mortems. Truth is all that suffers.'

Fee picked up the cups and put them in the sink. 'You're a rat, Will,' she said. 'Just you wait until you're on the receiving end of that kind of treatment, then see how you like it—'

He handed Fee his empty plate. 'So I take it, you'd never resort to such tactics?' he challenged. 'You're always absolutely honest, above aboard, never any deception?'

'Of course I am. Well, at least, I try hard to be. It's only fair.'

'Lesson number one, Fee,' Will said patronizingly. 'Fairness doesn't come into relationships. Not, that is, if you intend to remain magnificently on top no matter how difficult the situation.'

'You're wrong,' Fee answered flatly.

'Lesson number two is even more painful,' Will continued, ignoring her reply. 'Lesson number two is that ten years from now, when I'm ready to settle down, I'll still be able to select a younger mate and have a couple of kids – but you?'

Will smiled and stepped sharply to one side as Fee grabbed a teacloth and threw it at his head.

'What I'm telling you is for your own good,' he admonished, wagging his finger. 'When it comes to the mating game, men have all the advantages. Bar none. And you, who keep banging on about the importance of female choice, when you find yourself at what, forty-five? fifty? – you'll discover that choice is a young woman's illusion.

'In short, my darling,' Will was enjoying himself, 'you'll be just another middle-aged casualty. On the shelf. An independent, modern woman – who just can't get a man. But all is not lost.' He paused dramatically, then dropped onto his knee at Fee's chair.

'Call it a day now, Fee,' he pleaded, theatrically. 'We were made for each other. I'll give up my life of shallow deceit and throw away the pleasures of young flesh, just to be with you—'

Fee dismissed him cheerily. 'You're a vain, arrogant, selfish bastard, Will Evans,' she said.

He affected disappointment. 'But I thought that was exactly the kind of man you fell for?' he protested.

'Real bastards, yes,' Fee answered. 'Your kind, no.'

An hour later, Will Evans, back in his own flat, ruefully examined the scars of the night in the bathroom mirror. It was the first time in his life that anyone had exacted physical revenge upon him. Will knew that the experience ought to have made him contrite, ashamed, regretful . . .

He traced the path of a scratch with one finger. As there was only him and his reflection discussing the issue, he could afford to be honest. The scratches made him feel good; a veteran. He was no longer an ex-husband with little previous experience. He was now a man who had Lived.

He smiled and, as if on cue, the telephone rang. It was just after 7 a.m. Only his ex-wife rang him at that hour. He picked up the receiver gingerly.

'Hi, Will, Hilly here. Hilly Byrne. Remember?'

He grimaced and then sucked in his breath at the pain from the scratches. He and Hilly Byrne had met via the Internet. Within days, they had arranged to have an early-evening drink. Within hours, they had discovered that while they had little else in common, they could have an alarmingly good time in bed.

Briefly, Will had even seriously considered that this standard of sex, unknown to him before, might be the perfect foundation for a second marriage. But the bits before and after copulation increasingly became a strain, so, after a few months, they agreed that it was time to say goodbye. Or rather, Will suggested it and Hilly Byrne had no choice but to agree.

Will had been grateful to the Internet for widening his sexual repertoire but now, many weeks later, he did not relish a post-modem relationship.

Hilly revealed, however, that she was making a purely professional call, in her capacity as a television director. Will listened and then chuckled.

'I've yet to meet one,' he remarked. 'But I'll pass her on if I do.'

'Fancy a drink, sometime?' he added; a little test, just to see if Hilly was still interested.

'No, thanks,' she replied brusquely. 'Right now, I'm into a career thing. You know how it is.'

For the next several hours, Will's thoughts kept returning to Hilly Byrne's breasts. He found it extremely annoying.

'Now *that* is a *real* bastard.'

Fee was on the phone to her mother.

Helen Travers looked expectantly at the telephone receiver as if it might signal whether Fiona was playing straight or not. She could never be quite sure with her youngest daughter.

Fee had just been told that Charlie Jackson, her brother-in-law, a builder, had refused to obey his wife's instruction to remove the spiral staircase he'd installed in the centre of his living room only a few weeks before.

'Can you imagine how your sister must be feeling?' Helen demanded of her daughter.

'Gutted. Absolutely gutted—' Fee replied, deadpan.

Helen frequently regaled her with stories of the married lives of her two older sisters, Veronica and Elizabeth; the generosity of their respective husbands; the magnificent décor of their family homes; the cost of their latest holiday; the beauty of their now grown-up children.

It was intended to whet Fee's own appetite for marriage. Helen found it very disturbing, to have a still unattached daughter in the family: *one in her late thirties.*

Now, coming up to her daughter's thirty-eighth birthday, Helen had decided that something serious had to be done.

For Fee's own good, of course.

*

Fiona Travers should have been born on April Fool's Day. It was only Helen's categoric refusal to push for an almost inhuman amount of time that ensured that Fee was born at seventeen minutes past midnight on 2 April. Helen had spent a great deal of her time since then continuing to try to hold her daughter back from almost anything other than matrimony.

She had agreed to Fee going to university – the first from either side of the family to do so – only because the daughter of the woman next door had met and married her husband in the final year of her degree course.

'Don't study so hard that you forget to look,' were Helen's parting words of advice to Fee.

For as long as her daughters could remember, Helen Travers had conversed in clichés and homilies, some of them homemade.

'You make your bed, you lie on it,' Helen would instruct her three daughters. And, when advocating if not tolerance then no surprise at male infidelity, 'Marriage wasn't made for monks.' Another favourite was, 'Don't dig deep, unless you can fix what you find.'

When her girls were young, they took these then incomprehensible remarks as evidence of the mysterious wisdom of adults. As each moved into their teens, they recognized them as echoes of Helen's own fearfulness.

Born just after the First World War, Helen had never ceased to find life dangerous. She was caught in an eternal dilemma.

Men were treacherous, but since a woman 'on the loose' was an even more unpredictable commodity, a sensible female acquired a husband as speedily as possible.

'Women go bad without the protection of a man,' Helen frequently said. All her experience told her that women who refused to fit into the mould paid a price. The fact that her own conformity had probably cost her even more dearly she could never afford to acknowledge. Instead, a permanent air of disappointment hung around her.

Others, Helen would say, 'without naming names', had let her down badly.

Veronica and Elizabeth had been born when Helen and her husband, Jim, a welder in the local railway works, were in their twenties. Fee was a late accident. Helen had been thirty-seven and deeply upset to discover she was pregnant for a third time.

Veronica and Elizabeth took after her side of the family. They adopted their mother's ambitions early.

Veronica, a bank clerk, had walked up the aisle at twenty-one. She then had two children. Elizabeth, a florist, was two years older when she became the bride of Charlie and she, too, became the mother of two.

They were delighted to find themselves, at a very young age, living happily ever after. Admittedly, Veronica was now going through a bit of an upset, as Helen preferred to phrase it, but then nothing in life is absolutely perfect.

Not even happy endings.

In Helen's opinion, Fee took after her father. And she couldn't get much more damning than that.

Jim Travers had coped with married life by retreating to a garden shed for much of his spare time.

There, in an armchair with an electric fire in winter, he read westerns and manuals on how to raise the perfect budgerigar. Helen wouldn't let him breed birds. Helen wouldn't let Jim do much of anything – except take the blame for all the disappointments she had had in life.

Jim disappointed her even in death. He had a heart attack at fifty-seven, reducing his pension considerably. Fee was eighteen when her father died. After he had gone, whenever she was home from university, she would spend a lot of her time in his shed, reading his westerns, escaping from Helen's constraining expectations.

In so far as you can love a man who had withdrawn so much into himself, Fee had loved her father. Not least because he had introduced her to The Lone Ranger.

As she grew older, Jim Travers became only the first of a number of elusive men for whom Fee would fall.

A final reason why Helen viewed Fee with uncertainty was because of that terrible business with Great Granny Vera.

Helen had known that Veronica and Elizabeth could never do a Vera; but Fee . . . well, who could tell?

So, from almost the minute she was born, Fee was criticized, chastised, and threatened with dire punishment, not so much because of what she had already done, but as a deterrent against what she *might* do.

'Good girls don't make trouble,' Helen used to say again and again. 'They accept that others know best. You're a good girl, aren't you, Fiona?'

Infuriatingly, even at three years of age, Fiona chose to remain silent.

Now, while part of Helen wanted to see Fee safe, secure, *settled*, part of her deep down also wanted to see her daughter go desperately, badly, wrong. Perhaps because, as much as Helen repressed the idea, she knew Fee was increasingly becoming the person *she* might have been.

And Helen wasn't at all sure how she felt about that.

'So you'll definitely be there on Saturday?' she asked Fee for what must have been the tenth time. 'You know your Emily hasn't asked everybody to be a godmother, she's asked you—'

At 3 p.m. the following Saturday, a christening would be held at the church of the Holy Trinity, South Welsden. Emily was Elizabeth's daughter, Fee's niece. The christening would be followed by champagne, rich fruitcake and smoked salmon on bruschetta brushed with black olive paste at the house of Emily's aunt and uncle, Veronica and Les Haslem, since they had by far the largest garden in the family.

'How's that nice man Adam?' Helen suddenly asked Fee, hoping to catch her offguard.

'He's away,' she lied, to deter further questions.

'Away where?' Helen asked suspiciously.

'Away for a bit. Working, you know, the usual—'

'So he'll be back for your birthday?' Helen probed further.

'It's none of my business, I know,' she began again. 'But Adam has a lot going for him. I told Mrs Jackson next door, he's absolutely besotted with you. And don't forget, none of us is getting any younger—'

Fee knew how to derail her mother.

'Well age didn't stop Vera, did it?' she asked casually. 'I mean she wasn't getting any younger when she changed her life, was she?'

'What?' Helen squeaked down the line.

'I was just saying that age didn't stop Vera getting into her stride,' Fee continued conversationally. 'I mean, she must have been well past her forties.'

'And what made you mention Vera out of the blue like that?' Helen asked tartly.

'Oh, nothing really. I was just thinking,' Fee replied casually, trying to keep the smile out of her voice.

'Well, don't,' Helen commanded tartly. 'Not if you know what's healthy.'

Later, as Helen Travers plumped the cushions on her settee as she did several times every day – she did so like visitors to see them *nice* – she told herself that everything would have been so much easier if Fee had been, well, *dimmer*. Like her sisters.

She was fully aware that friends, relatives, *people who mattered*, believed that it was she, Helen, who was somehow to blame for Fee's lack of a spouse.

This condemnation was a bitter disappointment, since, really, what mother could have done more? Helen herself had no doubts about who was the real cause. Jim and his ridiculous cowboys. And, of course, Vera.

Vera had done her bit too.

If young Travers family members were present, Vera was always discussed by the adults in a semaphore of sign language and raised eyebrows.

Fee was fourteen before she was finally given a complete description of her great grandmother's alleged sins. An aunt drank one too many rum and blackcurrants at a wedding and out it all came.

It was Fee's first realization that bad girls become legends – which, of course, good girls never do.

Great Granny Vera, from Jim's side of the family, so the saga went, had married at twenty. Her husband, Arthur, was eleven years older, and a fishmonger. They had seven children and everyone said what a lovely family they made.

Then, when the youngest child was nineteen, and Vera was fifty-four, she suddenly disappeared. A fortnight later, she got back in touch with the family to give them the news.

She had run off to Hove with a painter of thirty-five called Bobby. Bobby used to call in the shop every Friday for a small piece of skate. Later, everyone agreed that the size of Bobby's skate should have been a clue.

Vera also announced that she had no intention of coming home – it was time for her to enjoy herself. The children were welcome to visit at any time. Visit, Vera had stressed, not stay.

Freda, the youngest child, duly called on her mother against her father's wishes. She reported back on the horror of it all.

Bobby, a striking young man with a wardrobe full of handsome suits was, in truth, a *she* not a he. The couple looked and behaved like a married couple but they were actually two of the same.

There was no better half.

Vera had lost her head was the general consensus. Deserting her family would have been bad enough; living in sin too awful to contemplate; absconding with someone so much younger, a disgrace. But to set up home with a woman . . . excluding men . . . not even *needing* a man . . . how unnatural can you get?

How downright *thoughtless?*

What's more, Vera had the brass nerve to live blissfully with Bobby for another twenty-two years until her death, 'waited on hand and foot'.

Of course, nobody in the family went to her funeral. They considered Vera long gone.

From that point on, while Jewish boys were Barmitzvahed as an entry into adulthood, at what was considered an appropriate age, Travers girls were Vera-ed. They were instructed on the fall and decline of their fomerly respectable relative but, naturally, never told about the happy-ever-after.

Decades on, Vera's ripples were still visible in the family. That was why Helen had been so relieved when Fee had moved in with Bill Summers – and perturbed again when he'd moved out.

As for Fee, she had been aware from an early age that she was a source of disappointment to her mother. But what had only recently begun to dawn on her was how much Helen needed it that way.

Chapter Three

THREE DAYS later, at seven thirty on the evening of her thirty-eighth birthday, Fee ordered a third glass of wine. The woman who sat at the till of the otherwise deserted wine bar was performing the equivalent of an archaeological dig on her cold sore. She moved reluctantly into action.

'You should have had a bottle,' she said accusingly, holding the fresh glass by the stem and placing it in front of Fee.

'I didn't realize he was going to be late,' Fee felt bound to explain. The woman shrugged as if to say she couldn't care less what excuses her customers provided for their personal excesses.

Fee checked her watch for the umpteenth time. As she did so, the cuff of her jacket caught the glass and, in an effort to hold it steady, she emptied her handbag on to the floor. She was on her hands and knees when she spotted Paul Denning's legs.

'Playing hide and seek?' he smiled. She attempted to conceal a sudden surge of pleasure.

Her birthday present to herself had belatedly arrived.

Of course Paul was late. He was always late. Anyone who knew Paul was aware that he always arrived on the second train, never on the train he'd promised.

That was Paul.

Paul, of course, did not know that it was Fee's birthday. Dear God, no. If he had any idea that Fee had chosen to spend

31

a significant date on her calendar in his company, he would have fled.

What Paul demanded of Fee was exactly what Will asked of his women: no strings. From the outset, Paul had indicated that the only role he wanted in Fee's life was a small role, a bit part.

The bit that's fun and comes with no obligations, promises or long-term plans.

Fee, of course, not only accepted his terms, but acted as if they were entirely compatible with her own. The whole point of Paul's attraction for Fee was not that he was hard to get – he had proved remarkably easy – but that he was tricky to hold on to.

For as long as she could remember Fee's predilection had always been for Mr Wrong rather than Mr Right.

She'd moved in with Bill because she realized, with hindsight, that she'd sought respite from the volatility that had so far passed for her love life.

If anything, Bill had only stoked up Fee's addiction for unreconstructed bastards, like Paul.

'It's been too long,' Paul said, ordering champagne.

'Has it?' Fee countered.

In Paul's company, she was always slightly on edge. He loathed what he called 'neediness'. So she was constantly worried that her real feelings might suddenly escape and destroy what he clearly regarded as pleasant little encounters.

Or were they so pleasant?

The question caught Fee by surprise.

Paul playfully kissed Fee's ear lobe.

'I missed you. Tell me you missed me,' he instructed.

'Of course, I didn't miss you,' she replied lightly. 'Much too busy—'

*

Paul Denning was forty-five. He had told Fee that he had been very briefly married in his twenties and speedily divorced. He had no children. Now he was a successful and highly ambitious barrister who split his time between London and Newcastle.

They had met six months ago, when Fee's firm had sent her and Will Evans to Newcastle on business. On the journey back to London, after those first series of meetings, Fee had casually remarked to Will that she thought Paul Denning had a smooth taste in clothes. Will's view had been that not even money could stop Paul Denning looking like a wide boy.

Fee had mentioned, just in passing, that she thought Paul was good looking in a leonine way – strong features, a mass of black hair with flecks of white. Hair long enough to signal he was more at the radical than the conservative end of the bar.

Will said he thought Paul Denning was far too impressed with himself; not just concerned with his high profile but his side profile and full profile as well.

Fee said that Will had to concede that when Paul Denning was around, life moved up a gear; he was impatient, energetic, almost rude at times, but he got things done – and he was fun. The project had meant long hours, relieved only by numerous bottles of champagne which Paul Denning had insisted was the only accompaniment to bad, fast food.

'What do you really think of him?' Fee had asked Will.

'What do I really think?' Will had given a quizzical look.

'In the company of Mr Denning, only one word comes to mind. And that word is—' Will had paused as if giving the question serious thought. 'Yes,' he finally said. 'That word has got to be – tosser.'

'That's only because you don't know what he's really like,' Fee had responded. She had sounded so defensive it had taken them both by surprise.

'Oh and you think you do?' Will had sighed and shook his head in mock-despair.

'And I thought you were old enough to know better,' he'd added.

Leaving the bar, an hour later, Paul took Fee's hands and kissed them both. His finger traced her jawline. As gestures go, it was a cliché, but Fee felt shy, exposed.

It had been twelve days since their last meeting and Fee had heard from Paul only on the previous morning. Then, in his customary fashion, he had sent a fax to tell her of his time of arrival.

To tell her, Fee reminded herself. Not to ask if she was free. And what about an apology for his tardiness?

'So, what have you been doing?' Paul asked in the taxi, cupping his hand over her knee.

Adam did not know about Fee's relationship with Paul. If asked, Fee would have been honest. She had never pretended to Adam that he was the only man she was seeing.

'I haven't done much,' Fee said in answer to Paul's question. 'I've had my car vandalized by a jealous woman, I was asked out – sort of – by a small, dark divorcé called Philip, who certainly knows his onions . . . and I received a proposal of marriage—'

'An average week, all-in-all?' Paul remarked drily. Fee noted that he didn't even bother to ask how she had responded to the proposal. That was another man's business.

'Dead average,' Fee smiled back.

How she hated all his game-playing – except, of course, when she was ahead on points.

A little later, the taxi pulled up outside a small, expensive hotel in Kensington.

Paul Denning usually spent the night at Fee's flat. After the initial pleasure, she gradually began to object to his automatic assumption that all that was hers in the flat was also his: the telephone, the fax, the bathroom, the contents of the kitchen.

'No beers?' he'd said on one visit, petulantly, opening the fridge door. 'I thought you knew I was coming—'

He'd then thrown what could only be described as a tantrum. At first, Fee had thought he was joking. Then, she had done her best to mollify him, finally borrowing a six-pack of lager from Will upstairs.

In anyone else, such behaviour would have appalled Fee. For Paul, she provided excuses. Over-stressed; too much work; she had been thoughtless . . .

The visits only ever lasted a night, but once Paul had also spent the following day with her. It happened to be a Sunday and he'd enjoyed himself so much, Fee hadn't seen or heard from him for three weeks. She had known better than to pursue him.

Paul was nothing if not suspicious of his own feelings.

'So how do I rate?' Paul's tone was light-hearted. He and Fee were in the large circular bath in the hotel a couple of hours later. Playfully, he had been batting soap froths with his hands, aiming at Fee's breasts. Bastards always field trick questions, Fee reminded herself as she lay soaking; say nothing.

'You're mad about me, I can tell. Go on admit it,' Paul teased, but Fee knew his intention was more serious. 'Go on, be honest.'

Be honest? *Be honest?* Several intimate encounters with men like Paul had meant that Fee knew she was equipped with few survival skills that worked – except one. Never speak the truth about the depth of your feelings.

Too much demonstration of female affection and the man fled; too little and his ego wilted, so there was a real danger he would take it elsewhere for emergency treatment. The challenge lay in establishing precisely the right balance. It also meant the death of all spontaneity and hardly any relaxation.

'Go on, how much do you really like me . . .?' Paul was getting more persistent.

'Why do you want to know?' Fee teased. She knew exactly

what Paul wanted her to say. 'I love you.' The mystery was – why *now?*

'I miss you when you're not around.' Paul scrutinized Fee's face for a reaction. 'That surprises me.'

'Thank you,' Fee replied.

'It's thrown me offguard. I mean, I didn't really have to come down today. I came mainly because I wanted to see you.' Paul avoided Fee's eyes by busily turning on the hot water.

'You know me,' he continued. 'Work comes first. Don't feel safe unless I've got more on my plate than I can handle . . . Here,' he added. 'Turn round and I'll wash your back.'

'The trouble with me is that when I get in too deep, I get frightened and back out . . . I hate myself for it, but there it is. That's me—'

Fee almost didn't need to hear the rest of Paul's pitch. He couldn't deal with personal emotions disrupting his otherwise orderly agenda. If his feelings for her were becoming untidy, he would put a stop to it by turning *his* problem into *Fee's.*

Next, he would say that she *deserved* something more than he could give and so . . . It was a circuitous route but one that Fee had travelled before. It always led to the same abrupt ending.

Paul squeezed warm water from the sponge onto Fee's back and rubbed hard. 'I tell myself that you can do better than me. I know that, you know that.' He sounded totally unconvinced.

'I tell myself that you need, no, you *deserve*, a relationship that's going somewhere. You need a steady nine-to-five man.' Paul made security sound as attractive as halitosis.

He spent what appeared to be a very long time sponging her shoulders, then spoke again. 'Look, Fee, there's no way of putting this gently. I've thought about this long and hard. It's going to break my heart, but for your sake, perhaps it's best we call it a day . . . I can tell you're not over-involved yet, so let's go out on top. Say our goodbyes before there are tears.

'I mean, we've had a bit of fun, no harm done – yet. But there will be if we go on. So let's stay friends. What do you say?

You're not going to cry, are you?' His tone was more curious than caring.

No, Fee was not going to cry. She could manage that. She could always manage that. For a short time, at least. But, naturally, her heart had stopped; her stomach had dropped into the hotel's basement; her bottom lip was twitching like a gundog chasing rabbits in its dreams. She let her hair fall forward to hide the signs.

Then she found her voice, playing the game hard to the end, 'You offered to soap my back,' she said lightly. 'Not grate it.'

A few minutes later, the deed was done. Fee was surprised at how easy it had been. She'd heard the thunder of hoofs, smelt the damp leather – and out the words had come.

'You're absolutely right.' She was smiling steadily, fighting hard against all her instincts. Instincts that told her to persuade him to change his mind, ask him to give them a second try, not say goodbye.

Instead, she said, 'You're right, this isn't going anywhere and it never will. I've been telling myself that for a while now, but I suppose I've been too lazy to do anything about it. I've got a tendency to drift . . . At least, that's what my friends say.'

Paul watched her, perplexed. He hadn't expected this. Every other time he'd tried his little strategy, the woman had cried, pleaded, negotiated, and finally the relationship had moved into extra time.

The manoeuvre had clear advantages for Paul Denning. It kept the woman on her toes, it confirmed his supremacy and it allowed him to dictate future terms.

Fee was not reacting according to plan.

He grew angry, extremely angry. What the hell did she think she was doing, mucking him about like this?

'You want to end it,' he said petulantly, forgetting that it was he who had initiated the proposal. 'Fine. It's ended.'

*

Fee stood in the bedroom and hid her tears in a hotel towel the size of a shroud. This was a first for her. She had seized the initiative. Usually at this point she'd be begging and bawling, promising to change. Change precisely what, she didn't always know, but the vague suggestion of improvement was usually enough. Some men seemed to like that. And Fee almost always assumed it was her who should be doing the improving.

At this stage, she would experience such a deep sense of loss it would overwhelm the little rational thought that remained. She would pledge anything and everything. Only later, if the man agreed to resume the relationship and the initial panic at abandonment had subsided, would Fee ask herself, is this what I really want?

Now, for the first time she had changed the rules of the game. But so what? She was still in a situation in which she didn't want to be.

Next door, Paul continued to soak in the tub, his eyes closed, humming tunelessly.

Fee was dressed and just about to let herself out when he emerged from the bathroom. His mood had changed dramatically.

'You're not really leaving, are you?' he asked, affecting surprise.

'I thought you were staying the night?' he added casually, as if the official severing of their relationship was no cause to leave early. 'Come on, don't go.'

'Of course I'm going,' Fee replied carefully. She had intended to keep conversation to a minimum, aware of Paul's ability to ensnare her again. Instead, suddenly, the words poured out. Words triggered not by several hours with Paul, but years of making mistakes with men who each believed themselves unique – but who, to Fee, were all too depressingly similar.

'You said, "Be honest." But that's not something I am in your company. I'm never open, honest, spontaneous . . . I'm confused.' Fee paused.

'Confused is the word. I've reached a point when I don't know if I'm expecting too much from the relationship or not nearly enough. Don't worry', she suddenly added. 'I'm sure it's nothing to do with you. It's probably my own fault.'

Privately she cursed herself. Of course some of it was Paul's bloody fault. Why do women always take it upon themselves to accept emotional responsibility?

'It's my birthday,' she announced suddenly as if she expected that, like a magic wand, it would transform the situation. Paul made no response. Instead he pulled her down to sit on the bed next to him.

He carefully massaged the base of her neck. He had a towel around his waist and smelt wonderfully clean.

He lowered his voice. He found resistance arousing.

'Look, Fee, it's OK. We'll stop seeing each other *regularly*, if that's what you really want. But it doesn't mean we can't see one another now and then, does it? For old times' sake? Just an occasional bit of fun?'

He was right, Fee thought. A lot of it *would* be fun. Aimless fun. But at thirty-eight, was that the way she wished to spend her time? The fact that she had even begun to think in such a vein she found unnerving. Live for today was Claire's motto, and let fate take care of the rest.

Paul was trying to ease Fee out of her jacket.

'So why not stay tonight, Fee? No strings? We're adults, aren't we?' In one smooth manoeuvre, he kissed the end of her nose, grazed her nipple with his fingertips and glanced down at his watch.

Fee saw him check the time. He had probably calculated that it was too late to book in anyone else, so he might as well persuade her to stay.

This man has the depth and maturity of a cartoon character, she chastised herself. So why on earth did she fancy him – as she most certainly still did?

She wavered. Perhaps this *was* her fate. Perhaps, after all, she did deserve the bastards she attracted?

'Well?' said Paul, kissing her ear lobe. 'What's it to be?'

*

Two minutes later, standing alone in the hotel corridor, Fee couldn't stop the tears.

'Grief and pain is inevitable and temporary,' she told herself firmly. 'That's all it is. For once, you've taken a considered decision. Do what they tell you in books. Congratulate yourself.'

Still, the tears kept coming. Somewhere deep inside her, in a place that she rarely risked visiting, she had already begun to create a future for herself and Paul: companionship, support, intimacy, shared goals, friends, achievements. All interwoven with lace hearts and pink ribbons and never a cross word.

Fantasy, pure fantasy.

'You stupid woman.' She said the words out loud as she rested against the corridor wall. 'You stupid, stupid, woman—'

She fumbled for the lift button, and as she did so a crumpled envelope caught her eye. It lay by the fake art-nouveau wastepaper basket. Fee picked it up and some instinct made her smooth it flat. One word stood out.

It might as well have read, 'Fool.'

In his hotel room, Paul Denning was left feeling – what? Upset? Peeved? Disorientated?

That was it. He felt *disorientated*. This hadn't happened to him in a very long time. Perhaps he was losing his touch? He gave himself a quick once-over in the mirror. Seemed OK.

Paul felt his annoyance grow. Fee would be back. Making up was part of the female game. Of course, she'd be back.

This evening still presented a problem. He hated his own company. And he felt niggled, very niggled. He knew that he had allowed himself to be outmanoeuvred. For a man who prided himself on his manipulation of female sensitivities, this was a disturbing development.

He reassured himself. Hadn't a former lover once called him feline, so instinctive was his understanding of the female psyche?

He poured himself a whisky from the fridge. He'd leave an interval of time – several weeks – then take careful steps to prove to Fee how much she needed him.

After that, he'd dump her.

'Do her good, to know she can't always be in charge,' he told himself with almost infantile savagery.

For now, he knew exactly where to find reassurance, how to regain control.

He picked up the phone, dialled a number and waited. Satisfyingly, he did not have to wait very long. His wife answered almost immediately.

On the journey in the taxi back to her flat, Fee ran through what she had read in magazine after magazine on the subject of how to bail out from a bastard successfully.

She knew the theory inside out; it was the practice at which she always faltered.

For the first time in years, she had weighed up the situation and taken the sensible decision to save herself from the pain that she knew would be bound to come further down the line. Very grown up. So why no sense of triumph?

What she felt was – flat.

'The Lone Ranger rides again,' she told herself wryly. 'Masked – and miserable.'

Gareth had been Fee's first boyfriend. She had been fourteen. Fee calculated quickly, if she excluded five years living with Bill and a couple of years with other lovers, that meant that she had been on the hunt for well over a dozen years.

Twelve whole years.

In the last couple of months alone, for instance, she had been 'matched' at dinner parties with a former white mercenary with three ex-wives, a fox-hunting army captain and a twenty-five-year-old DJ from Seaford, and somebody's ex-brother-in-law who had rubbed so much fake tan into himself he was almost the same colour as the walnut sideboard. Is that any way for a girl to live?

'Got any kids have you, miss?' the taxi driver interrupted Fee's thoughts.

'They're mine.' He nodded to a photograph of two small boys jammed into the visor.

'Little devils,' he added affectionately. 'How about you?'

'I'm not married,' Fee replied. 'Never felt the urge.' She knew she sounded defensive.

'Single? You lucky beggar,' the taxi driver laughed. 'If you take my advice, you'll stay that way. I'd love to be free again. No nagging, a duty only to yourself—'

Fee smiled briefly, remembering her father. He had been fond of talking about duty. He'd dutifully stuck with a marriage he hated, meeting the demands of a job he loathed. He'd lived dutifully, uncomplaining, dreaming of what might have been. And once he was dead, his sacrifices were forgotten.

Vera, on the other hand, had managed to balance a duty to herself with a duty to others. She'd cared for husband and children, then moved on literally to please herself. Her critics would say that she had caused her husband grief, embarrassed her children and appalled the family, but she had died content. And she was certainly remembered.

'What's that, miss?' the taxi driver asked.

'Duty,' Fee replied. 'I was just wondering how you balance it – a duty to yourself with a duty to others?'

The taxi driver chuckled. 'Once you're married love,' he smiled. 'You can't even afford to ask the question. Take my advice, stay well out of it.'

But Fee could tell from his smile that he didn't mean a word.

*

That night, Fee Travers weighed the two possible futures ahead of her. She attempted to assess her own sticking power. And, finally, she came to a decision.

Fee was certain about only one aspect of what she had decided: her mother was bound to take it personally.

Chapter Four

NELSON CHARLES WOLFF, aged eleven weeks, appeared to be enjoying his christening party. The rain, which had bucketed down throughout the church service, now made an interesting drumming sound on the kitchen roof. At the same time, his mother, Emily, was making lots of funny faces entirely for his benefit.

Emily Wolff was, in truth, registering her dismay. Two stains, each the size of a toy saucer, now decorated the front of her crème-de-menthe pure-wool dress. Fee, making sympathetic noises, would have called the colour green but Emily insisted it was crème de menthe. Something that cost £178 could not be called green.

Emily was annoyed with herself. She had inserted pads in her breast-feeding brassière, each cup the size of a Boy Scout's tent, but when Nelson had been baptized, the milk had absolutely gushed through. Fee, Emily's aunt, but only ten years older, had offered the loan of her navy jacket.

Emily had refused without much grace. Navy and crème de menthe looked, well, so *common*; like a flight attendant's uniform. Instead, she had borrowed a white angora cardigan with pearl buttons from one of the other guests. Fee considered the combination of angora and Emily's buck teeth an unfortunate marriage, but she kept her silence. Why stoop to Emily's bitchy level?

Emily didn't give a toss what Fee thought. She was a wife, a mother (twice over) and not even thirty. *And* she'd had a

Caesarean. Fee was a thirty-eight-year-old spinster, so what did she know about anything?

'A toast! A toast!' said Charlie Jackson, the proud grandfather. He was tall with sandy hair and a face deeply carved by squinting at the sun on too many golf courses. Fee liked Charlie; he was uncomplicated and amiable. But she also reckoned that, as a husband, his unflagging chirpiness might trigger murder. It would be like living with a mechanical, permanently wound-up Tommy Steele.

Fee made herself comfortable in the window seat of Veronica's and Les's spacious sitting room. She emptied her glass of champagne and immediately found it refilled. Good. She needed something to dull the memory of the better parts of Paul.

'Any luck?' the dispenser of booze asked, indicating his own wedding ring and pointing at Fee's left hand. Fee offered her lockjaw smile.

'Doesn't pay to be too fussy now, does it?' The man, the husband of a second cousin on her father's side, winked.

Older, unmarried women and the pregnant share a unique position in society, Fee had come to realize. Both are considered public property. Both are prodded and pummelled and asked deeply intimate questions by near strangers. And offered unwanted pieces of advice.

'Carrying a lot of weight, aren't you?' Fee had heard a woman, a stranger, in a department store tell Emily when she was seven months pregnant. 'Husband a big man, is he?'

Likewise, at all family events, christenings, funerals, weddings, Fee could expect the obligatory series of questions. 'Courting, are you?' 'Found Mr Right yet?' 'Career girl, are we?'

'Mind your own damn business,' were the words that came readily to Fee's lips as a response. Once, she had actually said them out loud. The reaction had been predictable.

'No need to get funny about it,' Emily's twice-married sister,

Stephanie, had snapped back. 'It's not my fault you're on your own.'

So, now, Fee just gave this lockjaw smile. And stayed silent.

'Satay?' Veronica asked in what Fee recognized as her hostess voice. 'Or miniature pitta pockets stuffed with feta cheese, roasted red peppers and rocket? Les says that goes down very well with champagne. Oh, it's you, Fee,' she said, recognition restoring her voice to normal. Then she added warmly, 'Are you all right?'

Fee took a good look at her sister. The last year or so, they'd only met two or three times. They phoned each other weekly, but recently the calls had been brief, skimming over gossip that didn't personally involve either woman. Fee recognized that this slow disconnection of their lives had been her fault.

In the time when they had been closer, the impression conveyed by Veronica was that all was well in her life, if uneventful. For Fee, love, career and friendships had dictated a much more irregular, unpredictable rhythm.

Fee sometimes envied Veronica; Veronica had never expressed similar feelings about Fee's life. So Fee assumed that her sister was untroubled. Helen had mentioned 'a small problem' but Fee had avoided considering what her mother's euphemism actually meant.

Looking at Veronica now, she was frightened by what she saw.

'Am *I* all right?' she answered awkwardly. Spontaneously, she wrapped both her arms around her sister, and avoiding the hors-d'oeuvres, tried to squeeze some optimism back into Veronica's lost, grey figure.

Veronica was almost fifteen when Fee was born. She had become Fee's minder and heroine.

At school, she had been tough and intelligent and spiky, a tomboy. She was a natural blonde, small in stature and with a repartee that made her feared and admired by both the girls and the lads. Everyone said that Veronica had a Personality.

At eighteen, something happened to her. She met Les. She toned down the cheek, became much more feminine. She grew her nails and took to wearing ginghams and pastels. Les was tall, good-looking in a rough-and-ready way, large in gesture and voice, amusing if moody, and described by some as 'a difficult man'. He had always been almost obsessed with Veronica.

He was her fourth boyfriend and the first to promise to keep her safe and care for her for ever. So when he proposed, she'd said yes. He'd wanted a woman to protect and pamper; Veronica had grown into the role.

Les had joined the army at seventeen and became a chef. On leaving the forces, he'd opened up a sandwich shop and taken evening courses in business management and marketing.

Ahead of the pack, he had moved on from corned beef and Branston pickle to walnut bread and pesto, and suddenly, in the 1980s, he was not at all surprised to find that he had a success on his hands.

Now, he owned a chain of seemingly recession-proof 'sandwich brasseries', plus an outside catering company. It provided quaint nostalgia items such as chip butties with HP sauce for record-company promotions and TV companies' jamborees.

Soon after Les and Veronica had married, Les had insisted that his wife give up her work in a bank. She had briefly done the books for Les in the sandwich business but it had made him uneasy. People, he said, would think he couldn't afford a proper accountant. So, to keep her hand in, Veronica had studied at home for accountancy exams.

She hadn't told her husband since it wasn't worth the upset. She had qualified, but had backed away from the battle that would have been necessary to persuade Les that she could go back to work.

Now, at almost fifty-two, Veronica was constantly told what a lucky woman she was. She had a doting husband, two lovely children

– Les Junior, eighteen, was in Zimbabwe, teaching for a year before university; Samantha, twenty-one, was in her final year at Manchester, reading law – lots of money, plenty of free time . . . what more could a woman want, for goodness' sake?

Unexpectedly, a couple of months ago, Veronica had provided the answer. What she appeared to want – or rather, what she couldn't help herself from causing – was a record number of deaths.

'I think I'm a killer,' Veronica had blurted out to Les one Friday night, in their local Indian restaurant. (Les was preoccupied with his attempt to create a new concept in sandwiches, a chapatti filled with a curry that didn't run down your fingers when you tried to eat it.)

'I'm a killer,' Veronica had repeated, as her husband, seemingly oblivious, experimentally folded and refolded the chappati on his plate.

'And if I don't go home now, I may do something terrible to that man who's walking towards us with mango chutney. I want to go home NOW, Les,' she had shouted, suddenly rising.

The only other time Les had heard Veronica raise her voice was in labour, twenty-one years before.

'It was a terrible shock,' he told his mother-in-law, later that night on the phone, after Veronica had been put to bed with a sedative. 'It wasn't even as if I'd finished my dinner.'

The next morning, Veronica had tried to elaborate further to her husband and mother. She explained that she had developed a drop-dead look in her eye; when she looked, people dropped dead. This didn't happen all the time but often enough to bring her to a point of deep despair.

'It's nerves,' Helen said, the spectre of Vera hovering over her shoulder. 'Take no notice.'

Les had tried to follow Helen's advice but over the weeks he found himself spending more and more time retracing his wife's steps, at her request, in search of mythical dead bodies. He found himself spending hours enquiring into the health of perfect strangers.

Veronica would phone her husband at work, distraught. Could he please call in at the hairdressers? She was sure she had done something terrible to the junior who had washed her hair.

Had Les seen the milkman that morning? Veronica swore she'd exterminated him early the previous day. And what about the nice young girl who delivers the papers? Veronica just *knew* she had caught her eye from the bedroom window.

'It's her age,' Helen reassured her son-in-law. 'It's the Change. It does funny things to some women. It will pass.'

Les tried to coax Veronica out of what he called her 'fixation'. 'This isn't like you,' he'd say gently from time to time. 'This really isn't like you, Veronica.'

'Oh yes it is,' she'd answer with more ferocity than he'd ever seen her display before.

'This is the real me, all right.'

The only two places where Veronica felt she was less of a danger to the public were her own home and the food hall of her local Marks & Spencer. There, everyone was so busy buying, nobody bothered to meet her eye.

After three months with no signs of improvement, Les decided that Helen was wrong. Whatever it was showed no signs of passing. He took his wife to a psychiatrist, whose diagnosis was that it was not the menopause. Instead, he implied that the difficulty might have its roots not in the Change but the lack of it; the lack of variety, challenge, stimulation in Veronica's life.

'She's a very bright girl, after all,' said the psychiatrist of his fifty-one-year-old client.

He also tactfully suggested that over the years, Les's inability to allow his wife to lead a life of her own might not have had an entirely positive effect on her confidence.

'She wants to please you, no doubt about that,' the psychiatrist explained. 'But she also wants to please herself. And to cut a long story extremely short, that results in her feeling she is highly damaging. You should give her permission to get out and about more. Be herself. You know the kind of thing I mean.'

Les didn't have a clue. He puzzled over these words, '*Be herself.*' Who else was Veronica, if she wasn't already herself? And he grew sadder and sadder. All he'd tried to do was look after the woman he'd never stopped loving and protecting, not once, in thirty years of marriage.

Still Veronica's body count continued to rise – at least it did in a corner of her mind which was the only part of herself that she could genuinely call her own.

'Did you go into the local shop on your way here?' Veronica asked as she steered Fee into a vacant space near the doors to the conservatory. Out of habit, Veronica picked up a plate of M&S spring rolls to offer to whomsoever she passed.

'No,' Fee replied. 'Why, should I have done?'

'Could you pop there for me, now?' Veronica whispered anxiously.

'If you've run out of cigarettes, why don't we go and get some together?' Fee suggested. Perhaps regular doses of freedom might be her sister's best chance of a cure?

'You and me go out?' Veronica patted her pale-pink suit jacket, and adjusted the neck of her cream and pink blouse, as if to check that she was still in the here and now.

'If we go, I'll have to keep my eyes down. You know, so I don't—' She gestured vaguely in the air, as if to conjure up the carnage of recent times.

Fee smiled encouragingly.

'You know I kill people, don't you?' Veronica said bluntly, her eyes filling with tears. 'I just look at people . . . and wham—'

'Yes, of course,' Fee replied, but she hadn't known at all.

'If we go to the shop, Les won't like it,' Veronica glanced around the room for sight of her husband. 'He gets nervous now when I go out. Doesn't know what to expect. Prefers me to stay in, quietly.'

Distractedly she put the plate of spring rolls down on the plush carpet. Josh, her three-year-old nephew, Emily's first child, promptly began to stamp bean sprouts into the carpet as if they were engorged worms.

'You promise to keep count . . . of the bodies, I mean?' Veronica asked her sister.

'Even if we get into double figures,' Fee replied solemnly.

Veronica gave her a sharp look but Fee was already on the move.

'Follow me,' she instructed, waving her hand, as if leading a posse.

Fee was a child again. She was with her father outside the garden hut, as they both rode their imaginary horses, always the rescuers, never the rescued.

Alec Clarke spotted the two women as they manouevred behind the baby grand piano, skirted round the shocking-pink love seat, passed the large portrait Les had commissioned of his wife and laced their way across the large room, now full of guests.

He bore down on them fast. Alec made it his business to bear down on Fiona Travers at every family occasion. He was her third cousin, a bachelor, thirty-seven years old but middle-aged from birth; a creature of habit since the womb. Routine was his religion.

Alec read *Horse and Hound* and the *Sun*. At home, he was cared for by Mrs Rogers, who had 'done' for the family for a legendary amount of time, a woman who knew the importance of a suet pudding in a working man's life.

Alec was intelligent; he could talk EU farming regulations better than most. He enjoyed a pint or two with the lads; he dabbled in a bit of shooting; he never felt the need to holiday. Alec was a very contented man, except for one concern.

He was the fourth and last generation of Clarkes and he needed an heir. Therefore, being a conventional sort of a chap, he required a wife. Romance was not a sport in which he had much interest or expertise. So, fifteen years ago, he had settled on Fee because she was a good enough sort. It was taking longer than he'd anticipated but he knew that she would see sense eventually.

'Better the devil you know . . . eh?' was one of his many attempts at wooing Fee.

Recently, however, a small niggle had entered his mind. Perhaps Fee had passed the best age for child-bearing?

'Fiona,' Alec bellowed. He stood between Fee, Veronica and the escape offered by the front door. He gave Fee a bear hug. 'Your ma says you could do with a bit of company.'

Fee and Veronica looked at each other.

'Kill,' Fee ordered Veronica crisply.

'It doesn't happen like that,' Veronica replied, glaring at Alec. 'It's not something I can do when I want. It happens when I don't want—'

'Not now, Alec,' Fee said curtly.

Veronica and Fee arrived at the sitting-room door, majestic with its stained-glass panel of a Spanish galleon, the name *Veronica* just visible on the hull. There was still no sign of Les.

Suddenly, the doorbell chimed.

Veronica dropped to the floor as if pounded by a concrete block.

'It's Amy next door. They've come to tell me I've hurt her. I know I have . . . I ruin everything, everybody . . . I'm useless, no good for anything, nothing at all . . . I'm dead wood. Just dead wood,' Veronica sobbed.

Fee knelt by her sister while Alec answered the door. Amy Court-Smith, fifty-ish, holding a christening present and dressed expensively and effectively in cherry red, with matching umbrella, hovered uncertainly on the step.

'Come on, Veronica,' Fee encouraged her sister to sit up. It was the first time she had witnessed the extent of Veronica's distress – and she was angry. Not at Veronica, but at the *possessiveness* which, she suspected, had brought Veronica to this.

'Amy isn't dead, you haven't killed her. You haven't killed anyone. Amy's here, look,' Fee attempted to coax Veronica who, so far, was refusing to open her eyes.

Amy Court-Smith had become a neighbour when Veronica and Les first moved into the house seven years earlier (paid for by the surprising success of Les's seared tuna with cranberry sauce and red onions on muesli bread). Amy had quickly ascertained that Les only had eyes for Veronica, but she continued to enjoy the challenge.

Now, she remained glued to the doorstep. As if unsure of the etiquette once you find yourself unexpectedly raised from the dead.

'It is me, Veronica, alive and kicking,' she sang out. 'Not at all deceased. Not at all.'

Fee used her cuff to gently wipe Veronica's tears, as her sister used to do when Fee was a toddler.

'Don't cry, Veronica, please don't cry,' she whispered softly.

'No, you'll only upset yourself,' Amy Court-Smith smiled brightly.

'Don't you mean, "You'll only get *more* upset"?' Alec suggested pedantically. 'I mean, she's already upset, so if you say—' he laboured.

'Shut up and go away, Alec,' Fee commanded. 'NOW, please,' she added as Alec proved reluctant to move.

'Why not show Amy where to leave her wet things?' Fee suggested.

'Oh, I know all that,' Amy replied, then read Fee's face. 'Oh, I get the point, yes . . . Alec, wasn't it? Yes, why don't you show me where to put my coat? Goodness me, you're a very well-built young man,' she added, placing a well-manicured hand on the sleeve of Alec's Viyella shirt.

When they had gone, Fee sat on the hall floor next to Veronica, who had her back to the wall, legs curled up under her. The light pouring through the stained-glass window dappled her face, darkening the shadows under her eyes and hollowing her cheeks.

'Veronica, this *has* to stop,' Fee spoke softly. 'You've got so much, you really have. You're a terrific mother, Les worships you, you're the best sister I could possibly have . . . And now Samantha and little Les are off your hands, you can go anywhere, do anything . . . you can start again. Veronica . . .? All you've got to do is get a grip. Pull yourself together.'

'That's what they all say,' Veronica answered bleakly.

Fifteen minutes later, Veronica, now calmer, repaired her make-up in her bedroom.

'Look at this,' she instructed Fee. She opened a wardrobe door to reveal a stack of shoeboxes, each neatly labelled to indicate the colour of the contents.

She pulled out a box labelled 'Beige', opened it and emptied the contents on the bed. Several bottles of pills fell out.

'I'm supposed to be taking them,' she explained flatly. 'Les thinks I am. So does Mum. But I won't. At least this way, I'm still the me I've grown used to . . . If I take them, I won't know who the hell I am . . .'

'What do you think might work instead?' Fee asked.

She couldn't see her sister's face, because she was looking down, apparently concentrating on making patterns with the pill bottles on the counterpane. Silence. Then Veronica very quietly replied. 'I really don't know any more. Probably nothing . . . It's probably just me—' She shrugged, her eyes filling with tears again. Fee felt fear.

Fear for her sister – and some trepidation for herself. Both, in different ways, drifting on a raft constructed of other people's decisions. Veronica was much further downstream than Fee; much more entangled in the expectation of others. So much so that Veronica appeared not to know that she had a right to achieve something more for herself than others were prepared to permit.

Fee picked up one of the silver-framed photographs on Veronica's dressing-table. It showed her at fourteen in a pale-green bridesmaid's dress, with Veronica in her twenties, standing beside her, a maid of honour and dressed in a deeper green. Two runner beans in front of a church porch.

Veronica managed a small smile. 'It was the day you found out the truth about Vera, do you remember? You were so pleased with yourself—'

Fee picked up a second framed photograph. It was of their father in his early forties, standing awkwardly by the mantelpiece in the family sitting room, dressed as a cowboy with a check shirt, fringed waistcoat and a stetson in his hands. Helen stood by his side, also in fancy dress; a self-conscious Lady of Spain with a spectacular mantilla.

'Do you remember the row?' Fee asked. 'Mum wanted Dad to go to the party as a matador and he refused point blank. He said no woman was forcing him into a pair of tights. And she asked why did he always put himself out to disappoint her.'

Veronica gave a small laugh. 'They started rowing again when Elizabeth was taking that picture. And Dad told Mum she could have him as Wyatt Earp or bloody nothing at all . . . so Mum said, "Why change what you're used to? I'll have what I usually get from you, nothing at all.' Veronica was laughing unnaturally hard now and Fee found herself joining in.

Veronica continued, trying unsuccessfully to control her amusement. 'Do you remember . . . in front of us all, Dad suddenly took all his clothes off and stood starkers in the sitting room with only his stetson for decency. He told Mum, "You want nothing, you've got nothing." And he wouldn't get dressed again until she'd gone out without him.

'You must have been about four at the time, Fee, and you thought it was the best fun. You ran out in the garden and shouted over the fence at the neighbours, "Our Dad's starkers in the front room". And Mrs Harris had said, "But it's only seven o'clock."

'It's the only time I can remember Dad making a real stand

against our Mum—' Veronica added wistfully. 'He should have done it more often—'

'Why?' Fee jumped off the bed where she had been sitting cross-legged and grabbed her sister's hands.

'Why what?' Veronica asked, puzzled.

'Why should he have done it more often?'

Veronica shrugged. 'Oh, I don't know, it might have done him a power of good now and then. He should've shaken Mum up every so often. And himself come to that. He used to tell us, "Go for it, cowboy," but he didn't listen to his own advice much, did he?'

'So why don't you make a stand? Why don't you tell Les what you'd really like to do – and go for it?' Fee asked.

Veronica blinked some tears away. 'I have tried . . . It's just not as easy as you make it sound. I mean, I'm actually quite happy. Look, Fee, I'm an ordinary sort of person. I haven't got it in me to suddenly start changing my life—'

'Oh yes, you have,' Fee replied firmly. 'And I'm sure Les would—'

She was interrupted by her mother's excited voice. 'Fee, are you up there?' she trilled. 'It's Adam. He wants to speak to you. Says he's got something important to ask you – again. Take it on the bedroom phone.'

Fee picked up the telephone, and listened for a few minutes. Then she said, 'Of course, I'll tell the family. They'll be the first to know.'

An hour later, Veronica was back circulating the christening party with plates of finger food. The sun had belatedly come out, so guests had moved into the garden. The extended family and friends admired the newly installed Japanese waterfall and Canadian-teak pagoda (both funded by sliced roast lamb and asparagus with redcurrant jelly on warm mint bread).

Fee had consumed a large amount of champagne and was now holding her godson, while his parents described his mental agility.

'A clever boy, a very clever boy,' said his father.

'Takes after you,' offered Emily, loyally. Then she turned to Fee. 'Are you ready, Godmum?' she asked.

'Totally prepared,' Fee replied. She carefully handed Nelson Charles back to his mother, now hot but happy in angora. Then, she took another sip of champagne. Les clapped his hands to gain the assembled company's attention. Fee spoke.

'Welcome, everyone, to this charming occasion. Thank you too, to Les and Veronica for their hospitality and congratulations to the proud parents, Emily and Peter.' Fee raised her glass in an informal toast.

'He is a gorgeous baby,' Fee said, more out of duty than admiration. Everyone in the circle around her nodded vigorously in agreement.

'But actually I don't want to talk about christenings. I want to talk about me.'

The muted conversations halted abruptly.

Fee clambered unsteadily on to one of Les's garden chairs. She stood upright, and said, 'I have an announcement to make.'

Helen raised her eyebrows at Les, smiled and mouthed one word, 'Adam?'

She congratulated herself. Her patience had paid off. Soon, she would have three sons-in-law in the fold.

Fee gave her mother a broad smile and continued, 'I have an announcement to make about which I am very, very happy. If my dear old dad were here, I'd be happier still.'

Helen gave a little turn and a regal half-wave, to the assembled company, savouring her moment.

'Congratulations!' Les yelled out and there was a ripple of applause.

'Who's the lucky man, then?' came a shout from the begonias.

'There is no man,' Fee began again. She beamed and gestured with her glass for a refill.

Silence descended on the group. *Surely to God, not a second Vera . . .?*

57

'And,' Fee paused, enjoying the suspense, 'there is no woman either. But I do have a number of people to thank for the situation in which I now find myself.'

Helen could feel her heart beating faster. Pregnant? Her one unmarried daughter couldn't possibly be pregnant, could she? Disappointment rose from her like dust from a beaten carpet.

Fee pressed on. 'My sister Veronica, her husband Les, Adam, Paul, even Alec here, probably Emily, definitely Horatio—'

'Nelson,' Emily interjected crossly. 'Nelson, he's called Nelson. Not bloody Horatio.'

Fee smiled warmly.

'My thanks to my dad, Jim, who was the first to show me that principles aren't just for cowboys. And, above all, my appreciation to my mother Helen, who has contributed more to my decision than she can possibly know.'

Fee took a deep breath.

'From this day forth, I, Fiona Constance Travers, am a fully fledged unrepentant spinster. I am putting myself on the shelf – permanently.

'I am no longer interested in the hunt. I will no longer seek out Prince Charming. I will no longer spend my days in limbo waiting for the right man, the right moment, the right reaction, the right proposal—

'I am now no longer "between men". I may have male companions. I may even, one day, have occasional sexual partners.' Fee could see her mother cover her face with her hands. 'But, for the foreseeable future, I intend to abstain. Get it out of my system, clear the head, you know the kind of thing I mean—'

'Poor girl,' Elizabeth whispered sympathetically to Charlie. 'Nobody's interested any more. Still,' she added, almost enviously, 'she's had a bloody good run for her money.' Charlie gave his wife a sharp look.

'I can hear that you are speechless with delight on my behalf.' Fee smiled. 'But I vow before you here and now that, just as many of you have worked hard at marriage – and let's be honest about it – worked hard with varying degrees of success, so I intend to work equally hard at being single.

'One purpose of this announcement is so that you can share in my happiness. I'm sure one or two of you,' she looked in her mother's direction, 'one or two of you might be interested to know that, yes, I have been asked for my hand in marriage. Three days ago, to be precise. And, this afternoon, I refused that proposal for a second time.

'Another purpose for this announcement is to make clear that none of you are under any obligation to fix me up.

'I have finally fixed myself—'

A few minutes later, Fee walked unsteadily towards the house in search of more alcohol to celebrate the launch of her maiden flight. Her relatives seemed unsure how to react. What do you say to a woman who has, as it were, shelved herself?

Sorry? Well done? Never mind?

Emily had run off in tears, justifiably upset that she – or rather Nelson – had been robbed of the limelight.

'It's not as if he's going to get christened twice,' she'd sobbed. And to think Emily had only asked Fiona to be godmother as a sort of consolation prize because she didn't seem to have anything that mattered in her life . . .

'That is it,' Emily vowed. 'I'll never feel sorry for a woman on her own again. It's true what everyone says, they only take advantage.'

As Fee moved into Veronica's and Les's turquoise and marble Italian-fitted kitchen, in search of a drink, she spotted her mother's rear end sticking out of the oven.

'It's not gas, it's electric, you know,' Fee suggested lightly.

'Of course I know,' Helen replied testily, carefully withdrawing her head so as not to disturb the iron ruts and mini-peaks that were her newly styled hairdo.

'I'm just giving Veronica a hand with the cooking. She *likes* her mother's help in the kitchen,' she added pointedly.

Fee poured herself and her mother champagne. Helen, normally teetotal, swallowed most of it in seconds. Then she hoisted herself up on to a particularly vicious-looking wire stool, a sieve on legs, by the breakfast bar, and tackled her daughter.

'All this . . . stuff—' she began. 'It is a joke, isn't it? A bit of nonsense? You don't mean it, do you? I've read about it in the magazines. You stop looking and then it happens—'

'No,' Fee answered firmly. 'I've stopped looking so it *won't* happen. Look, I'm being sensible. You'd approve of that,' Fee smiled enigmatically at her mother.

'Of course I can probably find a man to marry me,' she continued, 'but he'll either bore me to death or I'll end up like Veronica. If I can't trust myself to make a good choice, then I won't make a choice at all—'

'Too fussy. I've said it before, I'll say it again—' Helen interrupted. 'Expectations way, way too high. I knew it. I just knew, you'd be the one to let me down. What's wrong with making do? You couldn't say that your father and I were happy all the time but—'

'You weren't happy any of the time,' Fee interjected sharply, then continued in an even tone, 'And I don't want that. I can and have been perfectly content living by myself. What can a man give me that I can't give myself?'

Helen fell silent but her fingers betrayed her agitation. Fee watched as her mother carefully shredded a paper doily, letting the pieces fall into a pile like a small funeral pyre.

'Choice,' Helen thought to herself, 'has been the mustard gas of this generation. They're crippled by it. At least we were grateful for the little we had.'

'Your lot will never be contented,' Helen chastised her daughter.

'High expectations have been the ruin of your lives. And do you know what your generation is really missing? It's not love or babies or relationships that last. You mark my words, girl, it's a sense of shame, that's what.

'Shame kept us in line – and no bad thing. Less mistakes, fewer tears. My mother always used to say, "Where reality meets expectation, there contentment lies." Your lot will never know contentment.'

Fee played with her glass and said nothing. Helen muttered to herself. *That damn silence again.*

'Have you told Claire yet?' she suddenly asked. Claire Harper was single but, unlike Fee, sensible with it.

'Claire isn't back until tonight. She's on a business trip. We're having lunch tomorrow and I'll tell her then. She and I will grow old, spinsters together.'

The thought cheered Fee, now definitely drunk. 'If others are glad to be gay,' she told Helen, jauntily, 'we'll be ecstatic to be uno; happy to be unhitched, serene to be seriously single—' It was the kind of rubbish Fee thought up every day on behalf of F.P.& D. Ironic that now she would have to live it too.

'We'll see.' Helen looked quizzically at her daughter. Perhaps Fee was on some drug? Or maybe it was her hormones? An early menopause?

'You have no idea what you're letting yourself in for. Women don't like spinsters. Not when they're your age. You'll be cut off. You'll be seen as too much of a temptation for every woman's husband. But you won't listen will you? Not you . . . oh no, not you—'

A fresh angle of attack occurred to Helen. Weren't women creatures to whom things happened?

'You can't *choose* to be a spinster,' she declared. 'It happens *to* you. And we've never had a spinster in the family. No spinsters and no divorcees. I tell a lie.' She paused for thought. 'There was Aunty Lily. She never married. But at least she had the Great War to blame. Her fiancé was killed when he was twenty and she never looked at another man. Mind you,' she added, helping herself to more champagne, a sure sign of acute stress. 'Mind you, I don't think another man looked at her. She wasn't exactly a stunner, was our Lil. Yes, she was single all right but she had a good excuse. What's yours?'

Fee didn't even pause to reply. 'That's why things are different now,' she gently dismissed her mother. 'Us girls don't need excuses.'

Fee only wished that it were true.

Chapter Five

'YOU ARE *what?*'

Fee and Claire Harper were in a restaurant that Claire had selected for its HWA – Heterosexual Waiter Appeal. Except that Monday must have been his day off.

At first, they had been given a table directly outside the lavatories. Claire announced this was totally unnecessary since, as she was not suffering from any urinary infection, such accessibility was a wasted opportunity. She would appreciate being reseated. So, of course, they were.

Claire had fine bones, natural skinniness and pale blond hair. All three were virtues in youth but, according to her, did not age well.

'What happens in our family', she would say cheerfully enough, 'is that we move from baby doll to TOB in next to no time.'

TOB stood for Tough Old Bird.

Claire also had a tendency to act as if she was wing attack in the school hockey team. In her thirties, this had matured into a no nonsense attitude that made her, at times, appear abrupt and formidable.

What Fee admired most about Claire was her sense of entitlement. She could trot out a list of desires and expect most of them to be satisfied. In contrast, Fee had been brought up to believe that nice girls didn't *want*; they appreciated what they were given.

Twice, Claire had lived with a man. Each time, she had moved out within a year. If Fee's weakness was for the unattainable male, Claire's was for the man who literally had more balls than brains.

'Intercourse followed by incompatibility,' Claire would often say, cheerfully enough. 'That's the history of each and everyone of my love affairs.'

'But, God willing, when the time's right, fate will take a hand. Or, if it doesn't, I will.'

Over the years, Fee and Claire, in and out of relationships, had squabbled, suffered, sulked, celebrated and supported each other. Their bond of friendship was unbreakable. Or so they had always told each other.

'You are what?' Fee gazed at Claire, disbelieving.

'You are doing *what*?' Fee repeated herself.

She had intended Claire to be the first to know, outside the family, about her changed status in life. But Claire had her own news to announce.

'I'm getting married,' she repeated, keeping her eyes on the butter dish.

'In white, in a church with a page boy in plum velvet. And you, as chief bridesmaid.'

'What on earth do you mean?' Fee repeated as if the information could be made more simple.

Claire pointed to her finger, 'You know marriage . . . ring . . . wedding bells . . . honeymoon . . . happy ever after . . . all the usual thing—'

'You've fallen in love. Are you telling me you've fallen in love?' Fee asked accusingly, not least because she was usually the first to know if there was even a hint of passion in Claire's life. Never before had developments reached this fully blown stage without dissection, discussion, conferring.

'No,' Claire now had her eyes locked on to the butter dish as if she was willing the pats to perform a formation waltz.

'No, I mean I'm getting married. In just under four months.'

'So it *is* love?' Fee accused Claire again. 'How come it's such a big secret? You've never mentioned this before. It's that man, Angus, isn't it? The one with the bi—'

'The one with the bifocals? No, it's not Angus. It's someone you haven't met yet. He's not what you'd expect. I mean, he's not the kind of man I . . . well . . . you know—'

Fee resorted to flippancy. 'Are you trying to tell me he's stable, sane, teetotal and does not have the emotional development of a six-month-old baby?'

'Almost,' Claire smiled faintly and finally raised her eyes to Fee's face.

'It's like this,' Claire explained, her words tumbling out in an uncharacteristic rush. 'Soon after we met, he said that although I give the impression I can cope with anything, what I really need is someone who'll look after me. And he's promised to do that—

'And, Fee, I really do want to be looked after. I'm fed up with coping. And he's very decent and dependable. No surprises. No moods. He's very . . . well, *nice*—

'It's not love. But he's good enough. Probably too good . . . for me, that is . . . But he's definitely *nice*. And because it's not love, I'm sure it's got a better chance of lasting.'

'Oh,' she added, as if as an afterthought, 'he's not bad in bed either. Quite good, actually.'

'Are you trying to tell me that's the *last* thing on your mind?' Fee looked at Claire, disbelieving again.

Claire blushed.

Claire *blushing*? Fee couldn't remember it happening before. Not once.

Something about this affair, her instincts told her, wasn't quite what it seemed.

'*Nice?*' Fee repeated the word.

Claire squirmed slightly. 'Nice, yes. Someone who's good for me, who has the right priorities. Who doesn't want to work all the hours and make a million. Someone with a bit of balance in his life—'

Claire paused while the waiter, camp and concave, placed a plate of salad in front of her that looked like a section of hedgerow. Then she took a deep breath and tried again.

'The thing is, even I can see that the kind of men I fall for are the world's worst candidates for a permanent relationship. So I decided I'd organize a marriage for myself.

'And by . . . sort of coincidence, I met this man . . . and last night, when I got back from Chicago, I proposed—' Claire suddenly paused. 'Well, go on, say something. Say, "I'm really happy for you." Or something like that. I would if I were you,' she prompted Fee.

Fee was too busy contemplating the irony of the situation. The more she explored the implications of Claire's decision, the less confident she began to feel about her own. And the greater the rage she felt towards her best friend, not just because of her impending desertion but because she had so efficiently sabotaged one of the first real choices Fee had made for herself.

She reviewed her situation. Permanently single? From *choice*? On reflection, perhaps that should be semi-permanently. Or possibly even, single *for the time being*.

In fact, why not just ask Claire if her fiancé, her *nice* fiancé, had an older brother?

'Is he rich?' Fee asked, breaking her silence while Claire pretended to eat. If he was, she swore she would vomit on the spot. Claire, as a partner in a successful firm of headhunters, worked horrendous hours but earned what Fee regarded as absurd quantities of cash.

'No, he earns next to nothing . . .'

'Is that wise?' Fee couldn't stop herself. She had an irresistible urge to hurt. 'I mean, what you're saying is, you'll have to keep him in the style to which you are accustomed . . . difficult area that . . .' Fee knew she'd inflicted enough damage, so she didn't have to pursue the thought.

'Any mental illnesses?' she pressed on hopefully.

'Any physical impediments? Impotency? Firing blanks? Perfectly OK if he is. In fact, it's quite the fashion.'

Claire shook her head, smiled wryly and explained that her prospective spouse used to manage a trust fund. Then his wife had walked out and gone to live with his best friend. At that point, he had decided to do only what he wanted in life so long as it didn't cause harm to others.

Claire smiled a smile that Fee didn't recognize. 'He said he realized that because he'd been a workaholic, put money first, he'd lost his wife—' Claire's voice had taken on the texture of syrup.

'A man of principle then—' Fee commented drily. She didn't mean to sound as sarcastic as she did.

Claire ignored Fee and continued to try to extract some sympathy.

'You two have got something in common, you know,' she attempted with forced jollity. 'He teaches like you used to do. He's the deputy head of a junior school and he loves it. He's very good at drama, organizes the school play, lots of after-school activities, that sort of thing—' Her voice trailed away.

'That's a bit of an odd career for a man to choose, isn't it?' Fee questioned, hating herself for trying to insert a worm of doubt in Claire's mind, but unable to stop herself either.

'He's not a child molester, is he?' she went on, only half joking.

Again, Claire ignored the comment. It was almost as if she'd anticipated Fee's responses.

'So what's his name?' Fee asked, trying to postpone the time when she would have to give her blessing to the arrangement.

'Clem,' Claire avoided Fee's eye. 'And no, he does not wear an anorak,' she added spikily. She poured each of them more wine before she spoke again. It mattered to her that Fee approved. It mattered more than she could say.

'Look, Fee, all I've done is face facts. I'm not getting any younger and the pool of likely mates is getting smaller.

'Free to choose is one thing; "free" because there's nobody left who will have you is something else altogether. That's not single, that's second best.

'I want children. I want to have a family just like everybody else. But I'm working too bloody hard ever to allow it to happen. So, now I've decided to *make* it happen—'

Claire was unstoppable. Clem was kind. He was funny. He could iron. He had close friends. He put money into collection boxes. He read books. He climbed mountains in his spare time. He was everything to himself that a good wife should be. Oh, and he was thirty-eight.

'He's not very *needy*, is he?' Fee finally interjected, genuinely concerned. 'Are you really sure you know what he wants from you?'

'A relationship that lasts,' Claire replied promptly. 'And kids.'

'What about love?' Fee realized she was beginning to sound like a chief prosecutor.

'Well, that too,' Claire shrugged. 'Eventually. Anyway, he assumes that I do. Love him, I mean. I haven't said so in so many words, but he's assumed.

'And, when I asked him to marry me,' Claire added defiantly, 'he didn't even pause. Besides, anyone these days who trusts in personal chemistry and cards with red-velvet hearts has to be mad. I don't want romance, I want resilience under fire. Something that survives beyond the first five years.'

As Claire recited her reasons for arranging a marriage for herself, the more hostile Fee grew towards the unknown Clem.

She didn't have to meet him to know that he was a thiever of friends and a gold-digger.

'I'm nearly forty, Fee,' Claire was saying. 'I'm too old to change the way my heart behaves. So, now, I'm going to rely on my head—'

'Sounds as if you've got it all worked out.' Fee smiled, but her tone was sour.

She disapproved of bitchiness between friends. So, considering how little practice she had permitted herself over the years, she was both impressed and appalled at how adept she was proving to be.

Claire observed her warily. 'You're *jealous*, that's what it is, isn't it? You're actually *jealous*?'

'On my honour, I'm not,' Fee replied, retreating to the language of the school playground.

'So what's going on?' Claire peered at her friend. 'Didn't you say you had something to tell me? What happened at the christening? How's Veronica? And Paul . . . And Adam?'

Fee ignored her questions. Instead, in salute, she raised her glass.

'Congratulations, Claire,' she said. 'Clem is a very lucky man.'

Privately, she had made up her mind. Clem would have to go. It was the least she could do for Claire.

In her flat, that evening, Fee took the emergency action to which she always resorted when she wanted to waylay an impending depression.

She walked into her spare bedroom, opened the drawer at the bottom of the wardrobe – and took out her wedding album.

Or rather, it would have been her wedding album, if she hadn't said no to Bill's proposal.

Such was his confidence (or, more precisely, so great was his enthusiasm as an amateur photographer), Bill had already bought the album. It was covered in white plastic, decorated with silver bells. As a compromise, once Fee had turned him down, Bill had filled it with photographs of their first year of living together, then presented it to Fee as an anniversary gift.

Fee had held onto the album. It served to remind her that no matter how bad the current situation, it could never be as terrible as that period when everyone had continually told her, 'How happy you must be.'

Fee sat in her sitting room and turned the first page.

Bill.

A self-portrait taken in the bathroom mirror.

Bill Summers. Pleasant, slightly flattened face with very large eyes, blondish hair. Six foot. He always took up a great deal of space. Now, he burst out of the album.

They had met at a school fête. Fee was teaching and thirty; Bill was a surveyor, two years older and the brother of a fellow teacher. They went out for a year and suddenly everybody began to say, 'Wouldn't it be nice if you two moved in together?'

Bill had agreed it wasn't such a bad idea. Fee raised a few objections until one day her mother had snapped. 'Compromise, Fiona, *compromise*. It's what people *do*. Why should you be any different?'

Fee certainly hadn't wanted to be *different*. At least, she thought she hadn't. Not then.

She turned a page of the album. Several photographs taken of the two of them in the garden, all with other people in the frame.

For a long time, it was easy to overlook what was missing, mainly because they spent so little time alone in each other's company. They were either at work, or entertaining or being entertained or visiting relatives or shopping for the home. It was like playing at being married.

Bill also spent much of his free time working on his hobby. He preferred to refer to it as his project. He took great pleasure in photographing the patterns of leaves. He was holed up so often in his dark room, Fee began to call him her Prints of Darkness. Bill said he couldn't see what was so funny.

For Fee, life at home was routine and pleasant but somehow not *real*. She knew this wasn't how she was going to spend for ever. Bill was no trouble. He was uncritical, accommodating, amusing, all of which had made him good fun in courtship but, on a day-to-day basis, this particular cocktail began to taste, well, almost bland. She missed the occasional emotional bombshell.

'You couldn't wish for anyone nicer,' she was often told. Which was absolutely true. Fee longed for someone worse. She used to think such perversity was a sign of her adventurousness. Claire believed otherwise. It was, she told Fee, 'immature'.

'Look after Bill because if you don't one day when it's much too late you'll realize that you lost a very good man,' Claire would warn.

In the time Bill and she were together, Fee had switched careers from teaching to what was initially a lowly job in advertising. Just before they had split up, she had been recruited to F.P. & D.

She and Bill had been highly supportive of the other; each shared domestic duties and made no complaints about the long hours they worked. They agreed that they didn't want children for a few years, if ever. On paper, it couldn't have been a better set-up.

Much later, Fee realized that the fatal flaw in their relationship had appeared on day one. They worked hard, they played hard, they rarely rowed, they copulated efficiently but not spectacularly, they entertained to a respectable level, but *nothing between them had changed*.

She blamed herself.

She hadn't allowed anything to develop between them, no growing intimacy, no greater understanding. They were two people living side by side, going nowhere.

'Are you happy, Fee?' Bill would occasionally ask.

'Of course I am,' she'd reply. It was true. She was happy *in these particular circumstances*. 'That's all right then,' Bill would reply, apparently reassured.

Then, one night, he'd come back from his advanced photography evening class, begun five months earlier, and asked his by now customary question.

'Are you happy, Fee?'

She was about to give her usual response when Bill cut in, a muscle in his cheek twitching hard.

'Only I'm not.'

It was only then that she could afford to admit that what she'd been experiencing hadn't, after all, been a muted kind of contentment. It had been sheer bloody boredom.

Fee closed the photo album and shoved it under some cushions. Bill was now married to Erica, the woman who had taught him photography. Erica already had twins from a previous marriage and, within months, had become pregnant with Bill's child. She gave up her part-time teaching job and, almost two years on, was now a full-time mother to all her children, including Bill.

Everyone had said that Fee had been very good about Bill's behaviour. She was civilized, understanding. They sold the house, split the contents.

'I hope one day we can be friends,' he'd said, dutifully.

'Why not?' Fee had replied cheerily. 'It's no more than we've ever been—'

She glanced down and rescued a stray photograph that had slipped out of the album to the floor. It was a hazy head and shoulders of Colin Stevens taken in a booth. Fee couldn't help but wince.

About the same time as Bill's last call, Colin had provided Fee with a new milestone. He marked her recognition that she was in the grip of an accelerating addiction to men who confused love with grievous emotional harm.

They had met at a fund-raising supper and auction for Childlink, the Third World charity for which Colin worked as Director of Projects. Fee had attended as the guest of a girlfriend who was also employed by the charity.

'I hate these things, don't you?' Colin had said, asking if the seat next to Fee's was free. The following two hours in his company had sped by.

Colin was thirty-four, unmarried. Almost immediately, he had made the mistake of telling Fee that he was far too involved in his work to have much of a private life.

'But that's the way I like it, I suppose—'

'You love your work?' Fee had said, just to make sure that she really had come across yet another member of the wandering tribe of Unattainables. Colin nodded.

'The job involves a lot of travelling. So my time's not my own. But yes, on the whole I do.'

Fee moved into heaven. As always, it was only a temporary sublet.

Over the next six weeks, Colin invited Fee out several times. They chatted, discussed, mildly disagreed at times, and laughed a great deal.

Colin talked a lot about the importance of integrity and personal honesty. Fee blossomed on a diet of a couple of hours' sleep each night. The two put the kind of tentative questions to each other that people often do when they hope they share a lot in common and are fearful of discovering that the opposite may be true.

'Thrillers? Well, I'm not so . . . oh, you like them? Me? I love them. I really do—'

In this exploratory way, they had begun to build up quite an impressive list: Wales, walking, white burgundy, the books of Ross Macdonald . . .

Just when Fee really *knew* that something was happening between them, Colin announced that he had to go to the Middle East on a two-week trip. He'd call as soon as he returned.

On Saturday afternoon, three days later, Colin Stevens was kissing a woman outside W. H. Smith in Victoria Station when Fee bumped into them both.

'How have you been keeping?' he asked curiously, as if Fee was some sort of semi-putrid fruit.

Fee had smiled, with only the slightest quiver to her bottom lip. 'Fine,' she'd said.

'The trip, it was cancelled. Last minute thing . . . That's our train,' Colin had added, increasingly uncomfortable. The two women, unintroduced, smiled faintly at each other, uncertain of their respective positions in the hierarchy of Colin Stevens's life.

'I'll give you a ring, OK?' Colin said, grabbing the woman's hand.

Of course, he never had.

'You'd got to him,' Claire had announced that evening in her flat, pouring Fee a drink.

'You've got to him and he can't afford to let himself be that vulnerable. Men like him need to be in control. What they fear most is opening themselves up—'

'If that's the case, all he had to do was say so,' Fee replied. Claire looked at her as if to say, 'You think it's that simple . . .?'

'I *know* he was interested—' Fee insisted.

'Of *course* he was. If he wasn't, he'd still be here,' Claire replied reassuringly. 'But the crucial question is, what did you want from him?'

'What do you mean "want"?'

'Want . . . You know . . . W A N T . . . Did you drop any hints? Come on too strong? Come on too cool? Did you mention the long term . . . shacking up, marriage, what?'

'God, Claire,' Fee interrupted. 'I'd barely got round to learning how many sugars he had in his coffee . . . we'd only known each other five minutes. It just might have been nice to see what would have happened . . .'

'Fee, all you failed to do was examine the subtext,' Claire snapped in exasperation.

'What do you mean? Subtext?'

'If you have an emotional investment in a man, assume, until proven otherwise, that what he says and how he behaves is no guide to how he feels.'

'So how the hell do you know what's going on?' Fee asked.

'You let your instincts pick up on the subtext,' Claire instructed.

'If you're a clear, level-headed, self-confident, self-sufficient woman who knows what's good for her, then that's no problem—'

'And if you're not?' Fee asked ruefully.

'You're in trouble,' Claire announced. 'Quite a lot of trouble.'

After Colin, Adam's adoration offered immediate comfort. Then Fee met Paul and the subtext had grown confused all over again.

Fee sighed and neatly tore Colin Stevens's photograph in two. He had been very pretty. Probably too pretty for her. Anyway, from now on, men would only be intervals of light entertainment.

Never again would Fee see the fear of God pass across a man's face when she mentioned the word 'love', however innocuous the context.

Enough men had told her in the past that all they desired was 'something light', 'no commitments'; 'Let's be friends with a bit of a zip.'

Mostly her zips, Fee recalled.

She too was now one of the Unattainable; one of the elusive; one of the 'I'm-just-hopeless-at-involvement' types.

Why should a *subtext* be only a male perk?

Fee poured herself a glass of wine and walked out onto her balcony to drink it in the evening sun. A small private treat. A woman who had just declared a state of permanent independence might be feeling excited, elated, hopeful. Instead, she was weary. A sense of emptiness had been with her all day, which at any moment might slide into self-pity. She knew who was to blame. It was all Claire's fault.

Fee acknowledged she shouldn't mind so much about Claire's impending wedding. But she did. It wasn't that she was jealous of Claire, certainly not. She was irritated. That's all it was – irritation.

A woman caught Fee's eye in the garden opposite. She was sitting in a deckchair, reading a newspaper. A man appeared and sat on her lap, tickling her as she did so. She laughed and they kissed.

Fee felt a lump in her throat.

'I am alone but not lonely,' she told herself firmly. It was true. At least some of the time.

At 11 p.m. that evening when Fee was watching the late-night news, the phone rang.

It had to be Paul, Fee told herself. Relief flooded through her. Everything was bound to be on a different footing now that he knew she couldn't be pushed around.

As she reached for the phone, Fee smiled wryly at her own display of instant weakness. 'What's it to be, kiddo, self-deception or honest spinsterhood?' she asked herself.

The voice was male but it did not belong to Paul.

Fee smiled resignedly.

'Hello, Will,' she said.

'Hi, Fee, it's late I know. I'm really sorry . . . Can I ask a big favour?' He didn't stop to hear her reply.

'I've run out of petrol. I'm only twenty minutes or so from you but I don't want to leave the car here because I need it first thing. If you want to say no, I could try and find a garage. One that's open, that is . . . but it's late—'

'OK, OK,' Fee interrupted. 'I'll be there as quick as I can—'

'Thanks, Fee.' The pips began to drown Will's voice. 'You're a real mate.'

'What more could a girl want?' Fee said as she hunted for her car keys.

Half an hour later, Fee drove into a cul-de-sac in which several cars were parked. Two figures sitting on a low wall were locked in each other's arms.

Fee stopped the car and sat and watched for a matter of seconds. How peculiar. She'd never seen Will kiss anyone before. Not even his ex-wife. Not like that.

'Will,' Fee hissed, leaning out of her car window.

She had to call three times, before the name registered. He finally looked up and waved casually, as if she just happened to be passing by.

He kissed the woman again. She was faintly familiar to Fee. The woman walked away without giving her a glance.

Five minutes later, as Will poured petrol into his tank from the can Fee had brought, she asked casually, 'Why isn't your friend coming back?'

'She lives around the corner. That's why we're here,' Will answered.

'Why couldn't you stay the night with her then, instead of dragging me out?' Fee asked.

'I hadn't seen you for a couple of days. I missed you.' Will smiled.

He handed the can back to Fee and wiped his hands on the back of his jeans.

Then he said, 'Look, I can't stay with her. She lives around the corner with her boyfriend. I don't think he'd be keen to offer me a bed for the night—'

'God, Will, don't you care about what you do? Don't you ever have a conscience?'

'No,' Will replied cheerfully, leaning against his car, his arms folded. He observed Fee's growing indignation with amusement.

'My view is, if he was making her happy, she wouldn't feel the need to come to me.'

'That's not the issue,' Fee answered, wondering why she felt so angry when it was none of her business.

'What should matter is that you are being deceitful, dishonest, stealing a person who belongs to someone else. I bet you that's half the thrill for you . . . Well, in my view, that's just plain nasty . . . Nobody—'

'Whoa, whoa—' Will said, taking a step back.

He walked around his car and opened the passenger door, indicating to Fee that she should take a seat.

'Hop in and let Uncle Will hear all about it—'

Fee contemplated telling him to shove off but, instead, half an hour later, Will had the whole story: her decision, Adam's proposal, Paul, Claire, the christening, her mother's reaction . . .

Will had always been a good listener.

'So, what do you think?' she asked, turning to him uncertainly.

'Have you told Adam yet that it's a no?' Will asked.

'Yes. He's now saying he never really proposed in the first place.'

'Terrific,' Will replied.

'Have you told Paul that you've signed the pledge?'

'No.'

'Ahaa!' Will examined Fee's face in the street light and wagged his finger disapprovingly.

'Of course I haven't. It's not the sort of thing you say is it? I intend to stay single? I'm a matrimony-free zone?'

'No,' Will answered, thoughtful now. 'But you need to make some kind of public statement. For your own good. No turning back, that sort of thing.'

'What? A sort of disengagement party?' Fee sounded more flip than she felt.

He smiled. 'Of course, a greater cynic than me would suggest that you're having a little game with yourself. Don't look and, hey presto, the man of your dreams appears.'

Fee shook her head vigorously. 'That's what my mother thinks. But if I've learnt anything over the years, it's that the men of my dreams only give me nightmares. I want to get myself on an even keel. I want to stop wasting so much energy looking for the next great love which turns out to be as flawed as the last one—'

She hesitated. Even with a friend as close as Will, she was wary of revealing too much.

'Go on,' Will turned on the engine and the heater.

'One day, when I've stopped equating loving with hurting, perhaps I can give it all another go. And if by then there's no one around who'll have me, well, at least I'll know that I can manage alone. And that I can have a reasonably happy life. Does this all sound totally dotty?' Fee asked anxiously.

Will shook his head. 'It's just a bit of an unexpected blow. I realized that I'd have to wait for you, but I didn't consider that we were talking years—'

She swiped him on the back of his head. 'I knew I shouldn't have opened my mouth,' she said.

The following morning, Will Evans was woken by the phone ringing. It was Hilly Byrne again.

'We're desperate,' she began. 'We—'

He interrupted her. 'I think I've got the woman you're looking for. She's thirty-eight and whole-heartedly single. For now. Her best friend's getting married and they're both fairly competitive, so you'd better get a move on—

'About that drink—' he added.

'Give me her details . . .' Hilly demanded. 'Let's do the personal stuff later . . . if we really have to—'

Chapter Six

A T EIGHT thirty in the evening on the same day, Veronica Haslem sat in a chair in the ladies' lavatory on the fifth floor of Tendon Hospital. The room was chrome and glass. It had three toilets, a changing room for babies and, on one wall, the health trust's logo and motto were emblazoned in fashionable fuchsia.

'Dedicated to Health,' read the words. Underneath on the cream wall in orange lipstick, someone had written, 'But not at weekends and after 5 p.m.'

Veronica stared at her own reflection. In many ways, she was still waiting to grow up. Ridiculous really. Over fifty, and still waiting to grow up. Veronica felt no age. A no-age woman. Inside, she was no age; but, outside, the evidence told her that she was decaying.

She didn't look attractive. That's very hard when all your life your appearance has been so much a part of how others judge you.

People still told Veronica that she was 'a handsome woman *for her age*'. But she didn't welcome such consolation prizes. She knew she had become invisible. Men no longer looked at her; not in that way.

She settled herself more easily and readjusted her feet, propped up on an overturned plastic waste-paper basket. She took the lid off the takeaway cup of coffee. As she sipped, the cappuccino froth dissolved to reveal a disappointing grey liquid.

Veronica looked again at herself in the mirror and frowned. If looks can kill – how come it never worked on her? Suicide by glancing?

She opened her duffel bag. Black leather, one of her daughter's rejects. Once a high-fashion item, Samantha had now classed it as 'sad'. She pulled out a paperback. Her father had always bought them second-hand; coffee-stained and dog-eared, but he carefully wrapped the covers in cellophane and labelled each with the place of purchase, cost and date.

Two Guns at High Chapparel, First Edition, Bloomsbury Book Fair, £1, October 4th 1971,' she read out loud.

Even in her late teens, Veronica would join in when her father and Fee played cowboys in the back garden. Fee was always the sheriff, dad the baddy, Veronica the good guy who walks into town and straight into trouble.

She smiled at the irony. As it turned out, she'd never been in trouble in her life, not even a parking ticket. Until now.

'Get me a tea on your way back, Bob,' said a female voice outside in the corridor. 'One sugar and milk. And a Kitkat, there's a sweetheart.'

Veronica looked at her watch again. She had left home at eleven that morning, without quite knowing where she was going. Several hours later, nobody had realized she was missing. That was part of the problem.

Les was visiting a fast-food festival at Alexander Palace and wouldn't be back until late.

'That's nice,' Helen had said on the phone the previous night. 'You've got the whole day to yourself. Why don't you come and have a bite to eat with me? Or I'll come to you if you don't feel up to it.'

Veronica refused, explaining that there was still a lot of clearing up to do after the christening. Instead, she had left the house and walked. In the late afternoon, she found herself at the hospital.

Recently, she had made several trips to Tendon. She wasn't visiting a patient, but a memory. Her father had been treated here before he died from lung cancer.

She poured the remaining coffee down one of the basins. She had been in the place for two hours and not a single person had come in. This floor of the hospital was used in the daytime for ante-natal research. Now it was peaceful, apart from the occasional slam of a door, and the ping of the lifts.

In a strange way, she told herself, she was quite enjoying this business of being odd; at least it gave her something on which to concentrate. It gave a kind of structure to each day: planning ways to avoid the next kill.

It didn't use to be like this. Veronica had always been busy when the children were young, too busy to think. She was involved with their activities, she was a volunteer helper in the class-room, and she served teas in an old people's home every Friday afternoon.

The menopause had come early but without undue discomfort when she was forty-seven. She hadn't told anyone because who would want to know?

She prided herself that sexually she was the woman whom Les had first married. But if her heart was still in it, something had happened to her soul. How could she enjoy making love when she had all these deaths on her conscience?

Children gone, husband preoccupied; it was time to *do*. But what? Especially when most people simply looked through you.

'You're needed here, *at home*,' Les would say firmly if she brought the subject up. But there was no evidence that she was.

A swing door banged. Veronica jumped. If she saw someone now, had eye contact, she was bound to do harm. She picked up her bag and coat and locked herself into the first lavatory, sliding the bolt so fast she nipped the skin on her finger.

She heard the door open with a slam and something that sounded like a pram being pushed in. Several taps were turned on; the metal holder for the handtowel was banged; a lavatory flushed. Curious, Veronica went down on her hands and knees and peered under the door.

What peered back caused her to squeak in alarm. What she could see was Cleopatra's eyes. Black eyebrow pencil had drawn two arcs;

blue the colour of a peacock's chest coloured the lids; mascara was clumped like miniature furballs on the lashes.

'Are you OK?' asked a voice with a light Scottish accent. 'Only an awful lot of people recently have gone in there and not come out—'

Veronica looked with alarm at the lavatory pan as if some hand might shoot out and grab her round the neck.

'Not without a lot of help,' the voice added.

'I'm fine, thank you,' Veronica answered. She pulled the bolt. It wouldn't shift. She pulled again, then pushed, then shook it.

'It's a knack,' said the voice on the other side of the door. 'You have to sort of lift the door a wee bit, then pull the bolt back. I've told them they should leave instructions. One poor lamb was in there all night. Another woman had left her baby outside and nearly went mental. She was in there for half a hour before anyone realized. Take this duster,' the voice instructed. A hand appeared under the lavatory door holding a yellow duster.

'Give the bolt a bang with this wrapped around your hand.'

Veronica peered under the door again. This time she saw an extraordinary pair of very high-heeled electric-blue suede shoes, with peep toes and a small bow: 1940s rather than 1990s judging by the battered condition of some of the suede.

The voice continued, its owner having stopped to pull deeply on a cigarette. Smoke came over the door.

'So,' the voice continued. 'Are you ready? Bang and pull.'

Veronica did as she was told. Suddenly, the bolt shot free and the door swung towards her.

Outside was a woman, the like of which Veronica had never seen before, definitely decayed but defiantly dressed as if the flesh was still young. This woman would never consider herself invisible.

'OK are you, pet?' the woman asked.

'Thank you so much,' Veronica replied. 'I don't know what I'd have done, if you hadn't been here. Are you one of the cleaners?'

A cleaning trolley now held the door to the corridor half open.

'Cleaning? the woman looked horrified. She wore a white coat over her clothes.

'No, that was in the corridor,' she indicated with her head towards the trolley. 'I thought it would let a bit of air in because I fancied a fag. Don't mind, do you?' She waved the lit cigarette in her hand.

'Have a seat,' she suggested to Veronica as if the lavatory was her personal domain. 'Want a ciggy?'

Veronica shook her head and sat down.

'I'm a radiographer,' the woman explained, checking her reflection and licking the pale-apricot lipstick off her teeth with her tongue.

'I'm on the late shift. Come up here to see my friend in my break but she's already gone home. She's the one who told me all about people being locked in the lavatory and that. She's very nice. You'd like her,' the woman added. Veronica felt flattered.

'Everybody loves Emma. She's that kind of person. Mind you, I'm a bit that way myself. Important to enjoy yourself. Let people know you're here, hey?'

Words poured out of the woman like water from a punctured rain barrel. Lonely or lively? Veronica wasn't sure. Periodically, the woman reanchored her very thin french pleat more firmly to her head with kirby grips, talking all the time.

Under the white coat, she was dressed in blue and white check capri pants, a white jumper decorated with seed pearls and what looked like fading tea stains, and she carried a blue suede handbag which matched her shoes.

An aroma reminded Veronica of childhood. At first, she couldn't identify it, then she recognized it as a mixture of lily of the valley and Velouté, a foundation in a tube which her grandmother had favoured.

Veronica judged the woman to be in her early fifties, but the cruelly flat black hair dye distracted the eye so much it was difficult to tell.

Veronica never described anyone as 'plain'. Not when she herself had been so lucky in her looks. It didn't seem fair. But in all honesty, nobody could be plainer than this woman. Only the very widest of smiles, which revealed a set of unreal white teeth, offered compensation. But what fascinated Veronica most was the woman's apparent belief that she was someone worth looking at.

'Can't put a pound on,' the woman was saying with pride, hands on a tiny waist. 'No matter how much I eat. Are you all right?' she added, scarcely drawing breath. 'You look sort of . . . sleepy?'

Veronica had half closed her eyes for the woman's own protection. Sometimes the technique saved a person from one of her more lethal looks.

'Oh I'm really fine,' Veronica answered, wide-eyed again. 'Sort of—'

'Sort of?' the woman said, settling herself more comfortably in the chair, in anticipation of a lengthy story.

'I'm dangerous,' Veronica surprised herself by saying. 'I look at people and then they die.' She watched carefully for a reaction. 'Everyone else tells me that I'm imagining it. But I'm not. I'm really not.'

Veronica waited. The woman blew a couple of smoke rings and stretched her legs. 'My auntie used to do that,' she replied nonchalantly. 'Got through virtually the entire population of Wolverhampton.'

'What happened?' Veronica asked.

'Her husband divorced her. He said it was more than he'd bargained for. And, next minute, she's as right as rain. You got a husband?'

Veronica smiled. 'He's a nice man,' she answered truthfully. 'He just thinks everything can be fixed by a cup of tea and a sandwich. Well, in his case, I suppose it was . . . What I mean is, he makes sandwiches for a living and he does quite well. Les is fine. He's all right, it's me who's the problem.'

The two women sat in silence for a few minutes.

The woman lit up her second cigarette. 'My name is Rita, as in Heywood,' she offered. 'But my surname's Mason. My mother was mad about Rita. Mum's dead now. Died a cruel death – cancer, a couple of years back. What's your name?'

'Veronica. If I'd been a boy, my dad wanted me named Roy as in Rogers. He was Wild West mad. He died here,' Veronica suddenly added. Then, it happened.

One minute, she was composed, the next it was as if her very being had dissolved in grief.

'Oh God, what am I going to do? What am I going to do?' she wept. She put her face in her hands and cried and cried. She cried so long and so hard that the sound and effort eventually began to give its own strange hypnotic comfort.

Rita sat silent. Then, when Veronica had calmed a little, she gave her a box of tissues pillaged from the cleaning trolley.

She eventually spoke. 'Haven't got a car, have you? No, I thought not. Nor me. Look, my shift finishes in an hour. I'll take you down to the coffee shop, you have a nice hot drink, then I can take you home. I can get them to call a cab at reception. That's best, isn't it? Have you got some coins? Why don't you give your old man a ring, tell him you're all right?'

Rita offered Veronica a cheap plastic tube of lipstick. 'Here, love, try this. You could do with a bit of colour.'

'I'm all right, I really am,' Veronica protested, in the ridiculous way that the profoundly upset often do. 'I can find my own way home.'

Rita Mason was adamant.

'I wouldn't sleep in my bed soundly if I didn't know you'd got safely back,' she insisted. 'You and me together, we'll soon sort you out. Just watch.'

For some reason Veronica experienced a fleeting sense of alarm. Then she told herself not to be so silly, the woman wasn't commandeering her life, just offering a helping hand. She watched as Rita produced a pen and notebook.

'Give us your address, Veronica Rogers,' Rita Mason commanded. 'Then I can order a cab.'

Veronica was about to correct the woman and say, 'It's not

Rogers,' but then she asked herself, why bother? They'd never meet again. Instead, she gave Fee's address. She couldn't bear the thought of returning to her own empty house.

Two hours later, just after midnight, the taxi bearing Rita Mason and Veronica Haslem stopped outside Fiona Travers' flat. Rita insisted on paying the fare.

'I'll be fine now, I really will,' Veronica insisted, her original fears about Rita dissolving in the face of the woman's obvious concern.

'You don't get rid of me as easily as that, young lady. First, let's make sure someone's in,' Rita replied firmly, teetering down the garden path on the ridiculously high blue-suede heels.

'What do you think of this?' Claire held up a page torn out of a magazine. At the same time as Rita and Veronica were making their introductions, Claire, Gill and Fee were finishing supper in a wine bar close to Gill's house. They had gathered to celebrate the news of Claire's impending marriage.

Claire had brought a stack of wedding magazines and had already elicited a promise from a reluctant Fee to come with her to choose a dress.

Gill and Fee had to concede that the turnaround in Claire was impressive. All her adult life she had been scathing about various friends and relatives who had trotted up the aisle in an excess of white satin and tulle. Her wedding, she said, would be minimalist, in a Register Office, no fuss.

Now, suddenly, she had become a zealot for nuptials. The list was endless: a horse and carriage; bridesmaids; one pageboy; a trousseau; a honeymoon outfit; veil; gloves; shoes; marquee; flowers – on and on. For three hours now, Fee had been experiencing bridal white-out – and Claire hadn't even begun to flag.

'Funny to think that soon I'll be a wife, just like you, Gill.' Claire beamed. Gill gave a wobbly smile back.

'You loved your wedding day, didn't you, Gill? And you and Simon are still going strong?'

'Well . . . yes, I suppose you might say that. I mean you . . . we . . . one has doubts now and then – who doesn't? But, you know, on the—' Gill stumbled on but Claire wasn't in the mood for nuances.

'Oh, come off it,' Claire interrupted, hockey captain to the fore. 'Everyone knows you two are the perfect couple. Isn't that right, Fee?'

Fee didn't have an opportunity to reply. Claire had turned towards her and seized her by the shoulders.

'Now,' she boomed. Alcohol always made her loud. 'How are we going to get you sorted out, my old sausage? Gill says you and Adam are almost there—'

Gill interrupted. 'She changed her mind,' she told Claire crossly. 'She let us get all het up and then she changed her mind. Was that how it was, Fee? You know at times I've got no idea how your mind works.' Gill made it sound as if Fee was depriving her of a major civil right.

Claire moved into bossy mode. 'Right, Fee,' she directed. 'It's time to take you in hand. It's time you became *proactive*. Why don't you try a dating agency, for instance? Or go to one of those social clubs . . . They organize all sorts of events . . . or you could advertise in a lonely-hearts thingummy—'

'Claire,' Fee said, struggling to keep the lightness in her voice, 'what kind of a person do you think I am? Do I *look* as if I'm in need of a trainspotter? Do I *look* as if I'm only half alive without a man? Do I? I mean, do I *really*?'

She glanced at the faces of Gill and Claire. What she saw was pity. *Pity?*

She was incredulous. Claire with her highly suspect husband-to-be; Gill with a marriage suffering from a couple of flat tyres, and they felt pity for her?

Claire was speaking again. 'Go on, why don't you put a lonely-hearts ad in the paper, Fee? Isn't that a smashing idea, Gill? Wouldn't you do it if you were single? I've read about it. If you're older and you've got a career and your friends are all married, it's a perfectly respectable way of going about things—'

'Oh, come off it, Claire,' Gill snorted. 'We're talking about other people's rejects here. Emotional seconds. And let's make no bones about it. I mean, you wouldn't take a man like that if he came wrapped up in a free annual holiday in Bali, now would you? Be honest? So why suggest it to Fee?'

'I'm fine as I am, I really am,' Fee interrupted. This was plainly not the time to announce that she had rejected romance in all its forms.

'Of course you are.' Claire patted Fee's hand condescendingly. 'But don't worry, someone will come along. Nobody in their right mind wants to be on their own for life, now do they?'

Later, Claire and Gill shared a taxi home.

'What are we going to do about Fee?' Claire asked. 'When I'm married, she'll have an awfully big gap in her life.'

Gill considered the prospect with alarm. 'Claire,' she tried to sound as casual as possible. 'Could you ever steal another woman's man? I mean, a friend's husband, for instance? Especially if you thought it was your last chance. You know, this man or nothing, kind of thing?'

'Probably,' Claire answered flippantly. 'In fact, almost certainly. But that's me, Gill. If you're asking, do I think Fee would behave in the same underhand way, the answer is – never. You know that she has a thing about the sisterhood. Loyalty to women, all that stuff. Totally misguided, of course.' Claire turned to smile at Gill. 'If anyone's not to be trusted, it's me.'

Gill smiled briefly, unconvinced.

'Fee? It's Les.'

Fee was on her car phone. It had been almost two weeks since saying goodbye to Paul, and the chances of him resuming communication had become more remote by the day. So her heart no longer bounced when she heard the phone ring.

Adam, in contrast, called often. *Just for a chat, see how you are.* He dropped frequent hints about the midwife he was seeing. Did Fee know she had a lemon MGB? Did Fee realize quite how much he was enjoying himself?

Occasionally Adam would suggest that they meet for a friendly drink. So far Fee had managed to end the conversation without confirming a time or a place.

'Hello, Les,' Fee replied. Her brother-in-law sounded panicked.

'Have you seen Veronica?' he asked. 'I can't find her. She's not home. She's not next door. She's not with Helen. Fee, I'm really worried.' He was almost shouting.

Fee looked at her watch. Past midnight.

'I'm sorry, Les,' she answered, trying to keep anxiety out of her voice. 'I've been out myself all evening. When did you last see her?'

'She always leaves a note when she goes somewhere. I can't find it,' Les replied. 'She always leaves a note. No matter what she does, she always lets us know. You don't think she's done anything silly, do you?'

'Absolutely not,' Fee replied firmly, trying to sound as if she meant it. 'It's probably something simple like the car breaking down or—'

'Her car's here,' Les said abruptly.

'Perhaps a friend called and she went out on the spur of the moment. Or—'

'If she turns up at your place, will you give me a ring?' Les interrupted. 'I'm calling the police. It's not safe for her to be out . . . Not in the state she's in. I knew I shouldn't have left her on her own. It's all my fault.'

Then he was gone. As Fee pulled up at her house, she immediately saw the note pinned to her front door.

*

Ten minutes later, Fee arrived at the booth on wheels that called itself a café, parked alongside a bridge half a mile from her flat.

A handwritten sign announced, 'Open All Nite'. An ambulance was just pulling away. A policewoman was about to get behind the wheel of a car parked on the pavement.

'Wait!' Fee shouted. 'Please, wait—' A couple of taxi drivers propped up against a cab and drinking tea turned to watch her as she ran.

'Excuse me.' Fee had slowed down. The policewoman, constructed from the same rectangular mould from which so many figures in uniform appear to be made, waited for her.

'I'm looking for my sister.' She waved the note in the policewoman's face. 'She said she'd be here . . . The ambulance . . .?'

'Is she dark, getting on a bit, tight pants, high heels?' The man behind the counter in the van was anxious to share his information.

Fee shook her head. Relief overwhelmed her.

'Oh, well, she'll be the small, blonde one then, well turned out like, pretty in her day?' the man offered, satisfied that he hadn't after all been cheated of the thrill of informing a relative.

Fee's internal organs reacted as if they were being given sixty seconds in a blender.

'What's happened? Is she all right? Where have they gone . . .?'

The policewoman put up her hand to the café owner, as if stopping traffice. Obediently, he fell silent.

'It's fine, madam, the two ladies are perfectly OK . . . You didn't know the victim . . .?' The policewoman spoke soothingly.

'What victim?' Fee asked.

'I'll tell you what happened.' The man behind the counter could restrain himself no longer.

'The ladies were standing behind him in the queue. Nicely spoken middle-aged man, well dressed. The blonde one is right behind him. He suddenly falls down, she starts yelling. She's saying, "Oh God, no, oh God, no," . . . summat like that . . . "I've done it again . . . Help him, do something, I've killed him . . . all that palaver . . . We're all panicking like, thinking she's stuck him with a knife and all that. Then, that fella over there, the one wiv the mug, suddenly twigs, don't 'e?'

'He sticks a spoon in the geezer's mouth to hold back his tongue. He's an epileptic in 'e? Anyways, we gets the ambulance just in case. The blonde woman is still pretty upset like.

'Screaming her head off as a matter of fact with her eyes tight shut . . . So, the ambulancemen get her to hop in as well, see if they can calm her down a bit at the 'ospital . . . Then the black-haired old gel, says she's a friend and she's got to go too . . . they've gone to St Thomas—'

'Still, all's well, eh? Can I get you a cup of tea, love?'

At the hospital, Les had been summoned to take a sedated Veronica home. The woman who had looked after her introduced herself as Rita Mason. She had refused an offer of a lift from Fee.

'I'm sure Veronica would like to thank you herself when she's a bit better. Has she got your telephone number?' Fee asked, intrigued by Rita's appearance.

'Oh, she doesn't have to worry. Tell her I'll be in touch. I know where she lives now—'

'Oh no,' Fee interrupted. 'That's my flat . . . Veronica lives in north London. Let me—'

But Rita Mason was already halfway out of the door.

'See you then,' she said.

At the time, it sounded like such an innocuous remark to make.

Later, as Fee lay in her bed and waited for sleep, she thought of Claire's advice that she should resort to a lonely-hearts column. It wasn't such a bad idea – but not for quite the purpose that Claire had in mind. Fee began to compose a suitable ad. in her head.

'Confirmed spinster, no psychotic tendencies, thirty-five plus, requires female platonic playmate to deflect the pity of others. And have a good time.'

She'd forgotten something. Then, Fee remembered, '*Only genuine applicants need apply—*'

Chapter Seven

'FABULOUSLY FLESHY!'

On Wednesday morning, Imogen Banks stood in front of her full-length art-deco mirror in her warehouse flat, reasonably pleased with the overall effect.

Some years before, after several near-death experiences while on a variety of diets (the near-death of others, since Imogen tended to become homicidal when hungry), she had finally come to terms with being plump. Now, when she looked in the mirror, she no longer thought, 'Fat.' She had programmed herself to say, 'Fabulously fleshy!'

It worked – sometimes.

Today, she had chosen to wear a black suit with multicoloured buttons the size of small frisbees; bright red lipstick; red, yellow, blue and green ear-rings that looked like cascading Smarties and a small, emerald-green handbag. She also wore two watches, assorted gold bracelets and a pearl necklace.

If Fiona Travers's dress code was based on the premise that less was better, Imogen Banks had the firm conviction that too much was never enough.

Imogen also believed that selling yourself hard, cheating, deception, manipulation and emotional blackmail were all reasonable modes of behaviour in order to look after number one with any degree of success.

Anyone who claimed otherwise was a hypocrite and a wimp. Good girls, Imogen Banks despised. Bad girls, if they were feminists, she also loathed.

Feminism, as far as she was concerned, was the cause of her immense difficulty in locating her lifelong soul mate. It had scared off men; driven them into the arms of other males. The sisterhood sucked.

If anyone asked her for the worst punishment she could contemplate, it would be to share the company of women for purposes other than work. To share their company voluntarily *for pleasure* was unthinkable.

Did Elizabeth I or Boadicea or Jane Austen sit around with a gaggle of girls discussing homeopathic cures for cystitis or contemplating the spiritual meaning of menstruation? No, they did not.

Imogen had never had a female best friend in her life nor did she want one. In her view, females fell into two categories: rivals or wives. The rest she took pride in stepping on – or over.

As for the glass ceiling, Imogen Banks considered it as real as the unicorn. And she should know. She was the employer of a staff of a dozen females.

In her opinion, women in work were nothing but trouble – herself excepted. Gynaecological difficulties, eating disorders, neurosis brought on by lack of self-confidence, maternity leave, childcare difficulties, old mothers to take to the chiropodist, HRT implants needing to be replaced, lumps in the breast, and always banging on about the three S's – self-esteem, sex, and second-class citizenship.

Imogen would have preferred to employ men – but they were so much more expensive.

Astra TV was a company that Imogen Banks had set up while she was waiting for the real business of her life to begin: a husband, a home. She did not like babies. She did, however, wish to be a mother. She could see herself – a couple of stone lighter, hair bleached, complete facial reconstruction – cavorting on a beach in Maine with two pre-Raphaelite children, born toddler-size. In the distance, her millionaire husband would snooze on the deck of their all-white clapboard house.

While she waited for the fairy-tale to come true, she filled in her time by making her company a highly successful endeavour. She would tell those impressed with her profits and prospects that you can't change a business plan's nappy or read a bedtime story to an award-winning comedy series.

Everyone else except Imogen could see that her heart lay not with Mr Right and babywipes but in the family-free zone of the workplace. Still, if the woman wanted to fool herself, it was nobody's business but her own.

Imogen checked her watch; 6.45 a.m. She would be in the office, as usual, within half an hour. She locked her front door. After a massive investment in maximalist décor, Imogen's warehouse flat still made her feel as if she was squatting in an aircraft hangar, so she was always relieved to leave home. She hailed a taxi.

'See the news last night, it's terrible—' the taxi driver began, after she had given him Astra's address. His radio blared Country 'n' Western.

She leaned forward. 'Look,' she said. 'Could you turn the radio off and keep quiet? There's a good lad.'

Imogen Banks was always direct – except, of course, when being devious produced greater rewards. And nothing was beyond dissection – not even the allegedly mysterious process of falling in love. Deconstruction of a romance she found a doddle.

She could generally tell in the first couple of hours of an affair into which particular category it fell. Narcissism? Father fixation? Masochism?

She knew her own heart inside out. Or, at least, she thought she did. Over the years, a pattern had established itself. Man after man would come, see, be conquered – and then, infuriatingly for Imogen, return to his previous love – usually, his wife.

On a couple of occasions, she had even had the humiliation of seeing a married lover return to his previous *mistress.*

She could hook a man, play with him, land him on shore – but once he got bored with what at first were regarded as her unique attractions and later as her 'excesses', that was it.

Imogen believed that her 'excesses' were more accurately described as being too bright, too independent, too self-sufficient and far too bloody expensive for many men to handle. Still, she never gave up hope. She profoundly believed that for every human being there is Another.

If only his wife would let him go.

Imogen's belief in self-help, or rather help yourself, when it came to other women's men, did not cause her any worry. A married man was far more grateful than his single counterpart; thankful – at least in the early stages – that you were not his wife. A married man had certain constraints on his time, which allowed Imogen to proceed with her own life without undue pressure. Above all, a married man belonged to someone else. Imogen enjoyed stealing from her fellow woman.

Recently, however, the lack of permanence in her relationships had begun to trouble her. Not least because she had convinced herself that, until she settled down, she couldn't class herself as happy. Not properly happy. So she had decided to apply herself much more assiduously to the business of finding a man she could keep.

Imogen had read in a magazine that odour counts for more than ardour. Each woman gives off smells that are perfectly compatible with those smells of a specific male. Find him – and you have a partner for life no matter how few the interests in common, or how minimal the mutual attraction.

Imogen was now an inveterate sniffer.

If she couldn't smell out a suitable future spouse, then nobody could. But progress, so far, had been slow. She had developed a very keen nose – easily identifying brands of aftershave, deodorant, moisturizers and a wide range of stale sweat, but the stink of true love had eluded her.

This morning, as she paid her fare and waited impatiently for a receipt, she indulged herself in a warm-up exercise. She inhaled deeply, then told the bemused taxi driver, 'Chinese take-away; Mum roll-on and perhaps a little splash of Ralph Lauren's Polo?'

The offices of Astra Television, in an anonymous block off Baker Street, were decorated in stark black and white and red. Or, as the staff preferred, referring to Imogen's frequent outbursts, 'Black and white and bled all over—'

Imogen perched on her unnecessarily large desk in her office and looked down on the three women sitting in a semi-circle around her. They looked up at her expectantly, waiting for her to speak.

She opened her mouth. 'What we have is crap—' she said crisply.

'Crap,' she repeated. 'Every woman so far in the film hedges her bets far too much.'

She mimicked the voice of an interviewee she had just watched on tape, '"I'm really happy as I am but if somebody came along, well then, who knows?" Yuk! Can't even one of these bloody people be a bit more *positively* single?'

'This is a good idea.' Imogen banged her hand on the desk. 'So, we're going to find the right people if it kills us.'

'We have looked,' began Hilly Byrne, thirty-two, the director of the documentary now under discussion in its rough-cut form.

'Not hard enough, obviously,' Imogen snapped, jealous of Hilly's anorexia.

Two months earlier, Astra had been commissioned to make a fifty-minute documentary for television based on an idea proposed by Imogen. She had called it *The Perfumed Pound – the Rise of the Spending Spinster*.

The theme was the growing economic clout of an increasing number of heterosexual single women – how they plan for a husbandless future, how they spend now. And what impact their independence might have on the rest of society.

Imogen had been instructed to ensure that the film was 'upbeat, sexy, fun'. So, her team had hauled in the usual single female million-aire entrepreneurs with loads of dosh and not much dress sense.

Each had proved reluctant to commit herself on film to the idea that life without a man might have more perks than coupledom.

'Why can't one of them say, for instance, "Being single is sublime,"' Imogen demanded. 'Or something sassy, like "Who needs a husband to spend all my money?"'

'It's just a thought,' ventured Angela Stead, in her late twenties, one of the two researchers working on the film. She had slight scarring from teenage acne, and more dandruff than one might expect in an era of medicated shampoos.

'It's just a thought,' Angela pressed on. 'But what if your kind of spinster – happily single, determined to live without a live-in partner – suppose she doesn't actually exist?'

Three pairs of eyes turned on Angela. She had not been employed in television long enough to trade in integrity for ambition so, foolishly, she pursued her line of thought.

'I mean, there has to be a reason why every newspaper is filled with loney-hearts ads. And why does it feel as if there are more singles clubs than pubs in London now? Surely it must mean that everybody's out there looking for Mr and Ms Right.'

Imogen smiled coldly. 'I've sold the idea to a commissioning editor, Angela, my darling, allegedly on the basis of a massive amount of prior research, for which that commissioning editor has already paid handsomely,' she said. 'So, if these women don't exist, we'll bloody well have to invent them. Won't we? Now, let's have a little creative licence around here, OK? Find me a woman.'

It was then that Hilly Byrne made her second call to Will Evans. Within minutes, she was speaking on the phone to Fee.

Stress as well as hunger always made Hilly talk too much. It did so now.

'Will told me that not only did you fit the bill – being a spinster and all that – but that you'd be awfully articulate on the subject . . . He's very impressed with you, because he said you're so, well, together . . . and you don't look too bad either . . . So visually, it works too . . . I mean we wouldn't want to put on a dog because everybody would say she couldn't get a man anyway. If you know what I mean . . . You haven't been married, have you? Please God, you haven't been married.'

Hilly stopped, aware that honesty wasn't the best form of seduction when it came to asking a woman to reveal her soul to (hopefully) at least 10 million viewers.

Fee was appalled at her suggestion. And embarrassed. Embarrassed that Will should have told a stranger about her decision. Politely, Fee explained that while she was happy to be single, she definitely did not wish to advertise the fact on television.

'I've made a personal choice,' Fee said crisply. 'Not launched a brand of toothpaste.'

'My boss will kill me if you don't say yes,' Hilly said, opting for a woman-to-woman plea.

'Sorry,' Fee replied. 'I'm not the kind of person you're looking for. Really, I'm not.'

Hilly was right about Imogen's reaction.

'You silly cow,' Imogen bellowed, standing in the centre of the open-plan office. 'And she's a silly cow too. If she isn't sure what she thinks on the subject, you bloody well *tell* her.'

She kicked the plastic waste-paper basket hard, causing a shower of cold coffee from several half-empty paper cups to rain down on her skirt and legs. Hilly hid her smile.

'Bugger,' Imogen said, inspecting her mottled calves.

She turned her attention back to Hilly.

'Didn't you tell her it's only television, for God's sake?' she demanded. 'Give me the woman's number. I'll get her to say yes. I wish some of these people wouldn't take it all so *personally*. It's

not history they're making, it's entertainment. Pure bloody
entertainment.'

At 6 p.m., Imogen left the office and went home to change. She
chose black slacks and a black cashmere polo neck with flat black
loafers. She stripped herself of jewellery and removed a lot of eye
make-up.

Half an hour later, driving her white BMW, she made a call on
her mobile phone. She had been looking forward to this all day. A
woman's voice answered.

'Hello, is that Annabel Davidson?' Imogen asked in her lowest,
huskiest, sexiest voice.

'Who is it?' the woman replied.

'I expect you think Nigel is working hard at the office, don't
you, Mrs Davidson?' Imogen continued, her adrenalin racing so fast
she found it difficult to breathe. How she loved these moments.
Imogen sometimes wondered whether she engineered the premature
end to all her relationships in order to enjoy this mischief at their
demise.

'Who *is* this?' the woman asked again. In the background,
Imogen could hear young children shrieking with delight and the
sound of splashing water . . .

The bathroom in which Nigel had so often locked himself to
make his illicit calls to her.

The phone clicked and whirred and the woman spoke again, this
time from a room without any echoes of family life.

'Are you his girlfriend?' the woman asked in an even tone.

Well, well. Wives today know far more than they're given credit
for, Imogen thought to herself, with some admiration.

'No,' she answered truthfully. 'But I was. I just thought I'd do
you a favour since you were kind enough to let me have the loan of
your husband. He isn't with me any more, you know. But he has
gone back to Jenni Templeton.'

Imogen paused. There was silence on the end of the phone. She felt no pity. Any woman who allowed herself to become too vulnerable deserved all that she got.

Imogen resumed speaking. 'You didn't know about Jenni? Well, Nigel must have been with her on and off for a couple of years, before me. Now, he's gone back. That's where he is now. The number is 0171 651 4367. Give him my regards.'

Imogen had enjoyed Nigel for several months, but she'd found herself growing a touch too sentimental about him so it was just as well he'd decided to call it a day.

Men, Imogen Banks thought to herself, as she pulled up outside the office of Fiona Travers, who'd be without them?

'Men,' Imogen Banks said, as she sat opposite Fee in her office at F.P. & D., 'I mean, frankly, which woman in her right mind needs them? Of course, they're very important to me as friends, even for the occasional romp in the hay, but in relationships . . . forget it. I've known ever since I was a little girl that marriage and me are as likely as The Lone Ranger falling for Tonto—'

'The Lone Ranger . . .?' Fee brightened.

Imogen had arrived uninvited. Fee still had a couple of hours' work to complete before she could allow herself to leave for home.

'Do you know,' Imogen leaned forward conspiratorially, 'I've even been sterilized?'

'I see,' Fee said, unsure how she was supposed to respond. The woman sitting opposite was voluptuous but low key. She had an open, friendly face and expensive hair. Her hands, unlike the rest of her body, were small and delicate with manicured nails the colour of tomatoes.

Fee thought the nails were out of synch with the rest of Imogen Banks's low-profile image. But then again the woman *was* in television.

'Shall I share the experience of sterilization with you?' Imogen asked, pitching her voice to a more confidential tone. Fee rather hoped she wouldn't.

Sharing an intimate experience was the way in which Imogen had persuaded the most reluctant candidates to reveal their intimate secrets to audiences of millions.

In the cause of work, Imogen Banks had allegedly been frigid, adopted, abandoned, battered by a former husband, a recovering alcoholic and infertile. Only the presence of a 38B chest had prevented her once from claiming to have had a double mastectomy in order to become a member of the third sex.

She had no moral qualms about such activities. These weren't lies, they were the tools of her trade. Fiona Travers needed someone to push her just a little bit further than she might initially be prepared to go. If successful, Imogen could see not just a television documentary, but a heated studio discussion as well. And oceans of media coverage.

She could visualize the clamour, she could hear the soundbites. She could see the following day's newspapers.

NEW SPINSTERS MAKE MEN REDUNDANT! NEW SPINSTERS DEVALUE MOTHERHOOD! WHO WILL TAME THE TESTOSTERONE OF OUR YOUNG MEN, IF YOUNG WOMEN GO ON STRIKE! And even: AS THE MILLEN-NIUM APPROACHES THE FAMILY WRECKERS ARE ASKING – WHAT ARE MEN FOR?

She smiled at Fee across the desk. She might not know it, she thought to herself, but Fiona Travers was about to become the leader of a new movement. A very small movement, naturally, but one that could easily be exaggerated beyond all proportion.

Imogen didn't even begin to take Fee's refusal to appear seriously. Everybody wants to be on the box at least once but some people take longer than others to realize it.

Imogen weighed up her reluctant protégée. Reasonably attractive, but too subdued for the screen. What was required was someone who was stylishly pristine on the surface but who gave out the message that she was unmistakably wicked within.

A Wanted Woman, an outlaw from society's conventions. But, above all, an outlaw whom men might fancy, and about whom women would have to concede, 'Well, she could take her pick if she wanted to—'

'This woman – given a little bit of extra polish – could say that there's more to life than finding a man – *and stand a good chance of being believed*,' Imogen thought.

It was then that she took the decision. She would do whatever it took to make Fiona Travers the star of *The Perfumed Pound*. Even, God forbid, perform that most distasteful of acts: become her bosom friend.

The ringing of Fee Travers's phone temporarily halted Imogen Banks She attempted to eavesdrop on what sounded like a highly vocal parrot being put through a shredder. Fee looked at her watch several times, made pacifying noises and eventually replaced the receiver.

'I'm awfully sorry,' she told Imogen. 'I've got to go. A bit of an emergency.'

'Can I help?' Imogen offered instantly. An emergency was a gift from above. 'My car's here . . .' she added swiftly.

'No, really, I'll get a taxi. Look, I'm sorry I haven't been able to help you more but as I explained to your director, it's not really—'

Imogen reached for her coat, and waved her arms in the air, fending off the apology. 'Don't worry about that now . . . You'll never get a taxi at this time of night. You give me instructions and I'll drive. Let's go.'

Ten minutes later, just as Imogen had hoped, the car came to rest in a traffic jam in the Marylebone Road.

'Use this,' Imogen said and offered Fee her mobile phone.

More squawking, more platitudes and a second promise of a speedy arrival.

'It's an old friend,' Fee explained. 'Her husband is late home – and he's never usually late. In fact, he's an unnerving a creature of habit. Anyway, Percy . . . Persephone . . . their daughter – she's just seven – she says she's swallowed an open safety pin, the next-door neighbour is away and Gill needs someone to mind the twins while she takes Percy to casualty.

'Gill doesn't often call on me like this . . . actually, she sounded a bit surprised to find me at the office. Can't think where else she thought I'd be. Anyway, the twins are no problem. In fact, they are absolutely delightful. Almost make me wish I'd had children—' Fee added with a smile.

Imogen Banks gave her passenger a sharp look – was that a hint of ambivalence that she'd just heard? If so, some serious work was about to begin.

'I thought you said you liked tomatoes?' Fee glared at the twins.

Ivo and Euan sat in their pyjamas and dressing-gowns at the kitchen table, chocolate moustaches indicating that the first bribe of the evening had gone down well.

It was an hour later. Imogen had been able to ingratiate herself even further when Gill's car had refused to start. She had driven Gill and Persephone to hospital, leaving Fee in charge of cooking supper for the boys. And at nearly eight o'clock, there was still no sign of Simon.

'I thought you said you liked tomatoes?' Fee repeated, glaring at the two untouched plates of food in front of them.

'We do,' the twins chorused.

'I thought you said you liked fish fingers?'

'We do,' the boys chorused again, enjoying the game.

'I thought you said you liked baked beans?' Fee asked.

'We do,' the boys answered, chuckling with delight.

'So why aren't you eating the tomatoes and fish fingers and baked beans?' she asked as patiently as she could.

'Because we don't like them *together*!' the three-year-olds shouted, clapping their hands involuntarily with pleasure.

Ninety minutes later, when the boys were finally asleep, exhausted, and Fee was making herself tea, the front door crashed open.

'Ah ha!' said Simon, swaying at the kitchen door.

He grabbed the tin lid of the bread bin, held it like a shield and advanced, pretending to lunge with the rolled-up newspaper clutched in his other hand.

'Attack! Attack!' he bellowed. 'Where are you? I'll show you . . . What am I, man or minnow? Advance, you whore . . . Come out, come out wherever you are—'

Fee watched, embarrassed. Had she accidentally stepped into one of Gill's and Simon's fantasy games? Was meek and mild and, above all, silent Simon the raging bull of Endlesham Avenue?

Simon spun round as if on guard and suddenly spotted Fee, standing by the sink. He dropped the bread-bin lid on the table where it clanged. Then his whole body sagged, as if his vertebrae had collapsed *en masse*.

'Oh, Fee, Christ, how embarrassing . . . I thought Gill was going to be here—'

'No, it's me,' Fee replied, shrugging. 'Would you like some tea?'

Simon sat down at the table, one elbow in a portion of baked beans, and put his head in his hands. He rubbed his hair and looked up.

'Daft, aren't I?' he asked rhetorically, sounding deeply weary. 'I was banking on Gill being here, doing her Flaming Furies bit—'

He attempted a poor imitation of Gill's voice in a rage, 'What time do you call this? How dare you have a bit of fun . . . What woman would be mad enough to fancy you . . . You are seeing another woman, aren't you . . . Don't think I don't know . . . Well, two can play that game—'

Simon looked at Fee. 'You know the sort of stuff, I'm sure . . . No?' he added, because Fee was shaking her head. 'No, well, perhaps not. Perhaps it's a long-term-married-too-many-kids-no-room-to-breathe-is-this-all-there-is-to-life sort of thing.'

'Tea?' Fee asked again.

She poured two cups and sat opposite Simon. He was staring at her intently, his bloodshot eyes narrowed. Fee affected not to notice his interest.

'Percy's swallowed a pin. She seems fine but Gill's taken her to hospital to check,' Fee offered on the assumption that Simon might be interested in why the nest was empty.

'Pity.' Simon ran his fingers through his hair.

'Pity Percy's all right?' Fee asked, startled.

'No, pity Gill's not here. I wanted to make the grand entrance, then refuse to tell her where I'd been. Do you know, that woman's a bloody mystery to me?

'At times, I think all I remind her of is failure. Then she behaves as if I'm the most desirable man in town – at least to others – and she insists I'm having a passionate affair. With you, as a matter of fact. I don't think it's the affair she's bothered about. I think it's the idea that I might be having a good time when she's not—

'It's not a bad idea, though, is it?' he added, his eyes narrowing again.

'What, having a good time?' Fee asked.

'No,' Simon interrupted. 'Us. Having an affair. Going for it. Just a bit of a lark.'

Suddenly, he threw himself across the table, fish fingers and plates spilling to the floor.

'Simon.' Gill's voice rang out from the kitchen door in a tone that any two-year-old would recognize as bad news. 'For God's sake, act your age!'

Imogen was standing directly behind Gill. She saw a large ramshackle man with gingery-blond hair and freckles on the back of his hands, sprawled across the kitchen table. Instantly she knew. In spite of the haze of Worthington E, the sweat and the niff of congealed fish, to Imogen Banks, this poor, crumpled, downtrodden man smelt as good as the gods.

Here was The One for her

*

'Guess how many single women there are in Britain? Ten million . . . half a million are forty-plus and never married . . . a figure that's doubled in the last decade. You are not alone, Fee . . . You are part of a growing trend . . . You are ahead of the trend! You are a pioneer!'

Imogen, on the journey home, poured out statistics on the state of the British *femme seule* as she preferred to phrase it, for three miles. At a set of traffic lights, she turned to Fee to assess the impact.

'I'm not interested in pioneers; I'm only interested in cowboys,' Fee answered, smiling.

'Having one?' Imogen asked crudely, forgetting herself momentarily.

'No, of course not,' Fee replied. 'Being one. But that's a different story—'

Imogen decided to change tack. For the remainder of the journey, she affected no interest in whether Fee chose to appear in her documentary. Instead, she concentrated on disclosing more and more about herself. She chatted about her disastrous love life; her pledge to celibacy; her interest in the Third World and charities. (She wasn't entirely sure that Fee had a heart of gold, but she threw in a touch of philanthropy just in case.)

'My goodness,' she remarked as they drove into Fee's road, 'you must have a gift. I can't remember the last time I was so open with someone—'

Fee, flattered, was surprised to hear herself suggest that they have a drink some time.

Imogen gritted her teeth. 'Why not?' she smiled.

Chapter Eight

'IT'S SMOKED goose plus rocket with herb butter and Saxmundham mango chutney on rye,' Les said, examining the unlabelled contents through the Cellophane. 'It's all we've got, I'm afraid. Veronica took a turn for the worse on Wednesday. And that's the day she usually goes to M&S.'

'A cup of tea will be fine,' Fee answered. 'My kettle's bust and it takes hours to heat up water in a saucepan. I keep meaning to buy a new one, but you know how it is—'

Les sat down opposite her at the breakfast bar in his wife's kitchen and nodded glumly. He always thought of it as Veronica's kitchen, in the same way as the double garage was his garage, not theirs. It was Saturday morning and normally he'd be at work, touring his brasseries. It was his favourite day, watching the gannets. Instead, here he was, fifty-six and wife-sitting. And worried, dead worried.

Perhaps the shrink had been right? Perhaps it was all his fault? Perhaps he had been too over-protective? Les shrugged, as if to cast off blame. Don't be daft, man, he told himself sternly. He'd never denied his Veronica anything. All she had to do was ask.

'You want a kettle? Take ours,' he suddenly offered, as if to confirm to himself the extent of his generosity. Fee shook her head.

Les coaxed her. It suddenly mattered to him very much that she accepted this gift.

'Go on, take it. We've already got two. Veronica has one in her room. Had it there for a couple of days. She's not come out for over forty-eight hours now. She's got milk and tea but no sugar. And she loves a spoonful in her tea. Don't know how she's coping. Without sugar, I mean. She won't open the door to anyone.'

'Do you mind if I go up?' Fee asked.

'It won't do any good,' Les said, but he nodded his head, giving permission.

Veronica opened the door instantly. 'It's not locked,' Fee said in surprise.

'No, Les just expects it to be,' Veronica answered wearily.

The room still had the curtains drawn, but Fee could see that Veronica was dressed in a white frothy nightgown and an equally frilly dressing-gown. Her toenails were painted shell pink. Her face was bluey-white, as if despair had drawn every ounce of blood.

'They'll put me away if this goes on, won't they?' Veronica addressed the curtains.

Fee gave her a hug. Then she sat on the bed, at a loss as to what to say. At the christening, she had briefly believed that a couple of pep talks was all Veronica required to put her right. Now Fee knew, if her sister was to improve, it was going to take a great deal more than words.

'I've thought about what you said about change the other day,' Veronica suddenly said. 'But change is a terrible thing to do to the people you love, you know that, don't you, Fee? I mean, if they're not ready for it—'

She paced up and down, picking up speed as she became more agitated.

'Everyone liked me the way I was – Jason, Samantha, Les, Mum, you—'

'Me?' Fee replied, startled.

'Yes, you. I wasn't a bother then. I was just someone to chat to, someone who didn't get in the way. Now, you feel obliged. I've become one more thing for you to sort out—'

'Don't be ridiculous,' Fee protested feebly. For someone who wasn't supposed to be fully aware of what was going on, Veronica was proving uncomfortably perceptive.

Fee picked up the kettle, moved into the bathroom and filled it from the tap. She put teabags into two cups by Veronica's bedside table and, trying to sound casual, asked, 'When do you think this . . . um . . . ah . . . killing . . . began?'

Veronica stopped walking. 'Five months ago, I suggested to Les that I go back to college. Samantha was already settled, and Les Junior had just left home so I needed something to do. Something *real* to do.

'I'd decided I wanted to be a speech therapist. Help people find a voice.' Veronica gave a wry laugh. 'Help *me* find a voice . . . I'd applied to do a course and been accepted.

'Les was very nice about it. He said he thought it was a good idea but wouldn't it intrude on our lives a bit? Just when we've got a bit more free time to do things together, now the kids were off our hands.

'He said that if I went to college, he'd be forced to take up golf and then we'd never see one another. Was that what I wanted?

'What he said seemed fair and reasonable to me. He's worked hard all his life, it was time we had a bit of fun together—'

She fell silent. Fee, who had been stirring the tea bag in her cup, looked up. A tear was silently sliding down her sister's face.

'Go on,' she encouraged.

'I don't know.' Veronica shrugged. 'Perhaps I was more disappointed than I realized. Anyway, that's when it started—'

'Of course you were disappointed,' Fee reassured her sister. 'You've done your bit for Les and the kids. Why shouldn't you do something for yourself now? What's so wrong about that? All you're saying is, "It's my turn."'

'It's selfish,' Veronica replied. 'It's all right if you're single, like you, I suppose. But if you've got commitments, you can't. It's selfish and it's—'

Fee interrupted. 'Dad used to say, "You don't have to fight to be a Somebody, just learn to be yourself – that's the hardest job of all." Isn't the idea of you starting a new career part of learning to be yourself?'

'But he wasn't himself, was he?' It was Veronica's turn to interrupt, this time in anger. 'He wasn't himself, was he? And sure as hell, he wasn't a Somebody.

'He wanted to live in Cheyenne, ride the range, be a Wyatt Earp or Hopalong Cassidy . . . be a Somebody with a horse of his own. The truth was that our dad was a welder in East Calderton – and the only nag he knew was our mum.' She smiled grimly.

'You could never see it, but some people thought he was pathetic. Our dad wanted to live in a place where bad and good and duty and honour and rights and responsibilities are all dead simple. But it isn't like that in the real world, it's a whole lot messier.

'Look at me, Fee, I'm fifty-one years of age. I was brought up to be a good wife, a good mother . . . then suddenly, twenty years down the line, everything changes.

'Half of me wants to stick to what I know – the house, the home, making Les happy. I'd never want to be without him, so why risk losing him by expecting more? But the other half of me *does* want something different – a life of my own as well as what I have with Les. And I just don't know what to do. I just feel so useless . . . so destructive, always so *wrong*—'

Fee put her arms around her sister and held her, stroking her hair, while Veronica buried her face in Fee's shoulder and sobbed. A framed photograph on Veronica's bedside table caught Fee's eye. It showed Fee, Veronica and Helen at a family wedding.

What do women want? We're three generations – each with a different answer, she thought.

Her mother couldn't even begin to fathom Fee's decision to stay away from relationships since it was inconceivable to her that a woman could provide her own security. While Veronica's commitment to putting her husband's needs first no matter how much she had to forfeit herself seemed to Fee not just misguided but a positive danger to her state of mind. And what of Fee, what did she want?

Les Haslem's anxious voice wafted in from the other side of the closed bedroom door.

'Ask Veronica if she'd like a bowl of sugar, Fee. A bit of sugar in her blood might make all the difference.'

'She's in such a state, she doesn't know what she's about,' Les said an hour later, as he searched the sitting room. He was looking for a parcel he'd promised his wife that he would give to Fee.

'Perhaps, she's in a state because she *does* know what she wants, but doesn't like to upset anyone by saying so?' Fee suggested quietly.

She had great sympathy for her brother-in-law. Veronica had been dependent on Les all their married lives. He had done his very best by her, according to the rules that he'd been taught. Now, suddenly, Les had begun to realize it was an entirely new game. Was he going to lose Veronica to midlife ambition? Or to madness? Either way, it wasn't much of a choice for a man moving close to sixty and proud to say he was still in love with his wife.

'I always thought we had a good marriage,' he said mournfully, searching for the parcel.

'But you're talking as if it's all coming to an end. It doesn't have to be like that,' Fee pointed out. 'It could just mean that something different is beginning, something just as good—'

Les's look said he was far from reassured.

A few minutes later, he grunted as he retrieved a carrier bag from behind the sofa.

'The funny old biddy who took Veronica to hospital? She lent her a cardigan. I haven't got an address but I thought you might know where she lived? She made out you two were quite chummy—' he explained.

'Me and her?' Fee replied, alarmed. 'I'd never met her before in my life.'

Les raised an eyebrow in surprise. 'Anyway, I just assumed that you two might have had a lot in common, both being on your own and all.'

Later that night, Fee went to her bedroom window. The sky was clear except for the frail line of a new moon. She left the curtains open and undressed in the dark.

As she lay in her bed, her eyes focused on something on the chest of drawers. A ball of Cellophane that glinted in the street lights.

Fee got out of bed and picked the parcel up. It was a new electric kettle. Attached was a gift tag which smelt of violets.

Written in an open, looping hand, like a fishing net thrown haphazardly, were the words, 'Thought this might come in useful. All the best, Rita.'

How had the woman got into her flat? What had possessed her to want to give a gift to someone she'd only met for a matter of minutes? To reassure herself, Fee settled on an explanation. Rita and Veronica hadn't come into her flat but Veronica must have mentioned that Fee never had tea or coffee or even a kettle in the place. The doubts didn't fade but Fee returned to bed.

Fifteen minutes later, she got up and, for the first time in years, locked her bedroom door. Against what, she wasn't sure.

Chapter Nine

It WAS a strange land. One that reduced Claire Harper and Fee Travers almost instantly to tears.

'I feel so silly.' Claire sniffed.

'It's so irrational—' Fee said as she wiped her eyes.

'It happens to everyone,' explained the assistant, who had already introduced herself as Michele Canning, a handsome woman in her fifties. 'Either they cry because they thought it would never happen to them – or they cry because it has.'

Nuptia Europa, 'We speak five languages plus the language of love', was a bridal 'boutique' decorated in pink and maroon with spindly gilt chairs and a wall of mirrors. Along a second wall were racks of wedding dresses, labelled with exotic names: Bianca, Estrellita, Champagne, Zsa-Zsa. The third wall was lined with changing cubicles, each with its own heavy velvet curtain.

Muzak consisted almost entirely of the strings of Mantovani and the sound of the Carpenters – 'We've only just begun—' At steady intervals, the muzak was punctuated by a sharp hiss. Michele Canning explained that it was the apple-blossom air freshener which was automatically activated.

Claire and Fee waited while a large pink sheet was spread in front of them on the lush carpet.

'You know what they call me here?' Mrs Canning chatted as she gestured for Claire to stand on the sheet while she worked away with a tape measure.

'They say more Michele Can't than Michele Canning. I've been married twice and let down a multitude of times,' she chuckled, not entirely pleasantly.

'Shoes off, please,' she directed Claire.

'It's strange, isn't it? Marriage, living together,' she attempted to philosophize, instructing Claire to raise her arms above her head.

'It's what everybody wants – and nobody can get right. Or, at least, if they are getting it right, you don't hear much about it, do you?'

Mrs Canning was to the bride-to-be what the hunt saboteur is to the Master of the Hounds: a goader.

'I expect you're wondering how many men change their minds before the day?' she prodded. Claire registered alarm. As the dumper, never the dumpee, the idea had never occurred to her.

'Well, more than you'd imagine,' Mrs Canning answered her own question briskly.

'God, how awful,' Claire responded weakly. 'What happens then?'

Mrs Canning stopped measuring and folded her arms before speaking, 'Well, what you can't expect is a full refund. But, occasionally, we'll agree to a deal and buy the dress back from you—'

'I didn't mean that.' Claire looked pained. 'However do you pick yourself up again?'

'Horse's mouth, lovey? I can tell you. With great difficulty,' Mrs Canning's vowels had bounced from posh to a terrace in the East End.

'My little bastard took off – excuse my language – never to be seen again. He hadn't even paid for the honeymoon, as he'd promised—' She sniffed.

'Still, let's not look on the dark side. This is a time of joy, isn't it, ladies? Follow me, please,' she beckoned Claire into a cubicle.

'You'd be surprised about the significance of the cubicle,' Fee could hear Mrs Canning whisper. 'It becomes a real little confessional. Brides-to-be tell us all sorts of secrets. Out it all pours. But don't you worry yourself. I am the soul of discretion. Nothing passes my lips—'

Fee sat and waited while Claire tried the first of many dresses. 'Just to give you an idea, madam.' She could hear her chattering away betraying, in Fee's view, further signs of bridal brain damage.

'Should it be a buffet or a sit-down lunch?' Claire asked Mrs Canning. 'Or perhaps a formal dinner would be better? Then again, brunch has its attractions . . .'

On and on . . .

Perhaps, Fee thought to herself, this sentimental, *girly* woman is the real Claire? Perhaps the hard-headed person who persuaded me to take out a pension five years ago was just a mirage?

Mrs Canning's voice wafted out, 'Now, do you want ready made, or would you like us to design something especially for you? I know you'll forgive me for saying this, but my advice for the more . . . mature . . . bride is keep it simple. Simple, straight without ruffles. And why not go for eau-de-nil? Much more flattering than white to those of vintage years—'

Claire let out a strange nervous giggle.

Much to Fee's surprise, Claire – bossy, assertive, I-know-what-I-want-and-nothing-gets-in-my-way Claire – agreed to each of Michele Canning's suggestions.

Eventually, she emerged from the cubicle. She was dressed in a drop-waisted cream lace dress. Fee felt a tear trickle down her cheeks again. Why so sentimental?

It surprised her that shopping for a wedding dress should leave her as emotionally wrecked as watching *ET*.

'That's just for starters,' Mrs Canning announced dramatically. 'Come, come,' she beckoned Claire back into the cubicle.

A woman in her late forties took up a seat next to Fee. She too was blotting her tears.

'You've no idea how I've tried,' the woman said. 'I've begged and begged her, but she will have her way.'

Fee, nonplussed, nodded sympathetically.

'I've said, "Why marry?" Since her father died – God rest his soul – I've had the time of my life. Not that I don't miss him, mind. But if I should be lucky enough to fall a second time, I'd never marry. Think of the expense. Think of the mess when it all goes wrong. I've said to my Louise, "Why not just live together?"'

The woman leaned towards Fee conspiratorially, 'Better still, in my book, why don't they stay apart? He's not got that much between his ears. Not like my Louise. Doing well in the city, she is.

'If I had my time again,' the woman continued, neatly folding her handkerchief and tucking it into her bag, 'I'd stay single. Wouldn't you?'

'I am single,' Fee replied, smiling.

Spontaneously, the woman placed her hand on Fee's sleeve.

'Oh,' she said. 'I'm so sorry.'

Two hours later Claire and Fee finally emerged from the bridal boutique, Claire triumphant, Fee depressed.

They took a table in the brasserie next door. They ordered a meal and a bottle of wine and Claire toasted herself for expanding the number of bridesmaids from three to five. She had also just spent £32 on a piece of blue elastic. Fee said she could have run up a garter on a sewing machine in seconds.

'That is not the point,' Claire admonished. 'If I'm going to do this bridal thing, I'm going to do it big. Besides, I'm part of a trend. Loads of forty-ish women are choosing to become late brides. And when we go, we go—'

More to distract Claire from any further interminable discussion about 'The Arrangements', Fee asked, 'So when am I going to get my first sight of Clem Thomas? Or do I have to wait until I glimpse the back of his head during the wedding ceremony?'

'How about tomorrow?' Claire suggested. 'You can cook us supper if you like. Why not ask Adam?'

'No,' Fee replied firmly. 'Absolutely not. And, come to that, never again either.'

It seemed an appropriate moment for her to break her own piece of news. 'I've signed off,' she added.

'What do you mean "signed off"?'

118

'I've stopped looking. I've decided to stay single – at least until I've grown up. So, basically, that probably means I'm an Old Maid for life. To be honest, now the decision's been taken, I couldn't be happier.'

This wasn't, of course, strictly true. Paul was still a bruise on her heart. Adam, she hoped, continued to be on standby should her nerve fail completely. And, of course, Fee had yet to be tempted by anyone new. But if attitude of mind counted for anything, she was working hard on it.

Fee glanced at Claire. 'Aren't you pleased for me?' she prompted.

Claire wasn't. A barrage of hostile questioning ensued.

'What about children?' Claire hissed.

'I'll borrow other people's. I already do.' Fee answered. 'Next?'

'What about loneliness?' Claire challenged.

'I've got friends. Lots of them,' Fee countered.

'What about companionship when you're old and they're all dead?' Claire persisted.

'Euthanasia,' Fee said flippantly.

'What about your mother?'

'Well, that is more of a problem—' Fee conceded. 'But you know her, there's nothing Helen likes better than being bitterly disappointed. And spinsterhood is probably the very best I can do in that respect—'

'Are you doing it to spite your mother?' Claire looked relieved, as if she'd discovered an acceptable reason.

Fee laughed. 'Of course not. I'm doing it for survival. Relationships and me are like fags to a heavy smoker. Delightful at times but deadly in the long run. You've seen me in enough messes to know that . . .'

Claire refused to give up. 'What about sex? And falling in love? And not being able to help yourself, as you usually can't, the minute you see an unsuitable man? What about turning into a selfish, obsessive, batty recluse?'

'You're too flattering,' Fee replied mildly although her irritation was mounting.

She moved onto the offensive. 'Anyway, why are you so bothered?'

'Of course I'm not bothered,' Claire protested. 'I'm just concerned about you —'

But Claire *was* bothered. *Really* bothered. She couldn't quite figure out why. Unless, of course, it was the horrible fear that Fee might have more fun alone than she could ever experience as a wife.

Think single, think positive, Fee told herself as she stood on the platform waiting for a train home a little later. But wherever she looked, the message that came back was less than encouraging: *Think single, think odd, think sad, think unfortunate.*

At 11.05 on the Victoria line, on a weekday night, she could have sworn everybody had somebody – except her.

The woman to Fee's left, waiting on the platform, was in her early twenties. She had long brown hair tied at the nape of her neck, and wore little make-up. She was dressed in a trench coat and black boots, and she was standing on tiptoe.

The man she was trying to reach with her lips was a little older. He had a woolly hat on his head, an Aran jumper and black jeans. As he spoke softly to her, her eyes constantly travelled around his face taking in very detail – a lover's trawl.

The woman looked Fee's way and Fee, embarrassed, half smiled, half frowned.

Ahead of her was a giant poster advertising Caribbean holidays. 'For Couples Only' read the shocking-pink sticker across one corner.

A few minutes later a semi-drunk couple, perhaps refugees from a business conference, kissed passionately. The lip-lock lasted from the departure of one train to the arrival of the next.

'*I'm drowning in it,*' Fee told herself.

'It's true what people say – to be single is freaky, deviant, selfish, warped. Every couple in the whole world is having fun, feeling wanted. And I'm not.'

She boarded her train. As it moved out of the station, it flashed past a hoarding for a romantic comedy.

'Who do older spinsters have for role models?' Fee asked herself crossly. 'Nuns, psychopaths . . . and Diane Keaton.'

Three stops on, she watched as a couple boarded who were engaged in a furious argument. She couldn't hear the content, but she could read the hand signals and facial expressions.

You take me for granted. What do you really want from me? OK, that's it. I've had enough. No, don't go—

The woman stormed off the train sobbing; the man remained behind attempting to look nonchalant, but his foot jiggled up and down furiously.

'Get a grip, girl,' Fee told herself. 'An awful lot of relationships are made in hell. And who wants to live in hell?'

'Me,' a small voice replied.

Fee hoped it didn't belong to her.

Simon Booth was in love. He sat in the kitchen of his home, watching his wife make sandwiches. It was past eleven, the children were asleep, supper had been peaceful and now Simon exuded contentment. He was in love.

He poured Gill another glass of wine. She was wearing a turquoise jumper and leggings. Probably new, Simon thought, and attractive. A small curl had woven its way round the lobe of one ear.

Gill had watched the ten o'clock news and weather and had decided that as the next day was a Saturday and the weatherman had said that it would be fine, the family should go on a picnic. Now she was preparing the food in advance.

Gill, as always, hadn't actually consulted with Simon, she had just assumed that he would fall in with her plans. Simon, on this particular occasion, had other intentions for tomorrow afternoon. He closed his eyes, cupped his hands around his glass and stroked its curves, in anticipation of moments to come.

'Mustard or pickle?' Gill asked.

'Mmmm?' Simon replied. He tilted back in the chair, eyes still shut, hands behind his head, a playful little smile on his face.

'Mustard or PICKLE!' Gill yelled, unaccountably annoyed by the expression on her husband's face.

Without waiting for a reply she slapped pickle on a thick slice of ham. It was edged with glutinous off-white fat that reminded Gill of her own flesh.

Simon was speaking. 'If we ever had another child, do you think we'd call her something Frenchified . . . I mean with the Common Market and all that?'

Simon, eyes now open, stuck his finger in the butter and licked it in a way that made Gill feel nauseous. She hated it when her husband attempted to look cute.

'What on earth do you mean?' she snapped.

'Well, would we call her something French like Simone or Nathalie . . . or Imogen—'

A look of triumph spread across Simon's face. There, he'd said it. He'd said the word. He had brought his one true love alive in his very own kitchen.

Gill snorted with derision. 'Don't be so absolutely bloody ridiculous. I wouldn't dream of becoming pregnant again. How many sandwiches can you eat?'

Imogen . . . Imogen . . . Imogen . . .

Simon let the word run through his head. It was years since he'd felt so . . . unpredictable, so alive, so valued, so *male*. Imogen was exciting, vibrant, a career woman. And still she made Simon feel he was anything but an irritant. Imogen promised a new, different world – a world without planning, domesticity, sandwiches on a Saturday, *routine*.

Imogen had invited Simon to lunch to discuss 'a proposal'. She had then suggested that they make an assignation for the forthcoming weekend. Like an infertile woman who suddenly conceives, Simon was both stunned and pleased – and slightly disbelieving.

They had met twice more since and the so far platonic entanglement had already been transformed in his head to love. It kept the guilt at bay.

He had an irresistible urge to divulge his spectacular good luck to his wife – he'd always discussed everything with Gill – but he restrained himself. He focused instead on what she was saying.

'Do you know what Fee has told Claire?' Gill slapped peanut butter onto white baps with all the enthusiasm of a dominatrix abusing a pair of buttocks. A bread roll crumbled under her assault.

'She's told her she's staying away from men, never getting married. Who's kidding who? That's what I want to know. Who is damn well kidding who?' Gill glared beadily at her husband.

'Fee Travers is having an affair and I don't think we have to search very hard to draw up a short list of possible lovers, do we?'

Simon had grown immune to his wife's probes. 'Don't we?' he replied mildly. His attention had turned to a far more alarming thought: how was he to excuse himself from the picnic and the house *for the whole of Saturday afternoon?*

He couldn't use work as an excuse because Gill would ring. In fact, Gill would ring almost anywhere he happened to be. Would the mobile phone work on the river? What possible reason could he give for suddenly discovering boating in middle age and with twenty-four hours' notice?

'As for that woman she brought with her the other night . . . What a tart! Did you see the length of her nails? And the perfume! A job lot from a St Petersburg blubber factory if you ask me—' Gill chattered on and then stopped.

Simon had stood up. He was white and shaking. He grasped the knife out of Gill's hand, held it high – and plunged it deep into the butter dish.

Why did she always set out to break the only toys he had? Why did she always have to savage his dreams?

'Call this living?' he shouted. Then he banged out of the kitchen.

On reflection, Simon would have wished to have said something more directly to the point, or more poetic, but as war cries went, he told himself, it wasn't all that bad. *Call this living?*

In the hall, he hesitated further. Storming out of the house would be more spectacular – but he was a pragmatist. It would be uncomfortable sleeping on a friend's sofa. Better to evacuate the twins from their room, deposit them with Gill in the double bed and he could then sleep on the bottom bunk bed.

Better still, why didn't he leave the bottom bunk to Gill? Simon smiled. See what a positive influence Imogen was already beginning to have?

'And we've only just begun—' Simon told himself light-heartedly, vaguely aware that he'd heard the phrase somewhere before.

In the kitchen, Gill removed the knife from the butter dish and finished the bottle of wine. Simon had told her repeatedly that he had no romantic or sexual interest in Fee. So why the combustion?

'She thinks she's made a clever little move. Thrown everyone off her scent. But she's met her match in me,' Gill muttered to herself. 'Spinster? My arse.'

Her uncustomary crudity gave her a strange sort of comfort.

'Hello, this is Rita, Rita Mason speaking. We met the other day. I see you're out. I'm sorry to bother you but I was just wondering how Veronica was. Give her my best regards. Well, bye then—'

Fee opened her front door just in time to hear Rita Mason's voice leaving a message on the answering machine.

She sounded warm, concerned, *normal.* Fee was slightly ashamed of her earlier mistrust.

Admittedly, it was odd to leave a present for a stranger but Rita Mason hadn't made any demands, issued any threats, stalked the street outside. She was only enquiring after Veronica.

Just because Rita Mason looked distinctive didn't mean she was daft as well. All right, she had flirted, *seriously* flirted with every junior doctor in casualty, and had been oblivious to the fact that they'd assumed she was having a joke. But when was fancying yourself at fifty plus regarded as a crime?

In reparation, Fee picked up the phone and was about to return Rita Mason's call when she realized that she didn't have her number. She knew nothing about the woman except where she worked and that she had told Veronica that she was a radiographer.

Fee promised herself that on Monday she would drop into Rita's hospital on the way to F.P. & D. and leave the cardigan and some flowers as a thank you. Then that would be the end of that.

She moved towards the kitchen, flicking lights on as she went. Fee ignored the unwrapped kettle on the table and began to fill a saucepan with water. She was suddenly aware that she was not alone. Spinning round, she saw Will was standing in the kitchen doorway, leaning against the frame. He was holding a bottle of wine and a parcel. He looked as if he was enjoying a private joke.

'God, you gave me such a fright.' Fee slammed the pan down on the draining board crossly. Will handed her the bottle, put the parcel on the kitchen table and pulled her keys out of his pocket.

'You left these in your front door – again. Dangerous habit, you know. What if someone—'

Fee interrupted his lecture. 'Why've you got that peculiar smile on your face? What's so funny?'

Will shrugged. 'I can't help it. One minute you're turning your back on all males. The next you're being wooed by a woman with a dodgy sense of taste and a highly utilitarian muscle where her romantic pulse should be.

'I have my faults,' he added. 'But never have I given a paramour a kettle. Never.'

Fee opened a packet of chocolate biscuits and Will helped himself. 'She is not a paramour.' She glared at him, annoyed with herself that she was taking his bait.

'She's . . . well . . . she's nothing . . . I hardly know her.' She shrugged. 'Was it you who let her in? Why didn't you tell me?'

'I didn't let her in,' Will corrected. 'She called by when you were out yesterday and I offered to put the kettle in your flat. I thought the bedroom was a nice offbeat touch. She said Veronica had told her you didn't have one the other night when they came and failed to raise you.'

Will took the bottle opener out of the drawer and two glasses from the cupboard. He followed her into the sitting room, carrying the glasses of wine and his parcel.

'I'm not going to keep it, you know,' Fee said. 'I'll have to return it. I hardly know the woman.'

'Don't be daft, of course you won't,' Will chastised. 'It's only a kettle, what harm can it do? She probably flogs kitchenware in her spare time. Here,' he thrust the haphazardly wrapped parcel into Fee's hands. 'Here's a proper present. Have a look at it later, see what you think.'

'Why not now?' Fee asked, beginning to peel away the paper.

'Later,' Will instructed firmly and then grinned. 'I don't want to witness your embarrassment at my impressive generosity.'

At midnight, Fee sat on her sofa, alone, with Will's present, now unwrapped, in her hands. It was an ornate frame surrounding a tapestry on which several words had been embroidered.

Fee read aloud. 'Being an old maid is like death by drowning. It's a delightful sensation once you cease to struggle.' *Edna Ferber.*

She was touched. She read the words again: '. . . a delightful sensation once you cease to struggle . . .' And how long would that take, she asked wryly? Six months, a year, five years?

A lifetime?

'Oh, you'd be doing me a favour by taking it, you really would. So don't feel at all obligated—'

At 10 a.m. on Saturday morning, Fee had answered the door,

expecting Claire. She had felt unaccountably annoyed to discover Rita Mason on her doorstep.

'I was just passing and thought I'd ask after your sister,' she'd explained, smiling pleasantly. She had her hair in an incongruous pony tail, fastened high on the head like an American teenager in the 1950s. She wore shocking pink lipstick, drawn over the lips to give a fuller look, a white fluffy jumper and lilac jeans. The net result was a bizarre conjunction: very late summer disguised as early spring.

'I'm a bit busy,' Fee had answered and then was ashamed at her lack of hospitality. Rita Mason had put herself out for Veronica quite considerably; the least that Fee could do was to offer her a cup of coffee.

So, Rita Mason had been invited in and, ninety-five minutes later, showed no inclination to leave. Fee poured fresh coffee, too polite to hurry her along. She'd rehearsed a couple of excuses in her head but they'd been crushed by conditioning: nice girls didn't tell guests it's time to go.

Rita began to giggle coquettishly. Briefly, Fee misunderstood. Please God that the woman didn't fancy her. Then she realized that Rita was holding out her left hand for inspection. On her fourth finger was a very large piece of . . . glass . . . Fee decided uncharitably.

'That's how I got the kettle. Well, four of them actually,' Rita Mason confided. 'At our engagement party. Got a bottom drawer that's overflowing, so it really would help me out if you kept it. After all, what are friends for if they can't do each other little favours?' She smiled.

'But we're not friends,' Fee blurted out. 'I mean, I hardly—'

The smile broadened as the woman ignored Fee's words and picked up the cardigan which Fee had returned.

'My sister's asked for your address, so she can write and thank you . . . would you mind?' Fee asked, already ashamed of her outburst of rudeness.

Rita Mason produced a sheet of paper from her white patent handbag. 'Do you want my flat in London – or I can give you the address of my place in the country. It's a workman's cottage, nothing much but it's got a lovely large garden. That's in Sussex . . .?'

'I'm sure your London address will be fine.' Fee wondered why Rita Mason needed to tell her that she was a two-dwelling woman.

'Have you been engaged long?' she asked, genuinely curious. Rita stopped writing. 'A year. My fiancé, Roger, is in Saudi Arabia. He's a commercial diver. A little bit younger than me, but not so it shows. At least, that's what I like to tell myself.'

She ran her tongue over her front teeth, removing a pink smear of lipstick as she did so.

'We're getting married next year when he comes back for good. But there's enough planning to keep me busy. You know, big white wedding, lots of family, reception . . . the usual carry-on.' Fee wondered why she didn't believe a word.

'A friend of mine's getting married soon, too,' Fee offered, then stopped. Rita almost physically pounced on this snippet of personal information.

'Not to worry,' she smiled at Fee. 'I know exactly how you must be feeling. Pretty lonely, I'm sure. I know because I've been there. But don't let it get you down. Somebody special is out there for each of us. Look at me—'

Fee had spent much of the past hour trying not to. Rita reached out warmly. It was a gesture of sympathy but, for Fee, it assumed too much.

'I'm fine,' she defended herself, flustered. 'I'm perfectly happy the way that I am. Really, I am.'

'Brave girl. I know just how it is.' Rita rose to her feet. 'I've just had a terrific idea. You be ready Thursday evening and we'll see what we can do. No, no, no ifs or buts. I insist,' she added, stemming Fee's objections.

Fee sighed. Better to concede now and cancel arrangements later. Besides, she didn't want to interrupt Rita Mason's momentum towards the front door.

'I've got exactly the right group of women for you to meet,' her uninvited guest beamed, picking up her bag and coat. 'Real characters, mostly single. We sometimes go out for a meal afterwards. Of course, I'm not allowed any hanky-panky any more. Not since I've met Roger . . . but the others, well, that's a different story.' She raised her eyebrows.

'See you Thursday then, Fee,' Rita said at Fee's front door. 'I knew as soon as we met that we'd have an awful lot in common—'

Chapter Ten

S IMON WAS in a sweat. So much so, his body odour was even
beginning to overwhelm Imogen. It was 3 p.m. on Saturday
afternoon and the two were sharing a lift in a hotel in Bayswater that
Imogen had had occasion to use in the past. They were keeping a
respectable distance, just in case someone either of them knew
decided to use the same lift.

As far as Imogen was concerned all that stood between her and
her destiny as the second Mrs Booth was a report on Simon's sperm
count (why back a dud?) and an investigation into his present and
future financial prospects. Imogen did not believe that love is blind.
Or, for that matter, that love is broke.

She wore a black dress and a black and red check swing coat.
The shoes were patent high heels. 'You sort of buzz—' Simon had
said; he was not a natural romantic. And he knew that, by some fluke
of luck, he had landed a mistress totally out of his league.

This unexpected delight had given him inspiration. For instance,
Simon had solved the logistical problem of removing himself from
the house at a peak time for family activity quite brilliantly, even if
he said so himself.

He had waited until Gill was in their bedroom searching for the
twins' wellington boots, then he had shouted up the stairs.

'Emergency – at work! I'm not sure where at work . . . Well, it's
not actually in work but outside it . . . but to do with work . . . Must
go! So, it's best if I phone later—' Then he'd rushed out of the
door. And returned immediately.

'Did you hear all that, Gill?' He yelled up the stairs again.

'I thought you'd gone.' Her voice sounded neutral. Simon skipped out of the door. What a clever, clever man he was.

He had already put his best suit in the car and had attempted to change in the gents' loo in Hyde Park. It had not been a pleasant experience. But Simon blamed himself for being so naïve.

In the lift, he was now also blaming himself for being a virgin philanderer. If he had done this more often, he wouldn't be quite so jumpy. He clutched his briefcase more firmly. It contained toothbrush, toothpaste, condoms, clean underpants, mouth freshener, aftershave, deodorant and body lotion.

Whatever happened, he intended to smell sweet. (Simon was quite proud that he'd remembered the briefcase. This was, after all, supposed to be work. And his wife had a fine eye for detail.)

Suddenly, as the lift slid past the third floor, Simon's mobile phone began to ring. He panicked.

'Oh God, she's found us. She's tracked us down. Gill knows where we are. I knew this would happen,' he babbled, and began to push Imogen out on the fourth floor.

'Get out, get out. Get out now, for God's sake.'

'Simon, dear, you have a mobile phone,' Imogen stepped back in, pressed the button for the fifth floor. She mopped his brow with her silk scarf.

'Of course Gill doesn't know where you are. Answer it.'

Simon obeyed. It was a call from work. Could he come in, there was a bit of a crisis?

'Yes, I mean, no ... Look, just don't phone home. OK? Whatever you do, do not phone home. I'll try and come in later—' Simon could feel the sweat beginning to drip again.

For years, nothing had shaken Imogen Banks's belief in the concept that each of us has one true love. Now, she inspected the puddle of passion before her and, for the very first time, began to reconsider.

*

On Sunday mornings, Helen Travers always followed the same routine. She would rise at seven, take Minnie the dachshund for a forty-five-minute walk in the park, call in on her next-door neighbour, Penny McTaggert, for a cup of tea and, at ten, she'd begin her preparations.

She would place two slices of brown bread in the toaster and lay the kitchen table with black cherry jam, butter, one ripe banana and a pot of weak tea.

She would drink her first cup while glancing through the *News of the World* (not for reasons of salaciousness, of course, but in order to confirm her thoroughgoing disappointment in the declining standards of the young, the old, the Establishment and the rest of the world).

At ten ten she switched on the toaster. By ten fifteen, when the first chords of the *Archers* signature tune staggered out from the radio, Minnie would have eaten one slice of toast, and Helen would be chomping away on the other, smothered in banana and jam.

Heaven.

Helen had grown confident enough in old age to admit to herself that the combination of black cherry, ripe banana, melted butter and a fat wedge of warm toast was unmatched by absolutely any other satisfaction she had encountered in life. And *never* a disappointment.

This was, of course, a piece of information that she kept totally confidential. On the rare occasions when Helen had visitors, she ate more orthodoxly. But marmalade was always *such* a let-down.

Imogen Banks was dressed in a subdued dark-green trouser suit built for a woman with a lither figure since the jacket ended in a frill just above the hips. She put her finger to the doorbell of the semi-detached redbrick house, just at the moment that Helen Travers had switched on her toaster.

Imogen noted that the garden had yellow roses which almost

exactly matched the bunch she was carrying. The lawn was also the home of a grey gnome fishing in an even greyer well.

Helen heard the ring. She hid the banana and cherry jam concoction behind the bread bin (she didn't want anyone to jump to the conclusion that she was vulgar), shooed Minnie off the kitchen chair, and went to answer the door. Helen was not happy at the intrusion.

'Mrs Travers?' the woman enquired, holding out the bouquet of flowers. Helen looked at her blankly.

'You're not the Lib. Dem. candidate, are you?' she asked suspiciously.

'Oh goodness me, no,' Imogen smiled, noting that Helen had the same clear skin and strong bones as her youngest daughter, but the mouth was disapproving. It sat like a thin hyphen between the plump cheeks.

'I'm an old schoolfriend of Fee's and I'm on a bit of a treasure hunt—'

'Donations? Is that what it's about?' Helen responded, her hostility increasing by the second.

'Shall I come in and explain?' Imogen suggested. Helen said nothing but stepped to one side. The hall and sitting room were decorated in cornflower blue and cream.

'Tea?' Helen asked. She had become resigned to company and was now considering the next step. Should she allow herself to enjoy the experience?

'That would be lovely,' Imogen answered, her face registering as much enthusiasm as if she'd been invited on a free weekend to Barcelona.

Ten minutes later, Helen was back, Minnie following on her heels. Imogen dutifully made a fuss of the dog, admired the china, said she hadn't had such a good cup of tea in *ages*, praised the décor and, when her professional eye told her that Helen had sufficiently softened, proceeded with her investigations.

Two hours later, the coffee table in the small sitting room was covered in memorabilia. Imogen had explained that she was organizing a school reunion and was collecting information on each of the old pupils who had agreed to attend. These mini-biographies were intended as a surprise from the organizing committee to the old girls, hence Imogen hadn't asked Fee directly.

Helen had dutifully produced photograph albums, school reports and cuttings from local newspapers such as the time when Fee had won a travel scholarship for an essay entitled, 'Why I believe it's important to venture afar'. ('Afar' in this case had been the Isle of Wight.)

At one point, Helen disappeared upstairs and returned with a bright-green brocade dress.

'This was the first time Fee was a bridesmaid,' she explained. 'She's going to be a bridesmaid again in August, you know . . . Her best friend is getting married. That will make it three times and you know what they say—' She sighed.

Her language was that of a mother with a child who had never quite proved good enough; shortcomings were accentuated, achievements underplayed.

'You've clearly done something very right in the way you've brought up Fiona,' Imogen smiled. She knew that while Helen Travers might be disappointed in her daughter, she wouldn't take kindly to a stranger supporting her in that view.

'All three girls say I don't praise them enough,' Helen replied, her expression indicating that she thought this nonsense.

'But then I never heard any praise when I was a child. On the contrary, it was the habit then to cut us down to size. It never did me much harm—' she added defensively.

'Still, I'll be a lot happier once I know Fee is settled. Are you married?' she asked suddenly. Imogen, who was helping herself to several photographs of Fee, in her teens and twenties, in a range of unlikely hairstyles, was caught offguard.

'Married?' Imogen repeated, considering what reply might be the most beneficial to her own interests. 'Oh furiously,' she answered.

'What I mean is, we've been married for five years – on Saturday actually. It's our anniversary. And I couldn't be happier. He's been such a support to me. Totally devoted. Marriage has turned my whole life round—'

'But you don't wear a ring?' Helen queried sharply.

'Eczema,' Imogen whispered confidentially. 'The ring gives me terrible eczema—'

'Oh, I'll tell Fee about your marriage,' Helen answered, hungry for more propaganda to direct her daughter's way. 'I'm sure she'll be delighted.'

'Oh gosh, don't do that. No, that would be a bit of a disaster frankly,' Imogen smiled nervously. 'Remember this is all supposed to be a big surprise. You know, hush hush!'

Ten minutes after Imogen Banks had departed, while Helen was scraping the cold toast and congealed jam from her plate into the bin, a thought surfaced in her head.

Imogen was a very distinctive name. And she couldn't recall an Imogen in Fee's class – or the class above. Or the class below. In fact, she couldn't remember any Imogens at Farnleigh Comprehensive. Not ever.

Helen Travers shrugged. Another sign of growing old. Of course, there must have been an Imogen at Fiona's school. Otherwise, why on earth would such a pleasant person bother to spend a whole morning collecting another woman's memories?

Chapter Eleven

G<small>ERRY</small> R<small>ADCLIFFE</small>, aged fifty-six, was the founder and star of
G F.P. & D. He sat in the office of his employee, Fiona Travers,
and tried hard not to look. In fact, he'd spent most of his life, boy
and man, trying not to look but, more often than not, he couldn't
help himself.

The same excuse applied to those occasions when he stepped
beyond looking and uttered a few choice words. He couldn't help
himself. Sexual innuendo was a language in which Gerry was
particularly fluent. He frequently reassured himself that he would
never, ever, do anything that anyone could constitute as improper,
he was only being playful.

His female employees, of course, had a much simpler explanation
for their boss's behaviour. Behind his back, they called him a dirty
old man – charming to some at times, but to others, a pest.

This was more than a nuisance. If, for instance, Fee Travers
made a presentation that involved, say, the purchasing power of the
Church of England, Gerry would somehow introduce the issue of
whether teenage girls had wet dreams.

In truth, Gerry Radcliffe had not had carnal knowledge of
another woman since marrying Marie-Jeanne thirty years before.
Nevertheless he constantly implied in conversation that adultery was
his main form of exercise. 'It's his pride,' Mrs Radcliffe, born and
brought up in Toulouse, would say. And shrug.

The couple had four sons, all educated at public school and now
'jobfree'. It was a word that Gerry preferred to use but he was well

aware it injected a false sense of purpose into his sons' aimless and expensive activities. All four were now in their twenties but, to Gerry's incredulity, they continued to live at home.

Now, Gerry Radcliffe examined the posters above the sofa and on each wall, mementoes of previous campaigns. He let his eyes take in the flipchart and the mess on Fiona Travers's desk and the two dead bunches of flowers in elegant glass vases. Then, he had a second look.

At that point, the woman sitting opposite him on the sofa suddenly shoved a plump hand with short stubby fingers down her neckline and heaved on what Gerry Radcliffe presumed was her bra strap. The massive wall that was her chest shifted upwards, causing the slogan written on her T-shirt to rise and fall.

'Why lose out? Have a heart!' the words read in a lop-sided wave. The man sitting next to the woman – a Jack Spratt squeezed to the edge of the sofa by her voluminous proportions – cleared his throat. Gerry decided this was due more to innate nervousness than an attempt to warn him off. So he looked again.

Then he glanced at his watch. 'I'm sorry,' he told the couple on the sofa. 'She shouldn't be much longer. It's not like her at all. She's usually the first one in the office and the last to leave. More coffee? Tea? Mineral water?'

The couple silently shook their heads left to right in unison, then giggled at their synchronization. They were both in their mid-thirties.

'See how well suited we are? What did I tell you, Derek?' the woman whispered triumphantly. Derek, her partner, wearing an identical T-shirt, grinned his approval.

'You're right again, Babs,' he said. Gerry reflected that if the past forty-five minutes of desultory conversation between the couple was any guide, all they shared in common was their mutual desire to make a match.

'Just off to the loo,' he told the couple on the sofa. 'Back in five.'

Gerry was proud of F.P. & D.'s perspex and turquoise premises. Mrs Radcliffe had read somewhere that in ancient Greece turquoise was a colour considered conducive to thinking.

'I may have many failings but at least I know myself well,' he told his face in the bathroom mirror. He was a man who lived on a diet of delusion. He examined his features. A short grey crewcut, heavy eyebrows, square jaw. He dressed flamboyantly – always in bow-ties with colour co-ordinated spectacles, socks and waistcoats.

Gerry straightened his bow-tie, flicked cold water on his face and smiled. He was happy. If Fee co-operated, as she usually did, by 2 p.m. this afternoon the company would be saying welcome to a fat, profitable contract.

Babs and Derek, the couple on the sofa in Fee's office, were the unlikely point at which Gerry Radcliffe hoped the corporate good times might really begin to roll.

Fee drove into the office an hour late. She had left her flat on time. Just as she was crossing the road to her car, she had spotted Gill Booth, in a voluminous camel coat in spite of the spring morning, collar turned up, disappearing around the corner.

'Hey, Gill!' Fee had called out spontaneously. Gill had appeared not to hear. Why would Gill be so far out of her own area when normally she would be ferrying the children to school? And why hadn't she told Fee she'd be in the vicinity – or called in for coffee?

It was only when Fee was pulling away from the curb that the idea came to her. *Gill must be having an affair.* Four minutes later, something hit the rear of Fee's newly refurbished Fiat. It was a man in a Saab. He, in turn, had been shunted by Gill's battered old Volvo.

A queue of early-morning traffic had now formed in the street and the first tentative hoots had turned into a solid din.

Gill's face appeared at the passenger window of Fee's car. Fee turned down the window and was about to ask if Gill was all right when she spoke first.

'I'm watching you,' Gill had spat threateningly. 'If I was in your shoes, I'd be shaking.'

Then she had turned on her heel and, addressing the fast-growing line of protesting car drivers, she had shouted at the top of her voice, 'And you load of tossers can bloody well piss off!'

For Fee, this side of Gill Booth was a revelation. She had watched her friend grow, well, quite matronly in the last couple of years. Out of her mouth, Fee had come to expect monologues about the advantages of Montessori teaching not invectives.

She was impressed. And not at all bothered by Gill's warning. She had long realized that the only way of convincing Gill that she was not having an affair with her husband would be to explain in explicit terms how deeply unattractive she found him. But she couldn't bring herself to do that to a friend.

Continuing her drive into work, she thought again about Gill's behaviour.

'Jealousy, paranoia, heartbreak and a rear fender that resembles a boomerang are among the many least attractive results of this ridiculous business called love,' Fee said out loud, as she manoeuvred her car into her parking space.

'Thank God, I'm no longer involved.'

Babs Lockyer, thirty-one, and Derek Berry, thirty-three, had now been waiting in Fiona Travers's office for two hours. Each had phoned work to say they were sick. Both were glad of the extra time this allowed them to spend together, although conversation had long since dried up. There are only so many times, as life-long dedicated Elvis fans, you can relive the plot of *Jailhouse Rock* or discuss the less well-constructed *Blue Hawaii*.

They had been introduced seven weeks earlier, decided they were in love fifty-five minutes later and become engaged on the following day. A week ago they had been asked to present themselves at the office of F.P. & Daughters, so they could tell 'One of the Classic Love Stories of Our Times'. Except that, having arrived, nobody appeared interested in hearing their tale. Certainly not the cretin sitting in front of them who kept examining himself in the stainless-steel pencil holder on the desk.

At 10.15 a.m., a woman appeared in the office. She wore a black trouser suit, white T-shirt and gold ear-rings. Derek noted that she had shiny hair and she wasn't as pretty as his Babs – too skinny – but she'd do. And she had a nice smile. She was smiling now.

'Can I help you?' Fee asked. 'It's my office? Or are you waiting for me?'

Babs and Derek looked blankly at her. Then Babs said shyly, 'We've come to tell our story as an inspiration to others.'

'I see,' Fee smiled brightly. 'Look, why don't I bring us all some coffee? I'll be back in a mo.'

Babs and Derek resumed holding hands. Each had been silent and alone for so long it was now a privilege to share the silence with somebody else.

Fee found Gerry Radcliffe in one of F.P. & D.'s boardrooms. He was on the telephone. Also in the room was Gina Masters, his personal assistant for fifteen years. At the outset, she had handled the boss's predilection for talking dirty by feigning deafness for several hours. Now, Gerry rarely lapsed in her presence. It was too time-consuming.

'He's out for the rest of the morning,' Gina explained to Fee as she invited herself into the office and took up one of the turquoise chairs. 'So we've got to get through a lot before he leaves.' Gerry raised his eyebrows at Fee by way of a greeting.

Fee and Gerry Radcliffe got on well, not least because he had poached Fee from her previous employers. He also paid her £10,000 a year more – an increase that still placed Fee considerably behind Claire Harper, as Claire had quickly pointed out. Fee had proved a good investment for Gerry's company. But he remained wary of Fee.

First, because he secretly fancied her and intensely disliked the vulnerability this engendered in him – not least because, for all his talk, he wouldn't dream of ratting on his wife.

Second, he had become aware that while Fee always maintained she enjoyed her work, he sensed a growing disillusionment. Personally and professionally, he couldn't afford to have her resign now.

He was right about Fee's attitude to her job. Her working day appeared to have stretched to encompass almost every evening too. This was partly because of the growing success of the company and partly because Fee had difficulty in saying no.

In addition to the long hours, she was also becoming increasingly dismayed by the manipulation of people's emotions which was at the core of F.P. & D.'s endeavours. Initially, she had been able to ignore her doubts, influenced by Gerry's justification of his business.

'If Moses came down from the mountain with the Ten Commandments,' he'd explained more than once to Fee in the early days, 'don't you think he would have needed a little help with projection and packaging and finding a place in the market?

'And wouldn't it have helped if his followers had prepared the customers for his arrival? Now, does that little extra help invalidate the importance of the Commandments? Of course, it doesn't. It gives them an ethical boost. It's a public service.'

The hitch in this line of argument, of course, was that F.P. & D. spent most of its time flogging cars and designer labels and supermarket chains, not ethics.

'If it makes you feel any better,' Will had advised Fee at one moment of crisis, 'tell people you work with the EC.'

'The EC?' Fee had queried.

'The Emperor's Clothes,' he had answered with a smile.

Now, Fee watched Gerry on the telephone, coaxing and cajoling an irate client.

'Sales up 5 per cent?' he was saying. 'But that's bloody fantastic. Congratulations. I'm glad we listened to that suggestion of yours about the free plastic rose . . . such a clever touch. Oh, we thought of it, did we? Well, never mind, great minds think alike—'

After ten minutes or so, he put down the phone and blew Fee a kiss across the desk.

'Ready?' he asked.

'Ready for what?' Fee replied, always wary of Gerry's passion for the *double entendre*.

'Ready for the best break of your career so far.'

'Doing what?' Fee questioned.

'Repositioning romance . . . We're—'

Fee was up and out of the chair and on her way through the door. She'd heard enough.

'Have a heart!' Gerry shouted after her retreating figure. 'Have a heart, Fee!'

Forty minutes later, Fee and Gerry Radcliffe were fifteen miles outside London. They were being driven to a country house in Surrey, the home of Harry Macklin, millionaire founder of the Have a Heart! dating agency; also known as HAH!

It was then that Gerry Radcliffe remembered Babs and Derek. The couple were now enjoying their third hour of togetherness on the turquoise sofa in Fee's office.

He phoned Gina. 'Send them home in a cab. Make a new appointment. Promise them a free wedding. Oh, and why don't you give them a couple of those T-shirts I've still got in my office? The ones we designed for the Meat Marketing Board?'

'The ones with Love Me Tender and a piece of steak on the front?' Gina questioned.

'That's them, no other bugger will wear 'em.' Gerry Radcliffe smiled and turned his attention to Fee.

'Babs and Derek, lovely couple. I want you to meet them. I want you to realize where this business has traditionally been anchored so that you can understand how far it still has to go—' He searched his employee's face for signs of encouragement. Seeing none, he resumed his efforts. He wasn't a salesman for nothing.

'Now, about this Harry Macklin. He's the man who, I promise, hand on heart, will change your life.' His voice resounded with conviction. This came from the fact that Gerry always personally believed what he said, no matter how much others might consider it bullshit.

'He has money, he has vision – and he is about to give us a fat slice of the largest-growing market in Europe. Now, Fee, I bet your next question is, "What is the largest growing market in Europe?"

'Is it religion? No, it is not. Is it interior design? No, it is not. Is it men's fashion? No, it is not. Is it Japanese takeaway? No, it is not.' He paused for effect.

'The biggest market in Europe is L-O-V-E. I am talking ready-to-wear romance. Mail-order *amour*—' Fee's wariness was beginning to annoy him. He paid her to be positive, for God's sake.

He persisted. 'Harry Macklin owns the Have a Heart! organization. He's expanded it from a dating agency into a variety of associated ventures . . . a lonely-hearts magazine, a chain of social clubs for singles . . . a singles holiday company. You know the kind of thing—

'Fee, I can't believe that I'm offering you involvement on such a big deal. Am I good to you – or am I not?'

She smiled wanly, then replied, 'If you're asking me will I take on the Macklin contract, the answer, I'm afraid, is no, Gerry. I'm not interested.'

No.

It had been so easy. Why couldn't she manage to say it more often?

'No, no, no,' she repeated, relishing the sound.

Gerry laughed. 'Go on,' he chuckled. 'You never say no. At least,' he added, smirking, 'not if it's anything to do with work. You're not the type. You know that, Fee.'

'The answer is still no,' Fee repeated.

He ignored her. 'Macklin wants to put a couple of ideas to you. He wants to give you the once-over, see if he thinks you're up to the job.'

'No,' Fee repeated.

'Good girl,' Gerry Radcliffe smiled confidently.

He was about to pat his employee on the knee, but he remembered himself just in time.

'Watch,' the man commanded. He pressed a switch in his hand. The room darkened and suddenly the image of a gigantic carton of Pot Noodle appeared on two walls.

In the dark, somebody giggled.

'Watch,' the man instructed again.

This time, a portrait of Babs and Derek, gazing into each other's eyes, was projected. Behind the couple, the blurred face of Elvis Presley appeared again and again as a recurring motif on the wallpaper.

The man pressed another switch, the lights came on. The group was in a large study with a panoramic view which included a distant motorway. The décor was all white – white leather sofas, white rugs, two giant brass coffee tables, a small jungle of plants. A massive copper shield hung suspended over an open fireplace. The 'shield' consisted of two overlapping hearts engraved with the letters, HAH!

The man gestured for his entourage, including Fee Travers and Gerry Radcliffe, to take their seats around a glass-topped table.

'Pot Noodle,' he intoned. 'And Babs and Derek. What's the connection?'

No one spoke. Fee suppressed a smile and Gerry frowned disapprovingly. The man leant back in his white leather chair and folded his hands behind his head, biding his time.

The silence gave Fee the opportunity to assess her so far brief encounter with the HAH! organization and its founder.

Harry Macklin, the man who had set the riddle of the connection between instant food and besotted human beings, had a heavily nicotine-stained voice and a Manchester accent.

He was in his early fifties, a slim man with an incongruous pot belly, as if he'd swallowed a ten-pin ball. He wore white slacks, white loafers and a white cashmere jumper. He resembled an ageing crooner in search of a stint in cabaret.

He was over six foot tall, self-assured and while Fee couldn't deny that he was attractive, she was far from enamoured. She guessed that immaturity was probably his worst design fault. And he had a manner that she didn't take to at all.

Alongside him was a woman in her late thirties with a hairstyle ten years younger than her face. It was streaked in various shades of blonde and worn loose and long and curly. She wore denim jeans and a matching shirt, both studded with pale-pink *diamanté*. On her feet were high-heeled snakeskin mules. Her nails were also pale pink and carefully manicured. She was heavily perfumed and smelt like a tropical fruit salad.

Fee didn't like the way Harry Macklin had failed to introduce his female companion or the way in which he was abrupt with the Philippino couple who had served drinks earlier. Nor the way he refrained from granting common courtesies to the two so far mute young men in suits, who now flanked him and who Fee presumed were members of his staff.

'He likes you. I can tell,' Gerry Radcliffe had whispered almost immediately after their arrival, on the basis of no evidence at all.

Harry Macklin decided that enough time had been wasted. 'Well, what a lot of bright sparks we've got here,' he spoke quietly. His two men flinched at the softness of his tone.

'Pot Noodle and Babs and Derek? The connection is simple,' Macklin announced.

'Springsters, that's the connection. Springsters! Got it?'

Those around him looked blank. Macklin was enjoying his little entertainment. 'Pass out the portfolios, Serena,' he directed. The woman in denim obeyed his instructions.

'Read,' Harry Macklin ordered.

'Drinks,' he instructed one of his aides in the next breath.

'I'll have a—' Gerry Radcliffe began, relief in his voice.

'Sparkling or still? Water is all Mr Macklin drinks.' The aide paused, then added, 'Now.'

It took Fee Travers only minutes to digest the information she had been given. First came a potted history of the business and a background to the boss.

Twenty years ago, she read, Harry Macklin had owned a battery chicken farm. He had set out to find a wife, had no luck employing orthodox methods, and applied to a dating agency. He was appalled at the service. So, he set up his own organization, charging half the then fee. He also guaranteed money back if the agency failed to find a partner within twelve months.

Have a Heart! flourished from the outset. It had since married 2 million couples. How many divorces subsequently ensued the official history did not reveal.

Harry 'Mr Marriage' Macklin, was fifty-six and had five children, ranging in age from two to twenty-four, but none living with him. Still, the biography boasted, 'He is a truly interactive father.' Married three times, he had recently divorced.

The portfolio also had details on 'Lamoor', the property in which they now sat. An aerial photograph revealed that the swimming pool and every flowerbed were heart-shaped, while a maze had been constructed using the HAH! logo of intertwining hearts.

Fee noted that HAH! was a private company so there were no details of its profits. The solitary reference to money made HAH! appear almost philanthropic. 'Under the guidance of Mr Macklin and his accountant Serena Alwyn, several millions of pounds have now been generated in the business of making people happy.'

Fee raised her eyes and met the interested gaze of the woman in denim.

'You thought I was his girlfriend, didn't you?' Serena Alwyn whispered. 'Lots of people do. I'm not. I'm his accountant and managing director of the company. Not as dumb as other people think I look,' she added drily.

'I'd never go near Harry romantically, would I, love? Between you and me, what Harry knows about how to make a relationship work wouldn't fit on this.'

She raised a long pink talon. 'Still, the people who like us aren't bothered about how to make it work, they want to know how to make it happen in the first place. Isn't that right, love?' She nudged Macklin.

Fee could swear she heard him purr.

Five minutes later, Harry Macklin ordered the drinks to be cleared away, then took up position in front of a large flipchart, which had silently descended from the ceiling. He drew on it, 'HAH! 2005', and began to speak with a charismatic style that even made Fee temporarily suspend judgement and take heed.

'So who or what is a springster? Springsters are men and women of thirty plus – and unattached.' He flipped, revealing phrases that reinforced his words.

'They may have lived with someone in the past or been married. Springsters may come in many forms but one thing they are not. They are not Anoraks. They are no longer Babs and Derek.

'Anoraks have contributed a great deal to our success. Shy, retiring, solitary, less than successful with the opposite sex—

'But now it's time for HAH! to move on. The future lies with springsters!

'Our new customer is highly motivated. Confident about themselves and their appeal. But they are busy, busy, busy. They have insufficient free time to hunt for a partner and they may be working against their own biological clock,' Harry Macklin expounded.

'If they decide at, say, thirty-four, this is the time to settle down, they don't want to hunt for five years to find the appropriate partner.

'Springsters want it *now.*' The man was growing more excited as he painted his vision of future profits.

'HAH! will be to the millennium what Pot Noodle was to the seventies – a miracle of modern selling. We want to strip matchmaking of the stigma of shame. It's no longer a loser's game. By the time we've finished, it will be as common for a springster to come to us, the professionals' matchmaker, as it will for them to play a game of squash, hire a personal trainer or take out a mortgage.'

'We know what we want,' Macklin ended melodramatically, leaning with his knuckles on the table and staring intently at Fee. 'The question is, "Are you the one to deliver?"'

Gerry Radcliffe had her out of the front door before she had a chance to answer.

'Fee, you're perfect for this account,' Gerry Radcliffe insisted. They had stopped for a drink on the return journey. 'You know exactly what this is all about. You've got an instinct for what works and what doesn't work. Nobody can lift a product off the shelf like you.'

'What you're trying to say is that since I'm desperate and unattached, I'm the ideal target HAH! client.' Fee gave her boss a strained smile.

'Well, not exactly, I—' he struggled to find suitable words.

'Besides, I don't think it's natural.' Fee played with the ice in her gin and tonic. 'I don't think it's a natural way to find a partner by filling in forms, answering ads, going on blind dates. It's—'

She struggled to find the appropriate words. 'It takes away all the mystery and gives the chooser too much control. What I think I want might not be what I really need.'

Gerry looked at her, perplexed, so she tried again.

'For instance, I might believe that I should fancy a six-foot vegan who cares about the environment, only to discover that I have a passion for a very small man who works in an abattoir and who doesn't recycle so much as a widget. How can any questionnaire compete with the fact that most of us don't really have a clue what we want until fate takes a hand?

'Or, to put it more bluntly,' she added, 'if I discovered that a man I liked had been to a dating agency, I'd wonder what was wrong with him. Anyway, it doesn't matter what I think. The answer is still no.

'I've already got five projects on the go. I'm already working all the hours—'

Gerry shrugged his shoulders. 'OK, OK, but this is a big prestigious contract. Lots of coverage in the trade press. Make or break time for yours truly and others. So, if you're going to be uncooperative – and I don't want to have to do this, mind – I'll have no alternative but to bring in Diana. And you know how it is.' He refused to look at Fee as he spoke; instead he studied his beer mat intently as if reading his lines from its design.

'You know how it is,' he repeated. 'One seat vacant on the board, and two strong women candidates. Who's it to be? This could be the decider . . . doesn't have to be this way, of course, it's entirely in your hands—'

Diana Woods was six years Fee's junior and had been brought into the company eight months earlier to concentrate on expanding F.P. & D.'s interests in the rest of Europe.

Since Diana Woods's arrival, Fee had tried to do the right thing, as one sister to another. She had helped her colleague with contacts and ideas and passed work her way.

Fee would never describe herself as ambitious. She worked as hard as she could in a job, but had never set herself goals. For too many years she had seen the effects of disappointment in her own mother to take the risk of inflicting that on herself.

In contrast, Diana Woods made it plain from the outset that she was mad about goals – but not so keen to be a team player. Even Gerry, who had hired her, treated Diana with caution.

'So is it yes or is it no? Are you ready for big things? A seat on the board? Or are you going to disappoint me and tell me you just can't hack it?' Gerry asked again as he and Fee left the pub.

Fee bought herself time by pretending to concentrate on buckling her safety belt. Why not say yes? Why not call Gerry's bluff? A seat on the board had never been mentioned before – now see if he delivered.

She knew that she could probably make a success of the HAH! project – but did she want to flog the illusion that the best guarantee of happiness was in the arms of another? Not least when personal experience told her that the contrary was just as likely to be true.

'I just don't want to take this account, Gerry.' Her words belied the fact that her initial confidence was now ebbing fast. 'So the answer is still no.'

'Well, this isn't like you at all—' Gerry Radcliffe responded icily.

'Oh, but it is,' she corrected him firmly.

'It makes no sense,' a bemused Fee Travers told herself a little later at her desk, as she packed the day's work, as yet undone, into her briefcase.

'I'm already manless; in a couple of months, at this rate, I could also be jobless, Claire-less and broke. And all because I'm trying to take charge of my life? How big a price does someone have to pay for trying to take a little control?'

'Hi,' said a voice at the door. It was Diana Woods. She was wearing a bitter-chocolate suit and her auburn hair was neatly held in a tortoiseshell clip. Diana Woods was always perfectly turned out. While others might spend several hours a day on hair removal, manicuring, coiffuring and various forms of personal irrigation to achieve the same standard of perfection, Diana Woods gave the impression that she was so quintessentially female she probably developed in the womb with eyelashes ready curled and each toenail painted.

Now, she walked into Fee's office and raised a hand to lift a hair from Fee's collar. She was carrying a pile of papers under her arm, including a computer print-out, and was wearing a victorious smile. At least, Fee read it as victorious.

'Gerry told me to let you have a look at this,' Diana explained.

'Gerry's not here,' Fee replied unnecessarily. She knew this was his crude attempt to bring out Fee's competitive streak. Anything Diana could do – he was continuing to calculate – Fee would try to do better.

'It's about the HAH! contract. I've made up a dossier – a SIMPLE dossier.'

'Simple?' Fee questioned, then mentally rebuked herself for playing straight into Diana's hands.

'SIMPLE – Single Independent Mature People Looking for Encounters – Macklin'll love it, don't you think?'

Diana Woods didn't wait to hear her rival's reply.

Only on her way to her car did Fee remember that Claire and Clem were due to arrive at her flat in ten minutes for supper. It would take her at least half an hour to drive home, another twenty minutes for shopping – ready-made fish soup, ready-made chicken breasts and frozen fruit salad she could defrost in the microwave.

On her car phone, Fee dialled Will Evans's number. He never worked late; he left that to his conscientious female colleagues. He was, as she expected, at home. He agreed to let Claire and Clem in and give them a drink but he would have to leave soon after as he'd arranged to meet someone at the cinema.

'I now realize the role that I have in your life,' he had joked. 'I'm the keeper of the keys. By the way, that woman was on your doorstep again when I got back an hour or so ago.'

'Rita?' Fee's irritation came from nowhere with a ferocity that she found unsettling. She'd dumped a prospective fiancé, only to be saddled with a woman who had all the persistence of an unwanted spouse. How ironic.

'She didn't ask to be let in. She said she happened to be passing but never mind, she'd give you a ring. Something about Thursday . . .?'

Fee groaned. She'd have to invent an excuse to avoid Rita's night out. Perhaps an unexpected business trip? As her car joined yet another lifeless queue of evening traffic, Fee gave a wry smile.

She'd given Will an earful about personal honesty and here she was contemplating practising exactly his kind of deceit. Why not tell Rita Mason the truth?

'I don't want to be your friend because you remind me too much of what I could become.'

It sounded idiotic. It *was* idiotic.

Chapter Twelve

B ATHS.
Imogen Banks was indulging in one of her passions. She adored abluting, soaking, steaming, sponging, soaping, basically any activity that involved sitting in a great deal of water for a lengthy period of time.

Her own bathroom was large with a vast copper tub on legs in the middle of it. The room also had wooden shutters, copious cupboard space, a comfortable armchair, a sound system, television, a shelf of books, and lights that could be dimmed at whim.

Now, Imogen lay in the bath, her face the colour of spearmint green, the contents of a face pack. In front of her, on a specially designed bath tray she had bought in Hong Kong (if she was ever asked to appear on *Desert Island Discs*, Imogen intended to name this little gadget as her one luxury), she had deposited a half-bottle of champagne in an ice bucket, a dish of smoked mussels and a bowl of pork cracklings, a personal weakness.

She reread the report propped up on the tray. The news was mixed.

Simon Booth's sperm count was excellent – but his financial situation was not. Imogen had it on good authority that, by this time next week, he would find himself redundant. Imogen was relieved. She would have taken the news of Simon's infertility very personally indeed.

Probe-a-Partner, the source of this information, was an organization she had come to depend upon. It had been set up five years earlier and Imogen Banks was now a regular customer. As its name implied, it specialized in checking out the credentials of potential partners. Probe-a-Partner was more expensive than a condom but, in Imogen's experience, as preventative measures went, it was infinitely more reliable.

Its help had meant she had been able to tweak out a dozen or more fantasies – lies would be too cruel a word – from potential lovers before the dissembling had become too damaging. An invaluable asset when dealing in the world of married men.

Imogen turned on the hot-water tap to top up the bath. Simon's imminent joblessness was less of a problem than the fact that he was already becoming surprisingly time-consuming.

'After all, it wasn't as if he didn't have a wife and family to go home too,' she told herself grumpily.

If Simon remained unemployed for long, she would have him on her hands even more. This was a worry.

She placed Simon's reports in the waterproof 'Pending' box by the bath and turned her mind to Fee Travers. Imogen's requirements were simple. On film, Fee should be able to talk eloquently and with conviction about why she had decided to remain single. *Permanently* single.

'Permanently' was, of course, as relative as everything else in these modern times. Once the programme was broadcast, Fiona Travers could engage in serial matrimony until the end of her days for all Imogen cared – it was the next several weeks that were crucial.

What Imogen had to ensure was that Fee did not fall prey to a nasty little attack of love at first sight – or, for that matter, revive any past romances. Unless, of course, such an encounter helped to strengthen her resolve . . .

In the short term, Imogen had a still knottier problem to untangle. Fee had yet to consent to appear. Imogen's dilemma was therefore twofold. She had to change Fee's no to yes. And she had to engineer an incident that would persuade Fee that spinsterhood was fun, wise, and definitely the best possible choice for her.

Imogen soaked and soaked and soaked. And then the idea came to her.

She rapidly dried and chose a dark-green towelling dressing-gown from a choice of six hanging in a wardrobe in the bathroom. Then, she dialled two numbers.

First, she spoke to Helen Travers. She persuaded her that the plan she had concocted was actually Helen's own idea.

'It'll do her a power of good, Mrs Travers, trust me,' she said, nursing the receiver in the crook of her still damp neck.

The second call was to Hilly Byrne at home. If Imogen was working, she assumed everyone else should be too. Imogen asked Hilly to investigate the possibility of a live studio discussion after *The Perfumed Pound* was broadcast.

'But this Travers woman hasn't even said yes yet, has she?' Hilly queried sleepily. She was in the middle of sharing her free time generously with Will Evans. Imogen didn't hear the question since she had already replaced the receiver.

Now, Imogen excitedly stuffed several pieces of sweaty pork crackling in her mouth and rubbed her hands together. If she was truly honest (which Imogen Banks rarely was, of course) she would say that when it came to making love or making mischief, there was no contest. She preferred the latter any day.

She dialled a third number. Now, it was time for some real fun.

'Hello,' she said, pitching her voice slightly higher – a tactic she knew made her sound more vulnerable. 'Is that Bill Summers? You don't know me but Helen Travers gave me your number. You remember Helen? Fee's mother?

'Well, we both use the same vet. I bumped into her recently and happened to tell her that I'm looking for a very good photographer to provide some stills for a film I'm making. Helen mentioned you. Do you think you might be able to come and see me . . .? Oh, is it that late, gosh I *am* sorry,' Imogen gushed, so utterly enchanted with her own little brainwave that she had forgotten to check the time.

'Champagne?' Clem asked.

Fee smiled stiffly. This was, after all, her kitchen, in her flat. Granted, her best friend's fiancé was offering his own champagne. But did he have to look quite so at home?

'How much longer?' Claire's contented voice floated in from the sitting room. 'It smells wonderful.'

It did too. That was an added irritation to Fee. This was *her* kitchen, and she expected to be responsible for any smells or odours that emanated from it.

Clem opened the oven door, checked the casserole, closed it again and expertly began to mix a salad dressing. With *my* olive oil, wine vinegar and condiments, Fee reminded herself crossly. All the time, she kept a small smile on her face.

Everything in Fee's kitchen had its place. She wasn't obsessional or anything, but as there was no one else to disrupt Fee's order, she'd grown accustomed to the olive oil staying in the site reserved for the olive oil.

Nothing wrong in that. Absolutely nothing wrong at all, Fee reassured herself fiercely. But she knew her skin was turning pink. Perhaps, without even realizing it, she had become one of those selfish old bints who puts herself first. And second and third.

'You wouldn't have any fresh basil, would you?' Clem asked. 'I thought I'd chop a bit up for the dressing. Or don't you like it? It's perfectly OK without it.'

Fee didn't have any fresh basil. Is it a crime not to have fresh basil, Fee asked herself. Of course it isn't. So why did she feel as if she was lacking in every social grace, just because she couldn't whip a bit out of the fridge?

Come to that, there wasn't a lot of anything to whip out of the fridge. 'But why be apologetic,' Fee checked herself silently. 'This is my kitchen, I'll run it how I please.'

'I find basil quite useful to have hanging around,' Clem said conversationally, as he began to crush garlic into a mound of whipped yellow butter. 'Especially if your cupboard is pretty bare. Mine always is too—' he added hastily.

Patronizing bastard, Fee thought – and carried on smiling, saying nothing.

'Claire's told me a lot about you,' Clem remarked, smothering slices of French bread with the garlic butter. Fee noted that his fingers were long and sensual and delicate.

'There's not a lot to know,' she replied, sounding more defensive than she intended.

'Isn't there?' Clem looked at her and smiled. Fee was cross. Why did she feel so unnerved?

The evening had collapsed even before it had begun. First, Fee was even later than she intended. After the supermarket stop, something untoward had happened to the exhaust pipe. She had continued to drive, slowly, dragging it along the road.

The noise was like a troupe of giants performing a tap dance on a steel table. Rushing into the flat, she discovered she had been usurped. She had been demoted from hostess, best friend, judge of the future spouse – to gooseberry at an intimate supper for two. At least, that's how she saw it.

The cooking was all underway, the table set, the champagne chilled.

Claire explained that she and Clem had realized there was a hitch when they found the cupboards bare. So Clem had shopped around the corner.

'He loves throwing something together. He's very good like that,' she had added with a smug smile on her face.

Fee had walked into her kitchen, radiating hostility. It was all very silly and territorial, she knew, but sod it, it was her flat, and she wanted to regain control of the evening.

That's when Clem had offered her a glass of champagne, pulled out a chair, and produced a bowl of perfect olives. (Fee always had a problem with olives. No matter where she bought them or what she paid, they still tasted as if they'd been pickled in a can of gasolene.)

'If you're happy with the idea, why don't you put your feet up, while I cook?' he'd smiled. Claire had fussed around both of them for several minutes, until she had been dispatched to the sitting room.

One of her mother's sayings floated into Fee's mind: 'A man wrapped up in himself makes a very small parcel.' Was Clem Thomas wrapped up in himself? It would make Fee's night if that turned out to be true.

'Claire says you're funny,' Fee suddenly blurted out. She knew she sounded aggressive.

'Does she?' Clem replied. He was carrying out some fiddly operation with the filling in the baked potatoes.

'I like my food plain and simple, don't you?' Fee remarked pointedly. She was surprised at how childishly she was behaving.

Clem appeared unperturbed. Without comment, he left one potato plain. He wore jeans and a white T-shirt, only half tucked in to his belt. A battered brown leather jacket hung on the back of a chair.

In the past, Claire had always been a suit man. She placed great faith in the cut of a man's cloth. What Fee couldn't understand now was how Claire had suspended all her usual criteria and chosen a man so totally different from her customary tastes. How had they even made the first connection?

'All I did', Claire answered later with an enigmatic smile on her face, 'is stop being so instantly judgemental. You should try it some time, Fee. You really should.'

Fee examined Clem as he gradually covered every work surface in the kitchen with dishes, pots and pans.

'*Why doesn't he wash up as he goes along?*' Fee asked herself crossly but said nothing. Clem was tall and fit with regular features and brown hair which took off in different directions.

'Tousled,' Claire had called it – but then she would, now she had taken up permanent residence in the land of Mills & Boon.

You wouldn't call him handsome, Fee told herself with relief. Her best friend's future husband was no hunk. To be honest, Fee classed him as a five-out-of-ten man, but what she did have to concede was that – apart from his smile – he also had a pair of very impressive aquamarine eyes. Still, even those assets didn't push him up the ladder. Definitely *cinq points.*

'So what do you think of him?' Claire had whispered in the first half-hour, when Clem had gone to the loo.

'Clem?' Fee had replied, as if there were other contenders.

'Clem,' Claire said firmly. 'Hasn't he got a lovely personality? And he doesn't feel the need to impress. Give him time . . . you'll see—'

Fee gave him time. Roughly, a further sixty minutes. Then she made her decision. She didn't like the man. She would tolerate him for Claire's sake. But she didn't like him. She couldn't explain exactly why – there was just something . . . something . . . about him.

He was attentive enough to Claire. His manners were immaculate. He was amusing without appearing to show off. He could tell funny stories and he didn't expect to hog the conversation.

He was also relaxed and self-assured, without appearing big-headed. Surprisingly, Fee found herself talking far more than usual. In truth, she had hoped there would be more to dislike – a strong dose of boorishness say – or a total absence of humour. Still, her judgement remained inviolate. She didn't like Clem Thomas and she didn't trust his motives when it came to Claire.

His real problem, Fee decided, was that he was too good to be true.

Claire, of course, was behaving in a thoroughly ridiculous fashion in a way Fee hadn't observed before: acting as if she was fifteen. Fee gave her a couple of dirty looks but Claire was not to be swayed. She knew Claire well enough to know that these weren't the symptoms of love or even infatuation, but she was performing in a highly bizarre manner. As if she was telling Fee, 'Look what I've got that you haven't—'

'I haven't ever seen you like this before,' Fee accused Claire when Clem briefly left them to bring more milk in from the kitchen for the coffee.

'Well, perhaps you don't know me as well as you think you do,' Claire replied. She had meant the comment lightly but the remark had cut Fee deeply.

It wasn't how best friends behaved towards each other, was it?

Much later, after the two had left, Fee picked up the coffee cups in the sitting room and stopped abruptly at the kitchen door. She'd expected a tip but instead the room had been restored to operating-theatre standards of cleanliness. Unexpectedly, her anger grew, swelling and snarling.

She opened cupboards, examined shelves. Everything in its place, a place for everything, as her mother would say. Fee could find no fault. This level of thoughtfulness had to be treated with the utmost suspicion.

Fee had the hunch that Clem Thomas was about to bring out the worst in her. And, frankly, she couldn't wait.

At 2 a.m., Fee's telephone rang. The answering machine picked up the message. It rang again three times before dawn. In the morning, Fee discovered every message was from Rita Mason – and each was uncannily identical.

'I need to have a quick chat,' the voice said politely. 'But it's difficult to contact me, so I'll try again later. By-eee. Love, Rita.'

'I need to have a quick chat—' 'I need to have a quick chat—' 'I need to have a quick chat—' Didn't the woman sleep, for God's sake?

The morning's post brought a small parcel. Inside was an exquisite voile blouse. It was white with delicate embroidery on the Peter Pan collar and small pearl buttons. It looked as if it had been made in the 1940s and cared for; Fee liked it very much.

She opened the note that accompanied it. It read, 'Thought you might like to wear this on Thursday.'

An hour later, Fee walked into Will's office at F.P. & D. She had decided that something had to be done about Rita Mason.

'This is an unexpected pleasure.' Will smiled, offering Fee a chair. He let her settle before he said, 'I see that Diana Woods is hard at work on the singles account . . . Been here most of the night—'

'Has she?' Fee replied casually. The information, although not unexpected, hurt more than she had anticipated. *Grow up*, she told herself. *You've made a decision, you've said no, now move on.*

Will began to play with a pot of pencils on his desk, 'She's telling everyone that Gerry didn't think you were up to it, so she's been put on the job. Younger, fresher ideas, you know the kind of modest assessment Diana makes of herself in public from time to time—' Will watched Fee carefully.

Fee shrugged nonchalantly. 'If it makes her happy, let her say what she pleases,' she answered.

'But it's not very sisterly of her, is it?' Will dug deeper. 'I thought you gave Diana her first big account here?'

'I did,' Fee smiled tightly. 'Look, she can behave as shittily as she likes but I'm not going to let that panic me into working twice as hard as I'm already doing. Or use it as an excuse to behave as badly as her—' Fee paused, embarrassed that she had said so much.

Will nodded as if in agreement, then added casually, 'She acts as if she's got all the inside gen—'

'Inside gen about what?' Fee asked icily.

'Oh, forget it, it's just gossip.' Will was genuinely sorry he had raised the subject. He hadn't known whether to shield Fee from the rumours, or be open so she could deal with them herself. He was now uncomfortably aware that whatever route he chose, he would appear in the wrong.

'Well, what gossip . . .?' Fee pressed him, her cheeks already colouring.

'Look, it's nothing. Diana hinted that you and Gerry had been having an affair . . . hence all the best projects going your way . . . I said I thought it was crap. But you know how these things snowball. According to Diana, it all came to a head when you and Gerry went to Macklin's place. She said it took you twice as long to get back as it did to go—'

'Of course it damn well did,' Fee exploded. 'We stopped for a drink. Gerry wouldn't lay a finger on me or anybody else for that matter. He just likes to *think* he might. Will, why didn't you tell me this before?'

Will ran his fingers through his hair nervously. 'I didn't think it was worth mentioning. But now it's sort of blown up out of all proportion. And it's not fair to you,' he added stoutly.

He paused, expecting Fee to speak. Instead, she remained silent, gazing out of the window.

'So what are you going to do about it?' Will asked again.

'Nothing,' Fee answered crisply. 'Let Diana Woods do as she pleases. I haven't told Gerry yet but I've decided to take Veronica away on holiday. When I get back, who knows what I might do? Resign, quite possibly. For the last eighteen years, I've done nothing but work flat out. It's time for a change.'

'Fee.' Will looked at her quizzically. 'I wouldn't decide on anything in a rush. Particularly now. You haven't seemed yourself recently. Just because Claire's changing gear, doesn't mean you have to too, you know—'

Fee gave him a withering look and got up to go. Then she remembered the original reason for her visit, and stopped.

'I came in to ask a favour,' she said. 'It's Rita Mason. Promise me that, in future, on no account will you let her into my flat, no matter what she says?'

'No matter what?' Will repeated.

'No matter what,' Fee insisted.

Closing Will's door, Fee turned to find herself facing Diana Woods. 'Everything all right?' she asked disingenuously.

'Couldn't be better.' Fee smiled broadly, annoyed that this woman always had the effect of making her feel like the bottom of her own handbag: all odds and sods.

'Are you free on Monday?' Diana Woods asked. 'Gerry says he wants you there when I make my first presentation. If you can't make it, I'm sure he'll understand. I mean you've got an awful lot on, haven't you?' The smile came and went.

'Of course I'll be there. I'm sure we'll both learn a great deal,' Fee replied cheerily. 'You know what they say about me in the office,' she added mischievously. 'The woman who never says no.'

Back at her desk, Fee sat, depressed and lonely. Normally, she would have called on Claire for advice, or turned to Gill for distraction, or spent time with Will as a diversion. But Claire was house-hunting, Gill was hostile and Will was preoccupied with a woman he had yet to introduce to Fee.

In the early afternoon, a call came through.

'It's Imogen. Imogen Banks,' said a voice she didn't at first recognize. 'I've had a splendid idea. I've got to go to Marlow tomorrow. Then, I thought, wouldn't it be fun if you could come too? We could have a spot of lunch, a glass or two of champagne, enjoy the river. I don't normally take time off from work in the week but what the hell – and I thought we got on so well the other day . . .?'

Fee didn't even pause to think.

'You can't take tomorrow off. Macklin's coming in to take a look at the whole team,' Gerry Radcliffe protested furiously a little later. 'And whether or not you're working on his account, you remain a senior member of this company. I want you here.'

'OK. I'm telling you in advance, I'm going to be ill,' Fee retaliated. 'I'm owed three weeks' holiday which I'm supposed to take before next month, and you're saying I can't take a day off?'

'I'm warning you, Fee,' Gerry threatened. 'No good will come of this—'

She smiled back. Defiance had lifted her spirits.

'Surely it's much too early to tell, Gerry?' she replied flippantly.

Chapter Thirteen

Simon Booth was baffled. He sat in the café in the park at 11 a.m. on Thursday morning and stared at the piece of paper he held in his hands. It informed him that his services were no longer required. Fourteen years in the company but the business had now been bought out, taken over. His salary, position and length of service merited a relatively handsome pay-off but still he was baffled as to why there was no word of apology, no attempt at explanation. He was simply surplus to requirements.

He wouldn't tell Gill yet. Not until he'd worked out his own survival plan. Otherwise, his rescue would be one more area of his life that she would commandeer.

The last few years of his marriage had become a struggle. A struggle to resist adopting the same negative views of himself that his wife now held.

Simon's advancement in work had been rapid but, for Gill, not rapid enough. Their house was large but Gill had anticipated grand. They had a second home but Gill's choice would have been a manor house, not a converted barn. They enjoyed one longish holiday abroad a year, but Gill had always assumed that, by her late thirties, they would be boasting about two.

Simon knew that what galled his wife even more was her conviction (misplaced in Simon's opinion) that if he had stayed at home and Gill had become the breadwinner, the fruits of her efforts in this the second decade of their marriage would have been far riper and more plentiful.

Recently, Gill's frustrations and Simon's attempts to adapt to them while still salvaging some self-respect had reached a head. Even before the redundancy, it was plain to both of them that Simon had not transformed into the man Gill had assumed he would become.

Years ago, Gill had been seduced by a magazine article in which Simon, aged thirty-one, had been named as one of the young Turks in architecture to watch. At the time, Simon himself had been philosophical about such publicity. He was more than aware that, having been branded in print as a rising star, he would be wise, in real life, to set his sights far lower in the firmament. And this he believed he had succeeded in achieving rather well.

Simon Booth saw himself as a man of moderate talent enjoying an above-average income – married to a woman who now wanted something else.

So why did Simon remain with Gill? If asked he would say it was because of the children. Then he would add that he admired Gill's energy and ability and determination. Besides, if he left, Simon knew he would deny himself the pleasure of witnessing that momentous occasion – and it would come one day – when his wife was forced to concede that being one half of a moderately successful couple was infinitely preferable to being a nonentity on her own.

All this, of course, was before Simon's redundancy and the arrival of Imogen. The redundancy was a setback. Simon had never been out of work in his life before. Yet, here he was at nearly forty-five, dumped. Stranger still, he found the idea of being job-free hugely intoxicating. A reaction he put down to shock.

Even being in the park mid-morning on a weekday was like entering a new world. He'd already nodded hello to a couple of other men from his street. Men whom, he assumed, must be likewise unemployed.

Another perk of unemployment would mean more time to spend with Imogen. This unexpected courtship, although still intensely thrilling, was beginning to give Simon a vague sense of *déjà vu*. At least, it did when he allowed it to.

Just like Gill in their early days, Imogen had the unnerving habit of banging on about Simon's 'winning aura'. Just like Gill, Imogen appeared convinced that Simon was destined to achieve hugely. He had, Imogen frequently said, 'the smell of success'. In fact, she seemed to have a bit of a thing about smells. And, just like Gill, Imogen could be a mite, well . . . directional, even bossy.

Simon dismissed the word from his head immediately. *Bossy.* It was too mundane, too run of the mill to be associated with this highly charged spiritual and sexual liaison he was enjoying – no, *celebrating* was the word.

It wasn't the sex he was celebrating, it was the fact that he was finally doing something that his wife couldn't control, criticize or influence in any way. Simon Booth would probably have enjoyed the same sense of liberation if he'd secretly become a trainspotter or illicitly taken up ballroom dancing.

Of course, he felt guilty. He was by nature a faithful man. Of course, he worried about the price he might have to pay – not least in forfeiting time with the children. Still, if Gill could be persuaded to modify her aspirations, if she would only value him for what he was, then he might even consider giving up Imogen.

He found this line of reasoning reassuring, since it placed responsibility for ending the liaison not on himself but on Gill – who, of course, knew nothing about the triangle of which she was now a part. In the meantime, he would continue in his new role as a sexual lion, his conscience further eased by the awareness that, whatever the wrongs of the situation, he was feeling better about himself by the minute.

Simon Booth gave a small growl.

'Mozart and Ella Fitzgerald?' Fee had picked up a couple of CDs. It was eleven on a Wednesday morning and Imogen Banks was driving her to a pub lunch in Marlow via three or four Buckinghamshire villages. She had explained that the most suitable might become the setting for a new comedy series which Astra TV had been com-missioned to make.

'My dad loved Mozart and Ella Fitzgerald,' Fee replied. 'Bill was quite keen on jazz too, when he wasn't in his dark room.'

'Bill?' Imogen affected ignorance.

'Bill Summers,' Fee replied. 'We lived together for a while and split up a couple of years ago. He married a woman who already has a couple of children, and they've got one between them. He still calls my mother now and then.' Fee gave a mock-grimace. 'Naturally, she makes a point of telling me how happy he is.'

'Don't they always?' Imogen Banks responded enthusiastically.

'Salmon and *crème brûlée*,' Fee decided, running her eye over the lunch menu. The two women were sitting in the garden of a pub that Imogen had visited many times. They were both drinking Pimms.

'How many units do you reckon you drink a week?' Imogen asked. Fee began to laugh. She had spent most of the morning laughing. Imogen was self-deprecating and funny. Anything Fee had done, Imogen had tackled with an even worse record of success.

'Sixteen units, maybe?' Fee paused and glanced at Imogen. 'If I'm honest, more like twenty-six at times. Too much anyway.'

'Me too,' Imogen used her finger to push the mint and sliced orange further down her glass. 'I give up every Monday morning and by Monday evening, I'm telling myself a half-glass of red isn't going to do much damage.'

'Do you ever drink alone?' Fee asked.

'God, no,' Imogen looked shocked. 'Not because I think it's wrong, but because I never seem to *be* on my own. Except', she added hurriedly, suddenly remembering her man-free existence, 'most nights and in the mornings.'

The words sounded odd even as Imogen delivered them but Fee appeared not to notice.

'So, what's it to be, ladies?' A man with a handlebar moustache stood by their table, pencil behind his ear.

'Salmon and *crème brûlée* for two please,' Imogen smiled. 'And will a bottle of Sancerre do for you, Fee?'

'Fine,' the man replied. 'And what will you be drinking, madam?' he asked Imogen.

It was a joke he must have cracked dozens of times before, but everyone pretended otherwise. Later, when they ordered coffee, he produced two glasses of Sambucca on the house.

'I know you ladies love a bit of a *flambé*,' he announced, as he ignited the coffee beans floating on the surface. Fee and Imogen avoided catching each other's eye.

'Come again, girls, if your hubbies will let you out,' he shouted from the bar. The froth from the glass of Guinness in front of him had added a small snowdrift to the moustache and familiarity to his tone.

In the late afternoon, driving back, Imogen Banks reflected on the day. Professionally, it had been an astute move. She knew that Fee Travers had enjoyed herself. More surprisingly for Imogen, she too had had a good time. This was, of course, a severe challenge to the Banks theory that any time spent solely in the company of a woman was time wasted.

Fee interrupted Imogen's thoughts.

'I've been meaning to ask you something.'

Imogen tensed.

'The first time we met, you mentioned The Lone Ranger and Tonto. That intrigued me a bit.'

'Did it?' Imogen relaxed again.

'Yes, you're not a fan, are you?' Fee asked.

Imogen pondered the effort required to weave yet more deceit. She was tired. On this occasion, honesty, as it was less demanding, would have to do.

Imogen smiled. 'No, I don't know a blind thing about them. Except, of course, watching them on telly when I was a kid."Hi ho—"'

Fee smiled. 'Silver,' she prompted. 'The Lone Ranger's horse was called Silver. Tonto called him that when he first saw him in Wild Horse Valley.'

'Of course,' Imogen replied.

Fee laughed. 'When I was small, I wanted to *be* The Lone Ranger, live like him. The unknown man who does good and rides in and out of lives. The man with no past. My mother found that all very upsetting.'

'Why?' Imogen asked, offering Fee a mint.

'Her view is that only strange girls want to be cowboys or Robin Hood or Richard the Lionheart. Nice girls have heroines. She was keener on Cinderella, Wendy, Snow White – you know the kind of thing—'

Imogen nodded.

'So I kept The Lone Ranger a secret for years. My dad and Veronica, my sister, knew, and the boy next door, because he was always Tonto, but nobody else.

'Then, in school, we were asked to conduct a survey for homework. I decided to ask the girls in my class who their heroines were . . . I suppose we were all about nine or so at the time—'

'And?' Imogen asked.

'A lot of them didn't have heroines either. They were just like me. They had heroes instead.'

Imogen grinned approvingly. 'Well, if you'd asked me, I would've said the Sheriff of Nottingham. Trusted by no one and unfaithful to all. It must be nice to be wicked now and then,' she added hastily, in case her endorsement had seemed too convincing.

Forty minutes later, the car drew up outside F.P. & D.'s offices. Fee had some papers to collect (and her conscience to salve for truanting on a work day).

'Are you working tonight too?' she asked as she opened the car door.

Imogen hooted. 'Me? Certainly not. I'm flopping into a bath and then straight to bed. One of the many pleasures of living alone is that you can do what you want, when you want – and there's no one to say otherwise. Agreed?'

'Agreed,' Fee smiled.

'I'll give you a ring,' Imogen suggested. 'We should do this again some time—'

'Look, about your film, I'm sorry . . . I . . . it's just not me—' Fee began hesitantly.

'Oh, don't worry about that,' Imogen replied dismissively. 'I'm sure we'll dig up someone else to take your place. Plenty more where you came from—'

'Are there?' Fee asked, genuinely surprised.

Imogen Banks drove away, feeling very pleased with herself. It wouldn't be long before Fee Travers's no turned into yes. And then this unsavoury charade of sisterhood could thankfully come to a close.

Imogen contemplated her immediate future – romance and ratings – who could ask for more?

'Hi ho, Silver!' she yelled into the wind.

Two hours after saying goodbye to Fee, Imogen sat, not in her bed, but three tables to the right of the harpist in the Savoy Hotel in Piccadilly. She wore a lavender tailored suit, which exactly matched her underwear. She had also dressed in black gloves and large triangular gold ear-rings. She ordered a dry Martini and opened a copy of the *Telegraph*.

She looked at her watch and smiled contentedly. Somebody's wife would be missing a husband tonight; such a pity.

Chapter Fourteen

ROOM 12 of St Agatha's Hospital, Bellington, had a peachy-pink deep-pile carpet. The colour reminded Veronica of the powder-puffs that her mother used to have lined up on her kidney-shaped dressing-table when Veronica was seven or eight.

The curtains in the room were cream with large pink cabbage roses. The roses were exactly like those that had decorated a dress Veronica had bought at sixteen. It had taken every penny of her first three weeks' wages from a Saturday job as a waitress in a milk bar.

The frock was nipped in at the waist with a full skirt. The look was completed by a white waspie belt and sling-backs. Through the whole of that summer, every night before she wore her dress, Veronica would soak three net petticoats in sugar and water and hang them to dry on a line strung up in the kitchen. By the following evening, the stiffened petticoats would rub like barbed wire against Veronica's legs, but they made the cabbage roses stand out almost at right-angles from her waist.

Now, she lay in the large double-bed with its counterpane of cream and sheets of pink satin and tried not to think.

She had known for a while that she wasn't quite right – but anyone she mentioned it to in the family told her she was imagining things.

On one occasion, Helen had given Veronica the, 'you-don't-know-what-suffering-is-my-girl' speech which she used to deliver at frequent intervals when her daughters were growing up.

Helen's mother had had eight children, no money, no bathroom,

172

a stove in the corridor and an old man who drank. All the children, Helen included, had had to leave school at fourteen.

'We were poor and we weren't happy,' Helen would say grimly. 'But we took a pride in ourselves and we had none of this nonsense in those days.'

What exactly 'this nonsense' constituted, depended upon the subject in hand – it might be delinquency, the menopause, ME, single-parent families, too much self-absorption or, as in Veronica's case, a mental instability that had the audacity to develop into more than 'nerves'.

The sedatives made Veronica's thoughts bounce and bump together pleasantly. What she was less anxious to recall were the events of the previous day. Yesterday morning, she had locked the man who had come to read the gas meter down in the cellar because she knew an attack was imminent.

If Amy hadn't called in from next door, he would have been down there until midnight, when Les was due home. Les said that was the final straw. Veronica smiled. It was funny how similar Les had become to his mother-in-law. Helen was always announcing that something or other was the final straw.

Veronica turned in the hospital bed. St Agatha's was a private psychiatric hospital. Les had suggested that she have a couple of weeks' rest and then they could think again. Samantha was coming down from Manchester at the weekend. Les had promised to tell Fee in the morning but Helen had already been instructed that visiting wasn't allowed. That was Veronica's idea.

'You're nothing but a nuisance—' her mother used to tell her when she was small 'Always on the want—'

It's ironic really, Veronica told herself drowsily. I want for nothing now and I'm still a nuisance . . . a fifty-one-year-old nuisance so what's been the point of it all . . .?

But, of *course* there was a point. The point was that Veronica Haslem would rather hurt herself than anybody else.

Now *that* truly was mad. Or was that eminently sensible? Veronica could no longer judge.

At just after nine in the evening, at F.P. & D., Fee leant back in her chair and put her feet up on the desk. The desk light cast gentle shadows on the perspex and turquoise décor. It was like being underwater in a swimming pool. All was silent except for the distant hum of the cleaner's vacuum. Fee was happy.

She'd had an enjoyable day with Imogen. She was sure she'd taken the right decision not to overload herself at work. She had good friends and no man trouble.

Capitalize on the positive, Gerry Radcliffe always instructed his staff. So, Fee dialled Paul Denning's office number and left a message on the machine.

'Hello, Paul, it's Fee. If you're coming to London, it would be good to have a friendly drink. Speak to you soon.'

Show-off, Fee told herself and smiled. Paul would know from the tone of her voice, her choice of words, that their relationship had reached the stage of R.I.P. At least it had for Fee.

No ties, no tears.

'I am definitely happy,' Fee repeated – and crossed her fingers superstitiously.

'Happiness is not an entitlement, it's a reward just as easily taken away as given,' Helen always used to warn her daughters. And then she would demonstrate just how easily it could be forfeited, by stopping their pocket money or banning Saturday pictures as punishment for some slight misdemeanour.

'Bullshit,' Fee told herself cheerily now. 'Happiness is a state of mind for which I alone am responsible.'

Fee pushed aside the thought of who bore responsibility for Veronica's state of mind. She would phone her sister in the morning and together they'd organize a couple of weeks away.

Fee unlocked her drawer. She had taken to locking her drawers at night only after Diana Woods had worked in the firm for a couple of months. Fee had come in late one night and discovered her colleague at her desk. She said she had been looking for an *A-Z*, and Fee had directed her to the shelf behind her head.

Now, Fee removed a sheet of paper from the drawer. On it was the list made several days before of the pros and cons of a single life.

On the *cons* side, she had written: surcharges on holidays, no one to halve the household bills, coming home to an empty flat, unreliable sex life, making up numbers at dinner parties, planning ahead for the weekend, dinner with men who relive their marriages, divorces and the traumas of being an absentee father before the second course, other people's assumption that, because I don't have a partner, I am definitely not normal . . .

On the *pros* side, there was a blank. Fee picked up a pen and idly began to write down thoughts as they came into her head: converting the biggest room in the flat into a bathroom and nobody to complain; cheese on toast with HP sauce five times in a row and nobody to complain; no sex for a month and nobody to complain; friends to stay and nobody to complain; money spent and nobody to complain; time alone and nobody to complain; empty fridge and nobody to complain; disgusting personal habits and nobody to complain; work all night and nobody to complain . . .

Work.

The word brought Fee to a halt. Today's outing meant that she was now late in writing two reports. Fee calculated that if she put in two more hours tonight and came in early tomorrow, she could at least finish one. First, she needed a drink.

Gerry Radcliffe was the only member of F.P. & D. with a fridge in his office. He often boasted to his friends that his door was always open and the fridge well stocked and free to all employees. Everyone in the company knew, however, that no one helped themselves unless invited.

Fee walked into her boss's office and examined the contents of the fridge. Inside was an open bottle of Chablis. She took it over to

Gerry's desk, collecting a paper cup from the top of the fridge on the way. The desk was bare except for a couple of books on management, a notepad and two framed photographs of the family.

Fee put the bottle down. She scribbled, 'IOU half a bottle of wine,' on the first sheet of the notepad and signed it. As she did so, her elbow dislodged the books. They shifted slightly to reveal an internal F.P. & D. memo.

She was about to put the books back into place when her eye was caught by the word 'Confidential', today's date and the initials in the bottom corner of the top sheet, D. W.

Fee turned the first page – and kept on reading.

Diana Woods had analysed the last three projects undertaken by Fee – the relaunching of a line of soup to appeal to the young; the repositioning of a holiday company from downmarket to upmarket and the marketing and design of a new cable network intended for the affluent over fifties.

Each undertaking, at the time, had been judged a success within F.P. & D. The clients had also expressed their satisfaction. The repositioning of the holiday company had worked so well that Fee had been promoted.

So what the bloody hell was going on now? She sat down in Gerry's chair and took a swig from the bottle. Fee had been brought up to believe that if you worked hard, treated others as you would wish to be treated and avoided making trouble, you received your just rewards. And kept your friends.

The memo she now held in her hands indicated that somewhere along the line that plot had been well and truly abandoned, at least in this particular company.

It was unclear from the memo whether the analysis had been requested by someone else or initiated by Diana Woods. Either way, the overall message was one that reminded Fee unpleasantly of school: Fiona Travers could do better.

Who the hell did Diana Woods think she was?

Fee took another swig and settled down to read more carefully. The report was propaganda. Facts misused; remarks taken out of

context; predictions and estimations grossly exaggerated; the performance of rivals excessively polished. No outright lies, just extra-
vagant adaptations of the truth.

'Fee Travers's strategy is always adequate, occasionally rising to
good,' 'D. W.' had pronounced on the final page, 'but lack of proper
supervision, the absence of a competitive element and a tendency to
complacency has prevented her from rising to the excellent. F.P. &
D. has therefore paid the price.'

A lifetime's conditioning cranked into operation – Fee's first
reaction was that if she was being criticized then, of course, she must
deserve it.

Then, a stronger instinct rapidly took over: the knowledge of her
own experience in the field and the awareness that no one imposed
a tougher standard on Fee than she did on herself.

'This is rubbish,' Fee said out loud. But dangerous rubbish.

Half an hour later, back at her own desk, the memo restored to its
hiding place (under normal circumstances an ideal spot since almost
no one in F.P. & D. had ever been known to pick up a book on
management), Fee attempted to unscramble her reactions.

She knew she was good at her job; she also knew she was
hopeless at defending herself from someone who wanted her out as
badly as Diana Woods appeared to do. So what move should she
make next?

'Go on holiday?' Claire squeaked down on the phone. 'Have you
gone totally bananas?'

Fee had called Claire at home, not expecting her to be there. On
the third ring, she had answered. Fee outlined the situation and
when asked by Claire what she intended to do, Fee explained that
originally she planned to take Veronica away on holiday.

Even as she said the words, she realized how asinine she sounded.

'Do you really want to keep this job?' Claire demanded.

'I suppose so . . . well, I'm not sure,' Fee replied truthfully.

Claire exploded. 'Christ, Fee, you can be annoying sometimes. Gill's right, you *do* lack a sense of direction. It sounds to me as if someone is piling up the evidence for a case of dismissal, and—'

Fee tried again. 'Don't be ridiculous. Gerry hired me. I'm his choice. Why should he ditch me now? Look, I don't know if I want to keep the job but I do know that, when I go, I want it to be on my terms – not because I've been drummed out by Diana Woods and labelled as some sort of failure.

'Do you know it was through me she got her first big project?' she continued. 'Gerry wanted me to oversee her but I persuaded him that she needed to be given a chance on her own—' She fumed.

'So you think she owes you some kind of favour, do you?' Claire's voice was aggressive, irritated as she always was by Fee's *naïveté* when it came to business.

Claire continued, 'Did Diana Woods ask for your patronage? No. Did she expect any dispensations from you? No . . . She may even loathe the fact that you gave her a helping hand—'

'But she's a woman,' Fee found herself shouting down the phone. 'She and I are the only two women in this company at senior level. We're *supposed* to stick together, give each other help.'

Claire made a noise as if she was about to vomit. 'Oh Fee, do grow up,' she snapped. 'All this sisterhood stuff makes me ill. We're not in 1970 now – some of us are big girls. You can't assume Diana Woods's allegiance just because she's got a set of ovaries—'

'No,' Fee countered fiercely. 'But I still think it matters that we look out for each other. That's what really gets me. It's all so underhand. It's all so *macho* . . . It's only a job, for God's sake, why does she have to sacrifice every kind of value for *a job*?'

'Look, Fee,' Claire spoke more calmly, 'not everyone wants to be rescued by you—'

'And what precisely do you mean by that?' Fee asked icily. The earlier pleasure of the day had now almost completely washed away.

'Well, Veronica for a start . . . she might want to be left to sort herself out . . . and Will—'

'What about Will?'

'Will doesn't need your lectures about how he should or shouldn't behave with his girlfriends. Frankly, it's none of your business, is it?'

'I've only done that a couple of times—' Fee began defensively and then stopped. Claire was right. It *was* none of her business.

'Not so much The Lone Ranger, more The Lone Bloody Nuisance,' Fee told herself wryly.

'Fee, are you still there?' Claire's voice sounded friendlier. 'Look, I'm sorry to sound so crabby . . . it's just been one of those days. Clem and I have had a bit of a barney, nothing serious . . . and work's a bugger . . . and, well, don't take any notice of me—'

Fee registered the words: *Clem and I have had a bit of a barney—*

'Fee?' Claire asked again.

'Don't worry, Claire. You're right to say what you have . . . but what should I do about this memo? Do I have it out in the open? Shall I ask Diana Woods what she's playing at?'

'If it was me,' Claire replied, 'I wouldn't say anything until I'd proven my worth again to the company. Besides, aren't they going to wonder why you were snooping around Gerry Radcliffe's office, in the first place?'

'I wasn't snooping,' Fee answered. 'I nicked some of his wine and wrote an IOU note.'

'Well, destroy the note and replace the wine.'

'I can't, not at this time of night,' Fee protested.

'Well, just forget about the wine. Get rid of the note. Act as if you know nothing about the report. Isn't there a project you can turn into something really good – and quickly?'

'No, well, yes – and no,' Fee replied. 'Gerry's after a new account – Have a Heart!, lonely-hearts, computer dating, introduction agency, all that stuff. Diana Woods is working on winning the HAH! account – because I turned it down.'

'You did *what*? Fee, you have got to change your mind,' Claire instructed.

'But that's exactly what Gerry wants. I bet you, he set this whole bloody thing up—'

'Well, give him what he wants – make it a straight, clean fight with Diana Woods. Show how much better you do the job. And when you're on top, that's the time to bring up the memo and ask exactly what's been going on—'

'But I'm sick of broken hearts—' Fee began.

'Do it,' Claire demanded.

'Over my dead body,' Fee answered.

'Well, when it starts getting rough, don't pretend you didn't have a choice,' Claire warned.

An hour later, Fee Travers stood in her front garden, hunting in her handbag for her set of keys. She'd decided to work at home, as the office, to her, now seemed contaminated. At least, the flat was entirely her own domain, run according to her own rules – rules she understood and which offered no surprises.

She noticed that the lights were on in her sitting room. She'd left in such a rush she'd probably forgotten to switch them off this morning.

But where were her keys? One for the front door downstairs, one for her own door to the flat. Fee pushed the front door experimentally. Occasionally, someone left it on the latch. The door opened.

As she climbed the stairs, she detected a distant hum. The same hum as she'd heard earlier that evening at F.P. & D. The hum of a vacuum cleaner.

Outside Fee's front door, the hum was much louder. Somebody was in her flat – and she didn't have to think very hard to guess who.

'Here, don't put the cup down there, sweetie, I've just polished it.' Rita Mason pushed a magazine under Fee's coffee cup on the small table by the sofa.

She had spring-cleaned and 'slightly rearranged' the furniture. She had also washed up, cleaned out the fridge and made Fee's bed. Fee was speechless. She was so angry, she had made them both coffee in silence, while she endeavoured to compose the words in her head that would firmly and finally tell Rita Mason that she could not assume squatting rights in her life.

Fee glanced at Rita. She wore leopardskin capri pants and a bright yellow sweater, cut off at the waist. Her hair was tied back in a striped chiffon scarf. Her lips, painted pink, were in a pout; a child in a sulk.

'All I tried to do was help,' Rita squeaked in a little-girl voice.

She was acting as if she couldn't even begin to understand the reason for Fee's hostility. What's more, she was doing so with such conviction that anyone other than Fee might have offered Rita understanding and comfort. Fee was unmoved.

'Sit down.' She patted the sofa next to her. 'You don't look at all comfortable, standing like that—'

'Rita, look, I'd rather—' Fee began.

'See,' Rita indicated with a nod of her head, 'your keys are on the mantelpiece. When I saw them lying on the floor in the hall, I thought, "Oops, Rita. Fiona's going to be in a bit of a jam." So I thought I'd better wait in here until you got back and let you in.'

Rita Mason cheered up, clearly bored with being contrite. She took her time to fix a cigarette into a long, ebony, cigarette lighter and lit up. She inhaled, exhaled and continued to talk as smoke snaked around her words.

'Well, once I was sat here waiting, I thought, "Don't waste time, girl. Lend a hand." Of course, if I'd realized it would upset you—' Rita Mason's tone had become distinctly huffy. 'Besides, I was only doing your sister a favour being here in the first place.'

'Why, what do you mean?' Fee returned her cup to its saucer.

'See,' Rita smiled smugly, 'I knew that would make you sit up. Your sister gave me her address book for safe keeping when we went to the hospital. She was worried – very worried – and made me promise that I'd give it to you *personally*. On the night, it was all so crazy, I completely forgot. And I couldn't post it to you, could I? Not once I'd made a promise. I've left lots of messages on your machine,' she added reproachfully. Fee refused to feel guilty.

'As it turns out, lucky I did come by, wasn't it? If I hadn't, who knows who might have come in and ransacked your private things . . . The man opposite, he said you were lucky too.'

'Do you mean Will?'

'No, he's upstairs, isn't he?' Rita reproved her. 'I mean the man in the flat opposite.'

'There is no man opposite,' Fee replied flatly, annoyed that she had engaged in conversation. 'The flat's been empty for weeks.'

'Not any more it isn't,' Rita Mason responded robustly. 'He's quite a looker, if you ask me. Thirty-ish plus, definitely in the market for talent, if the way he sized me up is any guide,' she giggled. 'I explained to him that you were a friend of mine—'

Rita removed her half-smoked cigarette from the holder and stubbed it out in the ashtray.

'Don't mind, do you?' she asked Fee. 'Saw you didn't have any ashtrays around so I dug this out from the back of that cupboard in the kitchen.'

'Yes, I do bloody mind,' Fee heard herself shout. 'I do mind very much. And I mind that you go round telling everyone we're friends. We are not friends. I hardly know you. I don't like you being in my flat. I don't like you doing my cleaning. I don't want to be grateful to you for anything. Do you understand?'

Rita Mason's eyes filled with tears. She reached into a shiny pink bag decorated with seashells, fixed in place with lime-green raffia, and produced a ridiculously lacy handkerchief. It was identical to those Fee had bought again and again for her mother, in Woolworth's, when she was a child.

'I thought you liked me,' Rita sniffed.

Fee sighed deeply. This woman was human quicksand; the more effort you made, the more impossible it became to extricate yourself.

'Look, Rita, I don't know whether I like you or not. I haven't actually thought about you much. I've got a hundred and one other things on my plate . . . I . . . oh—' Fee exploded in frustration.

'I thought you looked like the kind of person who could do with a bit of company. I was obviously wrong. Or, at least,' Rita added pointedly, 'You prefer to think I'm wrong. Anyway, here's your sister's address book.'

She took it out of her bag and placed it on the coffee table. Then she jerkily smoothed her hair back with both hands.

'Don't worry about me, I'll be absolutely fine. You won't hear from me again. I'm sorry if I did the wrong thing, by coming into your flat. I meant well, I really did.' She gave Fee a watery smile. Then she added forlornly, 'Oh dear.'

'About tomorrow night—' Fee heard herself say.

'About tomorrow night,' Fee began again. 'Well . . . perhaps I could come out – but only for an hour or so—'

Fee stopped because Rita Mason had gleefully leapt to her feet, gathering her bag and coat.

'You won't regret it, honestly, Fee,' she said. 'You'll enjoy yourself, I promise. Once you've joined our little Thursday night gang, there'll be no turning back. You'll be one of the girls. Be round about seven-ish. Bye for now—'

'No, look I—' Fee found herself speaking the words to a closed door.

Rita Mason had gone.

Three hours later, Fee relaxed on the sofa, a cup of hot chocolate in her hands. The report was finished and the results, Fee told herself defiantly, were good – even by Diana Woods's distorted standards. Good, but not sufficient in itself to fend off a serious attack.

Fee stretched and yawned. Optimism was beginning to creep up on her again. The highs since she'd permanently signed up to spinsterhood had been fewer – well, almost nonexistent – but so too had been the lows.

'What I need . . . just to test my mettle, of course . . . is a little bit of temptation,' Fee told herself.

'Perhaps I *should* do Imogen's film,' she mused. 'Perhaps Will's right. I need a point from which there's no going back.'

She mimicked Imogen Banks's voices, 'Now tell me, Ms Travers, what makes the modern spinster fundamentally different from her traditional sister?'

'Well, Ms Banks,' Fee gave a mock-reply, 'the modern spinster is a woman who said no, when she could just as easily have said yes—'

'I should be so lucky, she told herself drily in her natural voice.

It was only later when Fee was searching for a T-shirt in a drawer in her bedroom that she realized her photograph album was missing. She looked again. She scouted the sitting room too. It was gone.

Rita Mason.

But why? What could she want with a pile of old photographs of people she's never known? And surely she must have realized that they would soon be missed?

'Enough is enough,' Fee decided. 'When I next see her, I'll tell her that's it. Plain, straightforward, brutal and to the point. Bye, bye, Rita.'

It was then Fee remembered. The last time she had looked at the album she had shoved it behind some cushions on the sofa.

It was still there. Reassured, it never occurred to her to check on the album's contents.

'She's just a harmless slightly dotty woman who wants to be your pal.' Will Evans sat bleary-eyed at his kitchen table.

Fee had tried and failed to sleep. At six thirty, she had gone upstairs to wake Will. He'd informed her crossly that he'd only just retired to bed.

'Why not stay out the whole night?' Fee asked, as she invited herself in to his flat.

'Mind your own business,' he replied lightly.

He had made coffee and listened to Fee's description of Rita's actions since their first meeting. As she spoke, Fee realized that it was she, not Rita, who appeared to be the prime candidate for neurosis.

Will extended his hand and began to count on his fingers. 'One, the woman gave you a kettle she didn't want. Two, she kept a promise to Veronica by returning her address book in person. Three, she's kindly invited you out for a drink because she thinks you might be a little lonely. Four, she does you a favour by taking care of your door keys. And, five, you mistakenly believe that she may have stolen an old pile of photographs for God knows what reason. Fee, please.' He smiled wearily. 'Let's both get some sleep. And if it makes you feel any better, have the locks changed.'

'It's not what she *does*,' Fee persisted. 'It's a feeling she gives off . . . it's as if she's got an appetite she can't satisfy. As if she's trying to take me over. Live my life for me . . . I don't know—'

'You say she's got a boyfriend who's abroad?' Will asked. Fee nodded her head in agreement.

'She's got friends that you're about to meet?' he asked again. She nodded.

'She's got a good job at the hospital and her own place?' Will persisted.

'Two places, one in the country,' Fee corrected glumly.

'So what Rita Mason's crime comes down to is that she imagines she is twenty-five and dresses like a 1950s Hollywood starlet. Hardly spine-chilling stuff, is it?'

'You don't know her,' Fee answered, disgruntled.

Will got up and patted her on the head. 'The truth is, Fee, neither do you. You've let your imagination take over. Far be it for me to warn you – but there is a danger in believing that every older single woman is a psychopath in the making . . .'

He was enjoying himself immensely.

'Rita Mason is just trying to be friendly. And – let's face it – in a few years' time when you're the only single woman on the block, and everyone else is *à deux* and with kids, you may be glad of the company—' he teased.

'Oh, bullshit,' Fee replied, cross with herself that Will's words had struck a nerve.

*

Les Haslem made himself a cup of tea and walked into the garden. The house was dead without Veronica. Empty, pointless, dead.

Over recent weeks, Les had begun to develop his own theory about his wife's condition. It came from knowing her and loving her for so many years. Veronica *would* get better but only when she had something or someone to get better *for*.

Once upon a time, she would have got better for him. But not now. He wasn't enough. He felt sad about that. But he was a practical man. If Les couldn't work out what would put Veronica right, nobody could.

All he had to do was *think*. If he thought hard enough, Les was sure it would come to him.

An hour later, Fee found him in the garden, sitting in the dark.

'Are you all right?' she asked. 'Where's Veronica?'

Les stood up, then pulled over a chair for Fee to sit on. 'She's not here,' he said unnecessarily.

'I know,' she answered gently. 'That's why I'm asking. I called in to see how she was and found the whole place in darkness. I only came round the back because your next-door neighbour told me you were here.'

Fee couldn't see her brother-in-law's face very clearly, but his voice registered his distress. 'Veronica's in hospital. I mean a . . . special hospital,' he reported. 'The doctor said it was best. She's under sedation. She's got so wound up thinking about what's going to happen next, she's exhausted. She locked the gasman down in the basement, did you know? Gave the poor bastard a bloody awful scare—'

'In hospital? Where? Can I visit her?' Fee asked, then before Les could give an answer, she added, 'What do you think about us going away on holiday? Veronica and me? Just for a week or so? I know you're busy and can't get away and all that . . . So she and I could go?'

It occurred to Fee that she was asking Les if she could take his wife away, as if Veronica *belonged* to him. Something about

Les made her slip into thinking that way. 'Perhaps I should ask Veronica?'

'No,' Les answered sharply. 'Don't ask her anything. It just adds to it all, you know. Besides, she's never been away on her own, not once in all the time we've been married.'

'I don't mean on her own, I meant with me,' Fee corrected patiently. But she knew that's how Les saw it.

'To tell the truth, Fee, I've been thinking of taking her away myself. She'd mentioned Italy but I was talking to a fellow the other day who'd just had a lovely little holiday in a nice hotel in Jersey. I think Veronica would like Jersey, don't you? Plenty of golf and all that . . .?'

'But Veronica doesn't play golf,' Fee replied.

'No,' Les answered. 'But I do.'

Later that evening, as she drove into her street, Fee Travers was annoyed to see that someone had stolen her parking space. Well, it wasn't hers exactly, it was just a space on the street – but she regarded it as hers.

As she walked towards the flat, a man, perhaps in his early forties, emerged from the offending car. He wore well-cut stone-coloured slacks and a blue shirt. He was lightly tanned and had features that Fee, once upon a time, would have found a distraction. Features she still found a distraction.

'You're in my space,' she blurted out ungraciously, to cover her embarrassment at being caught looking.

'I am so sorry,' he apologized with charm. 'I hadn't realized. Here, let me move, I'll—'

'No, no,' Fee interrupted. 'You stay where you are. You've got every right. I'm just a creature of habit.'

Well, she'd certainly managed to make herself sound fascinating, Fee told herself drily, a creature of habit . . .

She turned into her garden. 'Do you live here too?' the man

asked. He was by her side now, much taller, slim, athletic. He had his shirt-sleeves rolled up, a detail of dress that Fee had always found seductive. The man fancied himself, Fee decided, but then he had cause too.

He offered his hand. She noted automatically that he wasn't wearing a ring. 'Hello, my name's Edward Spannier, Ted to my friends. I moved in a couple of days ago. It's only temporary. I'm having a house done up around the corner and I couldn't stand the mess. So I'm here for a few months. And you . . .?'

'Fiona . . . Fee . . . Travers. I'm in Flat 3—' She experienced an odd sensation that at first she couldn't identify – then she recognized exactly what it was.

She was flirting. Not, of course, with any serious intent, all that was in the past. This was just practice.

'Flat 3 is opposite mine,' Edward Spannier was saying, holding very steady eye contact. 'Why don't you come in for a drink some time? I'm still getting sorted, so I hope you don't mind a bit of a mess . . .?'

Fee smiled in reply. Experience told her that whatever else Edward Spannier might be, he was most definitely a bastard. Already, she could feel the pull.

Chapter Fifteen

'HAVE YOU ever thought of using a bit of colour?'
It was seven on Thursday night and Rita Mason had arrived half an hour early.

She was wearing white boots that ended at the knee; a black and white Op-Art shift and white plastic hoop ear-rings. If the wardrobe came from the 1960s, the eye make-up remained a tribute to Ancient Egypt.

Fee was dressed simply in black slacks and a cream twinset and Rita Mason was making it clear she did not approve.

'Look,' she said, 'why don't we brighten you up a bit?'

She walked around the back of the sofa and suddenly pulled Fee's hair up into a pony tail. She pulled so hard it hurt.

'Ow!' Fee struggled slightly.

Rita ignored her reaction.

She took some hairclips out of her own hair – concreted into place with quantities of lacquer – and pinned Fee's hair into a pleat. Then she plunged into her bag again and produced a bright-red chiffon scarf which she tied around Fee's neck.

Fee attempted to remove the scarf. 'I don't think it's quite—' she began. Then discovered that Rita Mason's fingers were not to be prised away so easily.

'Come with me, young lady,' Rita directed and Fee found herself frogmarched into the bedroom. *Her* bedroom.

'Look,' Rita commanded, pointing at Fee's full-length mirror.

'See what a bit of colour can do? Wait here, I'll get my lipstick then you can try it on—'

She walked out of the room and, for a couple of seconds, Fee actually did as she was told. Then she came to.

What a nerve.

Fee took off the scarf, folding it as she followed Rita Mason back into the sitting room. She returned it along with the hairgrips.

'We've got to leave,' Fee said firmly, shaking her hair free again. She was cross with herself that she had heeded Will's advice. He had suggested that she stick by her original arrangements with Rita and then avoid making any future dates.

'Let her down easily,' he had suggested.

'So, where are we off to?' she asked impatiently, hunting for her car keys.

'You'll never guess,' Rita giggled, reapplying pale-apricot lipstick.

Fee's heart sank.

'Welcome, welcome, welcome, ladies,' said the man in the centre of a ring of chairs. He was in his late fifties. He had white, wavy hair, worn slightly long. He was of average height and dressed in a white suit with a pink shirt and white snakeskin loafers. A pink and blue cravat completed the ensemble. His fingers were decorated with two heavy American college rings. He was elaborately dressed but surprisingly uncamp in his mannerisms.

He also smelt of sandalwood, a lot of sandalwood.

'He's Gwynfor, Gwynfor Pryce,' Rita hissed in Fee's ear. 'He used to be a piano tuner until he discovered his gift. Go on, sit down, he'll be starting soon.'

Earlier, she had directed Fee to a part of South London that was unfamiliar to her. They had stopped in an ordinary suburban street except that, two-thirds of the way down, an ugly modern concrete building had filled the gap where several houses had once been.

'The Church of the Eternal Spirit' read a large sign outside.

Inside, Rita led Fee to a hall furnished in pine with deep purple curtains at several windows. The hall had none of the regalia of most churches, no altar, pulpit, stained glass or pews. Instead, on two walls there were vast murals depicting an army of what Fee realized were faintly recognizable, deceased celebrities, dressed in identical choirboy smocks, marching determinedly across several clouds.

'Aaah, Rita,' Gwynfor smiled, extending both arms, in the same theatrical fashion as the stars on the wall to his left. 'You're looking lovelier than ever. And this would be . . .?'

He took one of Fee's hands in his. It was large and warm and moist and strangely comforting.

'Her name is Fiona . . . Fee,' Rita said.

Gwynfor shut his eyes and inhaled deeply. 'Ferrous Fiona—' his voice rumbled in a rich, Welsh accent, as he closed his eyes.

'A woman made of iron—'

Fee refused to allow herself to feel any better.

Over the following ten minutes, a dozen or so women arrived and took seats in a semi-circle around Gwynfor. He greeted each in a highly personalized way. Fee was surprised that the women were so varied in age and appearance. Some were very expensively dressed; others were in business suits; a few were casually clothed by C&A and M&S and BHS. Rita introduced Hayley and Isobel, her mother, both very large women. Hayley wore a voluminous black smock but it was the quantities of gold that caught the eye, enough to stock a modest pawnbroker.

Her mother was even more extravagantly festooned. Gold hung around her neck and from several holes in her ears as well as on each finger.

'All right, Reet?' said Hayley by way of a greeting to Rita Mason. Hayley's top lip was decorated with beads of perspiration. She spoke as if she had difficulty drawing breath. Rita nodded in acknowledgement.

'Welcome, welcome, ladies,' Gwynfor intoned again. He stood in the middle of the circle, his hands outstretched, and spun around gently a couple of times.

'Mary, Alexia, Isobel, Catherine, Hayley, Rita, Ivy, Priscilla, Jay,' he continued until he had identified every woman present, 'And our newcomer—'

Fee realized that Gwynfor had already forgotten her name. 'Iron . . . iron. . . Irene—' he beamed at Fee.

Gwynfor took a seat next to the woman he'd called Beryl and, without instruction, the women linked hands.

'You on your own too, love?' Isobel whispered to Fee. 'I don't know where Rita finds you all. Lost a loved one? Well, feel at home here. We're all on our tods. Matter of fact, Ivy and Doris never had anyone in the first place. Enjoy yourself.'

Fee watched while Gwynfor began to breathe more deeply and rhythmically. She didn't want to be in the room; she didn't want to be part of a half-baked seance. How on earth had she allowed Rita to inveigle her into spending an evening here? Only one activity was likely to be more depressing than searching for a soul mate in the here and now and that was attempting to dredge one up from the dead.

'Don't you worry, pet.' Isobel had misunderstood the frown on Fee's face. 'No matter how low when you arrive, Gwynfor sends you away a Somebody.'

It took several minutes for the man's talent to begin to manifest itself.

'Is James there?' asked Ivy, a tremulous woman in a baby-blue top and floral skirt.

'Ivy's got a bit of a thing going with James the First,' Isobel whispered to Fee. 'He treats her ever so well. Says really lovely things sometimes. Know anything about him, do you. . .?'

Fee raised an eyebrow to indicate that a conversation might upset Gwynfor Pryce.

'Oh, he's well gone now,' Isobel replied. 'Once he's under, he can't hear a thing, he's like a —'

'Ivy, Ivy, Ivy.' Gwynfor Pryce was speaking in a strange falsetto and dribbling slightly. 'Are you there, my small child?'

Fee watched as Ivy blushed, the flush spreading down her neck and across her chest.

'Oh, James,' she sighed.

Twenty-five minutes later, Gwynfor Pryce was still going strong, his repertoire of male accents by no means exhausted. James the First had held a lengthy conversation with Ivy, in which he expressed more concern than passion. Just as well, Fee thought drily, considering his homosexual inclinations.

Isobel had had a bit of a barney, as she put it, with Harry, her common-law husband, about his final words. Harry, it transpired, had died of a heart attack two years earlier, watering the garden on a Saturday evening.

Isobel had been bitterly resentful that as the ambulance men had lifted Harry on to his stretcher, he'd whispered, 'Don't forget the busy Lizzies.'

Harry via Gwynfor spent several minutes persuading her that what he'd actually said was, 'Don't forget – stay busy, Izzie.' Isobel was unconvinced.

'He was a lying toad when he was alive, and he hasn't changed since,' she whispered to Fee cheerfully.

Late in the seance, Rita grew impatient.

'What about Fee, Gwynfor? Is there anyone there for Fee?'

Fee shook her head, embarrassed, like a child attempting to back out of a party game.

'Yes, yes, yes, I'm hearing something,' Gwynfor Pryce began in his own voice, then what emerged from his mouth was a discomfortingly female sound.

'Irene,' the sound said. 'It's Elizabeth. I have much to tell you. I'm hearing a . . .'

At which point, Hayley – satiated earlier by a brief communication with Buddy Holly – suddenly pitched forward on her hands and knees, causing the room to reverberate.

She lay on the floor, a duvet of flesh, twisting and contorted, fighting for breath.

'It's God's orgasm,' Beryl pronounced incongruously while the others rushed to help. Isobel reached her daughter first. She plucked an inhaler out of Hayley's voluminous bag.

'Asthma,' she explained. 'Gets it chronic. Especially if she's excited.'

Gwynfor Pryce looked pleased with himself. 'Just a channel, that's all I am,' he announced to nobody in particular.

'Just a channel. That will be five pounds as usual, ladies, please.'

'I knew you'd love it,' Rita Mason announced to Fee half an hour later. 'We'll make a regular thing of it, shall we? And you seemed to get on ever so well with the others—'

They were sitting in a pub in which most were significantly under thirty. Rita had giggled and flirted her way to the bar, squeezing past male bodies, unashamedly using her mammary glands as a battering ram.

A few men had been too stupefied to move; others had backed away in embarrassment. Rita had returned to the table with a gin and tonic for Fee and a Bacardi and Coke for herself, apparently convinced that all eyes were upon her for the most flattering of reasons.

'I've always found men attracted to me,' she confided in Fee. 'And it's not because I'm easy. God, no.'

Fee sat silent. She was half impressed, half appalled by Rita Mason's capacity for viewing life as she wished to see it.

'Do you know what I like about you, Fee?' Rita asked rhetorically. 'You're so similar to me. We could be sisters—'

'No,' Fee began, then realized there was little point.

She hadn't wanted to come to the pub but somehow she was here. She hadn't expected to see Rita Mason ever again, but she had. She certainly didn't wish to accept her gifts, but the kettle and the blouse were still in the flat.

What was even more bizarre was that while Rita seemed determined to hijack more and more of Fee's time, she had yet to show any interest in Fee as a person. No questions about her life, her relationships, her work.

'Who do you think Elizabeth was?' Rita asked chattily. 'Do you know any dead Elizabeths?'

Fee shook her head. 'Only Elizabeth the First, perhaps she fancied an old maids' reunion?' Fee suggested facetiously. Then she took a sip of her drink, to brace herself.

'Rita,' she began, 'I'm going away for a couple of weeks. A business trip. And then when I get back, I've got this contract which is really pressing. So I won't be around for a while. Perhaps later – after the summer, say – we could get back in touch?'

'No problem,' Rita Mason replied brightly. 'I quite understand.' Fee relaxed, surprised that her excuse had been accepted so easily. 'Of course, I understand. We've all got things to do, places to be, people to see—'

The two women chatted for another half an hour or so, then Fee drove Rita to a tube station on the Northern line.

'I'll give you a lift home, if you like. It's no bother,' Fee offered, impending freedom making her generous.

Rita cheerfully refused, got out, closed the car door, then stuck her head back in the passenger window.

'I've just had a great idea,' she said. 'You know my fiancé, Roger? Well, he's coming home on leave in a couple of weeks, just for a short break. Perhaps we could all get together? I'll drop by and let you know when he's arriving. OK?'

Fee's smile froze.

Chapter Sixteen

A 'FOR SALE' sign decorated the front of Nuptia Europa.
'It's an omen. A bad omen,' Claire wailed.

Worse news awaited them inside.

Michele Canning, the assistant who had done so much to cheer them on their first visit, announced that she was in love. Madly in love. And she found it deeply depressing.

'I can't enjoy the good bit,' she moaned, laying groundsheets on the carpeted floor in preparation for Claire's first parade in the dress she had selected. 'I can't enjoy the good bits because I know what's to follow. Pain. Grief. Heartache.'

'Oh come on, it's not that bad,' Fee offered.

'I thought you said it was,' Claire chipped in.

Mrs Canning was pulling a dress deftly out of its plastic shroud. 'Do you know what I think?' She didn't pause for an answer. 'I think falling in love with the right person is rare. It's a talent, like playing the cello or singing top-class opera. We've all been sold this myth that it can happen to anyone – but it can't . . . Now, where were we?' she added absent-mindedly, ushering Claire into a cubicle to be dressed.

Fee declined an invitation to join them and sat outside. Her turn to try on her maid of honour's dress would come later.

She idly picked up a magazine, only to find herself distracted by Claire's voice. She was whispering but she was still clearly audible. And what she was saying was all news to Fee.

Claire wanted a large house; Clem Thomas preferred somewhere much smaller and perhaps a place outside London too. Claire, brought up in the country, had no intention of returning to it, certainly not for pleasure.

'That's understandable,' Mrs Canning said.

And then there was money. Claire explained that she had more to spend than Clem.

'He's a great cook, Michele, that's why he doesn't see the point of restaurants—'

'That's understandable,' Mrs Canning said.

'But I try and explain that I've worked hard for twenty years and I like to enjoy my money. I don't want to eat in all the time and drink paint-stripper for wine, just to suit him—'

'That's understandable,' Mrs Canning said.

Suddenly, the curtains to the cubicle swept back and Fee jumped, guiltily.

Claire's face betrayed no sign of *Angst*. 'How do I look?' she asked Fee.

'You look absolutely beautiful,' Fee replied truthfully.

Later, over a glass of wine, Fee asked Claire casually, 'So how's it all going? I mean, you and Clem?'

'Really well,' Claire answered too quickly. 'No problems at all. Couldn't be happier.'

On Monday afternoon, a group of half-a-dozen or so of F .P. & D.'s staff, including Diana Woods, Will Evans and Fee were gathered in the company's viewing room, watching a large screen.

A series of brief scenes portrayed the frenetic work lives of two ridiculously young people. The scene cut to the woman, dressed in a long, floating, chiffon dress, running along a beach. She was being chased by the man, now in jeans. He caught her and pulled her to the ground. They kissed as the music swelled.

Over the images, a creamy voice said, 'Want to make a dream come true – but too harried, busy, overstretched? A desire for love but no time to let it happen? HAH! makes the running easy. It's what success is all about.'

In the dark, a ripple of applause is heard. 'Lights,' Gerry Radcliffe ordered.

'OK, let's hear it,' he instructed. 'This is Diana's first crack at the HAH! account. A good, strong commercial with a powerful message for the thirty-plus single. I'll save my comments for last – Fee?'

Behind Gerry's back, Will semaphored to Fee by putting a finger to his lips and shaking his head firmly. No need to be frank and certainly not fearless. Gerry had sent out enough clues: he was pleased with the product – why upset the boss?

Fee was about to heed Will's advice when the images of Ivy and Beryl and Doris and Joan and the other women at Gwynfor Pryce's meeting shimmered into view. Weren't they the stuff of future springsters too? Weren't they twenty- and thirty- and forty-plus and unattached? How could they identify with a commercial like this? Why should they be rendered invisible?

Briefly, Fee considered the fact that Diana Woods already had enough enemies in the company. Was it fair to add her own name to the list? Then she remembered the secret report and the spitefulness of its tone.

'I think the ad. is daft. Or, to be more precise, I believe it's inappropriate,' Fee spoke succinctly.

Carina Holt, Will's number two, drew her breath in sharply. Gerry picked up a pencil and studied its lead intently, always a bad sign. Will's signals became more frantic.

Fee continued. 'I think it's trite, condescending and a cliché. The market this commercial is trying to reach is twice as old as this couple. The new customers we want probably haven't the energy or the inclination to run for a bus never mind along a beach for a couple of miles.

'On top of that, why focus on a pair who appear passionately in love and only inches away from the altar? They don't look as if they need any help at all from an organization like HAH!'

Diana Woods broke in. 'We don't deal in reality here, in case you hadn't noticed,' she said frostily. 'We deal in aspirations, escapism . . . I'm sure—'

Gerry Radcliffe had stopped studying the pencil and was now inspecting Diana Woods.

She continued, 'My research indicates that women past forty don't have an image of themselves as independent singles, separate autonomies. They see themselves as grannies, widows, ex-partners, old maids . . . and, frankly, if we tap into that, it's not exactly a sexy selling pitch, is it? Women watching this, no matter what their age, will put themselves in the young woman's shoes—'

'Bullshit,' was Fee's response. 'They want to see themselves as the rounded people a lot of them are . . . They may not have a man but they've got plenty of other things in their lives . . . friendship, travel, food, cinema, music . . . Why not pitch at the woman and man – in their thirties or forties – who have full lives besides work, but who also would like some romance?'

Diana Woods snapped back, 'The market research shows that—'

'Then the market research is asking the wrong questions,' Fee interrupted.

At F.P. & D. such a comment was akin to suggesting at the Vatican that the only element requiring correction in the Old Testament was the plot.

Gerry Radcliffe resumed the inspection of his pencil except that, now, one eyebrow was raised.

'So, Fee,' he said slowly, 'you're arguing against Diana's meticulous use of our resource centre, computer searches, focus groups and her ten years of experience in the business?'

Diana Woods smiled smugly. Fee answered, 'She's forgotten two things.'

'And what's that?' Gerry asked.

'Common sense and intuition. If she'd used both, she would have come up with something better than a revamped ad. for Cinzano.'

'Prove it,' he demanded.

'Right,' said Fee defiantly. 'I will.'

Even as she spoke, she saw the satisfaction on Gerry's face.

He had set his trap well.

'Fabulously Fleshy!' Imogen Banks shouted triumphantly at her naked image in her full-length mirror. Her body was dimpled and copious, like a large bowl of whipped cream.

She wrapped herself in a towel. She was pleased with her lot. Simon was proving to be unexpectedly good company; funny, perceptive and, now the novelty had worn off, no longer overwhelmingly attentive. He was spending much of his time endeavouring to discover 'a project', any project that might carry him from his forties to retirement without losing face.

A project sounded so much more glamorous than a job and, potentially, somehow more cash-generating than a career.

Imogen had also secured a couple of new commissions. She had come up with a game show for the afternoon slot. *Mates & Mistresses* which pitted ex-wives against ex- (or present) mistresses on their knowledge of the male they had shared.

The second commission depended upon Fee Travers's performance in *The Perfumed Pound*. If all went well, then Imogen intended to make a documentary that would involve Fee travelling through the US talking to her American equivalents.

Imogen called in to her office to say that she was on her way. Kelly Owen, her secretary, said, 'A man called Bill Summers is here. Says he's talked to you a lot on the phone. Says you asked him to drop by . . . He's got his portfolio of photographs with him and seems desperately keen. I hope you want him for his body,' Kelly Owen added drily, 'because his pictures aren't up to much.'

Chapter Seventeen

A T SEVEN THIRTY in the evening, Shona Spannier, thirty-six, opened a bottle of red wine, poured a glass for herself and hid the bottle in the bread bin. She looked at her watch. Then Shona checked on the lamb in the oven. Naturally, she'd calculated that her husband would be a couple of hours late when she'd first put the meat in for roasting; so the lamb was still bright pink.

Shona drank from the glass, topped it up again and walked into her bedroom. On the large dressing-table were two silver-framed photographs of her sons, Theo, eight, and Oliver, almost ten. They had their mother's dark hair, angular jaw, tiny chin and almond-shaped eyes. Others said that they were good-looking boys.

Shona's eyes misted as she thought of Theo crying himself to sleep in the first few weeks as a boarder. The boys didn't object to school now but no one in her family or Teddy's had been sent away before and she hated the pointlessness of it all. Still, Teddy had insisted.

Suddenly Shona tensed. Was that a key in the door? She searched for somewhere to hide her glass. It wasn't that she drank too much but that her life was constrained by rituals. Teddy believed that the wine should be opened only after his arrival. It was one of the small courtesies. And, besides, his mother had always obliged his father in that way.

After a few minutes, Shona relaxed and wandered back into the kitchen. The Spanniers had been married for twelve years. When they first met, Shona had been a personal assistant; Teddy had his own small software business.

Teddy had since prospered. They were now about to move into a seven-bedroom house, although Shona would have been happy to stay in this smaller and cosier flat on which they had a temporary let.

Her husband had also become a business guru; he'd written a couple of books; occasionally he delivered a *Thought for the Day* on Radio 4. Shona was immensely proud of Teddy, which made it even more of a tragedy that he found her such an irritant.

Shona had tried to curb those aspects of herself which she knew Teddy found particularly distasteful. For example, she had toned down what others had described as her strong sense of humour ('Trying to hog the limelight' was Teddy's charge). And she had disguised much of her passion for her sons ('Over-possessive' Teddy had pronounced).

Shona regarded these 'compromises' as worthwhile since she found life so empty when Teddy was absent. His energy seemed to give her energy. Teddy said there wasn't much point in her finding a job because he needed her to be available. And, anyway, with her lack of skills, he'd pointed out on several occasions, she'd only earn peanuts.

She wasn't a joiner of clubs or a woman who liked to do lunch so, since the boys had gone away to school, she spent much of her time being bored. And having a drink. Sometimes she'd visit the house they were having overhauled. But if she made any suggestions to the builders or decorators, Teddy would simply overrule her.

Shona was about to pour herself a second glass when the doorbell rang. Automatically, she hid the wine glass in the canister that held the tea bags.

An hour before, Fee had left work early loaded down with homework on HAH! This included files, videos and market-research reports which she had had great difficulty in persuading Diana Woods and her team to relinquish. Gerry had given Fee a fortnight to come up with a fresh strategy.

Fee glimpsed the slip of white paper on her doormat as she opened the door. Rita bloody Mason. She trod on the note purposefully and walked into the sitting room, dumping everything on the sofa. As she moved towards the kitchen, a strange smell filled her nostrils.

Fee cautiously moved towards the bathroom. She opened the door as if she half expected Rita Mason to leap out at her, bread knife in hand. Instead, a stream of sewage seeped out lazily over the hall carpet.

'Oooh, nasty,' said the voice on the end of the phone. 'What time is it? Blimey! Gone eight.' A detailed explanation followed of how Jimmy was in East Four and Clive was in North London and Winston was flat out on a boiler . . . and—'

'Look,' Fee interrupted, 'all I want to know is can one of your plumbers fix this leak in my loo tonight or not?'

The man on the end of the phone decided not – not unless she was prepared to pay triple time.

'OK, OK, OK.' Fee conceded defeat. 'How early can you get here in the morning?'

The appointment confirmed for 8.30 a.m., the man's voice asked for Fee's address and her name. 'Is that Miss, Ms or Mrs Travers?' he queried.

'Mrs,' Fee answered immediately. 'Mrs Travers.'

Fee's annoyance at herself for lying was replaced with a more practical concern. She was desperate to go to the loo.

Fee knew that the public lavatories in the park across the way would now be locked. Will was out and the spare set of keys she held to his flat was no longer in the jam jar in the kitchen. He frequently helped himself if he'd left his own keys at work.

It looked as if she had no alternative. Mr Edward Spannier, her new neighbour across the corridor, was about to have a surprise visit.

'At least it's more original than asking for a cup of sugar,' Fee told herself. In her hall mirror, she hastily reapplied her lipstick and checked her appearance.

Old habits die hard.

'Oh,' Fee said when Shona Spannier opened her door. 'Oh, I—'

'Can I help?' Shona Spannier asked. Fee tried to keep the surprise out of her voice. 'You are . . . you must be . . .?'

Fee rapidly took in Shona Spannier's appearance. She was fine-boned, slim, understated. Shona Spannier opened the door wide as the realization dawned on her that, since this woman had neither coat nor bag, she must be a neighbour; a near neighbour.

'Come in,' Shona said. 'I'm Shona Spannier. Edward . . . Teddy . . . isn't home from work yet . . . Come in—'

She was already halfway up the corridor before she realized that Fee was still standing – or rather hopping – at the door.

'I'm Fee Travers. I live here,' Fee waved behind her head, 'and my loo has sprung a leak . . . and I'm absolutely desperate—'

Shona began to laugh. 'You poor thing. Help yourself.' She opened the door to her left.

Fee dived for the bathroom. It was ironic, Fee thought, that just when she needed it least, she found herself living opposite individuals who appeared to be candidates for the world's most perfect couple.

A few minutes later, Fee stuck her head into the kitchen. Shona Spannier was sitting at an immaculate breakfast bar. Fee now had time to note she was wearing expensively cut slacks and a cashmere polo neck. Her hair shone like the copper pots arranged decoratively on the walls. The glass front of the oven revealed that supper was under way.

'Won't you have a drink . . . stay for a bit . . .?' Shona Spannier asked.

'I don't want to intrude; it looks as if you're about to eat.'

Shona was already on her feet, gesturing to the other stool. 'You're not intruding, honestly. Teddy won't be home for ages . . . he's awfully busy . . . Please—'

Fee tried not to register surprise when Shona retrieved her glass from the tea canister. Shona smiled with embarrassment.

'Oh I don't usually keep it there . . . It's just, well—' She paused as if considering before she spoke, then ploughed on. 'Teddy doesn't like me to open a bottle before he gets home. It's just one of his rules. Well, rules makes it sound too strict. And he's not at all strict, he's very easy, most of the time—'

Shona shrugged and gave up on the explanation. She poured Fee a glass.

'Or would you prefer white? I've white in the fridge. I'm sorry,' she added as Fee took a sip and shook her head. 'It's probably not great—'

'It tastes wonderful,' Fee interrupted her firmly. 'It's exactly what I need. I've had one of those days—'

Fee inspected the kitchen. 'You've done a terrific job in here. It was so dark and dingy before. When did you move in?'

'Do you like it?' Shona asked eagerly. 'I'm afraid Teddy thinks it's too twee. The decorators came in last month just to freshen it up a bit and we moved in on Tuesday. No one else in the building seemed to be about except the very tall man upstairs. He always seems to be . . . entertaining—'

Shona caught Fee's eye and they both smiled.

'That's Will,' Fee offered. The Spanniers must have moved in on the day she and Imogen played truant from work and visited Marlow. That was why she hadn't registered their arrival.

'Does Teddy work long hours?' Fee asked, more to make conversation than out of genuine interest.

'Oh yes,' Shona Spannier's face brightened up at the mention of her husband. 'Especially now, he's hoping to become an MP – a Labour MP. He's at ward meetings every night. He doesn't tell me all that much. I mean, I don't blame him. I'm afraid I'm not all that interested. The House of Commons seems so . . . well, so self-serving.'

Shona stopped, alarmed that she had voiced a possibly contentious opinion.

'I'm so sorry, you're probably passionate about politics,' she apologized. 'I don't mean everyone is self-serving, just—'

Fee held up her hands. 'Don't worry. I agree with you entirely. I can't imagine a more miserable life than sitting in the House of Commons—'

Shona walked over to the oven. 'Are you hungry?' she asked. 'Why don't you stay and have something to eat? I mean, if you're on your own tonight, it will save you bothering later? Or perhaps you've already eaten? It's no trouble. I've made pea and asparagus soup and there's some lamb . . . It'll probably go to waste anyway . . . so you'd be doing me a favour.'

Fee lied and explained that she'd had a large lunch but then something about the woman made her change her mind. She said a bowl of soup would be ideal.

'This', Fee pronounced, 'is delicious.'

'Oh, I'm sorry, it's nothing really,' Shona answered dismissively. 'Nothing at all.'

An hour sped by, punctuated only by Shona's frequent glances at her watch. 'Sorry,' she apologized. 'It's Teddy. I always get a bit anxious if he's this late—'

Shona told Fee about her sons and how she missed them. She discussed her previous job and how she still kept in touch with her former boss, who even now tried to tempt her back.

Fee said little about herself but did mention that her best friend was marrying in a few months. And that she was ashamed to admit that she hadn't had the kindest of thoughts about the husband-to-be.

'Oh, I understand that completely,' Shona responded warmly and then added, 'Don't you find marriage really hard work some

206

times? It was the one thing I wanted to do well in life and I know I've failed miserably in lots of ways. Teddy is much better at it than me. He says I'm too demanding . . . How long have you been married?' she suddenly asked.

'I'm not,' Fee answered cheerfully. She was totally unprepared for the panic that crossed the woman's face. To make amends, Fee quickly added, 'I'm single, but I'm not looking. For a partner, I mean. No men, no misery.' Shona Spannier did not appear consoled.

Conversation after that withered away. Just as Fee was saying her goodbyes, there was the sound of a key in the door. Shona shot from the breakfast bar. She reapplied her lipstick, grabbing a tube from the small shelf by the window. Then she roughly shoved the two wine glasses into the dishwasher and deposited the bottle, not yet empty, in the bin, concealing it with a layer of kitchen roll.

'I may be wrong,' Fee said, 'but I take it that's Teddy at the door?'

Ten minutes or so later, Fee sat in her sitting room, feet on the coffee table, a mug of tea in hand, exuding gratitude for the most simple of pleasures. She was thankful that she owned her own place and could do with it as she pleased.

She was thankful that she did not have to live with a man like Teddy Spannier who appeared to delight in boxing in his wife at every opportunity.

She was thankful that she could spend an evening uncaged by a lover's mood.

She was thankful, above all, to be alone.

In Fee's hand was the note she had assumed Rita Mason had written. It had been posted under her door by her new neighbour, Edward Spannier.

'I'm having a few friends for an impromptu housewarming supper tomorrow night,' it read. 'Sorry it's such short notice. Please come if you can, Ted.'

No mention of Shona. No mention of 'we' or 'us' or 'My wife

and I'. Teddy had repeated the invitation as Fee was leaving their flat. The panic had returned to Shona's face. Fee had accepted – if only to prove to Shona that she had nothing to fear. And, perhaps, to prove it to herself. Teddy was out of bounds unless, of course, he was adept as a plumber. Then, Fee told herself, trying to ignore the smell of sewage now overpowering the flat, she would personally carry him over her threshold without a qualm.

Fee was outside, putting her rubbish in her dustbin, before going to bed at midnight, when she saw a familiar figure pressing her doorbell.

It was Bill Summers. At *midnight*? At her door?

'I've come,' he said enigmatically. 'How are you doing?' he asked, as he kissed Fee on the cheek.

'In desperate need of help,' Fee smiled.

'That's what I've been told,' Bill Summers replied, placing his arm protectively around Fee. 'That's why I'm here.'

Fee was so grateful that she didn't seriously consider the meaning of Bill Summers's words, until it was much too late.

It only took minutes for Fee to persuade Bill to put his hand down her lavatory pan. He had always been useful like that.

Fee supervised from the bathroom door. Bill had lost weight; he was less shambolic, more compact. He was dressed entirely in black. In their time together, Bill hadn't expressed much interest in clothes; somebody else must be doing his shopping.

He had also grown a beard and his hair was actually cut into some sort of style.

'Erica's doing a good job,' Fee remarked conversationally.

'Who?' Bill replied distractedly.

'Erica . . . your wife . . . mother of your child . . .?' she jogged his memory gently.

'Oh yes, of course. Yes, I'm very lucky. But she's away at the moment.'

Bill flushed the loo. It worked perfectly.

'All done,' he said, pleased with himself. 'All you've got to do is clear up the mess and cancel the plumber.'

'Lucky you dropped by,' Fee said, leading the way back into the sitting room where she had opened a bottle of wine and set out two glasses.

'Lucky?' Bill Summers repeated the word. 'Well, not lucky exactly—'

'Telepathy then?' Fee suggested flippantly.

'So where's Erica? Has she gone on holiday?' she then asked politely. 'I mean, it's late for you to be out, isn't it?'

'Holiday?' Bill answered vaguely. 'Oh, she's not on holiday. She's in Sweden for four months. Did you know she was Swedish? She's taken the children too and I find that hard. Much harder than I realized.' Bill blinked several times.

Fee realized that there were tears in his eyes. In all the years they had known each other, Bill hadn't cried once. But, then again, he hadn't been a father or a stepfather at the time. She found herself moved.

'At first, when they went, I thought I'd like the extra time . . . for my photography. I've gone semi-professional, did you know?' Bill brushed away a tear.

'But it's not the same without the kids around. I hate it. I've been to visit them twice. Then Erica told me that she wasn't on holiday, she was separated from me but she hadn't said. Now she wants a divorce.

'I said yes because I don't know what else to do . . . I can't bear to think of only seeing the kids once or twice a year . . . But I can't force Erica to stay with me if she doesn't want to, can I?

'I told her I didn't think she'd given us even a chance . . . That's what marriage is about, isn't it? Getting through the rocky patches—'

'I suppose it must be,' Fee answered supportively.

Bill gave a heavy sigh. 'But I didn't come here to talk about me.'

Imogen Banks had already given Bill Summers a very graphic

description of Fee's fragile mental state, her plummeting self-esteem. She had graphically described how Fee talked frequently about him and clearly had regrets that he'd left. And how she was never home before midnight, preferring to work long hours to keep her mind off what she referred to as, 'the five happiest years of my life'.

In the circumstances, Bill was bound to offer what help he could. Apart from anything else, it would take his mind off his own misery. And after the last few months, he had told himself, it might be nice to feel wanted again.

He smiled at Fee wearily. 'I came here to talk about you. Now, why don't you tell me what's been going wrong?'

Spontaneously, Fee reached out for his hand. For the first time in all the years she had known him, she was experiencing a new and overpowering emotion.

It was sympathy. She felt enormously sympathetic towards her former partner.

Sympathy proved to be an effective aphrodisiac. A couple of hours later, Fee and Bill were in bed. Fee had no concerns that this brief interlude might spell the end of her own commitment to the single life. This wasn't copulation, it was social work. She was simply doing an old friend a favour, giving succour.

The two didn't waste much time on words. Bill required physical reassurance; Fee's libido was only too happy to oblige. Fee soon realized she had much to thank Erica for – not only had she relieved Fee of Bill, she had also improved his lovemaking skills immeasurably.

At eight thirty the next morning, Fee was woken by the doorbell. She opened her eyes, saw the back of Bill's head on the pillow next to hers, and briefly found herself catapulted back in time. It wasn't a pleasant sensation.

The bell rang again.

'Plumber!' a voice bellowed. 'Mrs Travers! Mrs Travers!'

'Oh, God,' Fee moaned. She'd forgotten to cancel. She took the coward's way out and slipped further under the covers. After several minutes more, the man departed, cursing and swearing.

Bill opened one eye and smiled.

'I hope that's helped,' Bill said. 'You're a terrific woman, Fee, really you are. You shouldn't think for a minute that you're not worth having—'

Fee sat up. 'What on earth do you mean? What do you mean, *you* hope that helped? I thought I was the one doing you a favour? And, come to that, why *did* you turn up out of the blue?'

Bill rubbed his eyes. It was too early for thought. 'Why did I turn up?' he repeated as if his motives for visiting were as mysterious to him as they might be to her. 'Why did I turn up. . .?'

'Yes, why did you come last night? Why so late?' Fee's eyes narrowed. The finger of Helen lay upon Bill.

'Have you been talking to my mother?' Fee demanded. 'Did she put you up to this? What's she been telling you now? Doesn't she realize you're a respectable married man?'

'Separated and about to be divorced,' Bill corrected. 'It wasn't Helen, but yes, your mother has stayed in touch . . . Matter of fact, I've always found her very understanding, particularly about you and me . . . She knows you inside out,' he added darkly.

Bill Summers belatedly began to gather his wits. 'Actually, all that is irrelevant anyway. The fact is, I've been thinking about you a great deal recently. I was happy with you a lot more of the time than I realized,' he hesitated. 'Perhaps we could give it another go, Fee? How do you feel about having children these days? Only I'm quite keen myself—'

Fee stared at Bill, disbelieving.

'I don't like being on my own,' he was saying. 'I've never actually been on my own, not once, not since school . . . I've always had *someone* . . . So,' he gave Fee an affectionate pat on the knee, 'shall we give it another go? Frankly, I don't think either of us is going to do much better, do you?'

Helen Travers had had a disappointing morning. First, she had unearthed next to nothing at the car-boot sale. Now, her youngest daughter was sitting at her kitchen table, having arrived just after noon, without phoning to forewarn her first.

'If you'd told me you were coming, I would've cooked a nice casserole,' Helen chastised.

Fee countered, 'I didn't know myself until this morning. A couple I have to interview live close by so I thought I'd pop in—'

'And . . .?' Helen said.

'It's about Bill,' Fee answered bluntly. 'Did you ask him to come and see me? Did you tell him that I was interested in us getting back together?'

Helen had been looking forward to this moment. Something dark within her found profound satisfaction in proving her youngest daughter wrong.

'Of course I didn't,' she answered truthfully. 'You know I've always said that what you do is your own affair. But I can't pretend that people aren't beginning to talk . . . This isn't central London, you know. We have different views out here.

'And you don't have to live with the gossip day after day,' she ploughed on. 'They're saying you're . . . you know . . . like Vera . . . Or at least if they knew about Vera, they'd be saying you're like her—'

Fee burst out laughing at her mother's convolutions. It lifted the gloom that had descended when Bill had told her that, at her age, half a commitment is better than none.

Will had been right when he'd suggested that she needed to make a public gesture, something the neighbours would understand. A clear and unequivocal statement that not only had she, Fee Travers, *chosen* to be on her own – but that she intended to stay that way.

An announcement in *The Times*? The neighbours would never see that. An appearance on prime-time television would carry much more clout.

Fee walked over to her mother, who was standing with her back to the kitchen sink. She took the small, stiff, tense figure in her arms and gave her the warmest of hugs.

'You're right, Mum,' Fee said. 'Something has to be done. You've put up with far too much. I'm going to try and make amends. All right?'

'All right,' Helen smiled warily. 'I only want what's best for you—'

At lunchtime, Imogen Banks received a call. It was one she had been expecting, but not quite so soon.

'Oh, what a pleasant surprise, Fee,' she cooed into the receiver. 'Of course, I'm delighted you've decided to appear in the film. But tell me, what on earth made you change your mind? *Do* tell.'

As she listened, the receiver in the crook of her neck, Imogen tore up Bill Summers's business card and deposited the tiny pieces in her waste-paper basket.

Now The Lone Ranger had been lassoed, Mr Summers's services were surplus to requirements.

Chapter Eighteen

A T SEVEN TWENTY that evening, Fee arrived home with ten
minutes to shower and change before Teddy's and Shona's
supper party. She was greeted by a postcard from Les. It showed a
picture not of one of the sights of Jersey but an overflowing sandwich
and a list of Les's establishments.

'Dear Fee,' the card read, 'Veronica is much better. Her handicap
– on and off the course, if you take my meaning – is improving by
the day. Home next week, Yours, Les.'

Fee rang the hotel and asked to be put through to Mrs Haslem.
Back came the reply that Mrs Haslem was resting and not to be
disturbed. Fee left a message, sending her love.

Today had been easier at work. Not least because Diana Woods
had departed on a business trip with Gerry Radcliffe to Amsterdam.
As a result, the atmosphere in the office had defrosted.

Harry Macklin had phoned Fee and demanded rather than
suggested that she personally make use of the various facilities that
made up the HAH! empire.

'Act as if you're a client on the receiving end,' he had ordered.
'If the staff know you've been hired by me, you'll never have a clue
what's going wrong. Be a punter,' he had instructed. 'Pretend you're
putting your heart on the line.'

That, Fee had remarked to Will later, was rather like inviting a
recent recruit to AA on a wine-tasting tour of the Loire valley.

Imogen had called to suggest that they meet before filming
began in the following week.

'I thought we might take a look at your image. Modify it a touch here and there, visit a few clothes places I know. See a hairdresser. You know, the usual kind of thing—' she had announced breezily. Banks the Buddy had been replaced by Banks the Boss.

Fee was too busy to argue. Imogen also announced that she would visit F.P. & D. to consider the possibilities for filming.

'Will anybody object to us having access?' Imogen had asked.

'Probably,' Fee had answered.

'Good, that's settled then,' Imogen had replied crisply.

Fee had driven home exhausted.

Now, she allowed herself three minutes under the shower, then pinned her hair up to disguise the fact that it needed a wash. She chose a simple black shift dress and gold and jet drop ear-rings.

Fee might have pretended she was dressing to please herself. The truth was that she was dressing to see if she could still please anyone else.

'It's a delightful sort of crabby flavour . . . very smooth. One of your own recipes, Shona?'

The woman to Fee's left was eating fish mousse. Shona smiled nervously.

'Oh it's nothing really,' she apologized. 'Very quick to make . . . it's crab and fresh tomato . . . is it all right?' Shona turned to Fee.

Fee nodded and smiled. She was the most underdressed woman present. Supper, to Fee, implied casual. The women around the table looked as if they were attending a cocktail party in first class on a round-the-world cruise.

Shona was in a spectacularly well-cut, full-length, black linen kaftan, heavily embroidered with beads around the neck. One guest wore a silk lime-green suit with buttons like large gold knots of rope. Another was dressed in a bright blue dress with a sequinned bolero jacket. The third wore brown palazzo pants and a brocade Chinese jacket. All three guests had the kind of shoes Fee always associated with 1960s beauty queens – stiletto heels, strappy and gold.

She had arrived late and alone. Edward Spannier was embarrassingly open in his attention. Shona pretended not to notice her husband's interest. Fee quickly deducted that this was not, as she had assumed, a cosy impromptu housewarming supper for a few friends. This was more a wine-and-dine-and-win-influence affair to which she had been grafted on at the last minute.

The three male guests were fond of their own monologues. The 'conversation' consisted more of anecdote competing with anecdote than any interchange of opinions or information.

In the rare intervals between the male performances, the women made small talk, mainly about the cost of private schooling, the terrors of the Friday afternoon run to their country cottages and the limitations of the local village shop.

Fee said little. This was partly because she had nothing to say on these subjects and partly because she was aware that she had been judged before she had opened her mouth.

'Oh', the woman in brocade had pronounced before Fee had barely broken into the homemade bread roll. 'Don't tell me, you're one of those relentlessly driven unattached young women . . .?'

Fee had smiled non-committally. Ever since that initial comment, the woman had repeatedly made reference to her self-regarding spouse sitting across the table.

'Donald, he's a lawyer you know, Donald always says . . . Donald thinks . . . Donald and I believe . . . Donald . . . Donald . . .'

Fee took a covert look at Donald. Even if she had been in the habit of stealing husbands, Donald would have had to be accompanied by a very expensive free gift before he became remotely desirable.

The woman in brocade spotted Fee's inspection, misread it and immediately reached across the table for her husband's hand. He jumped, startled by this unaccustomed show of public affection.

'Christ, Janie,' he said, irritably, 'You almost gave me a heart attack.'

Pâté was followed by venison followed by a chocolate roulade with fresh cream and raspberry coulis.

'This is fabulous,' Fee said to Shona. 'It must have taken you all day to prepare. I don't know how you find the time—'

As soon as the words were out, she regretted them. She knew that what had been intended as a compliment had been interpreted by the other women around the table – although not Shona – as a poor-little-housewife dig.

The men, oblivious to these female nuances, chorused their agreement. 'Absolutely right, Fee.' 'Couldn't put it better myself, Fiona.' 'A terrific meal, Shona.'

'Look, why don't I make the coffee?' Fee offered, desperate for some respite.

Five minutes later, she was in the kitchen when Edward Spannier entered. She had her back to him but she knew who it was. It happened within seconds. He stood behind her. Without speaking, he ran his hands down her sides and lifted the skirt of her dress in one easy movement to her waist. One foot and a knee were used to wedge her legs further apart. Then, Edward Spannier attempted to insert his hands in Fee's pants, reaching for warmer flesh.

Fee paused for longer than she should have done; the boldness of the move had momentarily enticed her. Then she twisted sideways and stepped back hard on the man's other foot. Edward Spannier swore.

Fee turned. Her hair had fallen loose with the exertion. His face was that of a spoilt child's, shocked because he had been denied – and now disbelieving.

Edward bent to kiss her, pinning her arms. She shook her head partly to avoid his lips, partly to convey her disgust.

'Stop it,' she whispered fiercely, her anger growing. 'For God's sake, stop it.'

Edward paused. Fee Travers had certainly given him enough of a come-on when they had first met. If she wanted to salve her conscience now, by putting up a bit of a fight, so be it. Edward knew the type.

He abruptly pushed Fee against the kitchen cupboards and gripped her wrists. Fee kneed him, hard.

'Don't you ever come near me again,' she hissed. Edward Spannier groaned and swore again. Fee heard Shona herding her guests from the dining room to the sitting room.

'I'll be with you in just a tick, Fee,' Shona's voice came from the hall, as if warning that time was running out. Her proximity made Edward's actions seem all the more contemptuous to Fee.

'Are you listening to me?' Fee whispered, adjusting her dress, and taking several steps away from her host. 'Or shall I make it plainer? I find you a cheap, repulsive, self-regarding egomaniac.'

'Don't give me that crap,' he spat back, smoothing his hair into place. 'You're dying for it—'

Fee said nothing. Protest would only increase the man's certainty. Shaken, she picked up the tray of coffee and walked out of the kitchen, across the hall and into the sitting room.

Fee's hair fell against her cheek as she bent to place the tray on the coffee table. She had forgotten to repin it. All Fee wanted to do was return to the comfort of her own flat and scrub the evening away in the hottest of baths.

'Sugar?' Shona had repeated the question twice before Fee realized what she was being asked. God, Fee thought, how she hated all this fake civility.

'No, no, thanks—' she replied. Shona avoided looking at Fee.

'Skin the most perfect marriage and the flesh underneath is often putrid—' Donald the lawyer was saying about a divorce case he had recently handled.

'Thank God some of us can get it right,' he added as Edward Spannier, relaxed and smiling, joined the company and gave Shona a peck on the cheek.

'Everything all right, darling?' he asked confidently.

Chapter Nineteen

'WHAT DO you want? I've got fifteen-stoners . . . I've got still living with mother . . . I've got totally asexual . . . I've got Cliff Richard freaks . . . You name it, we've got it.'

Trish Castle was speaking in the largest boardroom at F. P. & D. Also present were Will Evans, Diana Woods dressed in a frown and olive-green trouser suit, Fee Travers, and a team of five who would be responsible for drawing up HAH!'s strategy. Also present, sitting at the rear of the room, were Imogen Banks and Hilly Byrne. They were conferring about what they would and wouldn't film to give a flavour of Fee Travers's life.

'We've also got every type of normal,' Trish Castle added. 'We've put them into focus groups of eight, across the country. Anything you want to know in terms of client reaction, they'll tell us.'

'Is it the right age range?' Peter Winford, Fee's junior, asked.

'Thirty-five-plus . . . single, widowed and divorced and plenty of NPs—'

'NPs?' Imogen Banks asked, although she'd promised to remain silent and unobtrusive.

'Novice partners,' Trish Castle replied. 'Thirty-five-plus and never had a relationship which lasted longer than three months. They also tend never to have lived with anyone—'

'Thirty-five-plus and never had a long-term relationship?' Imogen Banks queried. 'I don't believe it.'

'I can assure you—' Trish Castle's face was bright pink.

219

Fee smiled. As soon as she had agreed to take part in the film, Imogen Banks's hitherto subdued image had been shed as easily as a snake's skin. This morning, she was dressed in lime green with crocodile-brown accessories. She had also shoved a pair of large tortoiseshell sunglasses on to the top of her head. Imogen was about as unobtrusive as the seven hills of Rome.

The group returned to the business in hand. Fee ran over the plans for the following ten days. She had decided to accede to Harry Macklin's demand that she make use of HAH!'s facilities. This was not because she had any desire to please an F.P & D. client – she had begun to experience a strange sense of recklessness in that area ever since first saying no to Gerry Radcliffe. She had agreed to Macklin's request because it was probably the quickest route to discovering how not to do it.

'You're going to look after the new logo, Phil?' Fee was saying. 'And you—'

She was interrupted by a resounding crash as the door to the boardroom was suddenly thrown open. Gill Booth burst in, her maternity Monsoon dress billowing out, so that she resembled one of those more exotic Christmas baubles.

'Oh, God—' Fee murmured.

Gill dramatically pointed a finger at Fee and shouted, 'You lay another finger on my husband, you . . . you . . . cow . . . and you will be cocktail snacks for vultures—'

Diana Woods's frown cleared. Will Evans half rose from his chair in alarm. The scar from his previous encounter with an enraged woman instantly began to sting. Others around the table shifted and shuffled in embarrassment.

'You . . . you . . . you twat,' Gill shouted again. Then Fee realized that Gill was gesturing not at her – but at someone behind her chair.

'Not you, *you*,' Gill was yelling. She was looking straight at Imogen Banks, whose face was without expression. Hilly Byrne was on her feet, her tigerskin clipboard falling to the floor. She loyally placed herself between this madwoman and her boss, mindful of her next pay cheque.

'Imogen?' Fee queried, bewildered. 'Imogen and Simon?'

Gill advanced further into the room, oblivious to the reaction she was causing. 'You are screwing my husband,' she spat out. 'By the time I have finished with you, you won't only need a heart, you'll need a lung, kidney and liver bloody transplant too—'

She began to sprint across the room towards Imogen. Hilly reconsidered her display of valour and hastily returned to her seat. Fee stuck out her foot, tripping Gill who stumbled but didn't fall.

'You've got the wrong woman, Gill,' Fee attempted to explain. 'Imogen doesn't.'

'Oh yes she bloody does,' Gill snarled. 'There she bloody is – tête-à-bloody-tête—'

She pulled out a pile of Polaroids from her handbag. They were smudged but Imogen Banks was unquestionably the figure in every frame with a series of men, including Simon Booth.

Gill slammed each Polaroid down on the boardroom table.

'She does it with him . . . and him . . . and him . . . and him . . . and especially him—' She triumphantly produced a photograph of Imogen and Simon, their arms wrapped around each other in what appeared to be the rose garden of a park.

Gill suddenly turned on Fee. She bent towards her so that their faces were only inches apart. Hatred and pain and fear of abandonment had distorted her features beyond recognition.

'You bloody spinsters are all the same—' she hissed, unaware that spittle had dribbled down her chin.

'You're nobody's friend. Got that?'

Fee's bathroom, six hours later, resembled a toy park. Two pedal cars belonging to Ivo and Euan, Percy's bicycle, a plastic farm, a large box of Thomas the Tank Engine paraphernalia and a wooden doll's house cluttered the space between the bath and the loo. The spare bedroom was now occupied by the two boys; Gill and Percy had taken over Fee's bedroom and she had relegated herself to the sofa. It was the least she could do.

At least, that is what Gill had implied when she had phoned Fee at the office in the afternoon and announced that she had left Simon.

'Stay with me,' Fee had offered immediately. It had been a long time since she had been able to do anything for Gill. And they had been friends, of sorts, for years. Perhaps the good times would now return?

'Of course I'll stay,' Gill had replied.

Now, while Fee struggled to house a giant box of cornflakes in a food cupboard plainly designed for a couple who skipped breakfast, seven-year-old Percy was expressing disapproval at the contents of Fee's fridge.

'It's all so boring,' Percy pronounced. 'And you drink too much. Mum says you're one of those secret drinkers. All single people are. You drink because you're lonely.'

'Give me that,' Fee demanded, taking a bottle of white wine out of Percy's hands. She proceeded to open it, then poured herself a glass. Watching Percy, she took a large tumbler from the shelf, placed a tablespoon of wine in it and filled the glass with lemonade.

'Cheers,' she said, giving the tumbler to Percy. 'Today, I am drinking not because I'm lonely, but because I have you for company.'

'Is that good or bad?' Percy queried, her face wreathed in smiles at her first very own grown-up drink.

'We'll see, won't we?' Fee replied, not uncheerily.

In the sitting room, Gill lay comatose on the sofa. It was all too much for her. She was a woman who needed control. Now her life had undertaken an ugly transformation. *Nothing was planned*. She didn't grieve for the loss of Simon, but she was depressed by her own spectacular lack of judgement. She'd got the right man but the wrong woman; Imogen not Fee. Still, she consoled herself, it could just as easily have been Fee.

'It's all your fault, you do realize that, don't you?' she said as Fee came into the room and handed her a glass of wine.

Fee barely took in Gill's words. On the balcony, unsupervised, the twins were shaking her fuchsia vigorously. Pink and purple petals now lay scattered like battered confetti.

'Here,' Fee commanded Percy, who had followed her into the room. 'Put this on.' She handed Percy a video of *Singing in the Rain* – the closest her collection came to children's entertainment. Then Fee pulled the two boys down from the balcony's wrought-iron railings. They giggled. They were jubilant, intrigued by the possibilities for mortal danger offered by unexpectedly moving into a first-floor flat.

'It's gone,' Ivo said proudly. Fee glanced over the balcony and saw two of her cushions – two of her large, silk, cream cushions – lying on the flowerbed below.

'Christ, they're only cushions,' Gill commented sanguinely from the sofa, observing the changing emotions on Fee's face – anguish, outrage, resignation.

Of course, these were more than cushions. They were large and cumbersome and Fee had suffered extreme discomfort carrying them back on the plane from Thailand. Their hand-painted design – which would surely never withstand the trauma of dry-cleaning – co-ordinated beautifully with the cream and white sitting room. Or at least, it had.

Fee experienced a moment of blinding revelation. She recognized that if she didn't accept that a cushion was just a cushion at least for the period that Gill's brood was with her, she would surely go mad.

'Come and listen to the nice songs—' Fee coaxed the twins

instead. The three-year-olds obediently followed her into the sitting room and sat on the floor in front of the television alongside their sister.

'I'm drunk,' Percy told the two boys proudly. 'Really drunk.'

Three hours later, Gill was still reclining on the sofa. Fee had bathed and fed the twins and put them to bed after a chaotic game of hide 'n' seek. She had also fed Percy and read her a story. Then she had made an emergency dash to the off-licence, prepared supper for herself and Gill, cleared away, tidied, and had filled the washing machine.

She sat exhausted in the chair, drinking coffee and considering how much office work she had to complete before bedtime.

Gill had eaten hugely in spite of her emotional upset. Now, she was sipping brandy as if it was beef tea and she was a Victorian heroine wasting away with consumption.

'You do have to shoulder the blame for some of this, you know that, don't you?' Gill tried again to pin guilt.

'Do I?' Fee asked mildly.

'Yes,' she continued, a little colour coming back into her cheeks as she swigged away.

'First, you distracted me, because I was sure it was you who was up to something. And second, you brought that woman into the house. She took one look at Simon and that was it—'

'Whiff,' Fee corrected Gill gently. Gill looked confused.

Fee went on, 'She took one whiff. Imogen says it was Simon's smell that did it. That's why she behaved so totally out of character. She says she hasn't looked at a man in years. That's what she says.' She shrugged as if to absolve herself from responsibility for Imogen Banks's views.

Gill was unconvinced. 'And what about the others? She was kicking up a bit of a stink with them, too, was she?'

Fee sighed. 'Imogen claims there's a totally innocent explanation for all those photographs.' She glanced at Gill, who had almost emptied her glass.

'At least, that's what Imogen says,' Fee repeated. To be frank, Fee was beyond caring about the veracity or otherwise of Imogen's explanations. She now mistrusted her thoroughly but she had agreed to take part in Imogen's film, and she wouldn't go back on her word. Besides, she *wanted* to appear in the film.

'You don't know how lucky you are,' Gill began again, glancing accusingly at Fee. 'You've got no children, no husband, no responsibilities, nobody after you every minute of the day—'

'Just hang on a minute.' Fee's patience evaporated. 'For ages, you've been telling me how much I was missing by not having a partner, not being part of a family, not having babies, not being *wanted*.' She mimicked Gill's intonation on the word. 'Now, you're telling me the opposite—'

Gill waved her hand as if to magic away these contradictions.

'Anyway, the real issue is how shall I handle Simon?' Gill swirled the brandy dregs around in her glass. 'Should I have him back? Or should I refuse?'

'What if Simon decides he doesn't want to give it another go?' Fee asked gently.

'Don't be ridiculous,' Gill snapped.

'I will not ask my mother,' Fee reached for a towel in the bathroom and caught her shin on a toy bicycle parked dangerously near the basin.

'Shit,' she said.

'Shit, shit, shit, shit—' chorused the twins sitting in the bath. Will Evans hid a smile. It was the second night of the Booths' invasion. He had called in and stayed to cook supper and help Fee with bathtime. Gill had fallen asleep on Fee's bed. Percy was in the sitting room watching *Casablanca*.

'If I ask my mother to give us a hand, she will drive us all insane,' Fee repeated.

'How long are they staying?' Will asked, hauling Ivo or it might have been Euan out of the bath and turning him upside down to squeals of delight.

'Gill hasn't said and it doesn't seem right to ask, not while she's still upset,' Fee replied. The twin still in the water put his arms around her neck and gave her a kiss on the cheek.

'Got you!' he shouted happily. Fee kissed his tummy. 'Got you too,' she chuckled.

Will watched, smiling. 'You can see why some people do it, can't you?' he said, lifting the second boy out of the bath and standing him next to his brother on the mat.

'Do what?' Fee asked, pulling the plug and rescuing various bottles of cream and exfoliants and anti-wrinkle miracle cures which the boys had tossed into the water.

'Kids,' Will replied, breathless, wrestling the twins to the ground. 'You can see why people have kids.'

'Listen,' Fee reminded him, 'you're the man who broke his ex-wife's heart by refusing to have any. So what's made you change your mind?'

'Old age,' Will Evans replied. 'I'm beginning to feel I've done the no-dependants bit. After all, there's only so many table tops you can dance on, before it begins to be repetitious.'

By eleven, the children and Gill slept while Fee sat at the kitchen table and Will made coffee.

'I've got it,' he announced as he handed her a cup. Fee glanced at him and found herself feeling unexpectedly sentimental. Will was always there when help was required.

'What about Veronica?' Will suggested. 'She can give you a hand. You don't want your mother, Gill has forbidden you to tell any of your other friends, so why not Veronica? She's desperate to do something. In fact, you'd probably be doing her a favour. She'd love it.'

Fee shook her head. 'She couldn't possibly. She's not up to it.

What if she thought she'd killed off someone when she was here on her own with the twins or Percy?'

Will was undeterred. 'Gill will be here . . . When does Veronica get back from holiday?'

Fee looked at her watch to check the date. 'I'm not sure. She may be back now for all I know. Les has been very protective.'

'Perfect!' Will was rubbing his hands together. 'And what about that woman, Rita? Couldn't she help out too?'

Fee groaned. It had been four days since she had told Rita Mason that she was going away for a very long time. So far, there had been no word from the woman. No word, no telephone messages, no gifts, no unexpected visits . . .

Will was speaking again. 'Didn't Rita and Veronica get on very well when they were locked in the lavatory?'

Fee smiled. 'They weren't locked in *together*. Rita Mason works as a radiographer at the hospital and she rescued Veronica—'

'Well, now it's Veronica's turn to rescue you,' Will announced.

'Les won't allow it,' Fee responded.

'Now, what kind of an excuse is that?' Will asked.

An hour later, just before midnight, Veronica was on the doorstep with an overnight bag.

Fee was surprised to see her. She had phoned and left a message on the answering machine. Five minutes later, Veronica had called back, whispering into the receiver. She and Les had returned from holiday the day before. Les was now asleep. And no, Veronica hadn't received any of her sister's messages in Jersey.

'I thought you'd forgotten me,' Veronica said lightly.

Fee explained the situation. Asked several times if her sister felt up to it. And was still asking when her sister said goodbye.

Veronica wrote a note for her husband, called a cab and was soon helping Will to make up the sofa bed in the spare bedroom, already occupied by the twins.

Fee came into the room to find Veronica kneeling on the carpet, weak with laughter, out-foxed by its mechanics. Will was nursing three fingers, freshly jammed in the springs.

'Your sister's trying to kill me,' he complained. Veronica found that even funnier.

A little later, Fee joined Will in the kitchen, bringing with her Ivo, who had woken and refused to go back to sleep. Will offered to make him a cup of hot chocolate.

'I've left the details there,' Will said casually to Fee.

'What details?' she asked.

'Didn't you hear the phone go? It was Rita Mason. She said to tell you to meet her at seven fifteen at Floods wine bar in Waterloo Station. She said she's got something very exciting to tell you but it will have to be a quick drink because she's meeting a friend off the eight thirty-five. Look, I've written it all down.'

Fee took the note. 'God, she's got a nerve . . . I don't want to see her. I told her I couldn't. Where's her number? I'll phone and tell her I'm busy—'

'She didn't leave a number,' Will said. 'I thought you'd have it.'

'The woman *never* leaves her bloody number. I'll have to phone her at work,' Fee said, reaching for the phone book.

Will looked sheepish. 'She mentioned that she's taken a couple of weeks off . . . she's busy with family or something—'

'What family?' Fee replied, exasperated. 'She told Veronica she didn't have any. I told you there was something odd about her.'

'You'll just have to do what I do in difficult circumstances, and which you swore you would never stoop to,' Will suggested smugly, enjoying the irony.

'What's that?' Fee asked.

'You'll have to stand Ms Mason up,' Will smiled. 'Then hope to God she's not the sort who goes in for bloody revenge.'

Chapter Twenty

A T ONE A.M., Fee turned off the lamp by the sofa, leaving the flat in darkness. She was trying to make herself comfortable when she heard a small tap, more like a scratch, at her front door. It was followed by another tentative scratch, then silence.

She was certain it couldn't be Rita Mason, she'd already left her trail of demands for the day. Fee rose, opened the door and peered into the dimly lit hall. She could see nothing. A tiny sound came from somewhere near her feet.

Shona Spannier was sitting on the floor, her back against the wall, huddled almost into a ball. She glanced upwards at Fee and then hid her face on her knees. Fee bent to help her up. Only then did she see that Shona had a badly split lip while the whole of one side of her face was the puce and purple of a damaged damson.

'I'm so sorry—' Shona wept quietly. 'It's all my fault.'

Shona Spannier sat on the sofa, holding a mug of coffee between cupped hands as Fee searched for her favourite cardigan – thick and old and comforting. She failed to find it, so Fee draped her dressing-gown around Shona's shoulders. The rest of the household slept on.

'What happened?' Fee asked. 'Was it Edward?'

'No.' Shona shook her head vigorously.

'Are you sure?' Fee asked again gently.

Shona put the mug of coffee down and grief distorted her face.

'He wants the boys to leave school,' she burst out. 'That's how it started. It's taken so long for them to get used to it. Now Teddy wants them to leave and go to day school. Just when they've made friends, just when they're both beginning to have fun . . . Of course I want them home with me, but above all I want them to feel secure.'

'Is it the cost?' Fee asked.

Shona gave a brittle laugh. 'Oh God, no. He makes loads of money. Or he says he does. He wants to move them because he doesn't think it suits his image. He's trying to get selected, did I tell you? He doesn't think it's on as a Labour MP to have two sons in public school—'

Shona wiped a stray tear that had tracked its way down her bruised cheek.

'Perhaps he's right. I get so confused . . . Most times I go along with what Teddy says. He can be quite forceful, you know . . . but this time I said I thought it was wrong . . . Then Teddy said I was being typically inconsistent. One minute I don't want them to go, the next, I'm saying they shouldn't leave—'

'It's true. I am inconsistent, but I just want the boys to feel settled—'

Shona gazed at Fee, her eyes welling with tears again.

'And—' Fee gently encouraged.

'Suddenly, Teddy lost his temper. I was sitting on our bed, he was standing by the door. He ran at me and gave me such a punch, I was knocked sidewards off the bed. He wouldn't stop kicking me. I covered my head with my hands . . . but he wouldn't stop . . . Then he grabbed me by the hair and threw me back on the bed and the back of my head hit the bedside table.

'Over and over he kept saying, "Look what you make me do . . . look what you drive me to . . ." And then he just banged out of the flat . . . I thought you'd heard . . . I thought the whole street had heard—'

Shona placed both her hands flat on the kitchen table. They were blotched and bruised and cut where she had tried to protect her head from the kicking. A trickle of blood dripped onto the collar of Fee's dressing gown.

Words deserted Fee. If this had happened to her, she would find comfort in the sound of horses' hoofs, the smell of gunfire and leather. She could pretend to herself that she would ride to her own rescue. And teach the culprit a lesson he would never forget. But this wasn't her life, it was Shona's – and Fee found it difficult to understand why the woman was being so apologetic – as if she *deserved* the beating she had been given.

'He's right. Teddy's right,' Shona was saying, now more calm. 'I do drive him to it. He says he's never hit any other woman before me. It's all my fault. Oh, Fee. I don't want him to leave me. I want to make this marriage work, I really do.'

Later, Shona refused the offer of a bed for fear that Edward might return, make a scene, and frighten Gill's children.

'Let me call Will upstairs,' Fee offered. 'He'll put you up for the night.'

Shona looked horrified. 'You are not to tell anyone else what's happened. Nobody,' she insisted, her face whitening with anxiety, in spite of the bruises. 'Promise me you won't tell a soul. *Nobody*. Absolutely nobody?' Shona repeated firmly.

Fee sidestepped the promise. 'But how will you get help? How often has he done this, Shona?'

Shona backed away, as if in retreat from the truth.

'Not much. Just a few times, perhaps once or twice. Look, thank you for listening. I'm really sorry I woke you up. I'll be fine now. Really, I will—' She stumbled over her words.

She had slipped out of Fee's door and into her flat before Fee had time to react.

At eight the next morning, Fee knocked on Shona's door. She refused to answer. Fee then left a neutral message on her answering machine, since she also failed to answer the phone. 'Veronica or I will be at home all day if you need anything.'

'She's embarrassed,' Veronica said when Fee told her about the previous night's events.

'She's embarrassed and she feels ashamed.'

'But why?' Fee asked. 'It's not her fault.'

'No, but she believes it is.'

Two hours later, Fee Travers was sitting in a luxurious office decorated in pastel pink and dove grey, acting the part of a difficult customer. Given the circumstances, she was finding it easy.

The woman opposite her was encouraging Fee to construct the man of her dreams – in the hope that the highly advanced, first of its kind, HAH! computer, a service known as Inter-Act, might deliver a near approximation – a Mr Almost Right.

Two packets of cigarettes were stacked next to a sign that read Angie Baxter (BA Hons).

Angie Baxter was in her late twenties. Her make-up was of the painting-by-numbers variety. Peachy brown on the cheeks; chestnut eyebrow pencil, beige eye shadow; the lips had been given a very dark maroon outline, filled in with a paler pink colour so that the mouth resembled a guava cut in two.

She was dressed in a brown suit, a dazzlingly white top and several amber necklaces. The perfume was very noticeable – perhaps rose- or jasmin-based – as were the blonde highlights in her brown hair.

Ms Baxter was baffled as to why Fee Travers had found it necessary to sit with an uncompleted application form in front of her for forty-five minutes.

She had never witnessed anyone so confounded by the simple act of selecting the qualities you desired most in an ideal partner. Didn't the woman daydream, for God's sake?

'For each question, there are three boxes,' Ms Baxter tried again. 'All you have to do is tick the appropriate one. Let's start with something easy. Would you like a man who is *very* interested in politics, *not* interested or *mildly* interested?'

'It depends,' Fee replied honestly.

'Yes, well,' Angie Baxter answered, now slightly testy. 'We don't have a box for "It depends." People who aren't prepared to be a bit more black and white can't really complain about who they end up with – can they? And it's your money, dear.'

Fee had just written out a cheque for £750 for her introduction to the service plus £250 for six months' access to as many suitable candidates as the computer could dredge up.

'How about this?' Angie Baxter tried again.

'Would you like a man who is earning £20,000 and over; £40,000 and over or £60,000 plus?'

'It's difficult to say really, isn't it?' Fee responded chattily.

'Oh dear,' Angie Baxter said. 'Oh dear, oh dear, oh dear—'

Fee attempted to explain herself better. 'Look, what the man earns is less relevant to me than, say, how he treats the children of his former marriage. Or whether he has a propensity to domestic violence.'

Ms Baxter, slumped in defeat, sat bolt upright in alarm. 'Good God,' she said. 'We wouldn't dream of dipping into the nastier side of life . . . That's something you'd have to sort out between the two of you, much further down the line. This *is* about romance, after all—'

Fee improvised. 'All right then, I'd quite fancy someone who earns over £20,000 and who has a strong concern for the future of the planet.'

Angie Baxter paled. She had once had a job as a driving-test examiner. She had changed careers because the stress had proved too much. Perhaps brokering love was also beginning to prove too taxing?

She gave Fee a brittle smile. 'Oh God, darling,' she said. 'If you're a *greenie*, you should have said so from the start.' Relief mixed with contempt had entered the woman's voice. So *that's* why this client had been so *contrary*.

She began to enthuse, anxious to remove Ms Travers from her records, from her sight, from her memory.

'Organizations exist especially for you tofu types. I'm told it's quite fun. Lots of lentil love-ins, if you get my drift . . . I'm sure you'll find Mr Right there. Or perhaps I should say, Mr Green—' Angie Baxter enjoyed her little joke.

'No,' Fee announced firmly, picking up the pen. 'I'll stick with what you've got on offer. Now, do I want someone who reads one to two books a week, several books a week or—'

She looked up at the woman who was now beginning to chew at one of her perfectly manicured fingers.

'Oh dear, oh dear, oh dear,' the woman muttered, spitting out bits of broken nail.

At work an hour later, Fee attempted to delegate. She was scheduled to attend 'Get Going!' at 6 p.m. GG! was yet another sub-division of HAH!. It organized a range of events, across London, for unattached men and women. The events included dinners, night-club evenings, walks, parachute jumping, motor rallies, weekends away, discos and wine tastings. The cut-off age was forty-five. In order to gain access to events, the member had to carry a copy of GG!'s magazine, issued monthly by post.

Once a week, a recruitment drive was held in a London hotel. In vain did Fee attempt to persuade half-a-dozen colleagues to take her place. All refused on the grounds of pride.

'Jeez, Fee, what if someone saw me going in there?' Trish Castle protested. 'I'd die—'

'Get Going!'s recruitment evening was held in a large rambling hotel near Liverpool Street station. The exterior of the hotel had been modernized with a facelift of glass and marble. The inside still had corridors wide enough for a coach and horses and a permanent smell of boiled cabbage.

Fee walked in at 5.55 p.m., briefcase in hand, looking purposeful, as if she was heading for a business meeting. She reassured herself that nobody but nobody would assume she was a Get Going! candidate.

'Want the singles do, miss?' said a porter helpfully, almost immediately. 'Third floor, take a left and a right. It's the Duke of York Suite.'

Five minutes later, she entered a large ornate room. Five rows of chairs were arranged to face a table, stacked with magazines and Polaroids of groups of people having 'A Good Time' in a range of activities.

Fee's first glance around the other potential recruits left her surprised. Ages ranged from late twenties to a woman well into her fifties; two men and half-a-dozen women. An observer might have judged that when it came to finding a partner, most had the necessary assets and, one or two, a bit more besides.

A woman of indeterminate age with a large bosom, a pleasant unmade-up face and glossy brown hair, walked to the front of the group, and held up her hands for silence. A name tag on her chest said she was called Sandra.

'Hello, everyone,' she smiled. 'My name is Sandra. I'm a dentist, I've been a member of Get Going! for five years. And in that time, I've certainly got going.' She paused for laughter that never materialized. 'And there's nothing to stop you doing the same,' she added brightly.

'Look at me,' Sandra suggested. 'I'm tonight's volunteer recruitment officer. I look pretty normal, don't I? I'm a member of GG! not just because I want to meet someone special but because I want to *do* things! I'm sure you're probably a lot of doers too—' Sandra directed her gaze at Fee. Fee decided to inspect her feet, as did almost every other person in the room. Why should this seem so *embarrassing*?

Sandra redoubled her efforts. 'Whatever you do, ladies and gentlemen,' she beamed. 'Whatever you do, please don't feel defeated just because you're here.'

If the thought hadn't entered the heads of those in the room before, it now hung over them, heavy and oppressive like a monsoon sky.

'Well done, Sandra,' Fee murmured to herself.

Sandra instructed that they each introduce themselves to the person sitting to their left and their right. That done, she grinned enthusiastically. 'Now we've broken the ice a bit, I'm sure we're all feeling a lot better, aren't we?' Her perfectly flossed teeth glistened like spent hope in the gloom of the room.

'Is that you, Fee?' Percy sounded very self-assured on the telephone. Fee had called after slipping out of GG! meeting early.

'Yes,' Fee replied. 'I'm just checking in to see if everything is OK? Where is everyone?'

Percy was eager to supply the details. 'Mum's gone to give Dad a piece of her mind. Veronica's making an adventure playground in your study for the twins . . . and she's fine now she's stopped crying.'

Fee tried to keep the alarm out of her voice. 'Crying? Why?'

'Les phoned up and said that she should come home . . . so then Veronica cried . . . but now she says she feels much better. Do you cry at all, Fee?' Percy suddenly sounded concerned.

'Mum says we're all getting on your nerves. And unless we're good we'll be homeless, because you're used to being on your own . . . and you can't be doing with children.' Percy's words escaped in a rush.

'Look,' Fee tried to sound as reassuring as possible. 'I love having you stay with me . . . It's fun. Don't you think it's fun?' Fee was surprised that this glimpse of Percy's insecurity had brought her close to tears.

'How about if I bring home a big tub of ice-cream and we'll melt a bar of chocolate to pour over it and then you and I will eat the lot. OK?'

'You mean that we won't have to give the boys any?' Percy pushed a hard bargain.

'No, just you and me,' Fee agreed.

'Sounds OK. So are you coming home soon?' Percy asked.

'I've got to meet a woman I know for a drink,' Fee explained. Her watch said five past seven. She had considered standing Rita Mason up, as Will had suggested, but Fee was too well behaved, too programmed, to allow herself to do it. Besides, how would she like it, if it was done to her? Treat others as you would wish to be treated . . .

So, Fee cursed Rita Mason who had once again forced her into a situation in which she didn't wish to be.

'Listen, Percy, I'll try very hard to be back before you're in bed, OK?' she answered.

'Promise?' Percy pressed.

'I promise,' she replied.

Fee waited for Rita Mason in the designated wine bar for forty-five minutes. She never appeared. At eight, Fee left.

'It's not your responsibility,' Fee told herself as she waited for a vacant taxi. Forget her. But she couldn't.

'You're late and you promised and you said ice-cream and now there's no time for a story, you promised, you did—' Percy bombarded Fee with accusations as soon as she opened the front door.

The little girl, dressed in pyjamas and dressing-gown, had camped cross-legged in the hall for half an hour, waiting for Fee's arrival.

'She wouldn't budge until you got back,' Gill explained. 'She's like her father. Stubborn as a mule.'

An hour later, Fee put a happy Percy to bed, both had stuffed on chocolate-chip ice-cream topped by a melted Mars bar.

'Mummy would never let me melt a Mars bar,' Percy confided, as Fee made a nest with pillows and the duvet, just like her father used to make for her.

'She's quite right,' Fee said loyally. 'She has all the hard work, I just get the fun bits.'

'Do you know something?' Percy asked, sleep beginning to weigh down her eyes. 'That's exactly what Mummy used to say to Dad about us ... "It's all right for you, you just get the fun bits with the kids—"' Percy opened one eye and gazed at Fee. 'Do you think that's why he left us? Because we weren't fun enough?' she asked.

'Of course not,' Fee replied, but Percy had already fallen asleep.

'I'm going to take you away from all this,' Will Evans said, arriving unexpectedly half an hour later as Fee and Veronica tidied up the toys that littered Fee's sitting room. Gill was lying on Fee's bed, claiming that she was too emotionally exhausted to help.

'Come,' Will commanded.

'Go,' Veronica ordered.

Ten minutes later, Will and Fee were drinking wine on Will's balcony.

'We haven't had a chance for a chat for ages,' Will said. 'You must be sick of it all by now?'

Fee shook her head. 'I'm really glad they've stayed with me.'

'Masochist,' Will teased.

'No, really ... I've learned some lessons. For instance, Percy. She's been far more affected than the boys by the split. They're too young really. But she blames herself. She thinks it's her and the twins' fault that Simon has gone. Somehow these things—'

'Things?' Will interrupted gently.

'You know ... divorce, splitting up, leaving children confused about who's done what to whom and why ... you'd think we would have learned how to manage it all better by now—'

238

'Well, that's not your personal concern, is it?' Will reminded Fee gently, refilling her glass.

'That's the other thing I've realized,' Fee said. 'It's made me even more sure that I wouldn't risk having a child. It wouldn't be fair. If you're going to demand the right to have a child, you also have a responsibility to bring it up in security . . . and love . . . and I don't think I could trust myself, so—'

Will yawned ostentatiously.

'Sorry.' Fee smiled. Will shifted his chair and suddenly appeared embarrassed.

'Fee,' he said, 'I asked you to come up here to tell you something. Someone's moving in with me . . . Someone you know . . . Remember when you brought me the petrol, when I was stranded a few weeks ago?'

'When you were with the woman who was living with her boyfriend?'

Will nodded. 'Yes, well, what I didn't tell you at the time was that she was also the one who attacked your car—'

'The one who wanted a future with you?'

Will appeared flustered. 'She's moving in but it's nothing serious. At least, not on my part. She's moving in and we're seeing how we go. Day at a time, kind of thing.'

'Real commitment on your part at last, Will.'

'What I wanted to know was what you felt about it?' Will blurted out.

'Me?' Fee asked perplexed. *Why should it matter how she felt?*

Fee smiled. 'I couldn't be happier for you. In fact, I seem a damn sight happier at the prospect than you do, Will Evans.'

At 7 a.m., a couple of days later, Fee was on her hands and knees. She was crawling in the semi-darkness of her bedroom, groping under the bed for a missing shoe, anxious not to wake Gill or Percy.

'What are you doing?' The words were hissed directly into Fee's left ear. She jumped and Percy giggled.

'I'm going to work,' Fee whispered back. 'Don't wake your mum or the boys or Veronica.' What she didn't add was that her new family obligations were eating hard into her extended working day and she was worried about meeting the deadline on the HAH! project. God knows how women with full-time jobs and families coped.

Percy followed Fee into the bathroom. She watched silently while Fee applied her make-up and brushed her hair.

'You'll kill yourself,' she said knowingly. 'For ages just before we came here, Daddy was leaving very early like you, and coming home late and Mummy said he'd kill himself, if she didn't kill him first—'

Fee stopped brushing her hair, and crouched down to Percy's eye level. 'Do you know something, Persephone Booth, you are absolutely right, I will kill myself,' she said. Percy looked taken aback. It wasn't often an adult told her she was right.

Fee made a snap decision. 'What about Macdonald's for breakfast?'

Percy gave a small skip of pleasure. 'Shall I tell you something deathly secret?' she asked Fee. Generosity on Fee's part merited some reward.

'Promise not to tell? Well, Mummy says you're spoiling us rotten and it's all right for you because you don't have to pick up the pieces later—'

'Is that what she said?' Fee answered mildly.

Percy continued in a conspiratorial tone, 'I think part of Mummy's problem is that she doesn't have a clue how her own kids tick—'

'Breakfast,' Fee answered diplomatically.

At 9.30 a.m., having delivered Percy to school, Fee belatedly reached F.P. & D. Diana Woods was waiting in Fee's office. She glanced at her watch and said, sarcastically, 'If you're this late, it can only be love—'

'It is,' Fee answered flippantly, picking unnaturally yellow scrambled egg from the cuff of her suit sleeve. 'But not the kind you mean—'

It was late morning when the latest rumour was reported back to Fee. Diana Woods was spreading it around that Fee had 'gone gay'.

Sue Leith from accountants bumped into Fee in the loo. 'Congratulations,' she said warmly. 'Your F.P. & D.'s first. At least, you're the first to come out.'

Chapter Twenty-One

ANGIE BAXTER of Inter-Act was proud of the efforts that she, assisted by the computer of course, had made to find Fiona Travers a soulmate.

She had abandoned the attempt to make Fiona Travers complete a questionnaire. The woman was far too indecisive. How was it possible to reach the age of almost forty and know so little about yourself, never mind what you sought from a loved one?

Angie Baxter had married at eighteen. Her husband, Dave, was a fireman with a thriving business on the side, delivering fresh fish direct to the domestic door. The couple had decided they wanted no children, but they did own a lovely home, they had two cars, two cats, and an awful lot of desirable objects . . . such as piranha fish in a tank, a patio and a barbecue imported from Florida. Their next goal was garden furniture that cost £1,700.

Dave was exactly what Angie had wanted and vice versa. Neither had expected too much; each had made allowances for the other's irritations. Dave had darts and golf and wind-surfing. Angie had aerobics and a Chinese takeaway, a bottle of wine and a video with the girls every Thursday night.

Eleven years down the line, so far, so good. Angie was absolutely convinced that she would find no better than her Dave. He was sure that she too was 'top class'. On that basis, each endeavoured to please the other; they split domestic chores; went away for romantic weekends and regarded infidelity as beyond the pale. And, of course,

Angie's job helped no end because she saw on a daily basis what the alternative might be.

In truth, in her professional capacity of matchmaker '*par excellence*', Angie Baxter sometimes had to hide her disgust that others were so bloody unrealistic in what they expected from a relationship. I mean, a spouse could only ever be an ordinary human being, for God's sake, not a bloody miracle worker.

Now, she ranged through the files on her computer just to double-check. She kept returning to this man Munsen, Alan Munsen, age forty-seven, never married. There wasn't anything scientific in Angie Baxter's choice; she just had a hunch that Alan Munsen might be the type who could handle a difficult customer like Fiona Travers.

She reread the report Alan Munsen had written on himself – an exercise Fee Travers had yet to complete.

'I recently returned to Britain after fifteen years in Central America. I first travelled to the region to take a job as a hydraulics engineer. Later, I became an adviser to farming co-operatives on the best use of water. As a result, while colleagues have grown rich, I've made more friends than money, but I count myself a lucky man. I love the region,' Alan Munsen had written.

'I came home to the UK because a friend in Honduras, one of my oldest friends, died recently from a heart attack. He was forty-three and, like me, without partner or children. I've gradually come to acknowledge that the passions that have satisfactorily filled my life until now – sailing, books, painting, Spanish history – are no longer sufficient to distract me from the need to belong. I want to belong to someone or somewhere.'

Angie Baxter stopped reading and sighed deeply. The man had a lovely way with words . . .

At 10 a.m., two days later, Alan Munsen found himself in the lobby of a London hotel, drinking coffee with a stranger. It was proving easier than he had imagined. Not least because the woman opposite looked awfully like a lover he had known for a year or so before leaving Britain. Or perhaps it was just that the two women shared a similar air of wariness?

Fee Travers took in the battered face opposite her. The man was around five foot eleven. He was lean, and had an open face, deeply lined, bushy eyebrows and a thatch of grey hair. He wore jeans and a faded denim shirt. Within a few minutes of meeting, his sense of humour had emerged. Fee knew fairly quickly that although Alan Munsen wasn't the man of her dreams – as HAH!'s computerized skills had insisted – he was extremely likeable. It was only fair to tell him the truth.

'I'm not quite what I seem,' she began. Alan Munsen looked at her, baffled.

'Is that so?' he replied cautiously.

'I'm not bona fide,' Fee tried again. More bafflement.

Alan Munsen ticked off the fingers on one hand. 'Sex change? Call girl? Undercover detective? Married woman?'

Fee laughed. 'No, what I mean is that I'm not really looking for a partner. I'm carrying out research . . . for my company . . . I'm sorry . . . I should have said something straight away—'

Alan Munsen shrugged his shoulders. Part of him felt relief; courtship in an unfamiliar society could be an exhausting business. Courting in any society can be an exhausting business.

'How are you on friendship?' he asked. 'I mean would your husband mind if you acquired a friend, a male friend . . .?'

Fee smiled. 'I don't have a husband . . . or a partner for that matter, but friendship sounds like a good idea—'

'Suits me,' he replied, offering his hand and smiling. 'Let's shake on it. To friendship.'

Alan Munsen was by nature reserved, so, for him, this was the very best of beginnings.

At lunchtime on that same day, Fee decided that she could no longer pretend indifference to Rita Mason's continuing lack of contact.

'You don't owe her a thing,' Gill had advised bluntly. 'She annoyed you when she was around and she's annoying you even more now that she's disappeared. She's just one of those women who spend their lives attention-seeking. Don't indulge her. Write her off. She's probably inveigling her way into somebody else's life, even as we speak. Probably somebody with more money and less sense—'

Gill's words made little impact. Fee had to satisfy herself that Rita Mason was alive and well. If she didn't, she knew, the woman would remain with her for life.

Fee's first call was to Rita Mason's employer – the Tendon Hospital Trust.

'Hello, could I have the radiography department, please?' she asked, after waiting several minutes for the switchboard, serenaded by repeated renditions of 'Moon River'.

'Hello, is that radiography? I wondered if I might speak to Rita Mason?'

'Rita who?' a grumpy female voice asked.

'Rita Mason. She's one of your radiographers. I think she works shifts—'

'No Rita here,' the voice said, sounding slightly more amiable.

'Are you sure?' Fee asked again. 'She's called Rita Mason. She's very . . . well, very . . . striking—'

'Look, dear,' the voice had resumed its gruffness. 'I've worked here for eleven years and never, not once, have we had a Rita. Or, for that matter, a Mason. All right? Bye-ee.'

Fee paused for a few seconds and then called Veronica at the flat.

'You're sure she said she was a radiographer?' Fee asked her sister.

'I'm sure. She had a name badge thingummy on as well . . . And when we left a woman in the canteen said goodbye as if she knew her really well—'

Fee replaced the receiver, perplexed and uneasy. A few minutes later, she began to hunt through her bag. Rita Mason had given her address to Fee so that Veronica could write a thank-you note. *Where was it?*

Receipts, dry-cleaning chits, mouldy chewing-gum, old cinema tickets and general debris were excavated from the depths of her handbag before she finally found the address.

She tried Directory Inquiries. No number was listed under R. Mason. Fee had a couple of hours between meetings, later in the afternoon, so would pay Rita a visit. First, Fee would see if she could recruit Claire's help.

These days, Fee and Claire seemed to avoid more topics than they discussed. To Fee, Claire appeared defensive; while, to Claire, Fee always sounded hyper-critical. Still, both women shared a common, if unspoken, belief that if the small rituals of friendship could be maintained, normal communication might eventually resume after Claire's wedding.

Fee gave Claire a ring at work. 'Will you come with me this afternoon, please Claire? Rita's got a flat in Stockwell – quite a large flat from the way she describes it . . . And a place in Sussex. But I thought I'd start with the flat first. I'm sure there's a really simple explanation, but I just sort of feel obligated to make sure she's all right . . . Will you come?'

Claire was about to refuse. She was already overloaded. For the last week or so, she had rarely left the office before ten – much to Clem's dislike. He didn't argue that she should have more free time for him – but, even more annoyingly, that she should have more free time for herself.

'Of course I'll come. I can't think of a better way to spend my afternoon than in pursuit of the world's oldest teenager—'

Claire drove, Fee gave instructions. Number 14, Ivesham Street, was a large Victorian house on a road of mixed fortunes. The garden next door was decorated with a discarded sign that read, 'The Goodfellows Friendly Society'. The sign kept company with beer cans, sweet papers, weeds, four dustbins and a broken pushchair.

Number 14's garden was altogether better maintained and had six bells, neatly labelled, on the right of the glossy, navy-blue door.

'Can I be of assistance, ladies?' A thin but athletic-looking man, perhaps in his sixties, was walking up the path to where Fee and Claire stood, trying to decipher the names alongside the bells. They had already established that none read 'Rita Mason'.

The man wore a panama hat, a check shirt, a striped tie, a yellow cardigan and beige trousers. In his hand, he carried a string shopping bag. He was neat and dapper and only slightly faded. It was his feet that caught Fee's eye. He was wearing cowboy boots. Real cowboy boots. They were tan with small cuban heels, a gently pointed toe and an intricate pattern tooled on each side.

'Ladies? Can I be of service?' His tone was tentative, as if, in the past, such courtesy might have been used to mock him.

'How do you do?' Fee replied. 'We're looking for a . . . friend . . . Rita Mason?' she has a flat here—'

'We've got no flats here,' the man replied, shaking his head. 'Only bedsits. I've been here almost two years and it's never been any different. Big bedsits mind, but bedsits nevertheless.'

He produced a packet of mints and unhurriedly offered the packet to each of the women. They waited for him to speak again. He was enjoying his unexpected audience.

'A bedsit does me fine,' he said eventually, as he began to search through his pockets. 'I go down to my daughter's in Broadstairs a lot, you see. She wants me to move down there. See more of my three grandchildren, all boys. Good boys, too. But I'm city born and bred. Drive me mad, just the sea and all those old people withering up.

'I've got my friends here. I try to explain to Sissy, that's my daughter, that I've got friends here, plenty to do. But she won't have it. She watches too much television so she imagines that anyone who's drawing a pension is bound to be mugged or lonely. But not me,' the man chuckled.

Fee believed him too. He spoke again. 'Three times a year, I go on safari. Well, I call it safari, but it can be anywhere. Travel where I please, sometimes on my own, sometimes with my friend, Jimmy . . . Jimmy Roth. He's on his own too.

'Sold the house when Alice died and told the kids – I've got two sons as well – that there wouldn't be any left for them, I was going to spend it all. Why not? they'll only take it off me to pay the nursing-home bills.

'Now, where's that blasted key? I keep putting it in a safe place and then forgetting—'

Claire took the man's string bag so that he could hunt more efficiently.

'Now, tell me ladies,' he asked jocularly as he searched, 'Are you private detectives, Social Security people, probation officers, debt collectors, Inland Revenue bods or a relation of the landlords? If you're any of that lot, you won't get a cup of tea out of me, never mind any information—'

'We're friends,' Claire replied firmly. 'We're friends of this person and we haven't seen her for a while. That's why we're concerned.'

The man gave her a quizzical look then appeared to make up his mind. When he finally found his key and let himself in, he beckoned for Claire and Fee to follow.

'By the way,' he added, raising his hat, 'the name is Walter Wilfred Whiting. W. W. Whiting professionally – Walt, to my friends . . . Follow me. And don't let the lino trip you up—'

Walt's room at the rear of the house was light and airy with a vast window overlooking a long stretch of lawn and a small garden pond. The room held a sofa, a rocking chair and a footstool. The bed was hidden by a large Indian rattan screen. On the floor were two Afghan rugs.

The kitchenette had a range of earthenware dishes, perhaps Mexican or Portuguese. Carved wooden statues were scattered at random. Piles of books overflowed from one wall of shelves. A second smaller bookcase carried nothing but Westerns with names that Fee had learned at the same time as her nursery rhymes – O. Henry, Bret Hart, Max Brand, Zane Grey.

Claire followed her gaze, 'Don't start on that,' she ordered in a whisper, as Walt filled a kettle with water. 'You Wild West lot are like the bloody Freemasons. And I've got to be back in the office in an hour—'

One wall was covered in photographs. Some appeared to be of family gatherings; others were of a much younger W. W. Whiting with faces that were faintly familiar.

'Are you surveying my acting career?' Walt asked. He was carrying a tin tray decorated with brightly coloured Chinese dragons. On it were mugs of tea and a plate of Jaffa cakes.

'Did you see *Brighton Rock* with Dickie Attenborough?' he asked, smiling. 'Well, that was another film I wasn't in.' He chuckled.

'Now,' he said, handing out the mugs of tea, 'let's solve your little mystery.'

Claire and Fee began to describe Rita Mason.

'She's dark, probably forty or so,' Fee said.

'More like early fifties,' Claire interrupted.

'And she's thin, very thin,' Fee continued.

'Anorexic to be precise,' Claire interjected and, in case Walt Whiting wasn't up to scratch on contemporary labels, she added, 'Like a skeleton, looks as if she doesn't eat enough—'

Fee frowned at Claire, then said, 'Rita dresses in a very . . . well, very . . . interesting, some might say distinctive style—'

'What she's trying to say is that she's mutton dressed as lamb,' Claire offered bluntly.

'And why do you want to find her?' Walt asked.

'I'm not sure really—' Fee began hesitantly. 'What I mean is, Rita, this woman, sort of involved herself in my life . . . and, well, it's a bit complicated really. Basically, she said she had a fiancé and friends and so on, but the impression she gave was that she was quite lonely. Almost as if she wanted to live my life for me—'

'The truth is', Claire bent forward towards Walt conspiratorially, 'the woman is slightly dotty and Fee – quite unnecessarily – feels responsible. They arranged to meet for a drink and Rita failed to turn up. Her prerogative if you ask me.' She helped herself to a Jaffa cake and took a bite before continuing.

'Rita was very kind to Fee's sister, so Fee has assumed that she is indebted for life. As a result, this woman has weaved herself into Fee's life. Now, wouldn't you think that she might be grateful that Rita's disappeared? Not a bit of it, Mr Whiting.' Claire was enjoying herself at Fee's expense.

'On the contrary. We've now spent hours trying to track this woman down. Does that make any sense to you, Mr Whiting? It certainly doesn't to me.'

'Call me Walt,' W. W. Whiting instructed and then rose with a dramatic flourish.

'Follow me,' he commanded.

The trio walked up two flights of stairs and stopped outside a door numbered 7. In the hall, damp had enforced its own pattern, conquering what was once the Regency stripe on the wallpaper. Walt Whiting knocked on the door. There was no answer. He knocked on the door opposite and it opened almost immediately.

'Hello there, Jimmy, lad,' Walt Whiting said. 'Meet some new friends, Claire and Fiona. Claire and Fiona, this is my oppo, Jimmy Roth. Go to lots of places together, don't we, Jimmy?'

Jimmy emerged from his room. He was six foot four and lanky. He had a sparse supply of grey hair, cut very short, parted on the side and greased back. He wore a white shirt and braces hung loose from his waist. On his feet were carpet slippers. When Jimmy smiled, a full set of white teeth clicked their heels to attention.

'Nice to meet you, ladies,' he said, giving a firm handshake. 'Is this man causing you any trouble?' he added, nodding his head towards Walt Whiting.

Walt smiled. 'We're after Rose—' he explained. 'Have you seen her recently? These two young ladies think she may have gone missing. They're a bit anxious—'

Rita Mason's bedsit was a fantasy in pink, best seen with the help of discreetly dimmed lighting at night. In the daylight, it looked shabby and second rate. The bed, against one wall, was covered by an ageing pink quilt eiderdown, barely visible under a mountain of fluffy toys. The nondescript hessian carpert had been covered by two shaggy pale-pink rugs. A pink and silver leather pouf had been placed on either side of the gas fire. Above the mantelpiece was a mirror surrounded by a do-it-yourself frame made of seashells painted over with pink nail varnish.

A small table had been covered in a pink and white gingham cloth which had also been used to disguise an armchair. A wardrobe had been stripped and repainted shocking pink, the chest of drawers was cream and had roses stencilled on it with varying degrees of success. Along one wall was a dress rail stuffed with clothes. An army of battered shoes was visible under the bed. At the window, concocted as curtains, was a confection of pink net like a ballroom dancer's skirt. Fee's jumper – the one she had searched for the night Shona appeared at her door – hung over the back of a chair.

Fee briefly took in the décor but her eyes were drawn to a framed photograph on the mantelpiece.

'Who's that?' she asked Jimmy Roth who had, after some persuasion, used the spare key that Rose/Rita had left in his care to let the four of them into the room.

'Rose said it was her fiancé, Roger,' Jimmy Roth replied. 'But you can never be quite sure with our Rosie. She's a lovely lady, mind,' he added quickly. 'But she does . . . well, elaborate a bit. Embroider now and then . . . What you might call a bit of a fantasist . . . Wouldn't hurt a fly, mind.'

Fee picked up the photograph of Rose/Rita's fiancé. She knew the face well. It belonged to Bill Summers – and last time Fee saw it, it had been in her album at home.

'Nice enough looking lad, isn't he?' Jimmy Roth commented.

'Though what he sees in Rose, God alone knows. She must be twice his age. No offence meant,' he added hastily.

'I wouldn't worry too much about our Rose. Last time I saw her she didn't mention she was going away but there's no law against it, is there?' He smiled.

'Tell you what,' Jimmy Roth suggested. 'I've got her mother's address somewhere . . . Cardiff way she is. In her eighties, but still going strong . . . Rose once asked me to forward her letters there when she was away for a couple of days. 'Cept, of course, she didn't get any letters . . . I'll dig out that address for you, if it helps—'

Fee nodded. 'Thank you. But I thought her mother was dead. She told my sister that her mother had died of cancer.'

Jimmy Roth gave a resigned look. 'Aah yes, that'll be our Rose, all right, won't it, Walt? Chances are, she'll turn up when you least expect it.'

Fee didn't say so – but that was exactly what concerned her most.

Driving back to work, Fee initially said nothing. She was too busy trying to make sense of Rita Mason's jackdaw acquisition of fragments of her life – her photographs, her clothes. Was it eccentricity or something more sinister?

Claire broke into her thoughts. 'If I were you, I'd report her to the police. People can't go round stealing other people's identity like that . . . there's bound to be a law against it. Does Bill know he's in the hands of a maniac?'

Fee was forced to smile at Claire's hyperbole. 'She hasn't stolen my identity,' she protested. 'You don't know Rita. She's quite childlike in a funny way. Perhaps it's just that she sees something she likes and decides to help herself. No harm done, as she would put it—' Fee added wryly.

'Oh, come off it,' Claire responded brusquely. 'She's either mad or bad or probably both. Didn't you say she had your keys? I take it you've had your locks changed?'

'She did have my keys and, no, I haven't changed the locks. I meant to, and then I just forgot. So much has been going on.'

'God,' Claire braked at the traffic lights fiercely, relishing the high drama. 'For all you know, she could be foraging around your flat every day when you're out at work. She could be wearing your clothes, fiddling with your things . . . doing who knows what—'

'Hardly,' Fee remarked mildly. 'My flat's so jammed with bodies, she'd have trouble raising her arms above her head without the co-operation of the guests, never mind fiddling—'

It was odd, Fee thought. She ought to feel deep unease, certainly anger. But now, instead, she was beginning to feel something . . . something almost protective towards this infuriating woman.

She wasn't mad or bad, just terribly lonely. And, of course, the worst kind of liar. One who believes her own untruths.

'I don't need to meet this woman to know that she is one very tricky lady,' Claire pronounced. 'Very tricky indeed. The only question you need to worry yourself about, Fee, is what exactly is she after?'

Chapter Twenty-Two

T HE THREE women sat on the sofa, marooned by depression: Shona, Veronica and Gill. Shona had avoided Fee for several days. It was Veronica who had met her on the stairs and invited her in for coffee. Since then, she had come to the flat regularly – usually when Fee was at work.

At the opposite end of the sofa, Veronica perched precariously. She had supervised the occupation of Fee's flat expertly and become more resilient by the hour. But now, Veronica appeared drained.

Gill filled the middle of the sofa generously. She had rapidly put on weight. Simon certainly wasn't showing any signs of repentance. On the contrary, he appeared to be relishing his new life as a man with the run of a large family house. Gill had assumed that he would crawl back. She was now facing the unthinkable: Simon might no longer need her.

Gill, Veronica, Shona . . . Fee surveyed the three women from her sitting-room door. It was seven thirty and she had just spent a twelve-hour day at the office. The concern about Rita had refused to go away. While Diana Woods had conducted herself in such an amiable fashion that Fee knew it probably meant bad news for her.

Now, all she wanted was peace and solitude, her home to herself. Her home to herself in sparkling good order. Everything in its place; no dirt marks on the walls, no footprints on the duvets, no toy display in the bath, no television around the clock, no obligation to listen to the woes of others, no children's feuds to resolve, no food to cook.

'What I want to do is to mainline on selfishness,' she decided. 'And no apologies to anyone.'

Instead, she was greeted by Veronica, Gill and Shona. 'Greeted' was hardly the appropriate word. The women barely acknowledged her presence, although Shona attempted a small smile.

Fee opened the kitchen door and, childishly, let it bang shut loudly behind her.

'Take a pew,' Percy directed precociously, pointing to a kitchen chair. 'I'll get you a glass of wine.'

On the table, Percy had placed three pizza bases and was busy concocting various toppings.

'Nobody out there wants to put these two to bed—' she said, indicating her two brothers sitting on the floor playing racing cars with saucepans.

'Is Veronica OK?' Fee asked cautiously.

'Les came here and they had a big row on the balcony,' Percy explained. 'It was the usual stuff. After that, Mum had a big row with Daddy on the phone. Then the lady from across the hall came in and they've been sitting on the sofa like that ever since. Mummy always used to tell me that sitting around doing nothing was no good for anybody,' she confided. 'Something must have made her change her mind.'

An hour later, all three children were in bed. Fee had asked the women if they would like something to eat but the response had been minimal. Now she sat in an armchair and poured coffee.

Idly, she picked up one of the *Get Going!* magazines from a pile she had brought home. And an idea began to form.

'It will be a pleasure,' Will Evans said a few minutes later on the phone when Fee asked if he would babysit at short notice. 'So long as I can bring my friend.'

He arrived shortly, hand in hand with Hannah Jaspan, his new live-in lover.

Introductions were made and Fee, alone for a moment with the woman in her hall, soon discovered that while she might look frail, she talked tough and was not overly friendly.

'You've known Will a long time, haven't you?' Hannah Jaspan remarked frostily. Fee nodded. 'Well,' she continued, 'my view is that men like Will require definite boundaries. If he breaks the rules, I'm off.'

Fee wondered who Hannah Jaspan was trying to convince.

Once Will and Hannah were occupied in the kitchen making themselves a drink, Fee told the three women that their time on the sofa was up.

'We're going out,' she announced. 'And we're going to have a very good time.'

Shona spoke first. 'I couldn't possibly do that. It will only upset Edward.'

'Edward doesn't have to know.' Fee turned to Veronica. 'What's your excuse?'

'Les wants me home,' Veronica offered.

'One night won't make a difference. Now what about you, Gill?'

'I've planned to stay in and be miserable,' Gill answered determinedly. 'I don't see any reason for amending that plan.'

'You planned to be miserable last night and the night before that,' Fee pointed out. 'Look, I want to go out. I want you three to come out with me. I want you to do me a favour and enjoy yourselves. Please,' she added as an afterthought.

Fifty minutes later, the four were finally ready to leave.

'Where are we going?' Gill asked, her depression receding as her desire to seize control of the evening's activities became stronger.

'I don't like pubs. And I don't want to see a film. It's too late for the theatre and I'm far too old for ten-pin bowling—'

'This will change your lives,' Fee told the three women, smiling.

At the time, she had meant it as a joke.

*

The pub was cavernous and mock-Victorian. The basement where the Get Going! open evening was being held was already packed. As the four women descended the stairs, Gill caught a glimpse through the glass doors of a heaving mass of people – and refused to go any further.

Veronica, until that point unaware of what lay ahead, stopped to read the poster on the wall which welcomed guests to 'The best night out for sophisticated singles in London (25–45 age group)'. She too promptly stopped dead. Shona dithered, taking a step down and then retreating, causing mayhem with the steady flow of traffic.

She turned to Fee, panic-stricken. 'I didn't know we were coming to one of *these* things,' she whimpered.

She made the evening sound like Sodom and Gomorrah's annual garden fête. 'If Teddy finds out he'll be furious . . . He keeps telling me that he's got a reputation to protect,' she stuttered.

Fee restrained the desire to say, 'What? As a wife-beater and a bastard?' Instead, she took Shona by the arm and pushed her gently down the stairs towards the door, in the hope that the other two women would follow.

'Look, girls,' she cajoled, 'treat this as entirely a professional exercise. If it makes you feel better, tell yourselves that you're here on a different footing from everybody else—'

'You're here to do me a favour,' she continued. 'You're here to help me in my work. On that basis, where's the harm?'

Gill's substantial frame quivered, partly in disgust and partly because she was being jostled by each unattached Tom, Dick and Harry pushing past her in their haste to begin the hunt.

'God, Fee,' she said, pressing herself against the wall to avoid further buffeting, 'do you have any idea how humiliating this is for a grown woman like me? I have never felt so ashamed. So *exposed* in all my life. It's all far too degrading.

'Anyway I've no right to be here. I've got a man, thank you very much—'

'You have?' Veronica asked sceptically.

'All right,' Gill conceded. 'I've got a man who's been temporarily suspended from my life. But even if I hadn't, I wouldn't dream of visiting this unappetizing meat market—'

A woman, eyes and hair shining, wearing a simple floral dress and a big badge bearing the words, 'My name is Ellen', overheard Gill's last remark.

She turned and with missionary zeal put her hand on Gill's arm and smiled at her understandingly.

'I remember my first time too,' she said. 'It's nasty, isn't it? But I promise you, you'll walk into that room and suddenly the world is full of friends. Full of fun. Full of reasons to live. Trust in the power of the heart. We weren't meant to be solitary human beings.'

She gave another smile and waved goodbye. She was replaced on the stairs by a man in his late twenties. He wore a thick gold chain around his neck, a cheap blue suit and had the swagger of a man who survives on cheek. As he attempted to squeeze past the small group of women on the stairs, he took his time grazing Gill's body.

'The name's Steve. Going in are you, babe?' he asked her casually, ignoring the others. Gill blushed.

The door to the room down below swung open again and released a fresh swell of noise.

'Gill, I think—' Fee interrupted, assuming she would regard this as the final insult. Instead, Fee watched with surprise as Gill followed the unknown Steve down the stairs into the room as if he was the Pied Piper of Hamelin. Veronica and Shona fell in behind.

A little bit of flannel had worked as effectively as Velcro. Gill was stuck on Steve.

Three dances later, a flushed but exuberant Gill found Fee, Shona and Veronica sharing a table at the rear of the room. Veronica had cheered up considerably since – in spite of being technically too old for inclusion in GG!'s sophisticated singles age group – she had twice been asked to dance.

Shona was still fidgeting nervously. Fee was hating every minute. A singles night out, she had decided, was a wake for the death of subtlety. Those sitting alone looked deeply uncomfortable; others in groups could have been in any pub, anywhere. But still, what they all wanted and didn't have was another human being. It was all far too obvious for Fee's taste.

'We've exchanged numbers,' Gill grinned, more cheerful than she'd felt in weeks. 'Steve says he prefers to circulate at these dos, but he's promised to give me a call. Between you and me, I've got him begging for more.' She smiled coyly. The expression didn't look at all right on Gill. It reminded Fee of Rita.

'I'm sorry to have to say this, Gill,' Shona's tone was reproachful, 'but wouldn't your husband be upset if he knew?'

'I sincerely hope so,' Gill replied curtly. 'And what's more—'

'Excuse me,' a female voice interrupted Gill, 'would you mind if we joined you? Every other table is full—'

The woman had grey hair cut in a short bob. She wore no make-up but her features drew the eye; high cheekbones, full lips, bright-blue eyes. She wore a loose lavender trouser suit and a silver necklace. Gill, who always measured herself against all newcomers, mentally calculated her dress size as 14.

'This isn't really my sort of thing.' The woman smiled again. 'I wouldn't be here if it wasn't for my daughter, Chrissy.' She nodded at the much younger woman by her side.

'Chrissy told me it would do me good to go out for the night. But she didn't say she was bringing me here—'

'Glad we're not the only ones who've been duped,' Veronica smiled as she made room so that the two women could pull up chairs.

Chrissy was in her early twenties and attractive. She had blonde hair, the same high cheekbones as her mother and she wore a short terracotta-coloured linen shift with no jewellery.

Chrissy spoke up in her mother's defence. 'I think it's disgusting that all these events stop dead once you're forty-five. Mum's fifty-one, you don't mind me saying so, do you? And it's as if she's not expected to have a life ... I phoned around a few weeks ago and not one of the introduction agencies and dating places would take her on, not unless she lied about her age. I mean, fifty-one is hardly the end of the line, is it?'

The older woman, who had introduced herself as Jean Stoker, smiled and shrugged, half-embarrassed by her daughter's passion. Veronica extended her hand as an introduction.

'Hello, I'm Veronica Haslem. We're the same age,' she smiled. 'Tell me, Jean, how has fifty-one been for you?'

An hour later, the women were still talking, oblivious to the pounding pursuit for the mythical perfect partner that continued around them. Jean Stoker explained with their prompting, that she'd been a widow for thirteen months. She had married Trevor when she was twenty-five. He was seven years older and already had two small children, Tim, aged five, and Kate, two. His first wife had died of breast cancer. Chrissy, now twenty-three and a medical student in London, had been born three years after Jean's and Trevor's wedding.

'I miss Trevor terribly. We were a good team.' Jean Stoker gave a fragile smile. She explained that she had been a nurse when they met but she had given up work to look after Trevor's children, now themselves married.

'Did you like them?' Gill asked. She was curious to know what it must be like to have to care for the offspring of others, since she felt so ambivalent about her own.

'Tim and Kate?' Jean smiled. 'Oh yes. They were so young when I came on the scene, they've always called me Mum. I really did see them as an extra blessing. And Trevor idolized them ... he idolized all three of you. Didn't he, Chrissy? That's what he was planning to do—' Her words faded away. Chrissy gave her mother's hand an encouraging squeeze.

Jean Stoker, composed again, continued, 'Trevor was going to retire at sixty. He always said that he would make up for all the time he'd been away from home.

'It's not fair, is it?' Her voice fractured a little. Then she forced a smile. 'But what about this lot?' She changed the subject purposefully, indicating the rest of the room.

'I told Chrissy that as I've already had one husband, it seems only fair to stay at home and let someone else have a turn. But she wouldn't be swayed—'

'I just think it's time you had a bit of fun again,' her daughter coaxed.

'Have you ever considered an escort agency?' The suggestion, to Fee's surprise, came from Veronica.

'God, how can you be so tacky?' Gill remonstrated.

'Whatever gave you that idea?' Fee asked.

'I was just trying to be constructive,' Veronica answered matter-of-factly. 'If Jean wants a male companion but nothing serious, if the introduction agencies and what-have-you have decided she's past it, then the obvious step is do-it-yourself. Hire a suitable man for the evening. She pays for the privilege of choice. Men have done it for decades so what's wrong in that?'

'It's prostitution,' Gill protested. 'Nothing but prostitution.'

Veronica was unperturbed. 'Of course it isn't. I'm talking about company not copulation. Why not give it a go, Jean? If you need someone to hold your hand, I'll volunteer.'

Chrissy looked at her mother with alarm. Jean returned Veronica's smile warmly, flattered that she might be considered that adventurous. 'Thanks for the offer. But I don't think it's quite my cup of tea.'

'Pity,' remarked Veronica. She had begun to look forward to a little vicarious pleasure.

'It's yellow!!!! And it's number sixty-eight!!!!'

It was midnight. Fee had been cornered earlier on her way to

261

the loo and bought five raffle tickets. Now they were being drawn out of a hat.

'We have a romantic weekend in a two-bedroom thatched cottage—' the master of ceremonies, a fellow lonely-heart, roared into the microphone.

'I said ROMANTIC, did I not? In Devon. Who is going to be the lucky man or woman? What we need is a little snapette taken by our official photographer here for GG!'s very own magazine . . . plus a few words from the lucky, lucky person—'

'Now, who has that yellow SIXTY-EIGHT . . .?' People peered at each other in the gloom. Shona glanced down at the tickets which Fee had neatly placed in a line on the table, between the wine glasses.

'Fee,' she shrieked. 'It's you . . . You're sixty-eight . . . go on, go on, quick, quick—'

Two minutes later Fee was accepting a large gold-embossed envelope. A microphone was thrust into her face.

'Who's the lucky man to be then?' the organizer slurped. 'Where is that lucky chappie?'

Fee paused for only a fraction of a second, then she gave a wide smile. 'They are the lucky chappies,' she waved in the direction of her table. Veronica, Gill, Shona, Amy and Jean all waved back.

'*Women?* A bunch of women, oh no, no, no,' the organizer began to tut. His lips were so close to the microphone, the sound resonated like machine-gun fire *Tut . . . tut . . . tut . . . tut . . .*

'That's not allowed—' he went on peevishly.

'Oh yes it is,' Fee declared, her six-guns twirling.

Later, as the group of women made moves to leave, Shona was the first to broach the subject of the weekend.

She began hesitantly. 'Were you being serious about going away, Fee? Only Teddy's funny about that sort of thing. I'm afraid I'd have to say no—'

'And Les would go absolutely potty,' Veronica announced cheerfully.

Jean Stoker spoke up. 'Well, I'd love to come. If, that is, I'm invited, Fee? I'd be happy to take care of the food—'

'And she's very good at it too,' her daughter chipped in. It was more than Gill Booth could bear. Years of forfeiting a career to stay at home had done nothing if it hadn't transformed her into an excellent caterer. How dare anyone usurp that position? Besides, it would teach Simon a lesson. He wasn't the only one who could indulge himself.

'No, no, *I'll* do the food,' Gill interrupted, intoxicated both by her encounter with Steve and several large glasses of wine. 'And I'll organize the booze. I'll put it all on Simon's account. That should wake him up to the true bloody cost of philandering.'

Veronica gave a broad smile. She liked the company of these women. 'Well, in that case, I'll tell Les that one weekend away is neither here nor there. So that makes five—'

Everyone turned to look at Shona. 'Look, I'm sorry, I just can't—' she stammered. 'Teddy prefers that I'm around—'

'Is he that much of an ogre that he'd begrudge you a little time off?' Jean Stoker asked innocently. Shona avoided Fee's eye.

'I'm sorry,' she repeated, looking miserable. 'I really wish I could. But I can't.'

Chapter Twenty-Three

'NEVER HEARD of her,' said the woman in the radiography department of Tendon Hospital the following morning. 'Never had a Rita in the department. I told a woman the same thing the other day on the phone. That wasn't you, was it?' she asked Fee crossly.

'How about someone called Rose Sutton?' Fee pressed the woman further.

'Have you tried Personnel?' she suggested. 'They're sure to know who she is and where she works. Personnel is in West Wing, second floor.'

Walking to the lift, Fee remembered the woman on the till in the hospital cafeteria. Veronica had said that she had appeared to know Rita well. She probably wouldn't be on duty now, but it was worth a try. Particularly if it meant shortcutting the bureaucracy that otherwise lay ahead.

'Black hair, you say?' the woman repeated parrot fashion, in a pause between customers. The breakfast rush had passed.

'Youngish clothes? About forty-plus? Oh, I know who you mean. Forty-plus quite a lot.' The woman laughed.

'You're after Rosie, aren't you?'

Fee nodded, relieved.

The cashier became friendlier. 'I'll tell you who'll know where she is – the long-stay care unit, LSCU. Ask them in there about Rose.'

'What's a radiographer doing in LSCU?' Fee asked puzzled.

'Radiographer?' The woman chortled as she collected money from a customer for coffee and a doughnut which was staining a paper plate with transfusion-red jam.

'Radiographer? Our Rose? Not likely. She's been a cleaner here for . . . must be six or seven years. Friend of yours, is she?' the woman asked.

'No,' Fee answered so quickly that she immediately felt ashamed. 'Not, not at all . . . We've just crossed paths now and then.'

'Rose Sutton?' the sister in charge of the Long Stay Care Unit was busy but, as soon as Fee mentioned the name, she stopped checking through medical notes to give Fee her full attention.

'I like Rose,' she declared as if she expected someone to challenge her view. 'She's a good soul. The last time she was in here was about a week ago. We tried to get her on the telephone beforehand but none of us had her number. And, to be honest, officially she had no connection with him at all—'

'Him?' Fee asked.

'Peter . . . Peter Rutter,' the sister replied. 'He'd been in here in a coma for eleven months. Only twenty-seven. We couldn't trace any family. Rose came in to clean and sort of adopted him . . . she visited every single day . . . None of us knew anything about him, so she created a world for him. Brought in photos, pictures, flowers. Chatted endlessly. Sort of took him over, I suppose.

'He died at three thirty on Monday morning. It wasn't expected. Rose came in as usual a few hours later and Peter was gone . . . She didn't say a word, just turned around and left. We haven't seen her since. I called her supervisor and she said Rose hadn't turned up for her shift . . . You say she's not been home either?' The concern was genuine. 'Well, from what I can gather, she's got a lot on her plate—'

'A lot on her plate?' Fee prompted.

'She told me that she was looking after her sister's three children while their mum was recovering from breast cancer. If you're a friend, you'll probably know who I mean . . . funny names . . .?'

Fee didn't even have to think. 'Persephone, Euan and Ivo?' she suggested.

'That's them,' the sister smiled. 'From what I can gather, without our Rose, they'd be in a real mess.'

As Fee made to leave, the sister opened a drawer and handed her a large brown envelope.

'If you see Rose, can you give her these? She brought them in to brighten up Peter's room—'

In the lift going down to the ground floor, Fee opened the envelope. Snapshots of her own life slipped through her fingers.

On her way out of the hospital, Fee stopped at a phone box and called Alan Munsen.

His voice was warm and friendly and uncomplicated, no hidden messages, no sense of obligation, no hint of desperation. It was a relief to hear from another human being who was single but apparently uninfected by loneliness.

'I wondered if you might like to come to a family supper this evening?' Fee asked.

'I thought you said you didn't have a family?' Alan Munsen replied. 'Or am I confusing you with Annie from Saffron Walden who I met on Monday? As I recall, she has four children, two ex-husbands, and wants sexual excitement on a Wednesday night when the children are scattered with their fathers—'

Fee laughed. 'It's not my family,' she explained. 'It's one I seem to have acquired. How are you at handling several women and three children?'

'At my best,' Alan Munsen promised. 'What time and where?'

Fee replaced the receiver. Driving back to the office, she was surprised to hear herself humming.

*

The mood did not last. Diana Woods appeared in Fee's office as she was putting down the phone to Percy.

'Hope I'm not interrupting anything, am I?' she asked and smiled warmly.

'Your private life seems so . . . well, so chaotic these days, Fee, I don't know how you manage.' It didn't sound like a compliment.

'I popped by because I wanted you to be the first to know,' she added, her voice high on triumph. 'I've been made a director. I've got a seat on the board. I know you'll be pleased for me,' she added.

'The first thing I said to Gerry was, "Of course, I won't allow this to change a thing between Fee and I. I want her to know that she continues to have a free hand on HAH!"'

She turned and left before Fee could offer her congratulations. For this small mercy, Fee was grateful.

An hour later, Paul Denning called. He wasn't using his business voice. 'I'm in London, can we meet?'

Fee recalled the envelope she had picked up outside his hotel room a few weeks ago.

'Why don't you come to supper at my place?' Fee suggested. 'Come tonight. About seven thirty?'

'You won't regret it,' Paul Denning said.

At 7.30 p.m. precisely, the front doorbell rang. Fee's flat was superficially in good working order – toys shoved under beds and behind chairs, the lights dimmed, a table beautifully laid by Gill, who saw it as a chance to show Fee how it should be done properly.

Fee arrived home from work at seven and discovered there was little for her to do, except put the wine she'd brought in the fridge. The soup had been made, the chicken breasts were in the oven and the lemon soufflé was in the fridge.

So, by 7.30 p.m., she was fully prepared when she went downstairs to open the door to Paul Denning.

Fee smiled as he carefully put the flowers and champagne and casual jacket he had been carrying on the stairs. Then he took her in his arms and kissed her lips, her eyelids, the end of her nose. He ran his fingers through her hair and told her how much he had missed her. She too had missed the smell and the strength of him – and some of his weaknesses – but she said nothing.

The two walked up the stairs in silence. Paul kissed her again in the hall outside her door. Fee led him into her flat and into the sitting room. The French windows on to the balcony were open, the candles on the table had been lit, a decanter of red wine had been set in the centre.

Around the table, dressed in their best, sat Persephone, Shona, Gill, Veronica, Jean Stoker – invited by Veronica at the last minute – and Alan Munsen.

'Now,' said Fee, smiling at Paul, 'where shall I begin the introductions?'

'Since you ask,' Alan Munsen said to Fee a couple of hours later as they stacked the dishwasher, 'I think he's a bit of a spiv.'

Fee had found it revealing to have the two men at the same table. Alan had encouraged others to open up; he had teased Percy until she was delirious. Gill had even opened up to Alan in whispered asides about Simon's affair, referring to it, in front of her daughter as, 'Daddy's little hiccup'. Paul Denning, in contrast, had sulked. His interest in anyone else was minimal.

'Percy tells me that Paul was once a boyfriend of yours, is that right?' Alan asked Fee casually as he tipped the dregs of the cafetière down the sink. Before she could reply, he added, 'It's happened to me in the past too. I've been quite keen on someone, only to meet them later and realize what a fool I'd made of myself—'

At eleven, Fee slipped out of her flat as arranged. Paul had left earlier. She'd invented a story about a report at the office that she'd forgotten. Half an hour later, she was standing naked in Paul's hotel room. She undressed him and led him to the bed. The emotional distance that she now experienced in his company freed the inhibitions that she had previously been too fearful to let go. Paradoxically, because she no longer cared, she could be as demonstrative as she pleased.

Soon after, while Paul slept, Fee showered and dressed. He woke as she kissed him goodbye.

'Don't go,' he said. 'I've got something I have to tell you—'

Fee smiled and sat on the edge of the bed. 'Is it about your wife?' she asked carefully.

His features registered no surprise. 'What wife?' he replied evenly.

'Aah, so you've got more than one,' Fee gently mocked.

She reached into her handbag and gave him the envelope that she had found in the corridor outside his room. It was addressed to Mr and Mrs P. J. Denning.

Paul laughed and shrugged his shoulders. 'Silly girl,' he chided. 'It's a letter addressed to my parents. You should know better.'

'I do,' Fee replied.

'She's a cow. She's an absolute unadulterated bloody cow.'

As Fee let herself in her front door, the weeping and wailing floating down the stairs made it sound as if a Lebanese funeral was taking place. She walked into the sitting room. Alan Munsen was comforting Gill, who was sobbing uncontrollably on his shoulder.

He jumped up, relieved, when he saw Fee. Veronica beckoned her into the kitchen. She explained in a whisper, 'Imogen phoned to make arrangements to pick you up tomorrow. Isn't she buying you an outfit or something? Anyway, Gill answered the phone.'

'And?' Fee prompted her sister.

'And, Imogen offered Gill her condolences.'

'Why, who's died?' Fee asked alarmed.

'Nobody's died,' Veronica explained. 'It's Simon. He's been made redundant. Three weeks ago. And he never told Gill. Of course, she pretended she knew to Imogen, but once she came off the phone, she fell to pieces. I've never seen her like that before. She's quietening down a bit now . . . go and see if you can cheer her up—'

As Fee walked back into the sitting room, Gill's distress had become a touch theatrical. 'I've been mugged by destiny,' she sobbed. 'All my plans are in ruins. Why couldn't he tell me the mortgage hasn't been paid for a month?' She turned to Fee.

'Now I'll end up like you, just drifting through life. Why didn't I choose a man who can get a grip on a situation?'

'Perhaps because you wanted a man you could boss?' Alan suggested gently. Fee had to admire his guts. Gill gave him a withering look.

'We'll have to sell the house,' she announced. 'I'll get a job and Simon will have to be the house husband. I knew it would come to this. I said all along that I could earn twice his money—'

'Why don't you talk it over with Simon first?' Fee proposed. 'He might have ideas of his own? I mean, if you're going to get back together, it's his future too, isn't it?'

'Look,' Gill replied. The crying had made her eyes look like the ripe flesh of pomegranates. 'I've learned from experience that I tend to be right about these things and Simon isn't—'

'Yes, but how high a price will you pay for that certainty?' Alan asked. Gill glanced at him, uncomprehending.

He shrugged his shoulders deprecatingly. 'Of course, I'm not really in a position to speak, since I've never managed to sustain a long relationship, but—'

'Precisely,' Gill interrupted coldly.

Later, Fee walked with Alan Munsen to his car, relaxed in his company.

'Percy told me something in strictest confidence tonight,' Alan smiled. 'She told me, and I quote, "Will fancies Fee something rotten."'

Fee snorted. 'Nonsense. We've known each other for ever. Will's girlfriends are nothing like me. You should meet Hannah. She couldn't be more different. For a start she's a damn sight tougher.'

'Talking of tough,' Alan smiled wryly, 'how long have you and Gill been friends?'

'Long enough to put up with her being a bit over the top every now and then. She's been good to me in the past, very good,' Fee answered firmly.

'Well, there's nothing wrong with her that a little humility wouldn't put right,' Alan Munsen remarked lightly. 'And what about this Imogen Banks?'

Fee laughed. 'A little humility wouldn't even begin to make a dent on Imogen. She runs a television company. I suspect she more or less tricked me into taking part in a film she's making. Now, I can't go back on the promise but something tells me the whole exercise is something I'll live to regret.'

'The whole exercise in what?' Alan asked, curious now.

'Singling myself out in a way my mother isn't going to appreciate at all,' Fee sighed.

The battle in the hairdresser's had been long and fierce. Imogen Banks wanted Fee to have a style that was shorter, highlighted and, as she phrased it, 'more chiselled'. Fee emerged more or less as she went in – except for the extra sheen.

In the area of clothes, Fee conceded more.

'Red,' Imogen instructed the assistant in one of those shops which has an interior that resembles a ship's boiler room, re-created at great cost: pipes, nuts, chrome and steel. 'We're thinking lots of red.'

After several different outfits had been tried and discarded, Imogen announced that we were no longer thinking red, we might now be thinking cream.

'But I wear cream and black all the time anyway,' Fee pointed out. 'Why do I need to buy anything new?'

Imogen had already moved on. She was contemplating warm tangerine.

Warm tangerine proved surprisingly striking. Fee agreed to the colour but rejected the gold-chain belt and the scarf with the Chanel logo embellished all over it.

'That scarf says such a lot,' Imogen argued.

'On the contrary,' Fee countered. 'It says yesterday's shopper.'

'Oh I like that.' Imogen gave a happy smile. 'We'll have that in the film, darling. You won't forget now, will you? Write it down, just in case you do. "Yesterday's shopper"—'

Driving Imogen back to the office, Fee's car phone rang. It was Claire.

'I wondered if you fancied dropping by this evening?' Claire asked. 'Perhaps stay for something to eat?'

'But it's Saturday,' Fee pointed out.

'I know it's Saturday,' Claire replied curtly. 'Are you telling me that you're already booked?'

'Of course not,' Fee smiled. 'I assumed that it would be you who had something on. Or has Clem taken the ten-year-olds in his class off for a week in the Dolomites?'

'No, he hasn't,' Claire replied. Fee knew she was being defensive. 'He's got a few things to sort out—'

'But I thought he had moved in with you?' Fee asked.

'He has, he did,' Claire struggled. 'What I mean is, he's gone back home, just for now . . . until we can find somewhere that's big enough for both of us—'

'But your place is huge,' Fee persisted. Privately, this erratic behaviour on Clem's part confirmed her view that there was something inherently unstable about him.

'Look, Fee,' Claire replied. 'It was my idea that Clem move out. I'm not used to having someone around all the time . . . It'll be fine when we find somewhere that is new to both of us. I'm sure then I

272

won't feel so . . . so . . . well, possessive . . . as if he's playing with my toys all the time—'

'It takes time to adjust—' Fee offered sympathetically.

Her hopes were suddenly high: goodbye, Clem.

'A friend?' Imogen asked when the conversation had come to an end. Fee was to call by Claire's flat later for supper.

'A really old friend,' Fee replied and added deceptively casually, 'How about you, Imogen, have you got many women friends?'

Imogen opened and closed her mouth. The fish was landed, why lie any further?

'Well, to be honest . . .' She took a deep breath, 'I can't stand women. In my view, they allow themselves to be walked over too much. They whinge and whine.'

She picked up pace. 'Instead of changing themselves, too many sit on their backsides and do nothing, while they wait for society to change. They want the rules redrawn, special dispensations, extra help, soft options, the works—'

She was now elated by her own argument.

'I mean at what point do women begin to take responsibility for themselves, instead of banging on about the lack of choices each time the going gets tough? Why don't they assume power in situations, instead of wating for it to be handed to them? I mean, when are they going to live in the real world? It ain't easy for men out there, either, honey—' she added with a flourish.

'Take your friend Gill. She wants Simon to be the traditional breadwinner. She wants him to make her financially secure for life. At the same time, she's constantly whining on about how her talents are wasted just being a wife and a mother . . . She chose to put herself in that situation, for God's sake. She can choose to get herself out of it, can't she? Talk about having your cake and eating it—'

Fee interrupted, 'Imogen . . . But for women like Gill and me—

and you come to that – in our thirties and forties, we're part of a transition, aren't we?

'Percy says she wants some security in her life so she's never getting married . . . When I wasn't much older than her, my mother drummed it into me that a marriage certificate was the best kind of security a girl could have—

'It's a long way to travel in one lifetime—' Fee continued. 'So no wonder some of us hold back when we should move forward. Don't tell me there are moments when you're just as confused and weak as the rest of us, Imogen?'

Imogen thought it best to leave the question unanswered.

Chapter Twenty-Four

Les Haslem was sitting cross-legged on the pavement outside Fee Travers's flat when she arrived home that evening. Alan, Gill, the twins and Percy swirled around him. They were loading Gill's car. Fee experienced a sense of relief at the unexpected sight of the brood decamping. Once more, she would be queen of her own castle. But unexpectedly, a mild depression accompanied the relief.

'Les, why are you sitting on the pavement?' Fee asked, trying not to smile at the bizarre figure her brother-in-law cut. 'Why don't you come in and have a drink?'

'What have you done with my wife?' Les boomed.

'Veronica? I thought she was in the flat?'

Les glowered with rage. 'Don't you pretend you know nothing about it, Fiona Travers. Veronica's told me she met some woman at a party that you took her to. Now she's cleared off, probably with her. AND IT'S ALL YOUR FAULT.'

'I'm sorry, Les, I haven't a clue, I—' He was having none of it.

'Don't you bloody patronize me,' he roared. 'We were doing all right until you stuck your nose in. The golf had done wonders for her . . . then you had to turn Veronica into a skivvy. And now God knows what she's up to—'

'I—'

'I nothing,' Les bellowed. 'If my Veronica has become a lesbian, I'll sue you. Do you hear me? I'll bloody sue you for every penny you've got—'

Litigation over your wife's libido was an interesting idea, Fee thought. What if, after all these years, the inheritor of Vera's mantle turned out to be, not herself, as Helen had always feared, but Veronica, the daughter whom Helen assumed could do no wrong? Fee suppressed a smile at the irony.

'This isn't a laughing matter,' Les protested fiercely and winced as Gill clipped him on the head with the wheel of the child's bike she was carrying.

'I'm sorry, I wasn't smiling at you, really I wasn't.' Fee attempted to make amends. 'Look, Les, you'd be much more comfortable inside . . . If you come with me, I'll phone around. Someone is sure to know where Veronica is . . . Perhaps we could even see this as a good sign?' she suggested hesitantly.

'Good sign? How the bloody hell can this be a good sign?' Les yelled, staying put.

'What I mean is—' Fee stepped out of Alan Munsen's way as he walked past, carrying two suitcases. Then she crouched down and said softly, 'What I was trying to say, Les, was that Veronica is so full of life these days she doesn't have time to worry about the other . . . the other business . . . So that's a good thing, isn't it?'

'Not if she turns into a dike and deserts me,' Les pronounced grimly. 'A man has a right to save his wife from the worst side of herself . . . I'm here to protest. It's the only way any bugger in this family will take notice.'

Percy had stopped to listen to Les. 'If you're protesting,' she asked politely, 'does that mean you're going to set yourself alight?'

Half an hour later, Fee handed Les Haslem a whisky. It was Alan Munsen who had eventually persuaded him to end his one-man demonstration. He had put his arms around the man's shoulders and said, 'C'mon, mate, I know how you feel—'

That was all it had taken. Les had shed a couple of tears. Now, he was opening a bottle of wine for Gill who was sitting on the sofa, easing off her shoes.

'Just one glass,' she instructed. 'Then we're off. Sorry it's happened so suddenly, Fee, but I thought I'd strike while the iron was hot—'

'Mummy says Daddy's ready to eat humble pie,' Percy offered by way of explanation.

'Percy, why don't you take the twins and check under all the beds? We're bound to have left something,' Gill instructed.

'But I want to stay and listen—' Percy began, but she reluctantly moved towards the bedroom, propelled by the look on her mother's face.

Gill waited for the door to close behind her daughter before she continued, 'Simon has suggested that we give it another try. I laid down my conditions, he accepted, so off we go again. And Fee,' Gill looked uncomfortable, 'Fee, I want to say thank you. You've been wonderful to the children. And I know I've been a bit of a pig at times . . . So thank you.' She gave herself a small shake, as if to shed this unfamiliar sense of indebtedness.

'The first plan is to sell our house, and rent somewhere smaller. Can you believe that, all these years, Simon's never actually liked the house?' she added incredulously.

'Did you ever ask him if he liked it?' Fee questioned mildly.

'He's got a voice, hasn't he?' Gill snapped. Alan, carrying in a tray of glasses, raised an eyebrow.

'Look here, does anybody know where my wife is?' Les broke in plaintively. 'Will somebody tell me what's happened to the woman I married?'

'Oh, do pull yourself together, Les,' Gill responded impatiently. 'You're certainly not the first. Every bloody person I know asks that sooner or later . . . What's happened to the woman I married? Or, in my case, the man. To be frank, that's not the question that matters. The real issue is how you're going to cope with the partner you've got, however bloody monstrous.'

Fee patted Les on the arm.

'Look,' she offered, 'I'll give Jean Stoker a ring. She'll probably know where Veronica is. She and Veronica seemed to have taken to each other—' Les shot Fee an even more pained look.

'What I mean is, they have a lot in common,' Fee corrected hastily. 'And Jean is a really nice woman.'

A new thought added itself to Les's woes. 'Can you imagine what the *News of the World* is going to make of all this?' he wailed.

'Mr Sandwich discovers his wife prefers a different kind of filling—'

Alan Munsen tried and failed to stop himself chuckling. Les turned on Fee accusingly.

'You've helped to turn me into a laughing-stock, that's what you've done.' He was now more resigned than riled. 'And all I tried to do was make things better.'

Chapter Twenty-Five

JEAN STOKER had a secret. It was one that she never could have anticipated. And she was determined that, unless the situation became utterly impossible, she would not divulge it to Chrissy, Kate or Tim. It was a matter of pride.

The children had grown up in comfort. The five bedroom house in a village near Rye had an acre of garden, a river and a small orchard. Trevor Stoker – as husband and father – had looked after them well. He was a generous man and Jean had never had to bother herself about money or bills. They were his concern, Trevor used to say. It wasn't that Jean couldn't have taken charge of the money – she had earned her own living since the age of eighteen – it was that both she and Trevor could see no need.

Then, he had died.

Trevor Stoker had built up his industrial cleaning company slowly over the years. He employed a reliable accountant, told his wife frequently that the company's order books were full and, just before his death from a heart attack, announced that he intended to retire within three years. So Jean had assumed that business was good. Not long after Trevor's cremation, she had learned the truth.

It was a spring morning. The windows were wide open. Hetty and Victor, the two labradors, were asleep in the garden. Jean was alone. She had persuaded Kitty, Tim and Chrissy to resume their normal lives. Jean sat with her coffee on the table by the kitchen door, where Trevor had always liked to sit, and opened the several letters that had been delivered that morning. Three were bank statements. All were overdrawn – the most damaging by £17,000, on which the bank was charging 22.5 per cent interest.

'I think there's been some mistake,' she said politely to the person who answered her call. She had asked to be put through to the bank manager. That in itself showed how long it had been since she'd bothered with the financial side of life.

'Bank manager? Sorry, madam, I can give you your personal customer services guide but we don't really have managers any more—'

Ten minutes later an anonymous female voice which sounded as if it belonged to a twelve-year-old, made the situation plain.

'What I'd advise,' the young woman directed bossily, 'what I'd advise is to have a word with Mr Stoker's company accountant. Perhaps he can sort it out? Thank you for calling. Have a nice day.'

It didn't take long for Jean to discover what had happened. If only she'd asked earlier, when Trevor was alive. Four of her husband's main customers had recently reneged on their payments. At the same time, the company had landed a major contract, cleaning a series of European agricultural shows. Trevor had taken out a large business loan to update equipment. Just before his death, the new contract had been cancelled without warning.

As soon as the rubble that was her husband's financial 'security' became apparent, Jean's need to grieve was forced to take second place to survival. Not her personal financial survival – but the survival of the memory of Trevor as a man who had worked hard to do well by his family.

Six weeks after he was cremated, Trevor Stoker's company was sold for what the accountant said was a good price, 'considering'. The major debts were cleared; decent amounts were given to each child, as Trevor had specified in his will, but unbeknown to his wife at the time, he had remortgaged the house. The accountant explained that if Jean sold it and moved into a smaller place, say a two-bedroom flat, she might salvage a small annual income of around £8,000.

If she remained in the house, which was far too large for Jean – but which worked beautifully when all the family were gathered together – the gap between outgoings and income would remain a growing black hole. 'You could end up with nothing,' the accountant had pointed out bluntly.

The children believed that their father had left Jean a comfortable income and a secure home. Her ambition was to keep the house for a few years at least. Trevor had loved it and, for now, she wanted to be close to the source of so many memories.

She tried to find a reasonably paid job. Her efforts proved fruitless and demoralizing. She was highly skilled in all manner of areas; she had the benefit of a happy marriage; she had successfully managed one of the more challenging tasks, step-parenting; she had run numerous voluntary organizations; she also had several years of nursing experience, albeit a few decades ago, but none of this appeared to add up to much in today's modern, flexible job market.

Jean Stoker had also committed that most unforgivable of sins. She had grown older. Age might have implied maturity, understanding, a proven track record in certain aspects of life – instead, potential employers equated it only with a spent force.

She realized that not only were the chances of a new and challenging career slight, but she also found herself socially ostracized. Friends still invited her for morning cups of coffee but invitations to supper became rarer and rarer.

She knew her self-confidence was seeping away. Her financial and emotional insecurity was gradually becoming indivisible: she had little and was worth little.

Then Jean had met Veronica.

'This may change our lives, you do know that, don't you?' she had said on the third occasion they met.

'I hope so,' Veronica had replied simply, squeezing her hand.

Veronica had not intended to leave home without telling Les where she would be. It had just happened that Gill had announced she was moving back in with Simon and Alan Munsen was on hand at Fee's to help. So Veronica took the opportunity to drive down to Jean's to give her some moral support, on this the most crucial of evenings.

Then she'd been so busy planning with Jean, Veronica admitted later, that 'Les just slipped my mind'. 'Slipped my mind' was a phrase that Veronica said over and over again to herself, just for the sheer pleasure of the words. For the first time in a very long period, Veronica's head was filled with what might be – instead of what couldn't. And she was loving it.

In the early evening, she took Hetty and Victor for a walk while Jean prepared herself. She showered and washed her hair. Then, for the first time, she used the body cream that Chrissy had given her for Christmas months before. After several changes of outfit, she finally settled on a pale-blue dress which had been one of Trevor's favourites.

Jean added perfume, lipstick, small pearl earrings and, lastly, placed £200 in her handbag and checked that she also had her credit card, now little used.

'Good luck,' Veronica said, returning to the house in time to say goodbye. 'I'll wait here. And don't forget to phone so I know you're OK.'

Jean smiled shakily. 'Of course I'll be all right,' she replied. 'People do this all the time—'

Veronica crossed her fingers. 'Let's hope so. For both our sakes.'

It was only later that she remembered to call Les. He was upset. She knew she had been thoroughly inconsiderate but, try as Veronica might, she didn't feel a shred of guilt. Not any more.

'I'll have a gin and tonic, please.' Jean Stoker smiled at the waiter in the bar of the London restaurant which had been suggested. 'A large one.'

She tried not to watch the door. As instructed, she placed a copy of the *ABC* railway timetable in front of her. For the fifth time, she considered pulling out. It didn't have to be like this.

For the past couple of months, Jean had been working part-time in a wool shop. It was pleasant, undemanding – and poorly paid. Why not stick to that, sell the house, and tell the children the truth?

'May I take this seat, please?' the voice was close to her left ear, unusually close.

Jean jumped, then fumbled for the railway guide. She picked it up and held it against her chest as if it might protect her from the stab of Cupid's bow.

'Mrs Street?' the man asked again. He had an actor's voice.

Jean glanced up and sighed with relief. He was at least ten years older than Tim, her stepson. She had specifically asked for someone older which had initially caused consternation at the agency. The man was of average height, trim, dark-haired and with pale-blue eyes. He was dressed in an expensive, dark-grey, well-cut suit and a subdued tie. There was nothing about him that might embarrass her, nor offer any clues to an observer. He wasn't outstandingly good-looking, but he had a nice smile and he was confident.

'May I?' He indicated the chair to her left.

She nodded. The arrival of the waiter with her drink restored her equilibrium. She was, after all, the one who was paying.

'What would you like?' she asked. 'Whatever you're having will do fine.' He smiled.

At midnight, after dinner and a dreary musical which Jean had suggested they abandon in the interval, and more drinks, she had learned a certain amount about her companion's life while opting to skate over much of her own.

She had introduced herself as Jessica Street. He had said he was Mark Telling. He was forty, a senior psychiatric nurse with an ex-wife and three children to support and an interest in a sailing boat. Hence the decision to take this second job. It might all have been pure fantasy since the man wasn't being paid to tell the truth, but Mark Telling was also intelligent and funny and thoughtful and attentive, so it hardly mattered.

Jean Stoker soon stopped telling herself that everyone must be able to guess the nature of their relationship. Instead, she decided that they made a handsome couple. Who knows? Perhaps in different circumstances, Mark Telling might even have found her attractive?

The effect on her morale was more than worth the money. She could fool herself that she had a value.

Would Trevor – wherever he might be – raise objections? On the contrary, Jean decided. Her husband would have been delighted to see his widow smiling again.

At one a.m., in the taxi, she handed Mark Telling a white envelope in which she had placed a £40 tip. The fee had already been paid by credit card. He appeared surprised.

'If you would prefer,' he said carefully, 'I've booked a room.'

Jean Stoker looked at him, nonplussed. 'What for?' she asked.

'Well,' Mark Telling replied, holding the taxi door open for her, 'that's for you to decide.'

It was six thirty on Saturday evening and Fee knew Claire was lying. She knew because, first, it was totally unlike Claire to be so apologetic. And, second, her excuse was becoming more complicated by the minute. Normally, Claire was nothing if not to the point.

On the phone, she had babbled on for what seemed like hours. 'I'm really sorry, I know that we'd agreed that you would come round tonight but someone at work has fallen sick . . . and he was due to entertain a very important customer who's only in town for this one evening . . . and nobody else is available. So, of course, I've been lumbered. And it wouldn't look good if I turned it down. I knew you'd understand, so while this is short notice—'

On and on and on. After several minutes, Fee called a halt.

'Are you telling me you and Clem have made up?' she said flatly.

'God, no,' Claire answered instantly. 'Well, yes, actually—'

Pride prevented Fee from calling other friends to see if someone else might be free to come out and play so late in the day. What was so terrifying about staying in alone on a Saturday night anyway?

This was the first time Fee had had her flat to herself for days, so why not savour it? She knew the answer. It was because, far from being calm and comforting, the place appeared cold and distant and devastatingly empty without the sound of children and the overflow from other people's lives.

'Work,' she told herself firmly. 'You've got plenty of work to do . . . So, do it.'

She had already settled herself at her desk before something pulled her up sharp. Was she utterly incapable of having a good time alone?

An hour later, Fee returned to the flat. In her arms, she had flowers, a bottle of champagne, a face pack, a thriller, two tuna-salad sandwiches and a variety of choc-ices.

She opened the champagne and poured a glass. She had a bath, used the face pack, ate a sandwich and was watching *Casablanca*, enjoying her second glass, when the phone rang again.

'Who's that?' Helen Travers asked suspiciously when her daughter answered the phone.

'It's me, Fee. Who did you think it would be?'

'You're in then,' Helen said. 'Are you sick?'

'No. I couldn't be healthier,' Fee answered. 'I'm enjoying myself.'

'So you're entertaining then?' Helen sounded relieved.

'No, I'm on my own.'

'It's not possible.'

'What's not possible?' Fee asked, knowing the answer.

'It's not possible to be having a good time on your own on a Saturday night. Not at your age, not in your circumstances,' Helen insisted. 'I thought you said you were going to do something about all this?'

'I am. I'm doing it,' Fee replied.

Chapter Twenty-Six

'NO, NO, no . . . I never want to see you again. I hate you . . .
Do you hear me? I hate you. I hate you, I hate, I hate you—'

At just after seven on Sunday morning, Fee Travers woke to hear
a milk bottle smashing and a voice screaming so loudly it had woven
its way into her dream.

The voice belonged to Shona Spannier. Fee pulled on a shirt and
jeans and rushed to open the door of her flat. Shona was standing in
her dressing-gown in the corridor. To Fee's relief there were no
obvious signs of injury.

The main door to the house banged shut.

'Is it Edward?' Fee asked unnecessarily. 'Breakfast not done to
his liking?'

Fee didn't expect Shona to smile but she almost managed it.

Half an hour later, in Shona's kitchen, Fee made coffee and listened
to the explanation. Edward had come home at three in the morning,
drunk. He had told Shona she was hopeless in bed. So much so, he
had been driven to make alternative arrangements – namely with
Hannah Jaspan, Will's girlfriend.

'What an awful thing to do,' Fee burst out, concerned as much
for Will as for Shona. 'God, he's a rat.'

'He speaks highly of you too,' Shona remarked drily. 'Teddy says
that you propositioned him in the kitchen the night you came to
supper. And what you're desperate for and can't get is a 'good seeing

287

to', as he puts it. He told me he was too honourable to oblige – and, besides, you're too aggressive to be remotely fanciable.'

Fee opened her mouth to protest but Shona raised her hand and gave a bleak smile.

'It's all right,' she said. 'I've heard it all before. I've got a pretty good idea what actually happened but, if you don't mind, I'd rather not go into it—'

Fee handed her a mug of coffee and watched while Shona drank. Now her anger had died, she appeared small and defeated.

She spoke without looking at Fee. 'I thought he was going to start punching me again. He raised his hand . . . and something snapped. I'm taking the boys out for the day from school today . . . It seems silly, but I just wasn't going to turn up saying I'd bumped into a cupboard or fallen over the cat as I have a dozen times before . . . They deserve a mother with more courage than that—'

'So what did you do?' Fee asked.

Shona looked at her. 'Before, I've begged him to stop, I've grovelled, I've apologized all the time he's been hitting me and I've just tried to protect myself as much as I could . . . It's so . . . humiliating—'

'This time, I just told him that I wouldn't take any more. He was so shocked, he stopped.' She smiled wryly. 'And that's all it took. This time. Then he smashed everything in the kitchen instead.

'Oh Fee . . . my life's such a mess . . . And the one thing I want I can't make happen—'

'What's that?' Fee asked, giving her a hug.

'I want Edward to love me as he did when we first met. I want him to be interested in me again, genuinely interested . . . Pitiful, aren't I?' she added defensively.

It took over an hour to restore Shona's flat to order. She said that Edward was unlikely to return for a couple of days, if his behaviour on previous occasions was any guide. So, when it was done, Fee persuaded her to go out and have something to eat in the small café where she and Claire often had Sunday breakfasts – before Clem.

'Do you remember the cottage weekend I won in the raffle?' Fee asked over the second cappuccino. 'You said you couldn't come when we all first talked about it – why don't you change your mind? What about next weekend? I'll see if the others are free. You'd enjoy the change, you really would—'

'Perhaps that's what frightens me most.' Shona gave a shadow of a smile. 'Change in my present state seems even more terrifying than Edward in one of his tempers ... isn't that a terrible thing for someone of my age to admit?'

It was Monday morning, always the busiest time of the week. Les Haslem sat in his office and looked incredulously at the two women sitting side by side in front of him. His own wife and a quite pretty, faintly intimidating woman to whom he had just been introduced, Mrs Jean Stoker.

'If she did something with her hair, coloured it a bit, she wouldn't be bad for her age,' Les Haslem thought to himself, discreetly examining Jean Stoker's features. He then immediately felt disloyal to Veronica.

Just because his wife was behaving badly, very badly, was no reason for him to do likewise.

'You are asking me to give you my blessing?' he repeated again, disbelief lending a twang to every word.

'Well, that would be nice,' Veronica smiled brightly. 'But it's money we're really after—'

Veronica looked different, Les decided. She looked, well, *alive*. He couldn't escape the use of the word. His wife of thirty years was more *alive* than he'd seen her look in ages.

'Let me run through it again,' Veronica suggested to her husband briskly, aware that Les was still adjusting to her new-found assertiveness. She gave a sideways glance at Jean. It helped hugely having an ally.

'It's an escort agency. The owner is asking for £22,000 for the goodwill, present clients, advertising agreements which still have time to run and a guarantee that 25 per cent of the gentlemen will continue to work,' Veronica explained crisply. 'We've told him we don't want any of the female escorts. We're going for niche marketing.

'Our male employees must already have full-time professional jobs. And we insist on three references. We'll also investigate their character thoroughly with the help of a detective agency.'

Les was unimpressed. 'Are you seriously telling me, you want me to invest in a brothel?' he asked disbelievingly.

For some reason, both his wife and her friend found this very amusing.

'No, no, no, Mr Haslem,' Jean smiled. 'This is for older women who are fed up to the back teeth with sitting at home alone, or feeling ridiculous in pubs and clubs and dinner parties. We put the woman in control, she is buying herself a pleasant evening out, on a regular basis if she so chooses. It's all very discreet, very safe and I don't think it's been tried before, not on the scale we intend.'

'Jean here', Veronica indicated with her head, 'is going to be front of house. She'll deal with the clients and she'll be responsible for selecting the gentlemen in the first place. She's got more experience than I have—'

'Experience?' Les repeated, dazed.

Jean patted Les on the hand comfortingly. She'd liked him as soon as she'd set eyes on him. He was not unlike her Trevor.

'The deal is this,' she explained. 'We'd like you to invest. Veronica is putting up £8,000.'

'She is?' Les responded. He was unaware that Veronica had her own savings.

'And she's in charge of the money as she's the qualified accountant—'

'She's what?' Les answered. It was dawning on him that his

assumption that he and his wife had shared the same world for all these years was misguided to say the least.

Jean Stoker pressed on. 'I've got five thousand from a policy I'm going to cash in. We'd like a lot more of course . . . for recruiting new men, finding and decorating offices, designing publicity material and so forth. But £27,000 would do for now. So, how about it, Mr Haslem? Won't you help a little?'

Veronica knew Les had never in his life bought sight unseen.

'Put your coat on, Les. We want to show you something,' she ordered. Then she practically skipped out of the front door.

The taxi stopped in Shepherd's Market, in Mayfair. Jean Stoker and Veronica Haslem appeared to head for a busy Italian sandwich bar emblazoned with a neon-lit sign which read, 'De Marco's Dee-licious'.

Sandwiches, Les Haslem knew about. His produce could beat De Marco's hands down, he pointed out to his wife, but she was already ringing the bell of a door to the left of these premises. It was painted black and had a large brass letterbox and plaque on which was written the word, 'Ludus'.

Jean and Les followed Veronica in and up the stairs to a large room which overlooked the street. It was expensively carpeted in moss green. The room also held two large desks, six telephones and four chairs, one black leather sofa and a rubber plant. And nothing else.

A woman in a neat black suit and without make-up sat behind one desk, smiling and doing nothing while every phone rang.

'Is this it?' Les Haslem asked. He'd half expected semi-naked men draped in togas, posing around a sunken pool.

'No,' his wife replied, pushing him gently down on the sofa and placing a large, leather-bound photograph album on his lap. 'This is what it's about.'

Les Haslem flicked through the album, glancing at a variety of fully clothed men caught in the same ridiculous pose, gazing impassively across open countryside, as if in search of the Americas.

He closed the book with a bang and turned to his wife. He wasn't angry, he was uncertain, a much more vulnerable emotion.

'Do you honestly think that this is what women of your age want, Veronica?' he asked rhetorically.

Chapter Twenty-Seven

ON MONDAY, at F. P. & D., Fee struggled to complete as much work as possible before lunchtime. It was then that Imogen Banks and Hilly Byrne were arriving with a film crew.

In a lull, Fee gave Veronica a quick call. Les had informed Fee of his wife's reappearance but had not been very forthcoming. Jean Stoker answered. 'Veronica's just popped out to get a few things,' she explained.

'Is she all right?' Fee enquired.

Jean laughed. 'Why on earth shouldn't she be?' Then added, 'Hang on, I can hear her at the door.'

When Veronica came to the phone, Fee explained that she was checking to see if the two women would be free to share her prize this coming weekend.

'It's a bit difficult,' Veronica replied. 'We've got a lot on at the moment. Something really exciting has happened to us. To Jean and me.' Her voice was elated.

Before Fee could respond, she heard Veronica break away to have a hurried conversation with Jean.

'Fee, are you still there?' Veronica asked. 'We've had an idea. We think you can help us. Les is proving a bit difficult, well, very difficult. So we wondered if you might step into the breach? Please?'

'Is this anything to do with love, romance, relationships, that sort of thing?' Fee asked dubiously. She could hear the two women chuckling.

'Good God, no,' Veronica laughed down the phone. 'It's to do with money. Quite a lot of it.'

Diana Woods had proved extremely uncooperative when it came to filming Fee Travers at F. P. & D. until Gerry Radcliffe had stepped in. He pointed out that her envy was obstructing an opportunity for free publicity on a grand scale for the company.

Diana retaliated spitefully. 'And do you think Harry Macklin is going to be thrilled with the idea that the person in charge of his account is the one person who allegedly intends to remain a spinster for the rest of her life?' she asked.

Gerry admitted that he hadn't considered that aspect of the proceedings.

'Well, think about it now,' she snapped. At times, in Diana Woods's company these days, Gerry had to remind himself who was the boss.

'Fee will know how to handle it,' he insisted with manufactured confidence. He did not wish to be seen deferring to Diana Woods but privately he cursed himself. He was old enough to know that there was no such thing as a free commercial.

'All right, what are your indulgences? Go on, shock us—' Imogen Banks, for once soberly attired in a plain grey suit, sat with her back to the camera and questioned Fee who was dressed in her new, burnt-orange dress. She had liked it in the shop, now it made her feel like a traffic cone.

She had already been filmed having lunch in a restaurant she had never visited before. Then she had spent two hours in her flat, recording an interview that would, according to Imogen, provide the backbone of *The Perfumed Pound*.

Fee had been impressed by Imogen's research. Her aim had plainly been to uncover some trigger in childhood that might explain why Fee would choose to be what Imogen irritatingly kept referring to as 'that-female-modern-maverick-ms-otherwise-known-as-a-spinster'.

'Why am I single? It's just a choice, like any other,' Fee had repeated again and again. 'Women seem programmed to seek approval. Finding the right man is part of that search for approval. A few days before my thirty-eighth birthday, I received a proposal from a man of whom my mother would certainly have approved—'

'And?' Imogen asked excitedly.

'I decided that living my life the way I wanted to was more important than living my life in the hope of winning other people's blessing. I wanted to ride the range as a free woman—'

Imogen appeared crestfallen. 'Juicy, I want juicy. Give me something sexier,' she had demanded. 'Give me a good reason. Can't you throw in a bit of abuse or something? What about a family friend? Perhaps he put you off men? Cut, cut, cut,' Imogen bellowed at the cameraman in the same breath. 'Let's give her time to think. She's bound to have something nasty in the woodshed, if she tries hard enough.'

Fee laughed. 'I don't need time to think. I told you, it's a choice. It's deciding what will make me happier. It's saying that, on balance, I do better alone than I do with someone else. I'm not saying that that's right for everyone; I'm saying it suits me. Isn't that what healthy societies are about? A variety of ways of living a life?'

'Use the term, "Lifestyles",' Imogen instructed. 'It sounds so much more *contemporary*. Not, of course, that I'm trying to put words into your mouth, you do understand that, don't you, darling?'

Imogen signalled for the cameraman to begin filming again. Then she trotted through the list of accusations that Fee had heard many times before, not least from Claire and Helen.

'Was it all down to selfishness? Was she incapable of commitment? What about facing childlessness?'

Fee answered as patiently as she could. It was then Imogen brought up the question of indulgences.

Fee was beginning to find herself at ease with the camera. Or, rather, the interview had continued for so long, she had almost ceased to be aware of its existence. At the same time, she realized that Imogen had accumulated so much material she could edit it as she pleased. Fee was at her mercy and it was too late now to try and regain control. So she might as well relax; the damage was done.

'Indulgences?' Fee had repeated, then added, amused, 'You mean how do I compensate myself for not having what so-called normal people have?

'I'll tell you what I have by way of indulgences.' Fee leaned forward conspiratorially. Imogen had flushed pink with pleasure at the prospect of Fee finally, belatedly, divulging intimacies on film.

'I buy tuna-salad sandwiches and choc-ices and face packs and stay in on a Saturday night—'

'And you *like* that?' Imogen Banks asked, in genuine incredulity.

Late afternoon, Fee returned to her office. Imogen, without seeking permission and undetected, had inserted a camera behind a screen in the company's main boardroom. She knew when the meeting was scheduled to begin – 5.15 p.m. – because Will Evans had told Hilly Byrne who had relayed the message to Imogen. Spot on time, Imogen began filming. She needed a little *vérité*.

The meeting was to consider options for updating the image of a well-established but staid washing powder. Several F.P. & D. employees were present including Will, Diana Woods and Fee. Oriel Ashcroft, a junior colleague, was to give a presentation on what research had thrown up so far.

She spoke now to Fee. 'I tried to get you earlier but your mobile was switched off,' she said apologetically. 'Could I ask a huge favour? Dominic is ill and I'm desperate to get home at a reasonable time. Would you be able to do the presentation? It's all stuff you know. I'm sorry, I wouldn't ask normally, but he was so ill last night and he cried when I left for work this morning—' Her face was desperate.

Dominic Ashcroft had just had his third birthday and his mother was now four months pregnant. 'Of course that's fine,' Fee responded immediately. 'Here, why don't you go now, I'll—'

Diana Woods interrupted. 'Just because Fee has no family,' she said crisply, 'doesn't mean that every woman with commitments should dump on her at the slightest opportunity. Frankly, some of us who've been sensible enough to decide on our priorities and not have children are thoroughly fed up being asked to cover for sickness and school holidays and maternity leave and childcare problems—'

It was a speech to touch Imogen Banks's heart, secreted as she was behind the bamboo screen. She had to restrain herself from shouting, 'Hear, hear—'

Oriel Ashcroft burst into tears. Fee got up from her chair and walked round the table to comfort her. Then she turned on Diana Woods.

'Diana,' Fee spoke slowly to calm her anger, 'a seat on the board does not turn you into a ventriloquist nor make me your dummy. I'll make my own decisions about who I do and do not cover for . . . And the day that work automatically takes priority over family then God help us all. With or without children.

'You and I may not have babies, Diana,' she continued, 'but who's going to cover for you when it's your turn to care for an old and ageing relative?'

'That's very MDF,' Trish Castle piped up chirpily. 'The Mutual Dependency Factor . . . everybody needs somebody . . . It shows up strongly in the HAH! material . . . Still, I'm sure a lot of people feel the same way as you do, Diana.' She smiled obsequiously.

Diana Woods ignored her and marched out of the room, slamming the door behind her.

'Go home, Oriel,' Fee advised. It was then Imogen Banks came crashing out from behind the screen, applauding enthusiastically.

'Wonderful, wonderful. Couldn't have gone better if I'd scripted it myself,' she enthused.

'So what do you think?' Jean and Veronica had invited Fee to a pub lunch to put a proposition to her.

'Veronica gave me the idea when we met at the singles night,' Jean explained. 'Do you remember, she suggested that I use an escort agency? Well, Veronica and I talked about it later. I explained that I needed to earn money quickly, Veronica said she needed to develop some sort of interest of her own. We thought we could work together.' Jean was brimming with enthusiasm.

'Later, for research purposes of course, I contacted an agency and arranged an evening out. It was far less painful than I had imagined . . . but what I did find cheap and nasty was going into the office and looking at an album of photos beforehand. It was all so cold-hearted and impersonal . . . So that's when we came up with the idea of—'

'But what happened on the night?' Fee interrupted, her curiosity aroused.

'Mind your own business,' Veronica chastised her sister mildy.

Jean Stoker smiled shyly, 'Well, he eventually asked me to stay the night. He did it quite tastefully actually—'

'And?' Fee asked.

'Really, Fee,' Veronica remonstrated.

Jean blushed and shook her head. 'No, of course I didn't. To be honest, I didn't have the nerve.'

Over the next half-hour, Veronica and Jean explained their idea. 'A woman pays us a fee for six months. In return, she is sent a folder which contains a selection of our men . . . In addition to an up-to-date photograph, there will be personal details such as his day job and his interests.

'If she wishes to book an individual for a day or an evening, she comes through us,' Veronica elaborated. 'We split the fee with the gentleman 30 per cent to us, 70 per cent to him—'

'Two questions,' Fee said. 'Once a client and one of your employees . . . have met, what's to stop them striking up a private deal?'

'Not a lot,' Jean Stoker conceded. 'But we'll have drawn up contracts for the men, good terms and conditions and if they decide to prejudice steady work, holiday money and all the rest of it for the sake of one client, well then . . . It must be love.'

'What's the second question, Fee?' Jean asked.

'What do you want from me?' Fee replied.

'Twenty-seven thousand pounds, or more if you've got it. You're single. You must have something put away in savings. We approached Les but he turned us down flat. I could take the money from our joint account but, as a result of Les's attitude, I want this to be entirely my own thing. I want to show him that I can do it without him—' Veronica looked hard at Fee. 'This means more to me than a business, you do know that, Fee, don't you?'

'So it's not a hobby? A bit of a thing on the side?' Fee asked, straightfaced. Veronica threw a paper napkin at her.

'I've forgotten one thing,' Fee said. 'What about sex?'

Veronica sighed. 'Why is everyone obsessed about the same thing? This enterprise is about the provision of good-quality, enter-taining company for older women.

'If sex follows at some later stage between two consenting adults—'

'One paying,' Fee interrupted.

'Well now, that's nothing new, is it?' Jean queried. 'Anyway,' she continued evenly, 'I suspect that a lot of women will simply want companionship.'

Veronica was less certain. 'Times seem to be changing awfully fast. When I look at my daughter and how I was at her age . . . Are you sure we're not going to end up in court, Jean?' She shuddered. 'The Menopause Madams, how dreadfully embarrassing—'

'I'm absolutely sure we're not,' Jean repeated firmly, then turned again to Fee. 'So how about it? Will you invest?'

It was only since leaving teaching several years before that Fee had begun to earn decent money – and most of that had been absorbed into buying a house with Bill at the wrong time in the market and selling at a loss. She had £4000 in savings but she knew how she could obtain more.

She could resign from F. P. & D. She had signed an agreement with Gerry Radcliffe that should she leave the company, she would receive £25,000 on condition that she took no similar employment with rival businesses for a period of nine months.

'I wish I could help,' Fee replied, 'but I don't see how I can. I've got around £4000 in savings and not much else ... I'm so sorry,' she added as the smiles disappeared from the faces of the two women.

At home, that evening, there were three messages for Fee on her answering machine. The requests to ring Paul Denning and Bill Summers she ignored. It was the third call that intrigued her.

She recognized the voice instantly, deep and melodious and unquestionably Welsh. 'Hello,' the voice said. 'This is Gwynfor Pryce. Rita brought you to my meeting. Could you phone me, please? I'm feeling very troubled about her.' He left a number.

Alarmed, she called immediately. Gwynfor Pryce suggested they meet in person. Fee invited him to the flat. Half an hour later, he was at the door.

He was as flamboyant in his appearance as the first time they had met. On this occasion, he was dressed in a black suit, white shirt and a postbox red polka-dotted tie. He refused a drink.

'It's Rita,' he said. 'Do you know her well?'

Fee shook her head.

Pryce spoke again. 'She's been coming to our meetings off and on for a year or so. A week after you came, she gave me your telephone number. She said I was to contact you in the event of anything happening—'

'Happening?' Fee asked. 'What's happened? You said you were troubled about her? Do you mean professionally? Are you having premonitions?'

Gwynfor Pryce stared at his hands, and crossed and uncrossed his patent-leather shoes.

'I'll be frank,' he said. 'I've lent her some money and I'd quite

300

like to know where it is . . . She told me she was the warden in a block of old people's flats. She said the residents had helped to raise funds to pay for a week's holiday in Bournemouth. It had been stolen, and unless there was sufficient for a deposit to pay for the coaches and the hotel, the whole trip would be in jeopardy.

'She told me it would be covered by insurance but not in time to save the holiday, so I said, "No problem." I owed her one,' Gwynfor Pryce confessed. 'Over the months, she's brought no end of women into the group . . . Most of them living on their own, a lot of them professional, well off—'

'Women she's conned out of money?' Fee asked.

Gwynfor Pryce shrugged. 'Who can tell? But somehow I don't think so . . . She'd come with the same person for a couple of weeks, then she'd be on her own again. I think she's so lonely she frightens them off. She doesn't know what to do with people, if you know what I mean? Not in terms of friendship.'

'Well, she certainly knew what to do with you, Mr Pryce.' Fee teased him a little. 'I'm surprised you couldn't see her coming.'

Gwynfor Pryce looked sheepish. 'She's got a helluva silver tongue. She's very good at it. And I've met the best.'

He left shortly after. Fee went into her bedroom, opened the wardrobe and began to hunt through the pockets of the clothes she had worn when she and Claire had first visited Rita Mason's bedsit. She eventually found the slip of paper with the address of Rita's mother written on it, in Jimmy Roth's strong hand. There was no name, only the address: '48, Penshurst Terrace, Westcliff, Cardiff'.

Fee mapped out a plan. Today was Monday. She would finish filming with Imogen Banks and write the main report on the restructuring of Harry Macklin's Have a Heart! empire by Friday. On Friday evening, it had been arranged that she, Jean and Victoria would drive to the cottage in Devon for the weekend.

Next Monday would be the earliest that Fee could visit Rita Mason's mother. If a mother can't explain the mystery that is her daughter, then who can?

Chapter Twenty-Eight

'I T WAS a lie. Of course, it was a bloody lie.' Edward Spannier chose not to look at his wife, as he carefully scraped the uneaten dinner she had just served from his plate into the bin.

'This', he said calmly, 'is inedible.'

Shona Spannier watched her husband and allowed herself to savour the unfamiliar reaction she was experiencing. It was indifference. She was past caring. Shona knew this wouldn't last, she would no doubt torment herself afresh, but for now her indifference was intoxicating. It smelt of freedom.

'Did you hear what I said?' Edward demanded, his voice threatening. 'I said I lied about that bitch that Will Evans sleeps with. I wouldn't go near her even if she begged me for it.'

Shona sighed. 'What you mean is that she turned you down.' Edward crossed the kitchen in three steps, grabbed a fistful of his wife's hair and twisted it in his hand, forcing her face close to his. She could smell the alcohol on his breath; he was trembling with rage. How many times had she recognized this prelude to a beating?

A beating. Such a polite, hygienic, solid word which disguised the desperate, humiliating scrabble to protect herself. After the beating would come Edward's flight, followed by his return and then remorse.

'The only time I have any power in this relationship', Shona thought, 'is when I have the power to forgive him—'

Edward hit his wife hard. She bit her tongue. The salt taste of blood was strangely comforting.

She fell, knocking her temple on the side of the breakfast bar and toppling one of the stools. She landed on it awkwardly, so that a leg of the stool poked her hard in the ribs, making it still more difficult to draw breath. Instinct made Shona roll away as her husband raised his foot to kick.

Edward turned and made for the door. 'Don't go,' she called. 'Teddy, please, don't go.'

It was a scene the two had played out many times before. Edward stopped, his back to her. Shona slowly got to her feet.

'You stay in the flat,' she told her husband, her voice strong and even. A voice he hadn't heard before.

'You stay, Edward,' Shona repeated, 'because I'm the one who's leaving.'

'Fabulously, fortuitously, famously, fleshy,' Imogen Banks shouted at her reflection, her arms raised like a Broadway star.

'I love you,' she cooed at herself. 'You are so clever, so talented, so cunning—' As a reward, she popped a handful of chocolate-covered raisins in her mouth. So who said they shouldn't be eaten at six o'clock in the morning?

She selected a bright-blue jacket and a black skirt with a matching blue and black patterned top.

She had several reasons for jubilation. Whatever Simon Booth had told his wife, and whatever Imogen had said to Fee Travers, their relationship was moving along nicely. In fact, Simon was proving quite a tiger . . .

Better still, she had looked at what had already been shot of Fee and the contretemps at F. P. & D. That plus interviews with those who had loved and known her, basic information kindly supplied by Helen Travers, would make a very nice montage of the modern-day spinster.

Imogen's attempt to find some psychological explanation for Fee's rejection of men had, it was true, not come to fruition. But now she had decided to establish in the film that the problem wasn't Fee's – it was men's.

If men weren't prepared to shape up, then the women of the future would refuse to come to heel. Fee Travers was about to be recast. She was no longer a neurotic, but a woman ahead of her time.

Imogen didn't believe a word of it, of course. Most women she'd come across believed that bastards were to die for . . . But she knew good television when she saw it.

Fee felt like a dog. She had arrived at work at eight, having had only a few hours' sleep.

When Shona Spannier left her flat, she had temporarily moved in with Fee. Much of the rest of the night had been spent listening to Shona. All paths led to the same central dilemma: she didn't want to leave Edward – not because of her commitment to him, but because of her commitment to the institution of marriage.

She didn't want to leave him, but neither did she want to live with the man that he had become.

They both agreed, some time after 5 a.m., that Edward should be taught a lesson. It was only when Fee was making scrambled eggs that the idea came to her. It was wicked and deceitful. But in terms of creative thinking, it gave Fee far more satisfaction than anything she had achieved at F. P. & D. in a very long while.

Fee briefly outlined her idea to Shona who was appalled. She refused to have anything to do with it. But by the time Fee dished up their breakfast, her resistance had weakened.

'You're a bad influence on me,' Shona protested.

'I hope so,' Fee replied cheerfully. 'I really hope so.'

Imogen Banks knew that if she wanted Hampstead Heath, semi-deserted and approaching twilight, it was ridiculous to film at 11 a.m. on a weekday. Still, that was what Fee Travers's schedule permitted, so that's what had to be.

'Walk!' Imogen bellowed. Fee dutifully walked away from the camera and the ponds and towards the brow of the hill.

A jogger stopped her and asked the time. 'Cut!' yelled Imogen.

What she had sought, as an image for the end of the film, was Fee, a solitary figure, but striding confidently towards an unknown future. It was corny. It was a cliché. It had been seen before. But that's why Imogen knew it would press the appropriate emotional buttons, before the viewer pressed the only other button that mattered – the off switch.

Imogen's scenario was not working out well, however. Far from being solitary, Fee had been stopped more times than a King's Cross hooker.

'Let's wrap,' Imogen ordered. It was only a small blip. She could manipulate people better than a master puppeteer, she told herself with some pride. She was without match.

'So, have you thought about taking part in a discussion programme after the film?' Imogen asked Fee casually, as they drove back to F. P. & D.

'When did you say the film's going out?' Fee asked, equally relaxed.

'Three weeks. It's a fast edit—'

Fee smiled guilelessly at Imogen. 'I'm going with a few friends to a cottage for the weekend on Friday. I was hoping you might come?'

'Friends?' Imogen responded, suspiciously.

'Women friends,' Fee answered firmly. 'Five of us, including you.'

To Imogen, this was a prospect as enticing as a time-share in hell: fluctuating oestrogen and no men. Then she remembered that Fee still had to say yes to the studio discussion.

'I'd love to come.' Imogen smiled, then swallowed hard.

'That's perfect,' Fee grinned.

'Sweetheart Cottage' was neither romantic nor idyllic; nor, for that matter, was it a cottage. It was a pebble-dash former council house, perched in splendid isolation in a large and unkept garden, between a delightful village and a motorway which rumbled constantly with traffic. It was like being sited in the stomach of a half-starved giant.

'It could be worse,' Veronica had remarked brightly. 'We might have come in August with the holiday-makers. Then, the racket really *would* have been unbearable.'

Collectively, the women set about putting a good gloss on the situation. The garden had a stream and a hammock and was overflowing with wild flowers. The interior was comfortable and carefully decorated with chintz and blue china and oak panels, just as if the building did have a thatched roof.

The beds were comfortable and the fridge was large enough to stock the dozen bottles of champagne Imogen had insisted on bringing as a means of ensuring that the weekend would at least allow her the private pleasure of getting blotto.

Three bottles had already been drunk by the time it came to prepare the salad dressing, late on the Friday evening. Gill's absence (she was at home nurturing her relationship) had restored Jean Stoker to the position of head chef. She had brought a cold supper with her – but now four women jostled for the honour of making the vinaigrette.

Fee had absconded from the competitors' tent which the kitchen had become. She had always viewed prowess in the domestic arena as something to be avoided.

Much to everyone's surprise, Shona Spannier proved the toughest. 'I'm sorry,' she insisted, 'but until you've tasted my dressing, you have not lived. *I'll* make it—'

Much later, after brandy had been opened to follow the champagne and white wine, and life stories had been told, some more highly edited than others, and the conversation had grown increasingly boozy and giggly and infantile, Fee casually suggested that it might be fun if each woman told the others a secret.

A real secret.

Imogen Banks put up her hand. 'I'll start,' she offered. 'My secret is that I can't stand women,' she surveyed the others defiantly.

'All women?' Jean asked, impressed by Imogen's honesty.

'All women,' Imogen repeated firmly. 'Ladies, I warn you,' she wagged her finger. 'Never put your trust in old Imogen here . . . Never.'

Jean looked askance. 'That's not much of a secret, is it?' she challenged her bullishly, tipsier than she'd been since her stepdaughter's wedding. 'I'll give you a real one. How about this?' She paused for dramatic effect. 'I recently paid for sex.'

It was Veronica who broke the silence. 'I thought you said you hadn't?' She chastised her business partner in shock. 'How could you?'

'Surprisingly easily,' Jean answered smoothly. 'Did I feel guilty afterwards? No. Was I ashamed? No. Would Trevor have approved? Probably.

'It's been a year since he died and I came away feeling, well, restored. As an occasional diversion, I'd recommend it.'

Jean knew she had a captive audience. 'I doubt I'll ever do it again in my life – but the experience has certainly given me the confidence I was lacking to take off the brakes, change gear—'

Imogen was gazing intently at Jean Stoker. Fee knew exactly what she was thinking. Imogen was thinking Television.

Imogen examined the other women. This weekend might well turn out to be far more fruitful than she had anticipated.

'Whose turn is it now?' she asked eagerly. She was disappointed when Fee elected to speak.

'My best friend Claire is getting married in three months and I can't stand Clem – her husband to be,' Fee offered. 'I want Claire to dump him so we can go back to how we were. Isn't that horrible of me?'

'Yes, it is,' Veronica said. 'I didn't think you were like that, Fee.'

'No judgements allowed,' Jean interceded, inventing a rule.

'Do you really want to split them up?' Imogen asked. Fee could have sworn that, in the firelight, she spotted fangs.

'Sleep with Claire's boyfriend,' Imogen suggested brutally. 'Then threaten to tell her.'

Shona, Jean, Veronica and Fee looked at her with distaste. She held her smile but made a mental note to expose less of her true self in future. She had forgotten just how stupidly *sentimental* women are.

'Why?' Veronica asked innocently. 'Why threaten to tell Claire?'

'To cause trouble,' Imogen answered defiantly. 'Fee won't have to tell Claire, because Clem will tell her himself. Claire's not the kind to forgive ... She'll probably threaten never to speak to Fee again, but she'll forgive and forget. And Clem will have definitely been given the boot. Isn't that what you want, Fee?'

Bored, Imogen curtailed further discussion on the issue by addressing herself to Shona. 'Your turn now,' she directed.

Shona fumbled, 'I have got a secret ... of sorts. I've got a secret desire to teach my husband a lesson that he'll never forget—'

'You don't even have to tell us the details,' Imogen intercepted swiftly. Adultery. She'd been there, done that. Nothing in it, intelevision terms.

'Leave him,' she instructed Shona crisply. 'Who's next?'

'I couldn't. I can't,' Shona replied, looking towards Fee for support. 'I've got a responsibility to try and make this marriage work – for the sake of our boys apart from anything else. Besides, Edward wants to be a Labour MP and he wouldn't even think of giving me a divorce now—'

'Oh God, you bloody wives are all the same,' Imogen pronounced, exasperated. 'Dictate your own sodding terms to your old man, why don't you? What's the matter with you, woman?'

Shona looked at Imogen. She took in Imogen's voluptuous breasts and her small, surprisingly delicate hands and her full lips as she sat in front of the fire, aflame in a bright-red silk shirt. Fee was right; Imogen Banks was the ideal candidate for the job.

'You could do it,' Shona suddenly said. 'Imogen, you could teach Edward a lesson. He's always the one in control. Take that away from him. Just once—

'Please, arrange to go out with him, spend the night and before anything . . . well, anything happens . . . I'll burst in on you . . . For once he'd be on the defensive. I'd have something to trade—'

Imogen raised her hands in mock horror. 'And you call this *love?*'

Then she laughed dismissively. Such a prank certainly wasn't beyond her abilities but why on earth would she do a favour like that for a virtual stranger?

On Sunday morning, it was a group decision to go for a walk on one of the nearby beaches. Imogen lagged behind the others. Fee took her opportunity and joined her.

'About this studio discussion—' Fee began. Imogen looked at Fee dully. *Such a decent, bright, uncomplicated, straightforward clean-living woman,* Imogen thought to herself savagely, as she nursed her second hangover of the weekend, aware that Fee had drunk far less.

Fee smiled at Imogen. She had drunk less, in order to negotiate better. 'I've decided that I'll take part in your discussion,' she said, 'if you'll agree to what Shona wants—'

Imogen looked at her blankly. 'And what *does* Shona want?' she asked. Friday night's confessions had been buried by a hundred conversations since. *Why did women talk so bloody much?*

'She wants you to attempt to seduce her husband, Edward, so that she can – as she puts it – have a lever on him. I think she's mad. I think she should leave him and make a fresh start. But then—'

Imogen interrupted. 'But then you're not the one in favour of marriage—'

Fee corrected her gently. 'I'm not the one in favour of relationships which work for one person in the partnership but at too high a price for the other—'

'And what's in all this for you?' Imogen asked bluntly.

Fee shrugged her shoulders. 'Nothing. Edward's a bastard who deserves what he gets. And I feel sorry for Shona.'

'So, The Lone Ranger still rides the range?' she snapped as she stomped away.

'I take that as a yes then,' Fee shouted after her retreating back.

Chapter Twenty-Nine

A T 9.30 A.M. on Monday morning, Persephone Booth, aged seven and three-quarters, was not in school. She was wearing the school uniform of dark green and red; she had her school satchel, but, instead of standing in assembly, singing 'Morning has Broken' for the umpteenth time, she was sitting at Fee Travers's kitchen table, and she was negotiating hard.

'I've had enough,' she said matter-of-factly. 'I've run away. I'm coming to live with you.'

Fee, on the other side of the table, decided that was the best compliment she had been paid in months. Out loud, she said, 'You know it's not that simple, Percy. Mummy and Daddy would miss you for a start—'

Fee had telephoned Gill and Simon Booth as soon as Percy appeared on the doorstep. She left a message on their answering machine. She learned from Percy that she had been dropped off at school and walked out again, taking a tube to Fee's flat, using her pocket money. It was a journey to which she had become accustomed when Veronica had been temporarily in charge of the school run.

Percy looked at Fee as if she was a dimwit. 'Mummy and Daddy won't miss me. They won't even notice I've gone,' she announced. 'In the old days, Mummy used to shout and Daddy stayed quiet. Now, they both shout, all the time. The boys and me have had enough.'

'You choose your boyfriends,' she added. 'So I'm choosing my parents. You can be my mother.'

'But I'll be hopeless at it,' Fee protested.

Percy smiled grimly. 'I know you will,' she said crushingly, 'but you're still better than what I've got.'

Half an hour later, Gill arrived. Fee hadn't seen or heard from her for days and presumed that she had been too preoccupied with the joys of a rebirthed marriage. Judging from Gill's appearance, it looked more as if she'd spent several days and nights in a very hot sauna. She had lost a considerable amount of weight; she had dark shadows under her eyes, and she looked drained and drawn.

At the door, Fee whispered that Percy was sorry for the fuss she had caused.

'I think she's upset about all the upheavals at home. Perhaps she just needs a bit of a cuddle and some reassurance?' Fee suggested tentatively.

Accepting advice had never been Gill's strong suit. She strode into the kitchen purposefully, took one look at her daughter drinking hot chocolate at the table, and roared at the top of her lungs, slamming both palms down on the table as she did so, making the spoon that lay by Percy's mug jump as if electrified.

'How dare you!' she yelled. 'How dare you cause me all this inconvenience? Do you think I've got nothing better to do than criss-cross London all day just for you? You are a wicked, naughty, horrible little girl – and I've a good mind to give you away.'

Tears fell silently down Percy's face. The confident, cheeky girl who had been in the room only minutes before Gill's arrival transformed before Fee's eyes into a dejected and miserable small child.

A child who had already learned the lesson that there was only one reality, and that was the reality constructed by her mother. Percy knew she could give voice to no feelings, except those which her mother wished her to have.

Percy was unhappy; Gill preferred to call her wicked. Percy was distressed by the fear of losing her father; Gill insisted she was simply being wilful, seeking attention. Percy might have only the vaguest ideas about the concept of power but she knew that her mother had it – and she had none.

Above all, Percy just wanted her mother to say what she hadn't heard in weeks: I love you.

'I hate you, I hate you, I hate you,' she sobbed and ran into the bathroom, banging the door behind her. The two women heard the key turn in the lock.

Fee gestured to Gill to sit down. 'I'll put the kettle on. Give Percy a minute or two . . . It must be difficult—' she ventured.

'No, not at all,' Gill snapped sarcastically.

Fee tried again. 'What I meant was, it must be difficult for Percy. She probably thinks Simon or you are about to go off again . . . You know children, they like routine, they—'

Gill interrupted coldly, 'And what exactly would you know about it? You've never even had a child—'

'No,' Fee replied, 'but I've been one—' She refrained from adding the words that were running through her head, 'And I've learned how to survive a mother like you—'

Helen Travers was unsurprised by her daughter's news. Fee had never known when to draw the line.

Fee was telling her mother on the phone about the saga of Percy.

'So I said Percy could stay as often as her mother would let her. Gill was a bit difficult about it at first, but she came round later.'

'And?' Helen asked.

'Percy's going to stay the weekend after next.'

'Are you sure you know what you're taking on?'

'Probably not,' Fee replied cheerfully. 'But then who does when it comes to children?'

'But why in your case does it always have to be *other people's* children?' Helen asked pointedly.

*

Imogen Banks glanced at her watch for the third time in fifteen minutes. *Where was the man?*

She gave a perfunctory smile in the direction of the man's wife sitting opposite her on the olive-green leather sofa.

Where was he? And why was she feeling so nervous?

After all, the skills required to make this little exercise successful were ones that Imogen had practised again and again over the years. She glanced again at Shona Spannier. The woman might lack backbone but, Imogen grudgingly admitted, she made up for it with a sense of style.

She wore a simple white dress, pearl-drop earrings and heeled sandals. Her dark hair was swept up in a French pleat. The only make-up she wore was mascara and lip gloss.

Imogen didn't find it surprising that a man who had Shona for a wife should still feel the need to stray. In Imogen's experience, it wasn't an even better-looking woman or a greater degree of lust that drew men like Spannier away from the marital bed, it was the need to feel indulged – uncritically indulged.

'More coffee?' Shona asked. 'Or wine? Or a gin and tonic?' Conversation between the two women had long since dried up. The misapprehensions each had about the life of the other had proved too big a hurdle.

To Shona, unaware of Imogen's inability to permanently hold on to a man, this woman was sexy, witty, and content.

To Imogen, Shona was a wife. What more was there to say?

Shona was speaking again. 'I'm going to have a gin and tonic, why don't you join me? I'm sure Teddy won't be much longer.'

When Shona left the sitting room, Imogen got up and checked her appearance in the mirror on one wall. In order to survey the bottom half of her body, she took off her shoes and stood on a chair.

She wore black. It had to be black. A tailored suit with a low neckline. The suit was severe in its cut, which drew the eye to the neckline all the more rapidly. Black suit, black stockings, very high-heeled black shoes, small diamond clips at her ears.

Different men, same or similar outfit. Boring, really. The notion stuck Imogen forcefully. *Boring?* Imogen shook herself. *What a ridiculous thought.*

'Are you all right?' said a man's voice. It held a hint of amusement in it. Imogen took the hand that was offered and stepped down from the chair. Fee had been right. Edward Spannier was a good-looking man. He smelt of Christian Dior's Eau Sauvage, a faint whiff of cigar smoke and Chanel No 5 which might or might not have been wafted over him by his wife.

Imogen gazed boldly into his eyes.

'I don't believe we've met?' Edward Spannier said. He still had hold of her hand. 'Are you a friend of my wife's?'

Imogen smiled her slow, lazy smile. 'No, not at all,' she replied, taking her time to slip on her shoes. 'Actually, I may be renting this flat when you leave. The landlord arranged with your wife for me to see it and when he was unexpectedly called away in the middle of my viewing, she kindly suggested that I stay—'

'That's why I was on the chair,' Imogen added. 'I thought I'd spotted some dry rot.'

'Aah,' Edward Spannier replied.

And after that, it was almost too easy.

Claire brought the camcorder into F. P. & D. late the following morning. It was built into a small attaché case and designed for secret filming. Typically of Claire, having bought it in Hong Kong on a whim, she had yet to find a use for it. So she had readily agreed when Fee asked if she could borrow it and asked no questions.

Claire said she had a meeting near Fee's office, so she would drop in the camera.

For several days now life at F. P. & D. had been disturbingly quiet. The HAH! report had been completed, but progress had been halted because Harry Macklin was away in Thailand. Doing what, Fee was not inclined to ask. Diana Woods and Gerry Radcliffe were out of the office in pursuit of fresh business in Italy.

Will Evans had taken Hannah Jaspan on a walking holiday in Scotland. Walking was one of his hobbies, and so far the few romances he hadn't himself throttled in early life had been finished off by five days following Hadrian's Wall.

Fee had been glad for Will's sake that Hannah hadn't slept with Edward Spannier, but she had also been surprised to find herself faintly disappointed.

Claire placed the attaché case on Fee's desk. 'It's dead simple to use,' she instructed.

'Are you all right?' Fee asked. 'You look tired—'

'Thanks,' Claire snapped. 'Of course I'm tired. I'm tired of nobody being able to make a decision about anything and the wedding is only weeks away. Now, do you want me to show you how to use this thing or not?'

At seven that evening, Fee delivered the camcorder to Shona Spannier.

'She's phoned,' Shona's cheeks were flushed with alcohol and excitement. 'Imogen's phoned. He's taking her for dinner in Knightsbridge and she's already suggested this hotel she knows—'

Fee placed the camcorder on the coffee table, already doubtful that Shona would be able to keep a grip on the handle, never mind focus it on her husband at the appropriate time.

'What's special about this hotel?' she asked.

Shona grinned wickedly. 'I don't know what Imogen's told Teddy, but I know why it's special to us. It only has one set of lifts. I told Imogen I was too squeamish to burst into the bedroom or anything like that, so the idea is she kisses him in the lift and I capture it to add to our library of happy family videos . . . Imogen's quite smart about things like this, isn't she?' Shona giggled drunkenly. 'Makes me wonder what else she gets up to—'

Fee had picked up on one word. 'Us?' she repeated. 'What do you mean by "Special to us"?'

'I can't do this on my own,' Shona squeaked. 'I've never done anything like this in my life before. I need moral support. I need help. Besides,' she added, 'it was mostly your idea. And, anyway, I'm too sozzled to drive.'

'No,' Fee said firmly. 'This part has nothing to do with me. Call a taxi, Shona.'

At nine forty-five, the second call came from Imogen.

'We're leaving the restaurant. It will take us roughly fifteen minutes to reach the hotel,' she told Shona.

'How do you know?' Shona, with yet another glass of wine in her hand, asked, apparently more intrigued by the mechanics of infidelity than organizing her husband's exposé.

'Darling, you don't think this is the first time I've made this little trip, do you?' said Imogen. 'I flatter myself that you chose me because I'm a professional. I'm a genuine bad girl, not an amateur like too many women these days.'

It took Fee thirty-five minutes to make the journey from the flat. When the two women arrived at the hotel, Fee realized that Imogen had chosen well. It was expensive, exclusive and small. The reception area was to the left. Opposite the entrance was the one set of lifts. On the right, facing away from the entrance, were two chairs, high-backed and with wings.

Anyone could check in and walk to the lift without knowing who might be seated.

'How do we know that they haven't already checked in?' Shona said nervously.

'Don't panic,' Fee told her calmly. She directed Shona to one of the chairs and helped her to make sure that the camcorder was in position. She placed the attaché case on Shona's lap, the lens pointing towards the lift.

'As soon as they step into the lift, get up and walk towards them. Try not to swing the case too much,' she directed. 'Edward will probably be so surprised to see you he won't notice what you're carrying. Whatever you do,' she added, 'don't put the case down. If you do, all you'll get – literally and metaphorically – is a pair of heels.'

Fee regretted making the feeble joke since Shona instantly doubled up with mirth, laughing so loudly too many people glanced their way. She made her way to the reception desk and asked if Imogen Banks had checked in. The man consulted a computer.

'No.' He shook his head. 'There appears to have been a cancellation.'

Fee had never ruled out the possibility that Imogen might decide to turn business into pleasure – and take a genuine interest in Edward. But so soon?

Five minutes later, Fee returned to Shona. She had ordered coffee and brandy.

'Is there something wrong?' she asked anxiously, slurring her words.

Fee reassured her. 'It's fine. There was a mix-up. Imogen's on her way. She used her car phone when I was at the desk. They were held up at the restaurant but they should be here shortly.'

Shona swallowed more brandy. 'I'm awfully sorry to put you to so much trouble, Fee.' She waved the glass in the air. 'But do you think it would be all right if we went home now? I think I've had enough—'

Before Fee could answer, she heard Imogen's voice at the desk. She pushed Shona back into her seat, put a finger to her lips and indicated furiously with her other hand for Shona to press the 'on' button on the camcorder, disguised as a lock on the attaché case.

Instead, Shona sat paralysed. Fee peered around the back of the chair. Imogen and Edward were walking towards the lift.

'Shona!' Fee hissed. 'Shona, get up *now*!'

Shona said nothing and moved not at all. The lift had arrived, the door opened, Edward and Imogen stepped in. Fee stood up as Imogen, on cue, placed her arms around Edward as the lift doors began to close.

Shona suddenly let out an earsplitting scream as the attaché case fell on her foot. 'Aaargh!' she yelled.

The pain in her foot at least galvanized her into action. She was now hopping forward, brandishing the case as if it was a weapon of war, shouting, 'It's too late, Fee, it's too late, the doors have shut—'

Fee privately cursed Imogen. She of all people could have used a little imagination once she realized how badly the scheme was progressing. Shona stood in front of the lift forlornly, the case under her arm.

Then Fee realized that the lift doors were reopening. Edward Spannier's tongue was buried deep in Imogen's ear, while her foot, encased in plum-coloured suede, was stuck in the door.

'Gotcha!' Shona shouted in exhilaration.

Edward turned and almost sprang out of the lift, lunging at his wife's throat, oblivious to the camcorder recording his reactions or the small audience that had begun to gather. Imogen and Fee acted as one, shoving him sufficiently hard to send him sprawling. After years of marriage, Shona finally had her husband at her feet.

She gave Fee and Imogen a broad smile.

'Do me just one favour, Shona,' Imogen said, watching as Edward gathered himself together, promising all types of vengeance on 'you three bitches' before slamming out of the hotel.

'Do me one favour. Deal with him how you like, but please don't apologize while you're doing it. There's a good girl.'

'What will you do about Edward now?' Fee asked as they drove away from the hotel ten minutes later. Shona sat in the passenger seat, the small videocassette clutched in her hand.

Fee had decided to return Claire's camcorder on the way home, not least because she didn't like the possibility of returning to the flat at the same time as Edward.

'I'll have him back,' Shona replied. 'Except that now he needs me more than I need him.'

'Why not make a complete break?' Fee asked.

Shona sighed. 'He's all I know. It must be difficult for you to understand, Fee. I don't suppose you'd ever let yourself become that dependent, would you?'

'All too easily,' Fee answered. 'That's what keeps me running.'

It was after eleven by the time Shona and Fee arrived at Claire's flat. Clem Thomas opened the door. He was barefoot, wearing jeans and a T-shirt and glasses which he had pushed to the top of his head.

'Claire's not back from work yet,' he said by way of a greeting, then immediately apologized.

'I'm sorry.' He opened the door wider. 'Come in. Let me get you a drink. I've been trying to plough through a mountain of marking and didn't realize the time—'

He looked at Shona expectantly and Fee introduced them. 'Shona, this is Clem Thomas, Claire's . . . fian . . . fi . . . friend—'

Clem Thomas looked at Fee, amused that she found it so difficult to say the word 'fiancé'.

For the next half-hour or so, until Claire's arrival, Shona rambled drunkenly through her life story, sipping yet more wine while Fee stuck to coffee and Clem listened politely. Claire's arrival coincided with Shona falling into a doze on the sofa. Fee watched while Claire fussily collected up the papers that Clem had been marking on the large glass coffee table. And Fee said nothing when Claire tutted at the piles of books Clem had left scattered on the dining-room table.

'Well, you asked me to move back in—' Fee heard Clem Thomas say when the two disappeared into the kitchen together.

When Claire returned stony-faced with fresh coffee, insisting that Fee stay longer – 'You, at least, look cheerful' – Fee attempted to ease the tension by lightheartedly recounting the story of her experience with HAH!'s introduction agency and her meeting with Alan Munsen.

'He's had an even worse time than me,' she chuckled. 'He met one woman who said that she knew from his application form that they had a great deal in common. He thought that was a bit odd because she was dressed entirely in black and had hair dyed the colour of marmalade.'

'So?' Claire said aggressively. 'So, why shouldn't that mean they won't get on? Opposites can attract, you know—'

Fee shrugged noncommittally. 'Of course they can. But don't you think it's ridiculous to believe that a computer can come up with a perfect match?'

The question remained unanswered because Shona had risen unsteadily to her feet and announced she was going to bed. Fee steered her towards the front door. *En route*, Shona remembered her manners.

'Did I tell you what a lovely couple you make?' she addressed Claire and Clem drunkenly. 'It's a rare and beautiful sight. Something to treasure. You take care of her, understand,' she said to Clem. 'Tell me, Fee, how did those two meet? I adore a bit of romance—'

Fee laughed. 'Come on, Shona, it's time for bed.'

Shona swayed in the doorway. 'Did you meet at a party, Claire? Or on a train? I love train meetings. So mysterious . . . All those dark tunnels and wet platforms—'

Claire smiled. 'It was much more down to earth than that, I'm afraid,' she said. 'We'll tell you about it one day when we've all got more time—'

Booze had made Shona bold. 'That's a definite date then,' she shouted over her shoulder as Fee propelled her towards the front door. 'Don't think I'll forget . . .!'

*

Fee eventually managed to fold Shona into the car and pull the safety-belt across her body. 'I won't forget, you know,' Shona said, peering into Fee's face in the gloom.

She smiled sleepily. 'That man is so gorgeous, I will never forget.'

'Clem Thomas? Gorgeous?' Fee was now exasperated with Shona's physical floppiness, as she attempted to buckle her safety-belt.

'Shona Spannier, you really are talking bullshit.'

Chapter Thirty

'ARE YOU sure you won't marry me, Walt?' Fee asked, laughing. 'I could make you a very happy man.'

Walt Whiting chuckled. 'Don't try to distract me when I'm winning. OK, question number 4. What was Roy Rogers's real name?'

Fee shrugged, 'Haven't a clue.'

'Leonard Franklin Slye,' Walt answered with glee. 'You are rusty, girl. Your father would be ashamed of you. Question number 5. Name two types of cacti in the Arizona desert—'

Fee didn't hesitate. 'Prickly Pear and Organ Pipe . . . Both featured in *The Man from the T-Bar Ranch* by Gus Arnold—'

'Not bad,' Walt conceded. 'OK, your turn to ask the questions but make 'em tough—'

He had contacted Fee at work that morning and told her that the landlord had threatened to dump Rita/Rose's belongings in a skip if she didn't pay her rent.

'We pay monthly and she's a couple of months behind,' he explained. 'Jimmy and I have said we'll pack her stuff up but we've nowhere to store it. Can you help?'

Fee agreed to come at lunchtime. Walt Whiting had insisted on feeding her. Homemade vegetable soup had somehow led to a conversation about cowboys and that, in turn, had led to a contest to see who really knew the Wild West. Walt was ahead.

Fee looked at her watch. 'I'll have to go soon,' she said. 'Is there much stuff to store?'

Walt shook his head. 'Sad, really,' he said and then smiled wickedly. 'Unless, of course, she's kept all her best stuff for one of her other lives?'

Two suitcases, five black plastic bags and a box of books had been placed in the middle of Rita Mason's denuded room. Once she saw these few possessions, Fee knew she didn't want them in her flat. It wasn't the space they would occupy; that wasn't a problem. It was the fact that they meant that Rita could reintroduce herself back into her life again. And Fee wanted this loose end tied in the largest possible knot.

'I'll take the lot to Cardiff,' she announced. 'I'd planned to visit Rita . . . Rose's mother anyway. Then I got waylaid. I'm sure she'll have somewhere to keep her daughter's belongings safe.'

'Does she know Rose is missing?' Walt asked.

Fee shook her head. 'She's not in the phone directory so my guess is she's got a different name—'

'Well, there's a surprise,' he commented drily. 'When do you plan to go?'

Fee took only a few minutes to consider.

'Tomorrow. I can get there and back in a day or so and I'm owed lots of time off.'

'Tomorrow suits me,' said Walt. 'You don't mind if I come along with you, do you?'

Fee smiled at him, delighted.

'You're a man after my own heart, Walt,' she said. 'Are you sure you won't marry me?'

The next morning, they left for Cardiff early. The address wasn't difficult to find. It was one of a row of terraced houses, each with its own neatly kept front garden. Number 48 had a red door, net curtains and two empty milk bottles on the doorstep.

A small woman – under five foot – but solidly built, was weeding a flowerbed. Her face was tanned and deeply lined and her hair pulled back into a bun. Her energy was almost tangible and faintly frightening in its ferocity. She wore wellingtons, a large pair of what might have once been men's corduroy trousers and a plaid flannel shirt. She certainly didn't look like the type who would have a crush on Rita Heywood, as Rita had reported to Veronica.

'Yes?' the woman said curtly when she saw Fee and Walt Whiting at her garden gate. The accent was Scottish. She didn't return Fee's smile.

'I wondered it I might speak to Rita ... Rose, please?' Fee asked. The woman's manner made her feel unusually hesitant.

'Who?' the woman asked impatiently but Fee guessed from the way she seemed to square herself that she knew exactly who Fee was talking about.

She cleaned her hands on her trousers. 'I'm seventy-two years of age and I've never known a Rita or a Rose. Sorry I can't help,' she added and turned away to walk into the house.

Fee and Walt followed her. Fee decided she was tough enough to stand a little gentle harassment. The woman turned again to face Fee.

'I know you don't have a Rita or a Rose,' Fee began. 'But this person gave this address as her mother's home. I'm very keen to know if this person is all right—'

'Of course she's all right.' The woman folded her arms in front of her. 'She's always all right ... it's everybody else she brings trouble to—'

Walt Whiting raised his hat by way of a greeting. 'Madam,' he began graciously. 'We mean well, we really do. May we have a few words? Perhaps indoors, if that might be possible?'

The sitting room appeared not to have changed for thirty or forty years. It was overcrowded with dark, utility furniture and bric-à-brac which marched like a tin and china army across every available surface.

Family photographs were in abundance, the more recent ones incongruously framed in opaque lilac and turquoise and bright orange. None figured Rita or Rose.

'If you're looking for snaps of her, I burned them all,' the woman said bluntly. 'I knew in the womb she'd be nothing but trouble. And she soon proved me right.'

Fee sat down slowly on a straight-backed chair with a torn brown leather seat. It was the first time in her life that she had heard a mother openly express such dislike of her own child.

'Even as a baby I couldn't stand her. Loved the others, but couldn't stand her. She was selfish, always wanting, always after attention, always leading the others into trouble. She was the first of the four,' the woman explained without emotion.

'I told people that I didn't like her. Why not be honest? But it's not what you're supposed to say, is it? You can think it, but if you're a mother you can't say it. Well, I did. I've always called a spade a spade. And proud of it.'

The woman suddenly got up from the chair she had taken by the window. 'I'll make tea,' she said. 'My name is Thomasina Hastings. Don't bother to tell me yours. There's been too many over the years.'

The story of Rita Mason, as recounted by her mother, wasn't very long in the telling. Rita's name on her birth certificate was Mary Hastings.

'Plain Mary,' her mother said.

The Hastings had moved to Cardiff from Glasgow after the war so that Peter, Thomasina's husband, who had died in his sixties, could take up a job working for a ship's chandler. Rita had been born six months after the marriage, when her mother was just nineteen.

At fourteen, Rita became pregnant. The child, a boy, was born in a mother and baby home and then adopted. 'A year later, I told her to get out,' Thomasina Hastings's tone indicated she had nothing to repent. 'It was the lies. Always lying. Inventing stories. Being who she wasn't. "What's wrong with who you are?" I used to ask her.

'After she left, she went from one fella to another. The few times she'd come back, she'd be dressed to the nines, dishing out expensive presents. Always managed to get some boy to spend money on her. I told her to keep her presents. I believe in honest money.'

'So how was she earning a living?' Fee asked.

'Don't know. But I could guess. Never asked what she was doing or where she was living, because I knew she'd only give me lies.

'My guess is when she got too old to hook the men, she started to latch on to women. Called herself a lady's companion at one point. Frightened one old woman half to death. Wouldn't let her live her own life.

'The woman's relatives called the police to chuck Mary out of the house . . . Mary said she was only trying to do what was best by the old woman and her relatives were all thieves—' Thomasina Hastings gave a grim laugh. 'She's greedy, Mary is. Always was, always will be. Wants too much of what others have got—'

She leaned closer to Fee. 'I haven't seen nor heard from Mary in months and, if I were you, I'd forget about her too. If she's not doing harm, that girl, she's not happy . . . The other three have married, settled down, raised families, never caused a day of worry. But Mary?

'I used to look at her sometimes and think she's not my child. She can't be my child. She's nobody's child.'

At the garden gate, Walt Whiting, hitherto silent, laid a hand on Fee's arm. 'What ghosts in that woman, do you think, made her punish her daughter so?' he asked gently.

Shona sat in Veronica's kitchen with the large diary that normally hung on Veronica's wall. Each month was illustrated with a lurid watercolour in which a tinned peach had been crudely inserted into the scenery. The calendar had been a gift when Salamanca, 'purveyors of the world's finest canned peaches', had tried to woo Les Haslem as a customer.

Shona stared at this month's illustration. It showed a blood-red skyline on a tropical island. The 'sun' beginning to set was a large tinned peach.

'Look at June,' Jean Stoker instructed.

Shona did as she was told.

'Do you see the ring around the eighth?' Jean asked. Shona nodded. 'That's our deadline for the money. If we haven't raised it by then, we've lost our chance of buying the business.'

'Edward's been behaving exceptionally well since he tried and failed to find the cassette,' Shona said. 'Do you want me to ask him for the cash? He's so desperate that I turn up for his selection meeting next week that he'd more or less agree to anything. After next week,' she added resignedly, 'who knows what will happen?'

Veronica shook her head. 'No,' she said. 'We don't want his money, we want your help.'

Shona took a good look at Veronica. She hadn't realized when she first arrived, but now it was obvious: *something had happened to Veronica*. She had had her hair restyled and she was glowing. If Shona hadn't known that Veronica was fifty-one, she would have said that she had that early look of pregnancy. Her eyes had a sparkle, her skin had a gleam. *Something had happened to her.*

'So, Shona, will you give us a hand?' Veronica asked again.

'Me?' Shona queried. 'How can I help? I'm sorry, I wish I could . . . but it's so long since I had a job. I'd be more of a liability—'

'Nonsense,' Jean reassured her. 'If you can persuade Imogen Banks to do something she doesn't want to do, you can persuade anybody to do anything . . . Veronica and I have talked it over and we're sure you're perfect for what we want. So what do you say?'

Half an hour later, an agreement had been reached. Veronica checked her watch and told the other two women to move into the sitting room, turn on the television and she would bring in the wine. 'It's almost time.'

Les Haslem was upstairs in his office. He shunned the word 'study' as too pretentious. Hearing the women move from one room to the next, he closed his door and surreptitiously turned on his television too. He'd told his wife that he hadn't the remotest interest in what Fee had to say on the subject of marriage, spinsterhood or, for that matter, Brussels sprouts, on or off the box.

He knew he would warm to her again, given time, but she had been the catalyst for too many unsettling events in his life recently for him to entertain positive thoughts quite yet.

He changed channels, keeping the volume low. Give Fee her due though, he told himself, she had helped put a stop to Veronica's problem. For now. Les settled down to watch his sister-in-law's television début.

The Perfumed Pound was a third of the way through before Fee Travers was introduced to the viewer. By then, Les Haslem had been snoring gently for several minutes. 'Women's stuff' always had that effect on him.

Chapter Thirty-One

CHEESE AND pickle sandwiches, curling at the ends like a genie's slippers, and several bottles of warm white wine had been placed on a table along one side of the room. Half-a-dozen office chairs faced a large television. Two female researchers shepherded people to and from the make-up department.

Participants in the studio discussion that was to follow *The Perfumed Pound*, due to go on air shortly, had not been formally introduced. So, unsure of who was an enemy and who might be an ally, they said little and concentrated instead on imagining the various ways in which they might be about to make a fool of themselves on national television.

The bishop, of course, was more confident. TV studios were his preferred pulpit. He discreetly examined Fee Travers. She looked normal enough; feminine, well kept, quite attractive, not even overweight. In his experience, so many of these sorts of females were, well, large; starved of love, stuffed on chocolate wafers.

The bishop had already been tipped off by Imogen. She had told him that Fee was one of society's subversives. She was extremely anti-family. She was also in favour of the elimination of the institution of marriage and its replacement with annually renewable contracts, which should also be available to same-sex couples.

The bishop sighed. Life had become so much more complex since Consumerism had replaced Christianity in most people's lives. Once upon a time, it used to be 'I believe' or even 'I think I believe' . . . now it was 'I want; I buy.'

'I'd Like My Money Back' was the closest the average pew-filler came to redemption, he mused, on his second glass. Even marriage had become as dispensable as last year's cassock. It had all been so much easier when everybody knew their place . . . the rich man in his castle, the poor man at his gate . . . And the wife?

The bishop sighed again and glanced at the woman to his right. She wore a dark-brown trouser suit and open-necked cream shirt. The hair was cropped with one curl literally glued to her forehead. She wore brogues and a large gold ring on her wedding finger. The bishop was fairly positive that her spouse was unlikely to be male.

'Chris Odell,' the woman said, catching his eye and taking the opportunity to introduce herself. She stuck out her hand and the bishop found himself in a grip so powerful he could have sworn his own hand had been neatly folded in two, like a napkin on a side plate.

The woman smiled. 'I'm spokesperson for SOS . . . Save Our Spinsters . . . We want to reclaim the word 'spinster' and make it synonymous with joy, celebration, pride, choice—' Chris Odell spoke as if she had written one too many mission statements.

'We believe that a woman's natural choice is to be single . . . roam free . . . to opt for no long-term partner. Study nature, bishop. It's all right if I call you bishop, isn't it? I find, "Your Grace" politically indefensible—

'Well, bishop, study nature and what do we see? Females of the species copulating with whoever takes their fancy, then going on to live as independent beings in colonies of females. Is this taught in the national curriculum? Of course it isn't, it's far too revolutionary. But we know the truth. The truth is that marriage, wifedom, is an unnatural state—

'SOS's intention is to reverse the brainwashing of girls today. Too many mistakenly believe that spinsterhood means only one thing – rejection, misery, failure—'

The bishop tried and failed to suppress a yawn. 'Isn't that three things?' he remarked mildly.

'Don't get me wrong, bishop,' Chris Odell continued, oblivious to his reaction, 'I'm not talking about the patriarchy here. I'm talking the next step. We don't know where that step may take us, but we do know that the new spinsters will lead the way because who—'

The young researcher interrupted forcefully. 'Excuse me, but could you hold all controversy until we get to the studio, please?' she ordered crisply. 'The director is worried that if you do it in hospitality, there won't be anything left to say . . . Here we go,' she added, as someone dimmed the lights.

'I hope you enjoy the film, everybody.'

The Perfumed Pound was Imogen Banks at her best – or, at least, that's what she'd encouraged others to write in a number of television previews. The film focused on three women, a GP of forty-five; a woman who ran her own import-export business, aged thirty, and Fee, who received the most attention, as she was the least equivocal.

The women were each filmed, then interviewed on the advantages of living alone and how they spent their time and money. This was followed by observations from the people they had encountered in the years leading up to their decision to remain unattached.

Fee presumed that the aim of this miniature version of *This Is Your Life* was to establish in the viewers' minds that the three modern spinsters paraded before them were neither rejects nor closet lesbians. As it was, Imogen Banks had skilfully linked the three cameos with general statistics about the proportion of single women in each age group and how this compared with post-war and more recent figures. She'd also referred to the economic power that single women wielded – and which had not yet been fully realized by many in the market place. Les Haslem woke briefly to be told that 62 per cent of cars costing over £25,000 were purchased by unattached females.

Superficially, the film appeared fair but, to Fee, it conveyed the idea that she and the other 'female pioneers' were emotional cowards by any other name.

For instance, Claire, in a brief interview, commented, 'I believe that Fee's problem is not that she prefers to stay single but that deep down she's fearful of taking personal risks. If you call that exercising a choice, then yes, I suppose she's chosen to be a spinster. But it's not what I would call choice.'

'Thank you, Claire,' Fee muttered in the dark.

As she and the other guests watched the film, Angela Stead, one of the two researchers, ran through the line-up with the male presenter who was due to chair the discussion.

'One bishop, pro marriage, in favour of a government-sponsored campaign to make the institution more sexy to the average secular refusnik. Say "I do" and collect £50, sort of thing—

'One lesbian . . . spokesperson for SOS. Need I say more?

'One woman from the film. Let the others push her hard, so we can get some fireworks.

'One Catholic mother of six, married twenty-seven years, husband known to play around but other guests will probably be too polite to point this out. Pro-wives.

'One right-wing academic and free marketeer who believes that women have a spiritual and civic duty to marry men, on the grounds that matrimony saves a man from barbarianism. Argues that the shame and stigma which was once associated with the spinsterhood must be restored in order to push more women into marriage. Confirmed bachelor himself, of course—

'One Israeli-American psychiatrist, thirty-four, will say either that the rise in spinsters is a disaster, a feminist plot designed to undermine society. If it goes on, the crisis in masculinity will reach danger levels. You know, the usual kind of thing. Or, he'll argue that the rise in spinsters is a sign of the first real breakthrough in the battle of the sexes, the inevitable result of men failing to change to suit a more egalitarian society. It's a warning to men and, if heeded, may mean a renegotiation in the contract of marriage and a much needed revival in matrimony – i.e. spinsterhood is good news.

'In short, he'll say what you feel is most required to give it all a bit of fizz. The deal is he prefers his left profile to camera.'

Hostilities commenced between the guests even before the discussion began. It soon transpired that the bishop also preferred to have his left profile to camera, and he too laid claim to the one seat that made this possible.

'It helps my hearing, so I must insist,' he said firmly.

'I'm sorry, but I've already reached an agreement,' the psychiatrist countered.

Chris Odell intervened. 'Why do you men always have to be so puerile?'

'Sexist generalizations like that, madam,' the academic pronounced, 'are sloppy, insufferable and an indicator of the kind of trouble we'd all be in if women ruled the world.'

'Now, now,' the Catholic wife and mother of six began in a placatory fashion, 'we don't need to behave like children, do we? Why don't I take this chair and then we won't have a problem any more, will we?'

'Don't you patronize me,' the psychiatrist snapped.

Fee watched wearily. She had come not to champion a cause but simply to explain her decision. But, as the evening unfolded, the very small hope she had held that this might be possible had slid further and further away. Not least because Imogen Banks had told Fee that there would only be one other opponent; now she faced five. Still, Fee consoled herself, she had helped Shona to get her man. What more could a good cowboy ask?

Chris Odell moved to fill the chair next to her.

'Thirty seconds to go,' the floor manager warned. 'And good luck, ladies and gentlemen—'

*

For the next twenty minutes, the chairman allowed Fee's five fellow guests to criticize not what she had said but what they assumed she had said in the film.

At first, Fee was angry, then defensive, then resigned – not least because she was repeatedly denied an opportunity to speak.

It was only when the academic, drunk on Sancerre and self-admiration, began to lecture her that Fee decided that she had had enough.

He spoke languidly in the style of someone who is accustomed to being treated as a wit and intellectual for displays of rude and offensive twittery.

'I have to say people like you, good lady, who advocate wholesale social engineering just to disguise the fact that Cupid has skipped on by—' he began.

Fee smiled sweetly. 'Is there something about a spinster that you find intimidating, perhaps?' she asked, then added, 'May I just make three brief points? First, I'm not advocating anything. I'm not *advocating* being single. But I am saying that diversity in relationships is no bad thing.

'Second, two out of three marriages are failing, I would argue, because we place an unrealistic emphasis on the transformative power of love. We've become smitten with the idea that having a partner somehow makes you a more acceptable human being, ensures happiness, solves difficulties, absolves you from a duty to look after yourself.

'Romance has become the opiate of our times. Fairy-tale romance which doesn't require effort or sacrifice or disappointment. Most people want to buy into that kind of magic. So they panic and persuade themselves they've fallen in love when they haven't at all. Or they move into a relationship and accept behaviour which they otherwise wouldn't tolerate. Isn't it perhaps time that some of us, a few of us, said, "Enough"?'

Fee glanced around her. The bishop, the Catholic wife and mother, the academic and the psychiatrist resembled a chorus line of goldfish as they simultaneously opened and shut their mouths.

'Lastly,' she added firmly, 'logic tells us that while 97.4 per cent of the adult population will live in a relationship at some time, a good many of them may do so miserably. If we were more honest and, yes, braver, perhaps we'd discover that many of us were actually intended to live happily ever after . . . but on our own.'

Chris Odell suddenly rose to her feet, yanking the academic up with her as she did so.

'You're on your own,' she hissed at him. 'Listen to what she says.' Chris Odell raised a clenched fist, 'Stand single! Stand free!'

Everyone agreed that it had been bloody good television. Or at least, each member of Imogen Banks's team told each other that it had made bloody good television. The switchboard had been jammed with calls, three tabloid newspapers were in pursuit of Fee Travers and the psychiatrist was already sitting in a corner of the hospitality room, writing what he called 'an instant think piece' on the psychosis of the permanently unattached.

Imogen Banks gave Fee a print-out of the first shoal of calls. For every three men and women who had phoned to say that it had been a change and inspiration to hear the positive side about being unattached, one claimed that the desolation and solitariness had been vastly underplayed.

Two calls had specifically asked for Fee Travers. One was from a woman called Anna Clarke. They had met when she worked on the local newspaper as a reporter and Fee was in her first teaching job. Anna Clarke had left her telephone number and a message to say that she now lived in Pembrokeshire and she'd love to hear from Fee again.

The other call was from Rita Mason. She had tried to leave a message but she had apparently been cut off.

Fee immediately rang the number that Rita had left. A boy in his teens answered.

336

'No Rita here,' he said. 'Nobody here at all. It's a phone box. I was just passing—'

'Whereabouts are you?' Fee asked.

'Clarendon Street,' the boy replied, his tone wary.

'Clarendon Street, where?' Fee pressed.

'Clarendon Street, Bristol, of course,' the boy said and added, 'Got to go now. Bye.'

'So what happens next?' Fee asked Imogen over drinks in the hospitality room.

'Marriage,' Imogen replied, helping herself to another glass of wine. 'You'll get dozens of proposals. And all this nonsense will soon be forgotten.'

'You sound just like my mother.' Fee smiled. She would miss Imogen.

As Imogen was about to reply, Alan Munsen walked into the room. Imogen had advised that Fee should avoid her own flat for a day or so in case 'one or two newspaper people' decided to pester her. Alan had offered Fee his spare bedroom.

'Now how come I haven't met you before?' Imogen murmured, breathing in deeply as she was introduced. 'Fee is such a good girl most of the time but she's got this perfectly wicked habit of keeping her nicest friends to herself.'

The features editor on the tabloid newspaper with whom Imogen usually dealt had done her proud. Several days earlier, Imogen had provided him with Bill Summers's and Paul Denning's telephone numbers. It was Imogen's intention that her film and discussion should have their life artificially extended by copious amounts of follow-up coverage in the tabloid press. She had achieved this by orchestrating an exposure of Fee's far from loveless life.

The spinster who helps herself to husbands.

Paul Denning, for understandable reasons, had refused to comment on Fee Travers, but his wife, when doorstepped and provided with the evidence of her husband's affair, had proved extremely fluent on the subject.

Bill Summers hadn't realized he was actually being interviewed by the reporter; he had been under the impression he was clearing up a few points.

The next morning he was appalled to see himself across two pages of a tabloid. 'I was bedded but bored,' read the headline over an old photograph of himself and Fee, taken on holiday years before. It was the kind of smudged and unfocused photograph that makes everyone look guilty of something.

'I didn't *say* I was bored with Fee,' Bill Summers tried to explain on the telephone to an extremely irate Helen Travers.

'I'm very, very disappointed in you, Bill,' Helen lectured. 'I thought you were going to cheer Fee up. That's what Imogen said would happen. Instead, you behave like a rat. I suppose you got paid for all this tripe?'

Bill Summers took in this information. 'What do you mean, "Imogen said"? I thought she wanted to see me because she was interested in my photography?'

'Well, I don't know about that,' Helen replied brusquely, anxious not to be sidetracked from the main cause of her disappointment. 'What I do know is that she and I had great hopes of you and Fee making a go of it. So I can't tell you how upset I am with you, Bill. Very upset indeed.'

Chapter Thirty-Two

A T SEVEN thirty that same morning, several reporters had con-
gregated outside Fee's flat. There were also half-a-dozen
women bearing SOS placards who told anyone who cared to listen
that they were protesting against Fee Travers because she lacked the
courage of her convictions. She had refused to condemn marriage.

'Marriage Means Murder . . . of a woman's individuality,' read
one of the SOS leaflets which a protester handed to Fee as she
slipped by unrecognized into her own flat, followed by Alan Munsen.

Will Evans was waiting in Fee's sitting room with a pile of
newspapers. A second tabloid had 'exposed' her across two pages as
a husband-stealing neurotic. She Stole Our Spouses, the banner
headline said with photographs of Erica, Bill Summers's wife, and
Paul Denning's wife, a woman called Cora.

'My Nights of Passion—' headlined a second story, in which
Adam Williams had apparently given details of nights of lust – none
of which tallied with Fee's own recollections.

Other tabloids had also pursued the story. 'The Sham and the
Shame of the Celibate Spinster' proclaimed one feature. Yet another
said that Fee had taken over the leadership of SOS and intended to
urge Britain's women to break free from partnerships and 'Stand
Single! Stand Free!'

The psychiatrist with whom she had appeared on television the
night before had produced yet another 750 words on the social
significance of this new female rebellion, under a banner headline,
'Why Today's Woman Says No!'

Other columnists pontificated on the end of the family; the demise of the housewife; the ruination of romance; the collapse of the community and the selfishness of the solitary life.

'And where the hell have you been?' Will asked Fee, eyeing Alan Munsen extremely coolly. 'I saw some bastard had tried to break the lock on your French window so I came in to check that everything was OK.

'I've had blokes on the phone all night offering me hundreds to spill the beans on you—' He indicated the pile of newspapers he had just dumped on Fee's sofa. 'Why have you suddenly become big bait?'

Fee began to flick through the pages. Mortification, embarrassment, anger, contempt and a distinct feeling of grubbiness – each waited its turn to wash over her again and again. Why was she suddenly a target? The answer came in two words. *Imogen Banks.* No wonder she'd looked uncomfortable when Fee had asked what would happen next.

'It's horrible. It's all so, so unfair. As for Paul Denning's wife, I only found out about her after I'd finished with him. Why isn't he copping it for not being honest with me in the first place?'

'I would've thought it's obvious,' Will shrugged. 'Women, beware women. Much sexier, don't you think? The good news', he added, 'is that this will all be forgotten in a couple of days. And Gerry Radcliffe called to offer his congratulations. The message is on your machine but, basically, he's delighted with your HAH! report.

'He's delighted with the plug you gave F. P. & D. last night and he's even more delighted that Harry Macklin never watches television so he's unlikely to throw a wobbly. He suggests you spend today at home to recover.'

'And the bad news?' Fee asked.

'The bad news is that Diana Woods has what he calls some useful amendments to make to your report. And he wants the three of you to have a meeting before your presentation is made to Macklin.'

Fee grimaced. Five minutes later, the phone began to ring and it didn't stop ringing for several hours. The calls brought requests for radio, newspaper and television interviews. *Singled Out*, a magazine for the never married and the separated and divorced, due to be launched in six weeks, asked if Fee would consider writing a weekly column. A couple of publishers suggested that she produce a guide for older singles.

'A guide to what?' Alan Munsen asked, helping to field the calls.

'To anything she likes,' the reply came back.

At ten, when Veronica Haslem arrived, bringing fresh supplies of tea and coffee and sandwiches, courtesy of Les since Fee's cupboard was bare, the crowd outside the flat had swollen even further.

The SOS squad had been joined by Christian activists in favour of banning all divorce; a variety of foreign print and television correspondents and several curious passers-by. Shortly after, Fee agreed to a brief radio interview on her telephone, in order to clarify the misconceptions that seemed to be mushrooming around her.

'No, I am not urging wives to leave their husbands,' she explained carefully. 'No, I am not saying that living alone is always better than living in a relationship. No, I am not on sex strike. No, I am not bisexual. No, it is not true that I've never had a proposal. No, I am not without morals. I try and treat others as I would wish to be treated – with some respect and a sense of fair play.

'No, this is not a publicity stunt. No, I am not about to fall for the next man who comes along. No, Imogen Banks and I are not having an affair—'

When she replaced the receiver, Fee looked at Will and Alan who had been banished to the sitting room but who remained listening at the kitchen door.

'How many times does a girl have to say no before people accept that she means what she says?' Fee asked wryly. Wisely, neither man opened his mouth.

*

Will, unsettled by Alan Munsen's familiarity with Fee, delayed his departure for work. When he could no longer postpone leaving, he said to Fee casually on his way out, 'Oh, by the way, Hannah and I aren't together any more. She moved out . . . Last night actually. That's why I didn't see your programme.'

'I'm sorry.' Fee gave him a hug.

'I wanted her to stay but there you go—' Will shrugged wearily. 'She told me that I'd never make a proper commitment to her . . . so, for her own sake, she was giving me the push. That's a first, you know, Fee. First time I've been dumped in years. Must be losing my touch.'

He laughed without amusement, then closed the front door behind him before Fee could offer reassurance.

Coming back into the sitting room, Fee took a proper look at her sister. Veronica had taken off her coat and was peering out of the French windows at the crowd below.

'In the hope that you don't take this the wrong way,' Fee remarked, 'you looked dressed to kill.'

Veronica chuckled. She was wearing a dress and jacket in a warm, cherry red. Her hair had been cut shorter and she was wearing discreet gold ear-rings.

'If I didn't know you better, I'd say you've been indulging yourself with the housekeeping money and following in Jean's footsteps. You haven't acquired yourself a gigolo, have you?' Fee asked, intrigued.

Veronica sucked in her breath. 'Please,' she responded in mock distaste. 'We don't use the word. Far too common. The answer is no, I haven't . . . but, yes, I do have a new man.'

'Oh, Veronica,' Fee couldn't stop herself. 'Do you honestly think that's wise? After all you and Les have come through? He'll be devastated—'

Veronica smiled. 'This man is taking me out for lunch. I told him to pick me up from here. I knew you wouldn't mind. Not now I know you're in favour of women branching out. Stand Up! Stand Free!'

Fee groaned. 'I didn't say it, the other woman did,' she moaned. 'But anyway you're not free, you're married . . . Adultery just isn't your thing.'

'Isn't it?' Veronica chuckled.

At noon, Les Haslem pushed his way through the crowd to Fee's front door. When the doorbell rang, she checked from her balcony to see if it was friend or foe.

The sight of her brother-in-law was not pleasing. Fee visualized fisticuffs between Les and Veronica's new suitor with a quorum of the regional and tabloid press acting as referees.

'Quick,' Fee told Veronica. 'Les is here. You'll have to hide. I'll try and get rid of him but promise me that you'll never put me in the middle like this again. OK?'

To Fee's annoyance, Veronica did nothing. 'Come and sit here,' she directed Fee, smiling and patting the seat next to her. 'I've got something to tell you—'

Fee did as she was told.

'It's Les who's taking me out for lunch,' Veronica said simply. Fee could swear her sister was blushing. 'He's started to court me again. It's made such a world of difference. I feel as if I'm being listened to properly for the first time in years. I feel as if I matter to him again.'

'And what worked the miracle?' Fee asked lightly, trying not to sound cynical.

'After he'd refused to help Jean and I with our business, I had the row with him that we should have had in 1980.'

'1980?' Fee asked, mystified.

'When I wanted to continue doing the books for him and Les said no. I should have held my corner and I didn't. And from then on, rather than have a confrontation, I just gave in. The last few weeks with you and Percy and the boys and Jean have made me realize that Les doesn't always know what's best either for me – or himself. That I am entitled to my own life too.'

343

'So I told Les he could either accept that I'd changed and treat it as a plus. Or he could make life difficult for us both and I'd have to think seriously about whether I'd stay . . . I said I didn't want to be treated like a habit any more.'

'It was as simple as that?' Fee asked.

Veronica smiled. 'Of course not. At first, Les said he hadn't a clue what I was talking about—'

She stopped as Les walked into the room, let in by a departing Will Evans. Relief was written on his face. He gave both his wife and Fee a kiss on the cheek. 'Great film, Fee,' he lied cheerfully. 'Didn't know you had it in you. Although I expect you could do without the mob out there?

'Have you met my new wife?' he added, winking. 'That's what makes a marriage work, you know. Room to let each other breathe, change, allow each other to develop a life of their own. Haven't I been saying that for years, Veronica?'

Helen Travers was enjoying a new experience – first in her local newsagent's and then at her hairdresser's. She had expected embarrassment, discomfort, even shame. She had even contemplated cancelling her appointment for a shampoo and set.

After all, it isn't every day that your daughter's sexual habits are paraded across several pages of the newspapers and she's transformed into Public Enemy No. 1. It isn't every day you have reporters knocking on the door asking for photographs of your daughter as a bridesmaid.

Helen Travers had outwitted them on that one. She knew their little game. Three times a bridesmaid, never a bride . . . So she'd said no and shut the door firmly in their faces.

Betty Wilthorne from number 17 across the way had said that the reason all this spinster stuff had become a Talking Point was because it had struck the nation's nerve.

'Everyone knows that marriage isn't working and they're frightened that more and more women are going to be like your Fiona and go it alone,' she elaborated. 'And where will the country be then? If it was my daughter, I'd give her a good talking to—'

No one in the Travers family had ever struck the nation's nerve before. Vera had only reached the nerve of the immediate neighbourhood. Now, in the high street, on this beautiful Thursday morning, Helen was experiencing a new sensation. It was so potent it even distracted her from the gnawing ache of disappointment which she had carried with her for years.

'Saw your daughter on the telly last night, Mrs T.,' said Ahmed Patel in the newsagent's. 'Bloody good too. Very pretty.'

'Wasn't that your Fiona on the box, last night?' asked Mrs Oakford who worked in the chemist's. Wendy, who worked in the baker's, commented, 'On that quiz show, wasn't she? Very good too. She always was the clever one of your three, wasn't she?'

Helen Travers had suddenly become a Celebrity. All right, she was a once-removed celebrity, but it would do for her. By the time she reached the hairdresser's, she was on the offensive.

'Don't suppose you saw my daughter last night?' she asked Shirley, the receptionist. 'She was on the television. Pity. Never mind, I'm sure you'll catch her next time she's on. She's had loads of offers. She's thinking about switching careers . . . The female side of the family has always been photogenic, even if I say so myself.'

That afternoon, Fee spoke to her mother on the telephone. She had expected to be heavily criticized but, to her surprise, Helen was offering a modicum of enthusiasm.

'Have you read any of the papers?' Fee asked cautiously.

'Yes,' Helen replied airily, 'but I never believe a word I read.'

'Did you watch television?' Fee tried again.

'Yes, I did,' Helen answered cheerily. 'I thought you looked quite nice, all in all.'

'You weren't upset?' Fee asked warily.

'I wasn't *listening* to what you said, dear. I was too busy *looking*

345

at you,' Helen chided, and added, 'Tell Claire not to wear that yellow thing on television again. It makes her look awfully peaky.'

Later that evening, Fee decided that her mother had been right. Claire did look peaky. She sat opposite Fee, eating little and saying next to nothing. She and Clem had joined Will and Fee for a meal. The crowd outside the flat had almost dispersed but Fee had escaped undetected anyway by climbing over several garden fences at the rear of the house. Will had suggested a night out as a brace against what the next day's press coverage might bring. And to take his own mind off Hannah's departure.

After the meal, the two couples walked back to Claire's flat. Will and Clem went on ahead. Fee mentioned to Claire the attempts by Jean and Veronica to raise funds for an escort agency and their intention to turn it into a service for older women. Perhaps Claire might consider investing?

'Selling sex, you mean,' Claire commented waspishly.

Fee smiled. 'That was my reaction too at first. But it's not sex they're offering, it's company.'

Claire was unimpressed. 'Frankly, I find that appalling. Is that what we're supposed to regard as progress? Women now doing what men have done for centuries – buying flesh to satisfy their sexual appetite? God, what's wrong with a little restraint now and then? Why don't we wake up to the fact that just because we want something, it's not always good for us to have it? I mean, don't you find it sad, Fee, that, in this day and age, some of us have to *buy* another person's company?'

'Yes, I do – but at least it's an honest transaction, wouldn't you say?'

'But it's so . . . so . . . so *pitiful.*' Claire almost spat the word out. Fee didn't have to hear the thunder of hoofs to know she'd had enough of Claire's lack of generosity both to herself, on television, watched by several million viewers, and to others.

'It may be pitiful but it isn't deceitful, is it? Take your relationship with Clem. Don't you think you might be exploiting him just a little bit?

'Isn't what you're doing, to get something you want under the false pretence that you're in love, a lot more dishonest than a business arrangement in which the terms are clearly understood, payment is made and there's much less room for the manipulation of another person's feelings? Or, to put it even more plainly, Claire, are you really in a position to judge anyone else?'

Claire stopped dead, shocked at Fee's totally untypical lightning attack. 'What's happening to you?' she demanded. 'What's *really* happening to you, Fee?'

Chapter Thirty-Three

HARRY MACKLIN, founder of HAH!, broker of hearts, maker of dreams, lord of the lonely-hearts ads, arrived unannounced at F. P. & D. on Friday morning. He was dressed head to toe in his habitual white and was accompanied by his accountant, Serena Alwyn, who was dressed cleavage to calf in embroidered denim, an ensemble that was completed by a pair of high-heeled denim boots.

Contrary to appearances, they had not come to duet for a Country 'n' Western special. On the contrary, they had come to perform a spot inspection on the state of health of the springster – that upwardly mobile, deeply attractive, genuinely gregarious human being who was so busy achieving that he or she had little time to seek out a soulmate.

What Harry Macklin wanted to know from F. P. & D. was – had the springster been sprung? And to what effect?

He wanted to hear that F. P. & D. had not only pinned down the species but, more importantly, that Ms Fiona Travers had also discovered how to tickle the springster's fancy sufficiently so that he or she would shamelessly spend money on the business of love.

Gerry Radcliffe knew this and he was flustered. He was so fundamentally flustered – he had not expected to have contact with Macklin for at least another fortnight – that he was even too preoccupied to travel the valley that was Serena Alwyn's cleavage.

'Jesus Christ, Fee,' he exploded in Fee's office while Macklin and Serena Alwyn were given coffee in the boardroom. 'What do you mean, we're not prepared?'

'No, Gerry, what I said was that *you* are not prepared,' Fee replied evenly. She was still smarting from the latest dose of hostile press coverage in which she had yet again been castigated for what she hadn't said. This time by a posse of female columnists who managed to be even more judgemental than Claire. But then they were being paid by the poisoned word.

Fee continued, 'My report has been ready for a week, but you said Diana wanted to make some changes. It's those changes that haven't been included in the report. So that's why I'm telling you, *you're* not prepared. I am.'

A smile spread across Gerry's face. 'Bugger the changes. Stick with what you've got, kid. Are you able to do a presentation now? I know you haven't had time to prepare properly but can you do it? For me?'

Fee examined her boss, sweaty and agitated. He was dressed in the vibrant clashing shades of a fairground merry-go-round – tie, shirt, socks. When she had first come to F. P. & D., she'd regarded his colourful clothes as a visible sign of the liveliness and originality of his mind. Now, they just seemed a case of bad taste. Fee recognized that she no longer cared about her job, nor did she respect Gerry Radcliffe.

Job and boss represented good money – but in other terms both amounted to, quite literally, a fuss about nothing. And Fee knew she was reaching an age when she wanted her work to amount to a lot more than 'nothing', however well paid. But for now she'd play Gerry's game.

Fee spoke crisply. 'I won't do it for you, Gerry, but I will do it for a rise.' She glanced at her watch, to reinforce the message that time was at a premium. 'A rise which brings me into line with what Diana is now earning will be perfectly adequate, thank you very much.'

The mock-up of the commercial went well.

Fee had put together an ad. for television to convey HAH!'s change in the market. Working with Will Evans's team, she had devised a message that was simple but dramatic.

Glimpses of the lives of five men and five women, aged thirty-five to sixty, were revealed – in work, with friends, with family and alone.

Then ten faces appeared on screen simultaneously. The viewers are told that four out of these ten people are single and want to find a partner – but have a life so busy that it's difficult to find the time or the opportunity.

'Can you guess which four?' asks a voice. Six faces dissolve, leaving the four least stereotypical candidates.

The commercial ends with a tease. 'If you thought that was a surprise . . . you'll never guess how they found their ideal partner—'

'We run these as tasters,' Fee explained. 'We don't give an answer until we've got interest nicely built up through the media, billboards, TV. The first point we have to establish is that the most surprising people, highly eligible people, not just nerds, find it difficult to meet others.

'The second point is that we need to develop a different brand name and logo, something more oblique, for the new market you're seeking.'

'Oblique?' Harry Macklin asked, mildly concerned about the consequences of this line of thought. He had just rebuilt his outdoor swimming pool in the shape of two interlocking hearts. 'Oblique? You mean like a zigzag or something?'

'Precisely,' Fee smiled. 'A zigzag would do perfectly. It means nothing and so it can come to mean everything.'

Harry Macklin frowned. 'People like to understand what they're seeing. They don't want messages they have to unravel. Life is too much like a crossword puzzle as it is, I'm not sure—'

'Harry, you know you're always the same when it's time to try something new.' Serena Alwyn nodded in Fee's direction. 'I think—'

She stopped because Diana Woods had placed a second cassette in the video recorder and was indicating that she expected everyone's attention.

'If you've got anxieties, Mr Macklin, I think that's very understandable,' her voice oozed sympathy. 'May we show you one alternative possibility?'

The cassette proved to be the original commercial that Fee had criticized. She opened her mouth to speak, but Gerry shook his head. Harry Macklin watched the ad. – figures running along the beach, violin strings and sat for several minutes without comment. Then, abruptly, he rose to his feet.

'I'll buy the second,' he said curtly. 'But add another fifteen years to their ages—'

An hour later, in his office, Gerry Radcliffe put up a hard struggle. At length, he tried to convince Fee that F. P. & D. was a team, and that it didn't really matter that Diana Woods had been unprofessional.

It didn't even matter that, according to F. P. & D.'s research, her 'concept' would bomb more dramatically than chocolate-flavoured crisps. If that was what Macklin wanted, that was what he would get.

'But it makes it look as if we don't do our homework correctly,' Fee protested. 'Diana had no right to undermine us . . . And we have a responsibility to use our research appropriately. Otherwise why bother with research at all? Why not just give a client any old crap they want – and smile when they lose every penny they've got? What about professional ethics, Gerry?'

Gerry pondered the situation. What he had not yet told Fee was that two companies had made contact that morning, offering large contracts to research sections of the market which might attract mature single women – on the understanding that Fee Travers would be involved.

He gazed at Fee balefully. How could this woman continue to bang on about professional ethics and standards and responsibility when there was so much damn money to be made?

Then, he saw the light. As a matter of fact, Fee herself had switched it on for him earlier that morning. 'OK, OK, OK.' He slapped both his hands down hard on his desk, like a demented domino-player. 'You've got it. A seat on the board. Same salary as Diana. No more arguments. Now, can we get on with the business in hand?'

Will Evans lay with his feet up on the sofa in Fee's office and watched bemused as she cleared her desk.

'You are mad,' he said. 'You've gone completely barmy. You're the only woman I know who is offered promotion and uses that as a reason to resign. What is going on?'

'I'm beginning to see sense,' Fee answered. If she'd known the relief that resignation would bring, she would have gone months ago. Except then she would probably have lacked the courage.

'For once I'm doing what I want to do, not what everybody else thinks is best. And you've no idea how wonderful it feels—'

Fee emptied the contents of her desk drawer into the perspex waste-paper basket. 'I don't like the job any more,' she said. 'I was brought up to believe that if you'd got a job, you hung on to it, come what may. But why? Why if it brings out the worst in you and everyone else?'

Will grunted. 'Forty ain't an easy time to start again,' he commented bluntly.

'Thirty-eight,' Fee corrected. 'Just thirty-eight. I want to stop and really think about what to do next. I want to satisfy myself that I've done as much as I can to find Rita . . . I might even invest in Jean's and Veronica's business . . . who knows? If I do, I'll still have enough to take three or four months off. Most people never have that privilege—'

'Most people would be too bloody scared to do it, in case they never worked again,' Will commented. 'I've got to admit you've got guts. And to think you don't even have a man to fall back on.'

Fee threw a cushion at his head.

Chapter Thirty-Four

Gill Booth always knew that she was at her best when handling adversity – not her own, but other people's. Persephone was to spend Friday night at Fee's. Fee phoned on Friday afternoon and explained that, as she had unexpectedly liberated herself from her career, she could collect Percy earlier, after school.

Gill had, of course, insisted that Fee come round immediately to be comforted. On arrival, Fee had looked disgustingly cheerful. Gill nevertheless saw it as her duty to prepare her for the worst. 'Watch out for depression,' she warned, spooning tea-leaves into the teapot.

'It can come out of the blue. I suppose you realize that, now you've got no structure to your day, it will be very easy to let yourself go? Resist it,' she advised. 'I've done that, been there with Simon.'

Fee took her cue, relieved to change the subject. 'How is he?' she asked, attempting to clear a chair of junk so that she could sit down.

'Brilliant,' Gill's voice sounded only slightly shrill. 'He's happy as muck. He's finally got a project off the ground – a series of five-minute films for television. He's asking famous people which building they like, then shoving in a bit of history. A firm of architects has also asked him if he'll join as a partner, so everything's just fine, couldn't be better, it's absolutely marvellous – for him,' she added bitterly.

Fee decided she couldn't handle her own resignation and an

353

exploration of Gill's reasons to be bitter on the same day, so she remained silent. She noticed that Gill had grown her hair so that it looked not unlike, well, Imogen Banks's hairstyle. And she had moved into a far stronger look. Now she was wearing a shocking-pink shirt and pink and black leggings. The overall impression was that of a quite glamorous presenter of a Channel 4 show on do-it-yourself.

'I've never thanked you for the time we stayed at your flat, have I?' Gill asked, pouring tea and offering biscuits.

'Oh, you did,' Fee corrected her, preparing herself for the sting in this tale. Gill smiled. It was a touch condescending but then again, Fee told herself, perhaps she was behaving more sensitively than usual today.

'I never thanked you for the glimpse you gave me of what life would be like on my own.' Gill shuddered involuntarily.

'That bad?'

'Bad but manageable,' she surprised Fee by replying. 'It made me realize that if things do get absolutely unbearable between Simon and me, then I wouldn't totally collapse as a divorcee.'

She paused. 'The trouble is, trust has gone between us. That's like taking the foundations away from a building.'

She handed Fee a cup and sighed wearily. 'Still, looking on the bright side, I've come out of this learning a few lessons. I'm aware that I've taken Simon and the kids for granted. When I realized that Percy preferred to be with you – and Simon preferred to be with Imogen, and, for that matter, that I preferred to be with that hideous man Steve at the singles night than on my own, it was a bit of a revelation.

'Now I know that I couldn't be without Percy or Simon. Or, rather, I wouldn't be happy knowing that they were with anyone else but me so I'm determined to make more of an effort. Of course, they've got to do their share too . . . Funny business, love, isn't it? The rules seem to change all the time.'

*

Later, Fee recounted the conversation on the telephone to Claire, who was about to leave on a business trip to Ireland. She was dismissive.

'I don't call that love; I call that possessiveness,' she said. 'Strange how some people can't tell the difference. Possession is nine-tenths of the real reason for divorce.'

Early on Friday evening, in the video rental shop, Fee told Percy that she was as stubborn as her mother. They had argued for fifteen minutes about which videos they should hire. Percy wanted a Certificate 15.

'But you're only seven,' Fee argued.

'Nearly eight,' Percy countered.

'I'll do a deal,' Fee offered. 'You can have two PGs instead.'

'Done,' Percy said.

Ten minutes after dumping her overnight bag in Fee's bedroom, Percy was sitting on the sofa, feet up on the coffee table, pizza on her lap, video whizzing on fast forward through the ads and previews.

'You have no idea what it's like to have a bit of peace and quiet,' she said as Fee came in with a tray holding two Cokes, tomato sauce and napkins.

Fee ruffled Percy's hair affectionately. As she did so, there was a knock on the door.

'Here we go again,' Percy said resignedly. 'I knew it wouldn't last.'

An unlikely trio, Edward and Shona Spannier and Imogen Banks, stood on Fee's doorstep.

'It's my fault,' Imogen blurted out.

'Yes, it probably is,' Fee answered coldly, still smarting from the unwanted press coverage Imogen had orchestrated.

'No, I mean it,' Imogen insisted, and walked past Fee into the kitchen followed by the Spanniers.

'It's my fault,' she repeated, pacing up and down in front of the cooker. 'I warned all of you that I wasn't to be trusted . . .'

Edward Spannier sat down heavily at the kitchen table. 'I'm sorry,' he said to no one in particular.

'*You're* sorry?' Fee repeated, now completely flummoxed.

Shona looked at Fee bleakly. 'They're in love,' she explained. 'Edward and Imogen came to tell me. It's the first time in our entire marriage that Edward has owned up to an affair and taken responsibilty for it, so I know it's serious.'

'We're suited, Edward and I,' Imogen began, as if Fee had requested an explanation. 'The textbooks say that you tend to fall for people who are a replica of your inner soul. And, well, basically, Edward and I have discovered we're as badly behaved as each other. That's why I know it's going to work.'

'So why come to me?' Fee asked.

'It was Shona's idea,' Imogen said.

'I want you to tell her what kind of a man Edward is. You know what he's really like, don't you Fee?' Shona pleaded.

Fee sat down next to her. 'But I thought you and Edward had agreed on a working arrangement for a marriage. You live your life; he lives his?'

Tears welled in Shona's eyes and Fee felt like shaking her. 'It sounds all right in theory, but in practice it's . . . it's . . . it's horrible. Tell her what Teddy is like, please, Fee.'

'Even if I did, do you honestly think she'd listen?' Fee asked gently. Then she turned to Imogen. 'Is this because Simon has gone back to Gill? Is this on the rebound? For God's sake, Imogen, why can't you choose a man who comes without any strings. Just once? For everybody's sake?'

Imogen's face registered outrage. 'Gone back? Are you mad?' she yelled. 'Simon didn't *go* back.' She squared her shoulders and banged the kitchen table almost triumphantly. 'He was *returned*. It was never going to work, so I took a decision that was best for both of us.'

Imogen addressed herself to Shona. 'Look here,' she began briskly as if making a final offer in a Delhi souk, 'Edward and I deserve each other . . . I'm sorry and all that but do stop being so pathetic. You'll soon be glad that he's gone. In fact, in a year or so, you'll thank me for it. Honestly you will.'

The following morning was a busy one for Fee. She watched cartoons in bed with Percy; consoled Shona who had slept badly on the sofa, and then sat down with a list by her telephone.

First, she contacted Anna Clarke, the woman who had left a message after the screening of *The Perfumed Pound*.

'That's Fee, isn't it?' Anna guessed immediately. Within minutes, the years had slipped away. 'I own a secondhand bookshop near the Brecon Beacons,' she explained. 'Why don't you come and spend a few days?'

'I was hoping you'd say that,' Fee replied.

Then, she called Jean Stoker.

'Are you still short of £27,000?'

Jean sounded despondent. 'A couple of bank managers have laughed in our faces at the suggestion of a loan. Veronica's next-door neighbour, Amy, has decided to invest £8,000 so long as she can have a role as a talent-spotter. And your sister, Elizabeth, has produced another two grand, but if we can't come up with the rest by Monday, that's it. I'm beginning to wonder whether Veronica and I are just completely out of our depth on this—?'

'I hope not,' Fee answered, 'because if you are, it will be my money that goes down the drain as well.'

'What do you mean?' Jean's voice suddenly lifted.

'I've left my job,' Fee explained. 'I'll need to keep some of the pay-off to meet my overheads for a couple of months, but you can have the rest. I'll talk to the bank so that either you or Veronica can collect the cheque as soon as I get the money.'

'Boy, oh boy.' Jean was ecstatic. 'We are finally in business.'

'I've got two provisos,' Fee interrupted. 'I'd like a decent return on my investment one day. And I need a baby-sitter now.'

She briefly explained what had occurred between Imogen and the Spanniers and that she planned to go away for a week or so, but she was reluctant to leave Shona alone.

'I was wondering if you or Veronica might be able to stay in my flat so that Shona knows there's somebody at hand?'

'I'll happily stay – but I'm sure Shona will be fine,' Jean replied confidently. 'You watch, Spannier will be sick of Imogen in a couple of days and come running home—'

'That's what he might want to do,' Fee answered cheerfully, 'but, this time, I'm not sure Imogen will let him go—'

On Saturday evening, after taking Percy home, Fee visited Walt Whiting. He and Jim Roth were about to go for a pint in their local and they asked Fee to join them. Fee told them about Rita's call from a phone box in Bristol. Jimmy Roth said that a young Iranian student was now renting her room.

'Has she contacted that seance bloke at all?' Walt Whiting asked.

Fee shook her head. 'He said he'd tell me if she did. You don't think I should go to the police?' Fee asked. Jim chuckled.

'You won't be the first,' he smiled. 'She told me that she'd been reported missing twice before. The police can't do anything unless they suspect foul play . . . Nothing much you can do now until she makes her next move.'

Fee decided on the way home that Jim was right. Tomorrow, she would drive to Wales, visit Anna Clarke and forget about work and men and broken, lonely, hearts.

How did the quote that Will Evans had given her read? 'Being an old maid is like death by drowning. It's a delightful sensation once you cease to struggle.'

Fee realized that she had stopped struggling – almost without noticing.

At 7 a.m. on Sunday morning, Clem Thomas telephoned. Claire had flown to Dublin on Friday. Twenty-four hours later she had been rushed to hospital with a suspected brain tumour. He had only just been informed. He said he planned to catch the ten thirty flight. 'I'll come with you,' Fee immediately offered.

Chapter Thirty-Five

O N THE flight to Dublin, Clem and Fee said little. They drove straight to the hospital and took turns to sit by Claire's bed. They were informed that the original diagnosis had been incorrect; what she was suffering from was a rare strain of meningitis.

Fee thought of very little over the next forty-eight hours except her overwhelming desire that Claire should live. Live and resume being her normal bossy, blunt and, at times, aggravating self.

Sitting alone in the cream and white room, Fee was compelled to talk to a rarely conscious Claire – about the times when they had first shared a house, had first gone on holiday; about the sense of loss when each had bought their own flat; about the lovers Claire had introduced into their lives and Fee had endeavoured to like, only to find them dumped within weeks . . . about Clem . . .

On Tuesday, the third afternoon of Clem's and Fee's shared vigil, when Claire showed a slight improvement, the staff suggested that they should take a break and go for a walk in the grounds together.

For the remainder of the week, the afternoon walk became a regular occurrence. The two talked about everything and nothing. Gradually, the initial judgements that Fee had passed on Clem, she quietly revised.

Of course, Fee told herself, what they had in common was Claire's recovery. So Fee had no games to play, no traps to lay, no subtext – as Claire would call it – to decode. She could afford the risk of being herself because if she failed to come up to scratch, so what?

'How did you and Claire meet?' she asked Clem casually on one of the walks. He looked at her quizzically.

'Hasn't Claire told you?'

Fee shook her head. Clem smiled. 'We met through an introduction agency. I was fed up of being on my own but I couldn't stand the thought of going out night after night on the hunt. Besides, I wanted somebody older, who enjoyed their job but who'd come far enough in their career to be willing to enjoy their free time too.' He glanced at Fee again.

'I don't know if Claire mentioned it, but my first wife ran off with one of my closest friends. It's OK, a lot of it was my own fault. I hardly spent any time with her, I was too busy climbing the ladder. Well, that was a lesson that hurt, so I decided I'd take a lot more care the second time—'

Fee began to laugh, then in case he thought her insensitive, she hurriedly explained. 'You went to an introduction agency? I don't believe it. And Claire must have gone too? No wonder she kept suggesting that I give it a go.

'No wonder she never asked any questions about the HAH! account. She must have been petrified that I'd come across her brilliant c.v. when I was poking around doing research. But why didn't she just come out and say so? Why be so secretive?'

Clem shrugged. 'Pride perhaps? She said she didn't want us to tell anyone in case people jumped to the wrong conclusion. Presumably that we were two of life's social inadequates. I said fine because it didn't bother me either way. But you asked a direct question, so I thought I should give you a direct answer.'

Fee smiled again. 'Well, speaking from my newly acquired professional experience, I would say that you honestly don't look the type.'

'And my advice would be that you would be wise to keep more of an open mind,' Clem replied lightly. 'Or start taking your own research more seriously.'

*

On Saturday morning, six days after she was admitted, Claire sat up in bed for the first time and began to talk a little. On Saturday afternoon, Clem suggested to Fee that they cancel their walk so that he could go and buy the odds and ends that Claire had requested.

'How long will you be away?' Fee asked and then, in case Clem should think the question peculiar, she added quickly, 'What I mean is, I'll wait with Claire. I'll have to think about going back to London soon—' She paused to gauge his reaction.

'Of course you will,' was all Clem said. *Of course you will.* Polite, non-committal.

Of course you will.

Clem promised he'd return in a couple of hours. Fee sat by Claire's bed and watched her friend sleep. It was then that she admitted to herself what, on a deeper, less conscious level, she'd known for a day or so. She was in love.

She was in love with Clem Thomas. She missed him when he was absent; she was disorientated when they met. She assumed that he must have guessed, but he gave no indication.

Fee tried hard to reason. This emotion was a consequence of her concern for Claire. This emotion was base: it was because Fee wanted what wasn't hers. This emotion was a result of Fee's determination to wreck Claire's relationship.

Fee didn't know which explanation, if any, might be true. But she was aware that, for the first time in her life, she had fallen for a man not because of the distorted passion he engendered in her, or the contempt with which he treated her, or the possessiveness he displayed, but because, in his company, she was comfortable both with him and herself. She was at peace.

On Monday, eight days after Fee's arrival in Dublin, she decided that her choice of action were minimal. It was time to run.

Claire would soon be fit enough to return to London. Clem would then be on his half-term holiday from school and he had promised the hospital staff that he would ensure that she rested. Fee had had no signal from Clem that he was remotely interested in anyone except Claire. Even if he had given any encouragement, how could Fee possibly destroy Claire's trust?

Fee, I haven't been honest with you.' Claire was in a wheelchair, and the two women were sitting looking out of her bedroom window, drinking tea. Fee had arranged to leave Dublin the following morning. Claire had improved but she remained fragile and weak. Seeing her vulnerability, Fee was consumed with guilt. But for what?

Claire took a sip of tea. 'I haven't been entirely honest about Clem and myself.'

Fee's mouth went dry. 'Oh?' she replied casually.

'The relationship's been a lot tougher than I've made out.'

'Oh,' said Fee again.

Claire proceeded to recite the complaints that she had first voiced to Michele Canning in the bridal shop – unaware that Fee had been able to hear. 'It's not Clem, it's me,' she elaborated. 'I'm difficult to live with. Perhaps if there was more passion on my side, I'd find it easier, I'd make more allowances—

'I've been trying to change Clem into the kind of man he doesn't want to be.

'No, no, I need to tell someone this,' Claire continued as Fee began to interrupt. 'I've tried to customize him into my perfect man . . . make him more ambitious, smarten up . . . and, rightly, he's been resisting.

'I've realized since I've been in hospital that instead of pursuing some ridiculous ideal, I should value what I've got in Clem . . . I know that's what I should do—'

'I certainly would,' Fee answered emphatically. 'I mean if I were you.'

Claire smiled at her, relieved. 'You like him?' she asked. 'I thought you might, if you had time to get to know him properly. I think it was partly due to your influence that I kept seeing him in a negative light ... I mean, you haven't exactly been enthusiastic, have you?'

Fee smiled at the irony of her situation.

'Clem's told me that you know that we met through an introduction agency,' Claire added. 'I would have told you earlier but you were already so scathing, I knew your reaction to that piece of information would probably finish our relationship off.

'I suppose what I'm trying to say is that when Clem and I first got together, I genuinely believed that my determination to make it work would be enough. As I told you, I hoped that love might come later—'

'Yes?' Fee encouraged her.

'Well, I'm just not sure any more . . . I just feel so uncertain—'

Fee put her arms around Claire and gave her a hug.

'Look, every woman who's about to get married suffers from uncertainties,' she said supportively. 'On top of that you've been dreadfully ill and your resources are at rock bottom. Once you've had a good rest, I'm sure you'll feel really positive about it all again ... It might help if you talked this through with Clem?' Fee suggested.

Claire shook her head.

'No. Once Clem's decided on what he wants, nothing on earth can make him change his mind. And I know he wants me.'

'Of course,' Fee smiled weakly.

Of course. Of course. Of course.

Clem Thomas knocked on the door of Fee's hotel bedroom at 1.45 a.m. on the day she was due to return to London. When she opened the door, he was standing there fully dressed and he had his coat in his hand.

'Fee,' he began, his face drawn.

Fee took a deep breath.

'It's Claire, Fee, she's had a relapse. She's in intensive care.'

It was several hours before Claire stabilized. During that time Clem and Fee had sat either by Claire's bed or in a waiting room, shared with the relatives and friends of other patients.

Fee was ashamed of her sense of contentment in Clem's company. She was ashamed that, at times, she found herself fantasizing about the predicament they would have been in, if Clem had been sharing her hotel bed when the call from the hospital had come through. Above all, Fee was ashamed that she was trying and failing to concentrate on the well-being of Claire.

At breakfast time, Clem suggested that they go to the cafeteria for a cup of drinkable coffee. Fee, her conversation hobbled by exhaustion, spouted nonsense about the sinful pleasures of Irish hotel breakfasts.

'I envy you, Fee,' Clem suddenly said. 'I envy the fact that you've decided exactly what you want in life—

'You've got no messy relationships, no pulls in different directions. No distractions. I wish I could be so clear-headed. And Claire says that once you've set your mind on something, nothing on earth will change it.'

'She did, did she?' Fee replied and gave a ghost of a smile.

Clever Claire; never too sick to defend her own interests.

Fee postponed her flight for twenty-four hours. By the following evening, Claire was again out of danger. Fee said her goodbyes and promised to visit as soon as Claire returned to London. Claire told her that Clem was at the hotel, having a bath and a change of clothes.

'He said to send his love.' She smiled. And as Fee reached the door, she gave a small wave.

'I couldn't have a better friend than you, Fee. I really couldn't.'

*

Ten minutes after the taxi had been booked to pick up Fee from the hotel and drive her to the airport, she was still sitting in reception. She looked up, to find Clem striding towards her.

'I've been phoning your room, I thought I'd missed you,' he said warmly. 'I just wanted to say thank you for all your help and support. And I hope you won't take this the wrong way,' he added, a smile on his face, 'but you're not nearly as frosty as I first thought—'

Fee raised an eyebrow. 'I hope you won't mind if I tell you the feeling is mutual,' she replied lightly.

Further conversation was curtailed by the belated arrival of the taxi-driver. Clem saw Fee to the cab and leant in at the window as she settled herself in the back seat.

'By the way,' he added casually, 'I thought you ought to know. We've decided to postpone the wedding. It's Claire's idea. She wants to wait until she's on her feet and ready to go again. Understandably this whole business has shaken her.'

Clem stood back from the cab and waved. 'Have a safe journey, Fee,' he said. 'And look after yourself.'

On the brief flight, the same six words kept running through Fee's head. *I thought you ought to know . . . I thought you ought to know . . . I thought you ought to know . . .*

By the time the plane landed at Heathrow, Fee had settled on a straightforward explanation. 'I thought you ought to know . . . because Claire has asked me to tell you.'

Shona Spannier had dark shadows under her eyes; her normally immaculately groomed hair was greasy and scraped back in a pony tail. She was without make-up and, while she was still undeniably attractive, the baggy cricket jumper and blue jeans hardly enhanced her appearance.

It had been ten days since Fee had left London. She had had one brief conversation with Shona, who'd promised that she was coping. Shona had offered to meet Fee from the plane so Fee had assumed that she had survived reasonably well.

'I'm so sorry,' Fee said, without thinking. 'You look as if you've had a terrible time.'

'Oh, it's been more than worth it,' Shona replied airily as she directed Fee to the short-stay car park. 'We've managed to get so much done—'

'You and Edward . . . you've decided on a divorce? You've been OK on your own?' Fee asked sympathetically.

Shona burst out laughing. 'On my own?' she said. 'You have got to be kidding. The flat is filled to overflowing—'

'Gill hasn't left Simon again, has she? You haven't got her and Percy and the boys?' Fee asked.

Shona smiled and shook her head. 'Darling,' she said, 'what you are looking at is a hard-headed businesswoman. Wait till we get home.'

In Shona's car, a note in capital letters was stuck to the dashboard. On it, in Shona's hand, were written the words, 'IT'S NOT ALWAYS MY FAULT. THINK BEFORE YOU APOLOGIZE.'

She shrugged, embarrassed. 'The day after you left, I sat down with Jean and Veronica and we drew up two plans. One for our business, and one for my private life. Both are going well. Although,' she added, the tears not far away, 'it still hurts more than a bit.'

On the journey home, Shona detailed to Fee the deal that Edward had offered. Separate lives, no divorce, Shona's bills paid and an allowance – but he would continue to live with Imogen.

'In a couple of years, once he's in the House of Commons, he said that we could think again about the arrangement, but he didn't want any domestic upheaval now,' she explained.

'What did you say?' Fee asked, non-committally.

Shona smiled. 'I told him I was in no rush to give him an answer.

I'm much too busy with my own stuff to think about him at the moment.'

'Good girl!'

When Fee walked into her sitting room, she stopped dead at the door. The room was overflowing with flowers. Piles and piles of mail were perched precariously on the coffee table and overflowed onto the floor.

'Fans,' Shona explained. 'Oh, and offers of jobs . . . We've had people knocking on the door too, wanting to sign up to the movement.'

'What movement?' Fee asked, stunned by the extent of the response.

Shona shrugged. 'I don't know, the single women's movement, I suppose. The Nobody Breaks My Heart commando unit . . . Anyway, you're the head chief and honcho; it's been decided by popular vote.'

'Bloody Imogen,' Fee said.

It was close to nine by the time Fee knocked on Shona's door. She had promised that once she unpacked, she would join her for something light to eat. She would have come sooner but she had wasted fifteen minutes debating whether to call Clem Thomas.

Could she pretend she was enquiring about Claire? But why not call Claire direct? Could she pretend she'd left something at the hotel? But why not call reception? Fee knew these symptoms and she knew what she should do – avoid all contact.

She knew, but she rang the hotel anyway. 'Sorry,' came the voice of the switchboard operator, 'Mr Thomas doesn't appear to be in his room. May I take a message?'

'No, no, thank you,' Fee mumbled, confused and suddenly feeling ridiculously let down.

*

Now, Shona's door was opened by Veronica and Jean, both beaming. Jean offered Fee a glass of champagne.

'To the woman who launched a thousand chits!' she announced dramatically.

'Chits?' Fee asked, kissing each, before accepting the champagne. She followed them into Shona's sitting room.

'Well, not chits exactly, but very tastefully worded leaflets which will be placed in magazines and outlets which reach the clientele we're after.'

The room was a tip of used coffee cups, telephone directories and discarded paper. Two computers had been set up in one corner. On an armchair, a stack of portfolios of male models had been stashed.

'We've abandoned all that,' Shona indicated the glossy photographs. 'We're going to recruit ordinary men who've never done this sort of thing before . . . but who've been checked and cleared and achieved the standing of impeccable gentlemen.'

'I don't know,' Jean interrupted wistfully. 'There's something about a scoundrel—'

Over supper, the three women described how, during the previous week, they had worked round the clock – hence Shona's exhaustion. They had set up an accounting system, redesigned the logo, hired a talent scout, found new offices, set up advertising, arranged publicity and fought over the name of the new company.

'So what is it going to be called?' Fee asked.

'It wasn't easy,' Veronica replied evasively. 'Anything French sounded too saucy; we want this to be an incontrovertibly clean show . . . Anything obscure was, well, too obscure . . . We wanted something classy . . . but memorable—'

'So what's it to be?' Fee asked again impatiently.

'It's going to be called . . . Spannier's—' Jean announced with a flourish.

'Spannier's?' Fee repeated blankly. 'Spannier's? It sounds like a dry-cleaner's or a gambling joint. You can't have Spanniers. Besides, Edward, the would-be MP, will have a fit—'

'Precisely,' Shona said.

Veronica interrupted hastily, 'I know what you're thinking, Fee, that this is about revenge. But it isn't, is it, Shona? It's because we want the name to be anonymous but imply quality. Haslem sounds like a pork butcher's. And Stoker is a bit . . . industrial . . . We did consider Travers but that's a bit . . . dull—'

'We could have chosen a name at random, of course,' Jean added. 'But the more we thought about it, the more Spannier's sounded right—'

'And what's the selling line?' Fee asked, her professional training coming to the fore.

The three women looked at each other, then at Fee.

'You're her sister,' Shona nudged Veronica. 'You ask her.'

'Well, it's like this,' Veronica began hesitantly. 'It's not exactly a selling line, but we have thought of a way of attracting some pretty strong publicity. It would give us a wonderful kick start. And, of course, ensure that your money is soon returned to you with a healthy premium—'

Fee waited. In the distance, she could hear the thunder of hoofs. Something told her that, contrary to normal practice, the riders were travelling fast in the opposite direction – away from the mess in which she was about to find herself.

Shona could wait no longer. 'You know you've had this massive amount of attention in the press and stuff? We thought we could capitalize on that and intrigue people at the same time by not giving away too much information—'

'No,' Fee replied, but nobody was listening.

'So, we came up with – you! We'd use your photograph – because lots of people know what you stand for now – then we'd have the line, "Spannier's . . . there isn't a woman we can't tempt—"'

Fee took in the faces of the three women, each watching her anxiously. They had got to be joking, hadn't they?

'"Spannier's . . . there isn't a woman we can't tempt" . . . Don't you think that's clever, Fee?' Shona asked.

Chapter Thirty-Six

Alan Munsen sat on Fee's floor, his back against the sofa, a beer in his hand. Fee sat cross-legged next to him.

Earlier in the day, he had offered to help with opening envelopes and sorting mail. He had arrived just before lunch and insisted that he treat Fee to a meal out. Only now had he broken the news that he had a new job.

'I'll be working with a charity, advising on emergency water projects,' he explained, his face revealing his excitement. 'I'll be based in Amsterdam, and it will mean a lot of travel.'

'But I thought you'd decided you needed roots?' Fee teased him.

'I do,' he'd laughed. 'But I've come to realize I need to roam even more. Who knows? Perhaps one day I'll find someone who'll roam with me—'

'When do you leave?' Fee asked. She didn't want him to go. He pushed the hair out of her eyes.

'I'll miss you, Fee,' he said, as if that was an answer.

Suddenly, Fee found herself sobbing uncontrollably. Alan put his arms around her and stroked her hair, soothingly. When the tears stopped, she stayed in his arms. A safe place, a place where she no longer felt quite so alone.

Later, Fee attempted to explain. 'I'm sorry, I don't know why . . . it just sort of happened—' she was half ashamed, half embarrassed.

'It's not you, well, what I mean is, I'll miss you, a lot. Of course,

371

I will . . . it's not just you, it's everything.' Fee glanced at Alan who was sitting opposite her, a box of tissues in his hands. She cursed herself for being so tactless.

She tried again. 'I don't seem to have any anchors in my life any more . . . and I suppose it's a bit alarming. I suppose what's even more alarming is the fact that I don't have any anchors because I've chosen to pull up so many myself,' she laughed weakly.

'I mean, what with leaving my job . . . and sticking my head so far above the parapet on television, it was bound to be cut off in the press . . . and then—' Fee was about to tell Alan about Clem Thomas, but something warned her against it.

'And then, the news that you're about to leave . . . and Claire sick . . . it's all too much—'

Alan Munsen smiled. 'Change is bound to be frightening, isn't it? I find the idea of working in Holland pretty bloody terrifying, but what's the alternative? To stagnate slowly?'

As Alan talked, Fee recognized what was at the core of her distress. For all the weeks she had considered the option of life on her own, she had been cocooned from the real impact of that decision. She had been cocooned by the number of people who had been dependent upon her.

Jane and Veronica and then Shona and even Imogen eager for Fee to deliver exceedingly high ratings. And, of course, Rita Mason.

Each had gradually become less dependent. Once Alan had gone, there would be nobody. But why did she need to have someone reliant on her, in order to feel worthwhile?

'I've got a good idea,' Alan said. 'You're free, I'm free, why don't we go away for a few days? Get out of London? As mates,' he added hurriedly, as if to reassure Fee.

She smiled. 'How do you fancy the Brecon Beacons?' she asked. 'I've got a friend there I haven't seen for years. She's already invited me to stay and she said I could bring a friend—'

'Let's go,' Alan beamed.

*

'Open up, open up,' bellowed Will Evans amiably at Fee's door a couple of hours later. She was soaking in the bath, trying unsuccessfully not to think. She was exhausted by conjuring dreams of what life might be like, should she and Clem one day . . . Fee told herself she ought to know better.

At least her previous love affairs, however destructive, had had the advantage of two participants. Fee was sure Clem Thomas had no idea how she felt, and she was just as certain that he was immune from such feelings himself.

'Fee-o-na, Fee-o-na, if you don't let me in, I'll huff and I'll puff and I'll blow your house down,' Will shouted.

'Drunk,' Fee told the bathroom walls.

Will was drunk and celebrating. F. P. & D. had officially been awarded the HAH! contract. As a result of his contribution, he had been promoted. His job remained the same, but his title had changed from Designer to Designer-in-Chief, and he had been awarded a hike in salary.

Will explained to Fee that four days after Macklin's surprise visit to F. P. & D., he had returned. He had watched a presentation by Diana Woods, who had sold the bulk of Fee's research brilliantly.

'You'd've loved it, if you'd been there,' Will said insensitively, his feet on Fee's coffee table. She sat in her dressing-gown, curled in the armchair opposite, trying hard to stay awake.

'So let's crack open a bottle.' He pulled out a bottle of champagne from his coat pocket.

'I thought to myself when I heard the news of my long-deserved promotion, who do I really want to be with to celebrate this event?' He grinned blearily at Fee. 'Who really deserves to share the pleasure?'

'Your mother?' Fee suggested.

Will was undeterred. 'I thought if that old bat, Fiona Travers, is back in her nest, that's where I want to be. If you can't share a glass with an old mate at a time of your greatest triumph, when can you?

'Mind you,' he added, 'I've always known that I could be London's greatest art director. And you, Fee, have always shown a similar faith in me.'

'I have?' she asked, genuinely surprised. She watched while Will returned from the kitchen with two mugs and unsteadily poured champagne.

'Why not glasses?'

Will wagged his finger at her playfully. 'Now that is a very intelligent question. But I have an even better one to ask. Are you madly jealous because Diana Woods has stolen all your best lines, including the zigzag? Did you know that is the new HAH! logo?

'By the way, Gerry said to tell you that he'll have you back tomorrow . . . But what I want to know is this. Did you miss me? Did you miss your good friend, Will, when you were in Dublin?'

Fee smiled. 'Not a lot,' she answered, 'but then I had too many other things to think about with . . . with what was going on around Claire—'

Will leapt up, spilling champagne, and deposited himself playfully in her lap. 'Ahaa!' he shouted. 'So you did miss me. I knew it. Absence makes the heart and all that—'

Just as suddenly as he'd landed on her lap, he slid off and ended in a crumpled heap, sandwiched between her chair and the coffee table.

'Bloody hell,' he asked. 'What's that pong?'

Briefly, Fee was alarmed. Then she began to laugh. 'You old romantic,' she teased. 'Don't tell me, you can't tell the smell of flowers when it's under your nose?'

'It's that bloody Alan Munsen, isn't it?' Will moaned melodramatically. 'He spends far too much time here for his own good.'

'Veronica says exactly the same of you,' Fee responded over her shoulder as she went to make coffee.

'Aah, but your sister is incapable of knowing the difference. Alan Munsen sees you as his prey. To put it bluntly, any fool can tell, except Veronica, that he is desperate to get his leg over. But I, I am your protector! I will not permit this to happen!'

When Fee returned with the coffee a few minutes later, her protector was snoring loudly, his mug on one side, spilling champagne into the carpet.

I need to get away I've got a week off and I need to clear my head,' Will said. His face was as puffy as a duckdown duvet.

He sat at Fee's kitchen table, desperately shovelling fried eggs, bacon, bread and mushrooms into his mouth, in the hope that an excess of grease might conquer the worst aspects of his hangover.

'Let's go away together. You've got time on your hands, and so have I. What about it?' he suggested.

She sat nursing a slice of toast. She'd forgotten how being lovelorn affected the appetite. If time is a healer, Fee's one wish was to spin her life forward a couple of years.

'Fee, are you listening?' Will asked. She shook her head. 'I'm sorry I can't go away with you. I've already arranged to visit a friend in Wales—'

'Not to worry, it'll probably do me good to go on holiday on my own for once. I'll commune with nature alone in Mykonos—'

'You'll be fine,' Fee retorted with absolute confidence.

Half an hour later, she surrendered. She hadn't realized quite how desperately keen Will was to avoid his own company.

'OK, OK, you can come. I'll have to ask Anna first. Perhaps we can spend a couple of days walking?'

'Perfect, Welsh rain, lots of bitter, long walks . . .'

Fee decided she should tell him now rather than later.

'And Alan Munsen.'

'Come again?' Will slowly put down his mug of coffee.

'I'm telling you that Alan's coming too . . . You'll like him once you get to know him better, you really will,' she offered encouragingly. 'But if you want to pull out, that's OK too.'

'What? And miss my chance of telling everyone I had a threesome on holiday?' Will smiled. 'I'll look on the bright side. I'll bank on Mr Munsen suddenly having to stay at home.

The day before the planned drive to Wales, Claire returned to London. Fee had been in her flat and stocked the fridge and changed the bed linen. She had put flowers in the sitting room and fruit in the kitchen. Some of which she would have done anyway, some of which was motivated by guilt.

Claire's firm, accustomed to dealing with employees suffering from burn-out and breakdowns and various stress-related ailments, insisted on sending a chauffeur-driven car to collect Claire and Clem from the airport.

Fee was relieved. She would have had to invent a reason why she couldn't have been there herself. She left a note on Claire's bedside table, explaining that she had been urgently called away to Wales for a few days but she would phone before she left.

On Thursday afternoon, she took a break from helping Veronica, who had been receiving a steady stream of calls from male applicants, and phoned Claire. She found her tired from the flight but otherwise her recovery was proceeding well.

'I'll be back to work in a week, you watch,' Claire promised. 'Clem can't do enough for me.'

If Fee had been travelling alone to Wales, she would have left that night. She desperately wished to put a physical distance between herself and Clem Thomas. To be in the same city was too close.

Instead, aware that Alan was not due to pick her and Will up until nine in the morning, she made an excuse to Shona, put on her coat, and left the flat. She walked and walked and returned home when she was so physically exhausted she could think only of sleep.

Clem Thomas was sitting on her front doorstep.

Chapter Thirty-Seven

'I'VE GOT something to say,' Clem began. Fee had suggested they walk in the park. She saw the park as neutral territory.

He rushed the next few words, as if he'd been rehearsing them. 'I haven't a clue how you feel, I'm not even sure this should be said, but it's driven me mad for days, and I've decided that I've got nothing to lose by being honest.'

He stopped and turned to Fee. 'I've fallen in love with you.'

In the few romances Fee had read, in every film she'd seen, it was at this point that the heroine flings her arms around her one true love, joy overflows, a union is made, happy ever after beckons. But Fee couldn't throw her arms around this man. No matter how much she wished to, she couldn't because the image of Claire stood between her and him.

He ran his hand through his hair agitatedly, misreading her reaction.

'Look, I'm sorry, I knew this would be a huge mistake. I've embarrassed you. And I know that you're happy on your own and everything . . . so it's probably entirely pointless . . . And, oh God, this is a mess . . . but I just wanted you to know—'

'No, it's not, I don't . . . I mean, I do—' Fee struggled to find the words.

Clem Thomas looked away from her. 'It's hopeless. In Dublin, almost from the beginning, I realized that I was engineering time to be with you . . . I felt guilty because I didn't want to include Claire in our conversations . . . Then I tried to wean myself off you by avoiding you as much as I could.

'I told myself that if this continued to its logical conclusion, I'd lose you both . . . But', he smiled ruefully, 'love isn't a rational enterprise. So here I am.'

Fee took a step away from him, but he saw that her face had softened.

'And here I am too,' Fee replied. 'Why don't we go home?'

On the short walk back to the flat, they were silent, each trying to make sense of the words that had been said. Fee's mood swung from depression to ridiculous heights of elation. Clem had placed his hand on her arm, when it came to crossing a road, and she had leapt as if he'd administered an electric shock. Since then, he had carefully kept his distance.

In Fee's flat, Clem stood awkwardly like a schoolboy trying to remember his manners until she suggested that he sit on the sofa.

'Would you like coffee or tea or whisky or wine?' she asked, nerves making her sound like a beverages hostess.

'Would I like wine? Would I ever,' Clem Thomas smiled disarmingly. The situation was almost surreal, Fee told herself. 'He has just told me he loves me, it was the one piece of information I longed to hear most – and now we're behaving like strangers.'

In the kitchen, she desperately tried to organize her thoughts.

Clem seemed different from the men who she normally fell for – but she hardly knew him well enough to tell. And what about trust between friends? Loyalty to Claire? The rule that you never help yourself to another woman's man?

Can it be right that you take what you want, no matter how great the pain or cost to others . . .?

In Fee's hands, the cork suddenly came out of the bottle with a sound like the crack of a bullet.

'The Lone Ranger had it easy,' she told herself wryly. 'What would he do if he discovered that the good guy and the bad guy shared the same heart?'

Pouring wine, Fee was fumbling and shy. And nervous, as if she was on her very first date.

'In the park,' Clem asked, 'what did you mean when you said, "And here I am"?'

Fee looked at him. He was staring intently, as if trying to pick up on any sign she might give.

'I mean that I feel the same way too,' she said finally. 'But it isn't as easy as that.'

Clem scooped her up in his arms. But caution – or was it fear or guilt – unconsciously made her tense. Instantly, he let his arms fall.

'What is it?' he asked gently. 'If you feel the same way, then we have a right to take this chance of happiness. Everyone has that right—'

'Claire,' Fee said.

Clem put his finger to her lips. 'No matter what you decide, once Claire is on her feet and well again, I'm going to be honest with her . . . Not about us because there may be nothing to tell, but about me—'

'What do you mean? About you? She's certain you're in love with her—' Fee felt disloyal even discussing Claire in this way.

'I'm sorry if that's what she assumed,' Clem said. 'But I've never mentioned the word love, not once. What I have said, again and again, is that I care for her; she has qualities that I honestly believed I could learn to love. I—'

He looked helpless. 'Christ, the more I talk, the bigger shit I sound . . . What I'm saying is that I thought I had no judgement worth relying on when it came to love . . . But I did want a family, a future with another human being who was committed to make the relationship work . . . I think, deep down, Claire felt the same way too.

'I thought, for once in my life, I was acting like a grown-up by choosing the right person. It was my head not my heart that was involved . . . and now—' He ran out of words.

'And what makes you think your judgement will be any sounder when it comes to me?' Fee asked.

'You're the nicest woman I've met in a very long time,' he replied simply. 'That's why.'

Much later that night, Fee went to bed – alone. After talking for hours, she had told Clem that she needed time. She couldn't rush into a decision, not with so much at stake for herself, and for Claire.

'I'm going away for a few days,' Fee had explained. 'When I get back, I promise I'll have a better idea of what to do.'

'Why wait?' Clem had demanded. 'Why not trust your instincts?'

'Because my instincts have betrayed me too often in the past,' she had replied.

An hour into the journey to Wales, not far from London, something happened under the bonnet of Alan Munsen's car. Fee never imagined that she'd be grateful for a car breaking down, but she was now.

The first thirty-eight miles had passed painfully. Alan had attempted to make conversation; Will Evans had sat in the back and replied in monosyllables. Like a spoilt child sulking.

Fee was almost at the point of throttling him when the engine of Alan's secondhand Sierra suddenly cut out. The car glided to a halt on the hard shoulder.

'Terrific,' Will muttered.

'I'll walk to the next phone box and call the AA,' Alan offered. 'It's done this before a couple of times. I know it's fixable but I don't have a clue about these things—'

'Allow me,' Will offered.

'Are you sure you know what you're doing?' Fee asked. 'I mean, you didn't even think to put petrol in your car—'

Will gave her a dirty look. 'That', he said, 'was an entirely different situation.'

Fifteen minutes later, the engine reluctantly revved back into life. 'Good on you, mate,' Alan slapped Will enthusiastically on the back.

'Not bad,' Fee conceded. Will grinned. It was then Fee remembered that Alan had told her how he used to service cars in Guatemala that were almost as old as his mother. But she said nothing; this was Alan's ploy. For the remainder of the journey, Will was a far happier man. His superiority to Alan Munsen in at least one area of life had been firmly established.

By the time they stopped for a drink and a sandwich at a pub that Alan knew on the Welsh border, Will felt generous enough to compliment him on his taste. It was only a matter of time before the two men discovered they liked the same sort of jokes, both enjoyed walking and both had had childhoods lived on and around boats.

Fee who, inevitably but misguidedly, had felt responsible for the initial tension, retreated into silence while the men talked. She ran through the previous night's conversation with Clem again and again. What he'd said, how he'd said it, and how he'd looked when he'd said it.

Was this, as Fee wanted to believe, a proper, grown-up sort of love?

'Excuse me, is anybody there?' Will was talking into Fee's ear, his chin resting on the back of her car seat.

'Sorry, what did you say?' Fee replied with a start.

'We've been asking you for the last few minutes to tell us something about this woman we're all dumping ourselves on. Is she fanciable? Would she go for fine, upstanding, mature men like Alan and me – preferably one at a time? Have I packed six new pairs of boxer shorts in vain?'

Fee laughed. If all else in her life failed, she told herself, at least she was fortunate in the company she kept.

'We should be there in half an hour or so,' Alan said. 'Speak woman, the floor is yours—'

'Once upon a time,' Fee began, in a soft, mock-Felicity-Kendall-style voice, 'there was a beautiful young single woman of twenty-two, called Fiona Travers, and a married woman of twenty-nine, who was naturally not quite so attractive as Fiona—' She was interrupted by the simultaneous groans of pain from the two men.

Fee persisted. 'Now this not-so-attractive twenty-nine-year-old—'

Anna Clarke had been employed by a local newspaper, the *Huxley Chronicle & Echo*. She was married and had just returned to work after having her second son when she came to cover a story at Lillieshall Primary School where Fee was teaching.

Anna was exceptionally tall and far too thin. She smoked too much, so that her voice had a rasp. Some people assumed that because she was skinny and she chain-smoked, she must suffer from her nerves. The truth was that she ate like a horse, drank copiously and smoked because she loved it.

Fee enjoyed Anna's subversive sense of humour. They also shared in common a monumental capacity to drift. And as both had recently drifted into Huxley, they became friends.

Anna and Fee moved to London within months of each other. Anna became a freelance writer and had a third son. Her husband, Neil, established a business making china for themed restaurants. Anna's career progressed too, but, for her, every step up the ladder seemed to produce still more conflicts of responsibility between work and home – conflicts from which Neil had made himself immune since he had long made it clear that his sole priority was his job.

Eventually, Anna and her family moved to Stoke on Trent, closer to Neil's two factories. Fee visited a couple of times. Then, Anna moved again – and Fee lost contact. Until the telephone call after *The Perfumed Pound*.

'What she told me then', Fee said, bringing the story up to date, 'was that she divorced Neil five years ago. She must be . . . forty-seven or forty-eight now. She runs her own bookshop and she writes horror stories. She told me that two of the boys, Daniel and Charlie, are living with her and the eldest, Dylan, is at university.'

'Great,' Will commented acerbically. 'So we're about to spend a long weekend with a depressed divorcee with sado-masochistic tendencies.'

'Conway & Rigsby, Booksellers of Repute – New and Secondhand Books, first-edition science fiction and horror a speciality—'

'Look!' Fee shouted as they drove along the B-road that led into Newyddfach, the village to which Anna Clarke had come after her divorce.

'Conway & Rigsby, that's Anna's shop—'

The posters had been stuck haphazardly on a brick wall surrounding a recreation ground. What caught the eye was the psychedelic background, a different one on each poster.

'I bet that's Dan's work, he was always the artistic one,' Fee said.

Alan Munsen feigned mild alarm. 'You don't think this weekend is going to be a sixties sort of experience, do you? Only it was a decade that passed me by—'

Conway & Rigsby was at the top of the high street, just around the corner from the village green. It had a thatched roof, and it literally overflowed with books. Even window-boxes had been conscripted into use to hold books, while trestle tables set up outside were stacked with secondhand paperbacks. In the rare space between books, homemade jam and marmalade were on sale.

The door of the bookshop had been painted sunflower yellow and it was open. To one side of the door, a large shabby emerald-green velvet Victorian armchair on casters was balanced precariously on the uneven flagstones of the pavement. Sitting in it was a woman

384

who was too preoccupied with the book in her hand to notice a car had stopped. Fee opened her door, unsure at first, until Anna Clarke glanced up.

'Well, if it isn't my old mate, Fiona Travers,' she roared, jumping out of the chair with such vigour that it rocked and rolled.

She had put on weight, which suited her well. Her black hair was cut short and streaked with silver. She wore cream trousers and a matching loose top. Around her neck she had a scarf in cream and turquoise and lime green and tangerine. She was barefoot and she had a cigarette in her hand.

'Cut back a bit,' she laughed at Fee, waving the cigarette. 'Only forty a day, and only if I sit outside for a smoke. The boys won't allow it in the house.'

Introductions were made. 'And which one—' Anna had asked, her eyebrows raised in semaphore, when Fee had linked arms with Alan and Will.

Fee had laughed. 'Neither,' she'd replied. 'They're both much too fussy to fancy me.'

She sensed that the two men found Anna a little overwhelming. She was large, loud and loquacious.

'Daniel!' she shouted to the open window on the first floor of the cottage. 'Look who's here.'

A boy of seventeen or so, paintbrush in hand, stuck his head out of the window. He had blond hair, olive skin and was tall like his mother.

'It's Fee. You remember Fee? If you're terribly nice to her, she might even buy one of your paintings.'

Daniel grinned and retreated back into the room.

'Is that his studio?' Alan asked politely.

'Good God, no,' Anna laughed heartily again. 'Property's far too valuable for that. It was the shop's store room but Dan's redecorating it so we've got more space to sell books. People come from all over. Bloodthirsty sorts of people . . . What time is it?'

'Three thirty,' Will replied obligingly.

'Jolly good.' She smiled. 'Just about time for a drink. Hop in the car and I'll show you where we live.'

As Anna climbed into the back seat, her three guests exchanged slightly dazed smiles. This was undoubtedly a woman who could convince anyone that they were having a thoroughly good time. To resist might prove even more exhausting.

The house was five minutes from the bookshop, down a lane and hidden by a small orchard. A large, almost wild garden with a gazebo and a hammock came into sight first. The house itself sprawled in an L-shape and was covered in lilac and ivy. The ground floor of the front of the house was dominated by three sets of French windows. A large table and chairs took up space under an old oak tree in the garden. Another held a tree house.

At the rear, where Alan parked, there was a chicken coop and two barns. Two mongrels were introduced as Spick and Span. Only a jaunty air of neglect and chaos prevented the three outsiders from deciding that what they saw before them was a portrait of rural perfection.

'You men sit there,' Anna ordered, pointing to the hammock and chairs in the front garden. 'We'll sort out the drinks. Fee, follow me.'

They went through into a low-beamed sitting room. It had three sofas in front of an open fireplace, and an assortment of armchairs from different periods in British history. Multicoloured rugs, many-hued cushions and throws vied for attention with the walls, on which there were a number of powerful abstracts in oil.

Books, candles and flowers were in abundance. The overall effect was one of surprising tranquillity; the room was vibrant but far from jarring.

'I've made Pimms,' said Anna in the kitchen. 'We'll have a glass or two here and let the men drink theirs in the garden. You mentioned B. & B. but I wouldn't dream of it. We've got far too much space. It would be indecent. And besides, you and I have got a lot of catching up to do—'

'What about the shop?' Fee asked.

'Oh, if anyone turns up, Dan will give me a bell. We do most of our trade at the weekends anyway. But that's not what pays the bills; my own books do.' She nodded towards a bookcase crammed with paperbacks.

'But don't attempt to read a page of those,' she added, as she picked up a tray of drinks and went towards the kitchen door, 'unless your Japanese is up to scratch and your stomach is strong. Back in a tick.'

Fee examined the books. There were over thirty paperbacks, some in Japanese, some in what she guessed to be Swedish or Danish. If the covers were any guide, the plots were not of the type that sent nice girls to sleep smiling. The author named on each was A. F. Clarke.

Anna returned and began to explain the origins of her relatively new craft. 'A year after Neil and I divorced, he moved in with a twenty-three-year-old aerobics instructor. I didn't give a damn about that. But what I did mind deeply was that he took every weekend off to be with her. She'd managed what I'd failed to do in all those years we were together. In that time, he barely took five minutes away from his job to be with me or the boys, never mind two whole days.

'It was totally irrational but I could have quartered Neil alive, parboiled him and buried his living remains in maggots. But I realized that might not be best for the boys.' Anna gave a dry chuckle.

'So, instead, I sat down and wrote a novel of revenge. It was so violent, so lacking in taste, so gruesome and unacceptably disgusting, certainly from a woman, that it was rejected by fifteen British publishers. Finally, as a last shot, I sent it to an international agent who specializes in selling horror abroad. I also reverted to using my initials.

'Now, I'm a star in Japan. Except, of course, they believe that

I'm a male recluse who has locked himself away on an island to protect others from his evil impulses. It's a load of old bull, but if it helps sales, who needs personal fame as well?'

'And what about Neil? How do you feel about him now?' Fee asked.

'Absolutely nothing.' Anna's smile broadened. 'He often comes to stay to see the boys. I'm quite fond of him in some ways but it's also always a special pleasure when he decides it's time to go. All in all, I'm quite surprised to find that I've never felt healthier or saner in my life.

'I write horror for pleasure. It's a great release. Matter of fact,' she added, pouring the Pimms and lighting up another cigarette, 'I do an awful lot of things for my own pleasure now. And about bloody time too.'

Fee raised her glass in a toast. 'Well, here's to you,' she said.

'To us both,' Anna corrected.

Later, Fee walked with Anna to the bookshop to lock up. Dan was sitting outside with a man. He had a large moustache, a shock of dark brown hair, which circled a small bald patch, and he wore a large and well-worn jumper, jeans and sneakers. Anna enthusiastically threw her arms around his neck.

'Tom, my old lover, what are you doing distracting my son from a decent day's work?'

Tom smiled. Fee noticed that his face had lit up with pleasure when Anna came into view.

'I was trying to persuade him to come fishing tomorrow, but he says he's promised to give them a hand setting up for the barbecue and pig race.'

The man looked enquiringly at Fee. Anna excused her bad manners. 'Fee, I want you to meet the man who at one stage improved my Saturday nights no end.'

'Mum,' Dan remonstrated.

'Tom Lewis, this is an old and dear friend, Fee Travers. She has come here to have a good time. So what decent men do you know? Bring them to supper tonight. Is Tilly coming with you?'

Tom shook his head. 'She's off to stay with her sister in Cardiff for the weekend. They've got some mischief planned no doubt. See you,' he waved cheerily.

Later, as Anna checked locks and bolts at the shop, she explained her relationship with Tom Lewis. He was fifty-five and had been widowed for eight years. His wife had been killed by a hit-and-run driver. Tilly, Matilda, the youngest of his two daughters, was now nineteen, and at university in Aberystwyth. His older daughter, Megan, twenty-two, was an assistant chef in a restaurant in Cardiff.

'She cooks like an angel and wants to have her own place eventually—'

'What about Tom? He seems a lovely man,' Fee asked.

'He writes children's books. Very good ones, too. A couple have been turned into television. He came to live just up the road from us about three years ago. He decided he'd fulfil a lifelong ambition and become a rural hermit.'

Anna burst out laughing. 'The only drawback is that he's not cut out for the job. He's the most naturally gregarious man I've met.'

She grew serious. 'Until about a year ago, he used to spend two or three nights at my place or I'd go to his, and that suited me – and all our kids – perfectly—

'Then he suggested that we live together. I tried to explain that, for the first time in my life, I'd got control over what I did. Twenty-four-hour contact with Tom – or anyone else for that matter – might have eroded what I'd only just won for myself.' She shrugged.

'I tried to explain to Tom that what I wanted was the pleasure of his company. I didn't want to wash his socks, or administer to his few neuroses or put up with the friends of his that I didn't like—

'In other words, selfishly I suppose, I've outgrown living together, marriage. It's no longer such a massive thrill to know that somebody else is dependent upon you.'

'How does Tom feel about it?' Fee asked.

'He says I'm trying to have my cake and eat it. We both agreed to go back to being just friends. And that seems to be working out fine. Some day, he'll find someone who appreciates him properly.'

She laughed wryly. 'He tells me that I'm too bloody self-reliant for my own good. And how about you?' She gave Fee a curious look. 'Are you as self-reliant as you seem? Or is there some dark dungeon of dependency that you're about to reveal?'

Fee was glad that Dan's reappearance meant she didn't have to give an answer.

Chapter Thirty-Eight

A NNA COOKED the first two courses for supper – stuffed mush-rooms, followed by fish casserole. Will helped with the veg-etables, Alan made chocolate mousse. Fee was delegated to provide the bread, so she drove to the nearest town and bought bread, cheese, olives and wine. By eleven, the table was scattered with an assortment of empty bottles, as well as dying and newly lit candles and a couple of boxes of chocolates brought by guests.

Around the table, apart from Anna, Dan, Charlie and Tom, were Henry Stathers, a divorced farmer, obediently brought by Tom and Leatrice Fitzgerald, a retired dentist in her sixties who, Anna had told Fee, spent her winters working as a volunteer in a children's hospital in India.

'Lea was the first person I met when I moved here,' she had added. 'You'll love her.'

Much to Fee's embarrassment, Henry and Lea had watched *The Perfumed Pound*. Henry said he believed that women were biologi-cally programmed to nest. 'I know,' he added as if that concluded the argument. 'I see it on the farm, all day, every day.'

'What do you think, Lea?' Alan asked. Lea gave a throaty laugh. She was short and stout with almost a child's round face. Her hair was white, short. She wore a navy blue crêpe-de-Chine trouser suit and striking Indian silver ear-rings.

Lea shrugged. 'On love,' she said smiling, 'nobody listens to anybody. But my personal view is that it's a lot healthier if it comes from more than one source.'

'How many sources have you got?' Will asked cheekily.

Before Lea could reply, Anna broke in. 'She believes that it's almost impossible for a woman to have a relationship with a man in which she doesn't lose more than she gains. Go on, tell them, Lea—'

Lea smiled. 'It's the old cliché, a relationship works best when the man is a little more in love with the woman, but how often does that happen? So my view is, if I can't have a relationship on terms that are attractive to me, then I won't bother at all.' She gazed around at the other guests and smiled mischievously. 'Now, do I look as if I'm suffering?'

The men agreed to clear the table and wash up. Anna made herself comfortable in the sitting room; Lea and Fee sat outside on the garden steps. Once settled, Fee probed until Lea revealed a little more of her background. She explained that her parents had both been doctors – and the house had always been filled to overflowing with relatives, patients, friends and siblings.

'My parents were obsessed with each other, to the emotional exclusion of everyone else. We children – five of us – always knew we mattered less.

'The trouble with obsessive love is that one or the other person is bound to disappoint – constantly,' Lea chuckled. 'The rows we witnessed as young ones were something shocking. It made me think that true love must be the most terrible affliction that could befall anyone. And it was best to steer clear at all costs.'

'Have you had any regrets about being on your own?' Fee asked.

Lea shook her head. 'No, not seriously. In my thirties, I lived with a couple of men, but I didn't consider either relationship a long-term set-up. I've always assumed that I was responsible for my own happiness.' She looked at Fee keenly.

'Each and every one of us is different of course. What suits me may not suit you. It's best to keep an open mind—'

Moving back into the house, she linked arms with Fee. 'I forgot to mention one of the perks of being an old maid,' she said. 'Once people realize that I've genuinely *chosen* to live alone, that I might even be enjoying myself, you should see how quickly the pity turns to alarm.

'Suddenly, I'm a threat . . . I'm dangerous. Watching that change still gives me a bit of a buzz.'

Late on Saturday morning, Fee could no longer keep her problem to herself. She and Alan and Will had been helping Dan and Charlie to rebuild the stone wall that kept the pigs enclosed. She and Will were left alone, while the other three had driven to the rear garden of the bookshop to collect more stones from a disused outbuilding.

'You can't possibly be serious?' Will had said, sitting down heavily on the half-rebuilt wall.

She had expected sympathy; she had assumed he would half listen, allow her to talk; then say something appropriately noncommittal, such as, 'It's a really difficult choice.' Then she would feel a lot better, not least because she would have made her affection for Clem Thomas just a fraction public.

Instead, when Fee had blurted out her secret, Will's mood had turned thunderous. Now he was angry, almost raging.

'Fee, I'm flabbergasted.' Her face turned crimson. 'I can't believe you'd behave in such an appalling way. What about all that bollocks you spouted on telly?

'And you had the bloody cheek to lecture me on my behaviour with Hannah! Jesus Christ, and you've turned out to be the bloody Mata Hari of Maida Vale—

'How could you creep into bed with that jerk when your best friend is practically crawling towards Heaven's door in hospital?'

Tears welled up in Fee's eyes.

'I haven't been to bed with him. I haven't been anywhere near him, not physically. I thought you'd—'

Will was goading her now. 'You thought I'd what? Tell you to do whatever you felt like, and bugger the consequences? Come to that, what about Alan?' Will asked. 'He's a bloody nice bloke. Too nice to be treated like this—'

Fee was bewildered. 'What do you mean? He and I agreed right from our first meeting that we'd be friends and nothing more—'

'Oh, so that makes it all right, does it?' Will asked sarcastically.

Fee's guilt began to recede, fury taking its place.

'Now just hold on a minute, Will Evans,' she heard herself shouting. 'Absolutely nothing has happened between Clem and me. Nothing. Nor will it. I'd hoped you'd give me advice, not act like bloody Oliver Cromwell.

'Besides,' she added sarcastically, 'I thought *you* were the love 'em and leave 'em, what's a little lie between friends specialist? The who cares about principles and honour and honesty, that's very *passé*?'

Fee's face and hair were streaked with dirt, her hands were filthy, every bone in her body ached from the unaccustomed exercise, and now she had to face this emotional barrage from a totally unexpected quarter. Annoyed, she realized that her voice was quivering.

'Christ.' Will panicked. 'I can't stand tears. Please don't cry, Fee.'

'I'm not crying,' she corrected him huffily.

'Hey, you lot,' Alan Munsen shouted cheerfully from the kitchen door. He was waving two cans of cold lager.

'Coffee break. You two look as if you need it.'

On Saturday afternoon, every shop in the high street was putting up shutters. The road had been blocked to traffic and detour signs put in place. A modest fair had taken up residence on the village green, the beer tent was already doing business – and a brass band was playing with gusto. At 6 p.m., the annual pig race would be run, if the four pickets protesting against cruelty to pigs could be persuaded to remove themselves from where the start line was normally organized, outside Roberts the chemist.

Charlie, Anna's youngest son, was entering Jezebel, as he had done every year since the Clarkes had arrived in the village.

'I hope she can maintain her unbeaten record,' Anna grinned.

'What's that?' asked Alan, who had enjoyed himself hugely giving a hand here and there.

'She always comes last,' Charlie replied with not a little pride.

At 5.55 p.m., the protesters were tempted away with the promise that the pig race would be discussed at the next parish meeting. At 6 p.m., at the sound of a whistle, eight pigs bolted in various directions, but more or less down the high street. Jezebel opted not to move at all, until Charlie tempted her to follow him at a sedate pace by flaunting her favourite treat, a packet of cheese and onion crisps.

'Do you think this is cruel?' Fee asked, as she watched while the winner, a monstrous black and white sow, happily peed all over her owner's shoes. 'I mean to the pigs, not to the owners?'

'Not as cruel as women can sometimes be,' Will retorted pointedly.

Later, as the others made their way to the village barbecue, he pulled Fee to one side.

'I'm sorry,' he apologized. 'I'm sorry I was so cross. I'm sorry I've reacted so badly. I've done some thinking since this morning, and I realize I've made a complete and utter tosser of myself.'

Fee couldn't help herself. She laughed. She laughed both because Will appeared so abject and because she had no doubt that he would boomerang out of this trough of despondency quicker than she could say, 'It was nothing.'

Will didn't smile. Instead, after a number of false starts and several minor detours, he explained that his feelings for Fee had changed since she'd moved into the flat below his.

'I'm fond of you, Fee. Very, very fond. Too fond actually,' he floundered.

'Why do you think I keep popping in for a drink? And suggesting I make you a nightcap?'

He had lied to her about Hannah Jaspan's attack on Fee's Fiat. 'She didn't think it was mine; she knew it belonged to you. She was jealous. When she jumped me in your hall, she was trying to get at you.

'That's why she left in the end.' He allowed himself a small smile. 'She said that she'd given it a good go but she wouldn't carry on playing second fiddle to you—'

'I hadn't realized,' Fee said unnecessarily.

'Why should you?' Will shrugged. 'I'm as good at hiding my feelings as the next man . . . Besides, I knew I couldn't inflict the requisite amount of suffering on you that you seem to require before you can be attracted. Oh, excuse me,' he added sarcastically. 'Clem Thomas is different of course. Well, I've met him a couple of times and, if you ask me, I don't think he's what he makes out to be. But then I would say that, wouldn't I?'

Fee shook her head, as if to remove physically the doubt that Will was trying to plant. He stared fixedly into the middle distance, a muscle in his cheek twitching. Fee couldn't respond in the way that he wished, so the silence between them grew.

Eventually, he spoke. 'Look, Fee, let's forget that I said anything. Let's continue on as we did before . . . And whatever you decide . . . about Clem Thomas, I mean, it's fine by me. So we're still good mates. OK?'

'OK,' Fee replied. But they both knew that something between them had been permanently lost.

At the barbecue, Tom Lewis revealed to Fee a new talent. He could sing. He could even sing and play guitar at the same time. As rhythm guitarist and lead vocalist of Henry and the Has-Beens, he stole the show, not least because there was nobody else even attempting to compete.

The Has-Beens had originally agreed to play for an hour, but they played for over two. The group consisted of the local butcher on bass, a primary schoolteacher on lead, the village postman on drums and fifteen-year-old Charlie doing an excellent job on keyboards.

At midnight, after two encores of 'Rock Around the Clock', Henry and the Has-Beens took their final bows. The money raised, Tom announced, would go towards the £50,000 required for new operating theatres in Leatrice Fitzgerald's children's hospital in India.

'If you know anyone who is good at money,' Lea whispered in Fee's ear, 'we're desperate for cash.'

An ideal, if unwilling, candidate came to Fee's mind almost immediately.

Much later, Anna and Fee were each curled up on a sofa in Anna's sitting room. The fire had been lit and they had made coffee. Everyone else in the house had retired to bed. Charlie had staggered home drunk – a first, at least as far as his mother was aware. Then, in the way that fifteen-year-old boys sometimes do, he had indulged in projectile vomiting for a considerable period of time in the bathroom. It had taken the two women an hour to clean him and the room up.

Anna thanked Fee for her stoicism under fire. 'Do you know, Fee, I always assumed that you and Bill would have children.'

Fee refilled her cup before answering. 'I used to have periods when I felt vaguely broody but it was more to do with looking fabulous in a maternity smock. And Bill didn't seem very bothered either.

'I think, years ago, I was put off by what my mother did to us . . . Elizabeth, Veronica and me. She was so determined that we should be these perfect, well-behaved little girls whom the neighbours could find nothing but praise for . . . that we were reared on double doses of criticism. If you want good growth,' Fee added drily, 'I'd assume approval is a much more efficient fertilizer.'

She sipped her coffee. 'Anyway, at some point I suppose I must have decided that I wouldn't want to take the risk of grinding down a child of mine in the same way . . . But you know me—' Fee shrugged self-deprecatingly. 'I drift into situations . . .' She turned the attention away from herself. 'You don't seem much of a drifter these days, Anna. Did the divorce make the difference?'

Anna shook her head and picked up a large framed photograph from the table closest to her. The photograph was fuzzy but it showed a youngish woman, in a paper hat from a Christmas cracker, pulling a face at the camera.

'She made the difference. You probably don't remember her, Fee, but you met her at my house in London. Ros Cambridge?' Anna jogged Fee's memory. 'She was an actress . . . and she'd written a couple of plays for the fringe?'

'What's she doing now?' Fee asked.

'She's dead,' Anna replied, her voice several tones lower. 'She died six years ago this September. September the fifth actually—' She returned the photograph to the table, moving it slightly, so that when the curtains were drawn back it would face the garden.

'I'm so sorry . . .' Fee stumbled. 'What a waste; she must have been very young—'

'What a waste?' Anna sounded bitter. 'That doesn't even begin to match Ros's views on the subject.

'She was only thirty-three. She found a lump on her breast, same old story. She had a boyfriend whom she'd just met, she'd wanted children, her career was just beginning to take shape. She knew right from the first diagnosis – no matter how much crap the doctors told her – that die she would, and soon. And, Christ, did that make her angry.'

Anna lit a cigarette but left it unsmoked. 'What Ros categorically refused to be was brave; on principle. She refused to play the dying game.

'On the contrary, she raged, she shouted, she drove almost everyone away with her anger and her distress. A lot of people didn't like it at all . . . they wanted to visit someone who wouldn't make a fuss, wouldn't remind them of their own mortality . . . wouldn't make them feel guilty.' Anna fell silent. Then she stubbed out her cigarette savagely.

'Considering how many millions of people experience birth and death, the details of both are two of our best-kept secrets, don't you think?' she asked tartly.

'Were you with her when she died?' Fee asked gently.

Anna's face brightened as if the humour mined from a memory had eased her grief. 'Ros didn't want to stay in the hospice. She wanted to be at home.

Once she'd become seriously ill, a lot of people fell away, including the boyfriend, poor love.

'So, when she said she wanted to be at home, I was happy to look after her for that last month.'

Anna glanced again at the photograph and smiled.

'Ros died the way she'd lived. On the evening of September the fifth, she had a terrible row with her GP who'd suggested she might want to return to the hospice for a couple of nights, so that the pain relief could be better controlled.

'She told him she'd never felt better. That evening she asked if we could watch *Coronation Street*. She was shameless in her addiction to soaps. Later, she had a bit of a weep, like a child who's lost, then she died in my arms.'

Anna sat silent, tears sliding down her cheeks. After a few minutes she took a deep breath and began again.

'What struck me about Ros was the extent of her regrets. She had so many. I thought the least I could do in memory of her was to shake my own life up a bit – while there was still time.

'On the day of Ros's cremation, I made a list . . . what I enjoyed and what I didn't like about my life. Even I was surprised at how much my "let's wait and see" attitude had almost paralysed me . . . Neil, I'm afraid, was the first to go. And here I am.'

She took a swig of cold coffee. 'Do you know, Fee, for the first time in my life, I'm actually doing what I want to do. I love writing, I love this village, I love the shop. It hasn't been easy. At first, the boys hated the move and being apart from their father. But now they see more of him than they ever did when we were together.

'If I made a list tonight about what I like in my life, it would be an awful lot longer than when Ros died. So I thank her for that every day.'

The two sat silent for a while, then Fee came to a decision. 'Can I ask your advice, Anna?' she asked. 'Supposing, hypothetically, your best friend had decided out of the blue to marry. She sees this, rightly or wrongly, as her last chance to settle down and have a family. Suddenly, when you least expect it, you fall in love with her husband-to-be. He claims to feel the same way about you.

'The catch in this hypothetical problem is that you have a highly unreliable record when it comes to choosing men. And you know next to nothing about this particular man . . . You also care for your best friend.

'So what's it to be? Love, which may or may not be good for you and will certainly mean sacrificing friendship? Or forfeiting what may be your last chance of a soul mate?'

Anna chuckled. 'I can tell you straight away that whoever is facing this hypothetical situation ain't no spring chicken,' she smiled.

'What do you mean?' Fee asked defensively.

'If she was twenty-one, she wouldn't even be considering the ethics. She'd have made off with her lover man without so much as a wave goodbye,' Anna smiled. 'If Ros was here, she'd be all in favour too.'

'And you?' Fee pressed.

Anna shrugged. 'In my book, soul mates come cheap – friendship, my sweet, is so much harder to keep, don't you think?'

At the pub at lunchtime the following day, Fee made two calls. One was to Imogen, the other to Clem who was staying at Claire's flat. Imogen expressed delight at being asked for her help. She welcomed a chance to restore herself in Fee's eyes. Why, she couldn't exactly say. She certainly had no intention of liking the woman.

'Why don't I pick you up from the station?' Imogen suggested. 'Make it around lunchtime tomorrow and I should have something by then—'

'That soon?' Fee asked.

'My dear, we *are* dealing with one of the best.'

When Fee dialled Claire's number, Clem answered immediately, almost as if he'd been waiting.

'How's Claire?' Fee asked, hating the deception.

'She's asleep here on the sofa but doing well. How are you?' Clem asked evenly. His tone was warm.

'Could we meet?' Fee asked.

'Shall I come to your flat?' he answered.

'No,' Fee replied. 'Could you come to the park, to the café? Where we first talked. Tomorrow evening around six?'

Fee returned to the table. Tom was peeved that Anna had spent the past hour discussing Mexico with Alan. 'When are you lot thinking of going back?' he asked so pointedly that Fee had to smile.

'Well, I've got to go tomorrow, I don't know about Will and Alan. Weren't you two talking about doing some serious walking?' she asked.

'I'm in no rush, how about you, Alan?' Will responded. 'Fancy a couple of days in the hills? Tom says he knows a couple of good B. & B.s—'

'I certainly do,' Tom nodded emphatically.

The following morning, Alan drove Fee to the station.

'What do you think of Anna, then?' she asked casually. His reply was equally relaxed. 'An interesting woman. Very interesting actually.

But probably not enough of a roamer for me. Besides,' he added, giving Fee a quick look out of the corner of his eye, 'she seems pretty settled with Tom. And he's a decent sort of a bloke.'

'Anna and Tom are just friends. Good friends but nothing more . . . And do you know, she's always been a bit of a gypsy at heart—'

'And what does that mean in plain English?' Alan asked.

Fee laughed. 'It means, I suspect you're in with a chance—'

On the platform, Alan reached out impulsively to hold Fee's hands in his.

'Whatever you're up to now,' he said, studying her face, 'you know, there's always an alternative. Even if he isn't me.'

Chapter Thirty-Nine

'OF COURSE, you'll have total artistic control, darlings, if that's what you'd like,' Imogen Banks purred.

'And if I can't persuade just one or two of your clients to show the courage of their convictions and appear on camera, well, then I'm not Imogen Banks. And, my word, think of what a slot on television will do for your profit margins?'

My word . . . That's precisely what was making Jean Stoker uneasy: Imogen's word.

She and Veronica were taking tea on Sunday afternoon in Imogen's cavernous warehouse of a home. Shona had refused to come; how can you deal directly with the woman who has stolen your spouse? But her pride hadn't prevented her from realizing that one television documentary on the subject of Spannier's, due to open in a matter of weeks, would be worth thousands in terms of free publicity. The *correct* kind of free publicity: discreet, high class, unsensational, neither coarse nor bawdy.

Imogen beamed at the two women. 'Do you know how many viewers tuned in to watch *The Perfumed Pound*? Ten million. Helped admittedly by an excess of coarse fishing and football on the other channels, but 10 million nonetheless—'

'And, since all the fuss in the paper about Fee's—' Imogen searched for an acceptable description. 'About Fee's *stimulating* past . . . they're talking about a repeat. SOS is thrilled, of course, because its membership has simply shot up. Into the stratosphere.' Imogen gestured towards the ceiling, exaggerating wildly.

'Fee *will* be thrilled,' Veronica commented drily. 'She's already had more letters than she can handle from women asking for her advice as an agony aunt.'

She mimicked a Birmingham accent. 'My husband and I have been married for five years. I'm bored. Is it time that I found my independence and became single again, this time for good? I would like to be empowered. Please advise soonest, PS, s.a.e. enclosed . . . Yours, Helen from Handsworth—'

Jean smiled and stirred her tea, choosing her words carefully. 'What does Shona's husband think about you publicizing Spannier's, Imogen? I assume you know he intends to become a Labour MP? Our venture isn't exactly the monument to culture that he'd choose to be associated with, is it? What does he think about you giving it even more publicity? I mean, this is what we're about—'

Jean read from a leaflet, constructed from expensive, heavily embossed paper. 'Spannier's . . . Gentlemen carefully chosen for their intelligence, charm, humour and sensitivity—

'Gentlemen who have been professionally screened to ensure that you have the utmost confidence in your own security and in their discretion.

'Gentlemen whose aim is to make your evening a memorable one . . . Credit cards accepted . . . Make your choice in the privacy of your own home or visit our salon—'

'Who's doing the "professional screening"?' Imogen asked. 'Only I can recommend an extremely good company.'

'We know,' Veronica smiled at Imogen smugly. 'Gill Booth has already told us. Simon found the business card for Probe-a-Partner when he was staying with you. He told Gill; she told us—'

'I see,' Imogen, tight-lipped, reminded herself to replace her waste-paper baskets with a shredder in every room.

She moved on briskly. 'Anyway, you were asking about Edward? He has his ambitions and I have mine and we've decided that while we'll each give the other emotional support, what we do in practical terms is our own concern—'

'So it's going well then?' Veronica asked. She had decided that Imogen Banks must be a very unhappy woman. Why else would she set about ruining other women's relationships with such gusto?

The only drawback in this analysis was Imogen's demeanour. On every occasion that Veronica and she had met, Imogen looked far from unhappy. On the contrary, she was impressively jolly. Veronica had come to the conclusion that Imogen's conscience had been rendered obsolete years ago. Still, there was something about her that Veronica couldn't help but like.

'Marvellously well,' Imogen beamed. 'So, what do you say about the idea of a film?' she asked again. 'I need an answer soon—'

'Have you thought of a title?' Veronica asked, still concerned.

Imogen didn't even have to think, she'd had the title ready for days.

'How about, *The Women Who Do?*' she suggested.

Her guests went pale.

Imogen rapidly backtracked. 'All right, how about, *The Women Who Don't?* . . . Or, *Never Say Never*— Or perhaps it's best if we negotiate that little detail a lot later down the line?' she added hurriedly.

Veronica's face was disapproving. 'We need to talk to Fee,' she announced firmly. 'She's back tomorrow. She's one of our major investors and she's already had the experience of putting herself in your hands—'

Imogen smiled brightly, very, very brightly.

'What a wise decision,' she commented condescendingly. Her mind was already working on what she might offer Fee to encourage her to give the endorsement that she required.

'What a *sound* move.' She smiled.

Driving to her office later, the solution as to what she might offer Fee came to Imogen in a moment of startling clarity.

405

Clem Thomas.

Clem was what Fee wanted more than anything else in the world. Or, more precisely, Clem's head – on a platter. Why else would Fee have phoned from Wales to commission Probe-a-Partner to carry out an emergency search on Clem Thomas's background and his present circumstances?

Imogen prided herself that in spite of their relatively short acquaintance, she could read Fee like a book. It was her private opinion that Fee had traits that, if they had not been severely repressed from the moment she was on the breast, would have developed into a Machiavellian nature to rival only her own.

Fee was a bad girl camouflaged as good.

Imogen began to devise a strategy. Fee presumably was hoping for negative material on Clem Thomas. Once acquired, she would then find some way of feeding Claire the information. Claire would dump Clem. Fee would be single – but no longer alone. The Lone Ranger would have her Tonto back with barely a mark – except, of course, on Claire's finger, where the discarded engagement ring might have left a small indentation.

What Imogen had to do was deliver to Fee what she required. Only at a later stage would Imogen point out her indebtedness.

Fee's train was due to arrive at five minutes past noon. At eleven fifteen, Probe-a-Partner delivered its preliminary report to Imogen's office. A more detailed report would follow in forty-eight hours.

Imogen glanced rapidly through the details of Clem Thomas's past and present life. She made only three additions. One was to add an extra previous wife; the second was to insert a hefty over-draft in place of two healthy accounts; the third was to omit a reference to Clem Thomas's period as a banker and replace it with the following line: 'Occupations until 1986 when entered teacher training college, varied, mostly non-manual, including civil servant, clerk, salesman.'

Imogen was pleased with her five minutes of effort: from a king to a jack. Or even a knave.

On the train, Fee tried to read but failed. She drank tea, stared out of the window, went to the loo several times and imagined she saw Rita Mason standing on the platform at two stations at which the train stopped.

Every once in a while, Fee would allow her imagination to fly. Then, she would smell Clem Thomas's skin, recall the way his eyes smiled . . .

Imogen waited at the entrance to platform 9 at Euston Station looking anything but ordinary.

She was wearing a shocking-pink suit, a mauve and pink patterned blouse, pale-pink strappy sandals and a matching handbag. A slight drizzle had transformed her naturally curly hair into something resembling a soldier's busby, but, apart from that small defect, Imogen was happy to confess that all was going extremely well in her world.

She had her man; she had her staff literally now working around the clock, and, soon, she might well have another commission which would guarantee her position in television as the populist chronicler of the modern woman.

Imogen Banks was no fool. She realized that a less confident female than her, would assume that it was all going just a bit too well. Something had to give. The villainness always pays a price. But such was Imogen Banks's self-confidence, she didn't even attempt to touch wood.

'Have you read this?' Fee asked. She was being driven back to her flat by Imogen and she had the file on Clem Thomas in her hand.

'I couldn't; it was sealed,' Imogen lied. 'Anything unexpected?' she asked innocently.

'Yes,' Fee replied. 'Clem has a daughter.'

This was one truthful detail that Imogen had assumed Fee wouldn't find surprising. The man was in his late thirties for goodness' sake. Of course, he was likely to have some offspring.

Fee continued. 'He had a daughter by his first marriage. His wife left and took the daughter with her . . . it says here that they went to Australia. He hasn't seen either of them since. I wonder why he didn't tell Claire?'

'Perhaps he has,' Imogen suggested lightly. 'How many times has he been married?'

Fee was silent as she continued to read. Much of the report tallied with what Claire had told Fee about the man. But there were worrying differences too. She looked out of the passenger window, assessing the information, before replying.

'If Claire goes ahead – you know they've postponed the actual day, don't you? – well, if she goes ahead, she will be the third Mrs Thomas. She thinks she's the second,' she told Imogen.

'Ahaa!' Imogen said gleefully. 'And what about his work and life and times? What did our Mr Thomas do before he was a teacher?'

'He was a banker,' Fee answered instantly. 'Made a bit of money.'

Imogen glanced at her briefly. 'In the circumstances, hadn't you better give that a quick check too? This bloke's clearly not what he seems . . . You can pat yourself on the back, Fee. You always had your suspicions, didn't you?'

Fee gazed at Imogen, lost in her own concerns. She felt sick. Did this new information mean that, after all, Clem Thomas was the classic bastard who'd left a trail of emotional messes in his life? Or was he a decent man who'd made a few mistakes?

Imogen drew up outside Fee's flat. She refused an invitation to come in since she was off to a working lunch. She also showed that she was miffed.

'I must say, Fee, you don't look very cheerful. I would have thought this stuff on Clem Thomas would have made your week,' she complained. 'It would certainly make me think twice if I was Ms Claire Hastings. Looks like you'll soon have your playmate back in the sandpit – so why the long face?'

'When you get the full report, could you let me have it as quickly as possible?' was all Fee said.

Opening her front door, on Monday afternoon, Fee could see that still more mail had been delivered and had been piled neatly on her coffee table by Shona or Veronica. What also caught her eye were what appeared to be five large white cardboard suitcases.

Fee opened the lid of one case. Yards of cream and apricot tulle sprung out like a jack in the box dressed for a *pas de deux*. Claire's bridesmaids' dresses had been delivered – but why to her and why now?

The telephone interrupted Fee's thoughts.

The voice at the end of the line gave her a jolt.

'Hello, Fee, it's Claire . . . Clem said he thought you were home today or tomorrow and that you'd phoned a couple of times for a progress report.' Claire sounded relaxed but there was something extra in her voice.

'Clem's had to go to his parents. His father took a fall down the stairs. He might be there for a couple of days. I know you and he arranged to meet but he says he'll call you as soon as he can.'

'I see.' But Fee didn't see at all. If Claire was this well informed, why was she also being so civil?

'Fee,' Claire spoke again. 'Would you be able to call round later? I really need to talk to you – it can't be said on the phone.'

Fee's mouth went dry; she took several deep breaths.

'Are you there?' Claire asked.

'Yes, yes, sorry, I'm a bit tired, I was up most of Saturday night and I haven't quite caught up yet,' Fee answered. 'I'll come about three, is that OK?'

Claire sounded enormously relieved. 'That's terrific,' she said.

Replacing the receiver, Fee consoled herself that 'terrific' was hardly the response you'd expect from a woman who knew she'd been betrayed.

Claire was dressed and remaking a window-box in her front garden when Fee arrived. She had lost weight but otherwise, Fee decided, she looked surprisingly well. She didn't have to wait to discover why.

'I'm pregnant,' Claire burst out, smiling broadly. 'Twelve weeks pregnant. I knew in Dublin but I didn't mention it because the doctors were worried that I might miscarry. You should see your face. You look pole-axed.'

Fee swallowed hard. 'It's . . . I'm . . . Oh, gosh, I don't know what to say,' she responded truthfully. Then she flung her arms around Claire and kissed her on both cheeks.

'Now,' Claire looked at her best friend straight in the eye. 'About you and Clem—'

Fee reacted like a child caught in the act. 'I don't know what you mean,' she spluttered, the colour rising in her cheeks.

'Well, let me explain,' Claire replied amiably, directing Fee to a deckchair. 'Let's start from the beginning. Clem and I are a mistake. If I marry him, I'll end up destroying his confidence and my peace of mind. I thought I could settle for an accommodation, an understanding – but I realize that, for me, that's too much of a cheat on what life might have to offer—'

She raised her hand to silence any interruptions. 'No, let me say my piece. I've thought about this a great deal—'

'It's ironic really, I believed Clem was in love with me. Now I realize he was seeking the same from me as I was hoping for from him – a relationship without the risks. We've both been damaged by emotions disguised as love, and we both believed we could settle for something safer.

'The only trouble is,' she gave a wan smile, 'if you remove the risk, you also remove a lot of the reason for sticking through the bad times as well as the good. I realize now that I can put up with the domesticity but I've got to have the desire as well.'

She took Fee's hand. 'When I saw you and Clem together in Dublin in a situation where, for once, you weren't showing your teeth at him, I realized that you had far more going for each other than I could match . . . I tried to convince myself otherwise. I tried to convince you too . . . but it just became more and more obvious. And when you came back to London, poor Clem was like a lost soul . . . I don't want to watch that for the rest of my married life—'

Fee gazed at Claire, stunned by what she was hearing. Eventually, she found words. 'Have you talked to Clem about this? Have you told him about the baby? Have you decided what to do about it?'

Claire nodded. 'You know how I've always said babies need two parents? Well, you can't always have the ideal situation. I'm going to do the very best I can on my own – but hopefully with some help from Clem.'

'You're going to keep the baby?' Fee repeated. 'You do know what's involved? You do know you'll be exhausted and probably broke?'

'Look, if you're worried I'm going to ask you to babysit, just say,' Claire gently teased.

Embarrassed, Fee recognized that the force of her response had less to do with Claire and perhaps more to do with her own decision not to have children.

'I'm sorry,' she apologized.

Claire patted her hand. 'I didn't tell you but Clem already has a daughter . . . She lives in Australia with her mother who's not keen for Clem to visit. It must seem to him that he's about to lose a second child, but I've promised it doesn't have to be like that—'

'Poor Clem,' Fee said spontaneously. 'How has he reacted?'

Claire gave a weary smile. 'He says that the trouble with single women today is that we hold too many of the cards . . . But, given the circumstances, he would say that, wouldn't he?'

Fee's thoughts chased each other crazily. Clem and she could do as they pleased. Claire was not so much giving her blessing as

411

positively pushing her and Clem together . . . so why was Fee even more muddled and uncertain than before?

'I want to ask a favour,' Claire asked, then dissolved into laughter at the look on Fee's face.

'It's purely practical,' she reassured her. 'Nuptia Europa is closing down. They said they'd sent you the bridesmaid's dresses but I'd agreed to pick up my dress . . . Would you mind doing it for me? There is a perk in the job,' Claire added. 'You can have the pleasure of telling Michele Canning that not only is the wedding off, but the bride has been dumped and is up the spout, and her fiancé has run off with the maid of honour. I can't do better than that, can I?'

Edward Spannier sat at the desk in his hotel suite and thought of a good, round, solid figure – one that could easily be divided four ways – and wrote out a cheque. Then, he sighed heavily.

He saw himself as a rational, disciplined, organized kind of man. A man of ability. A man who was accustomed to achieving what he wanted. He had therefore surprised himself in the last few weeks.

At first, he had assumed that his defences had been temporarily weakened by that sexual boll-weevil known as lust. Lust, he could handle. Rather well, in fact.

Then he'd decided that the cause was much more prosaic. He was under the weather. Finally, he'd been forced to recognize that, for the first time in his life, the plain truth was that he couldn't live without a woman. A particular woman.

After fourteen days, what Edward Spannier had begun to find almost as appalling as his personal weakness was the woman to whom he'd fallen victim. She was just so damn *unsuitable*. For a start, he practically had to make an appointment to see her.

She had too many opinions, very strong opinions. And again, she had this highly disconcerting habit of walking away. Just disappearing, leaving him high and dry.

So far, Edward had lost his temper on three occasions. Justifiably, he would say. Each time, it had plainly been Imogen's fault. Each time, he had attempted to make her accept responsibility. And she had walked away. Laughing. *Laughing?*

Of course Edward was not denying that Imogen Banks was a woman of passion, fire, intelligence, zest, ability, talent. What's more she knew how to court success and make money. He had certainly found a woman who was his equal. For years with Shona, Edward had told himself it would all have been so much better if his wife had been able to match him in brain power and repartee, so why was he finding Imogen such heavy weather?

Why was he catching himself in unguarded moments recalling Shona?

Imogen Banks, dressed in a cream lace and satin négligé of a kind most frequently seen in Hollywood movies of the 1940s, walked out of the bedroom and across to where Edward was sitting.

She was barefoot, so he failed to hear her until it was too late. She kissed him on the top of his head and picked up the cheque in one easy movement.

'What a lot of money,' she commented lightly. 'And made out to whom? To Spannier's? Darling, you're not buying me a season ticket to your wife's little endeavour, are you?'

Edward Spannier wished he'd had his dinner. At least then he would have had more strength to survive the row that he now knew was pending.

'I've decided to make them an offer, buy them out, close the business down before it gets under way. End of story.'

Imogen's face froze. 'What on earth do you mean?' she asked in a tone Edward hadn't heard before. 'What on earth do you mean, you're making them an offer? They haven't even got anything to sell, yet.'

Edward nervously twisted the ring on his little finger. 'I want Shona and her associates to sell me the business,' he repeated.

He had expected that Imogen might rail at the amount of money he was prepared to offer his wife; he was not at all prepared for the way in which she actually reacted.

Imogen's apoplectic anger gave her the appearance of inflating

413

her hugely in size. Her bulging eyes and vast breasts reminded a startled Edward of the imposing ships' heads in Portsmouth harbour, which loomed above him when he visited as a boy.

'You stupid, stupid man,' Imogen bellowed. 'How dare you do this to me? How dare you sabotage a perfectly good undertaking—

'Don't you realize,' she shouted, putting her nose inches from his. 'Don't you realize that I am on the point of persuading these women and their clients and the men on Spannier's books that they should appear in a film? It would be a *coup*. A major *coup*. The best kind of entertainment – human weakness in all its shapes and sizes. And what do you do?'

Imogen raised her hand and bunched it into a fist. For one terrible moment, Edward actually believed she was going to punch him hard. Instinctively, he flinched.

'Don't you dare blink at me like that,' she shouted at the top of her voice. 'Let me make this clear. End of Spannier's. End of my bloody film. End of our sodding relationship. Got it?'

She pushed up the sleeves of her négligé as if preparing for action.

'Now, are you coming to bed or not?'

An hour later, Imogen was up and dressed. It was late, but not too late. She left a brief note for Edward, then got into her car and began to drive.

On the way, she telephoned Fee.

'How did it go with the information I gave you?' Imogen asked.

'Fine,' Fee answered. She sounded tired.

'Did Claire realize what a bastard her future husband had been?' Imogen chuckled, then, before Fee could answer, she added, 'I've got a favour to ask, Fee. I want you to persuade Veronica and Jean that they should let me film the launch of Spannier's. They want your opinion. You don't owe me any favours, I know, but have I or have I not been useful of late?'

'I'll do a deal,' Fee offered.

414

'Well, there's a surprise,' Imogen replied drily. 'If you're going to suggest that I send Edward back to his wife, that's no problem. He's already longing for what he left. I can read the signs. And, frankly, once that initial bonking mania wears off, it seems to me that it tends to decline dramatically into the ordinary, wouldn't you say?'

'Look, Fee,' Imogen smiled at herself in her driving mirror, 'I just happen to be driving right past your road. OK if I pop in for a few minutes?'

She left Fee no time to reply.

Fee had waited fruitlessly for a phone call from Clem. Perhaps the situation with his father was worse than expected, she reasoned. He was sure to call later. Imogen's arrival was almost a welcome diversion.

'You're a troublemaker, Imogen,' Fee remarked amiably. 'A troublemaker who has no personal morality at all.'

Imogen affected puzzlement. 'Morality, you say? Well, darling, speaking as one woman to another, which you know I'm usually loath to do, I can tell you that I'm up to here with morality.' She indicated the top of her head.

'Why should I deny myself the pleasure of another woman's husband?' Imogen asked, warming to her subject. 'Why should I speak the truth if it fails to achieve what I want?'

Fee shrugged. 'Perhaps because in the long run you damage yourself as well as others round you . . . ?'

Imogen smiled broadly and put a hand on each hip. 'Come on, sweetie, you're the professional who sells hot air. You're going to have to do better than that.'

Fee smiled non-committally. 'Imogen, you said you wanted me to persuade Veronica and the others to agree to you making a film about Spannier's. Right?'

Imogen nodded.

'Well, I'll do that if you'll give me a hand. I've met a terrific woman called Lea Fitzgerald. She needs money for a children's hospital in India . . . You could raise the money in five minutes, blindfolded . . . Is it a deal?'

Imogen put her face in her hands and pretended to sob copiously. 'Do I have to? Have you really brought me to this, Fee? Is there no other way?'

Finally, she gave a sigh of resignation, enjoying herself hugely.

'One condition,' she announced. 'Nobody but nobody is told that I've helped. Spinster I can live with. A spinster of the parish who does good? I'll cut my throat first.'

Imogen left at nine. There was still no call from Clem. Fee fretted, then cursed. Weeks ago she had promised herself there would be no more waiting for a man to phone, so what was she doing now?

Fifteen minutes later, Veronica knocked on her sister's door. She and Jean and Shona wanted Fee to take a professional look at the prototypes of the publicity material and catalogues for Spannier's laid out on Shona's kitchen table.

'I'm sorry,' Fee apologized. 'I can't. I'm waiting for a call. And I need to be here when it comes.'

'It's not the mysterious Rita, is it?' Veronica asked.

Fee shook her head.

'Leave you answering machine on,' Veronica urged. 'We want you to see all the stuff so we can send it off in the morning. We need a fresh eye . . . Mum says it looks OK but—'

'Mum as in our mother?' Fee questioned.

'I've got no reason to doubt her authenticity,' Veronica remarked mildly. 'She's developed a taste for notoriety since your television appearance . . . Did you know she's given an interview to the local paper?'

Fee smiled. 'What does she think of her eldest daughter running an escort agency?'

Veronica put on an exaggeratedly pained expression. 'Please, Fee, "escort" is not the word we like to hear. "Associates" is much more refined and open-ended. What does Helen think? Well, naturally, she's very disappointed—' The two sisters burst out laughing.

'Actually I think she'd prefer it if I went back to knocking off strangers at six paces with a single glance of the eye . . . So long as I did it quietly . . . But now that we're so far down the line with Spannier's, I think she sees it as her duty to be critic-in-chief. Tell us where we're going wrong. And, to be honest, she's weeded out two or three men who've asked for jobs and turned out to have faked their c.v.s.'

Veronica made her way to Fee's front door. 'Is there anything I can do?' she asked. 'I know you've got something on your mind. Can I help? What's wrong?'

Fee gave a tired smile. 'What's wrong? You mean apart from no job, not a lot of cash in the bank and a surplus of bridesmaids' dresses cluttering the flat, which is already overflowing with enough mail to keep a team of agony aunts busy for a year?'

'No,' Veronica said. 'I mean what's *really* worrying you? Come on, come and have a drink at Shona's and tell your big sister all about it.'

'Claire's pregnant,' Fee said abruptly.

Veronica's face softened. 'Oh, you poor thing, now I understand—'

'Well, if you do,' Fee replied honestly, 'I certainly don't—'

Chapter Forty

'**S** SSH!' JEAN Stoker hissed.

She was standing in Shona's hall, the door open, a finger to her lips.

'I was just going to come and tell you,' she whispered to Veronica and Fee.

'Tell us what?' Veronica asked, puzzled.

'Tell you that he's here.' Jean nodded with her head towards the closed door of the sitting room. 'Edward. He's in there . . . He arrived about ten minutes ago, when we were in the kitchen. He doesn't know we're here but Shona doesn't want us to leave, in case he tries any rough stuff—'

The three women tiptoed down Shona's hall and into the kitchen. The table and breakfast bar were covered with material for Spannier's launch, including an expensively bound catalogue which Fee flicked through.

It was Spannier's first crop of 'associates'. Each man had been shot in the same style, in casual clothes, on a park bench, as if in a holiday snap, relaxed, smiling, informal, but the effect was professional.

'We didn't want those awful James Dean-type poses—' Jean said, answering Fee's unstated question.

'Didn't the photographer cost a lot . . . there must be seventy or eighty pictures here?' Fee asked.

Jean answered, 'No, he gave us a special price . . . on the understanding that if we become successful, we'd carry on using him. Summers? Bill Summers. It was your mother who suggested him.'

Fee closed the catalogue. 'Well,' she said. 'I'm delighted that someone is managing to profit from my past mistakes.'

In the sitting room, Shona Spannier was standing in front of the French windows. Opposite her, also standing, was her husband. This was the first time in over a fortnight that they had seen each other – and Shona's overwhelming emotion was one of mistrust, a mistrust of herself.

Edward Spannier had his hands in his pocket and appeared anything but contrite. He glanced at Shona, then looked away. Anyone less fluent than Shona in her husband's body language might read this as a sign of guilt. Shona knew that boredom was more likely an interpretation.

'I've talked to Imogen about the situation,' Edward was saying. 'I've told her that I can't see our relationship going anywhere. It was an aberration on my part. I let it all get out of control . . . it's unusual for me. I'm sorry.' The words were mechanical.

Of course he had not discussed the issue with Imogen. He preferred to keep his options open. In the unlikely event that Shona spurned him, he knew he could still fall back on Imogen.

Shona appraised her husband. He was, as always, immaculately turned out, cool, unemotional – except in anger. She was reassured. After all the recent turmoil, at last life had returned to its familiar pattern; its vocabulary of denial and deceit.

'I've made it clear to her that the relationship is over,' Edward said, examining his cuticles. 'What's your response?'

Shona didn't know whether to sob or sigh. She sighed. 'Are you saying you want us to try again, Teddy?' she asked.

'Yes, so long as you accept a couple of provisos,' he added, as if Shona and not he had been the errant partner.

'Teddy, would you excuse me for a minute or two, please?' Shona suddenly excused herself and walked out of the sitting room.

It was only a flesh wound but the look of surprise on her husband's face gave Shona a small thrill of satisfaction.

'He wants to come back,' she told the three women in her kitchen.

Fee responded instantly. 'You don't need him, Shona. Tell him to drop dead. You're beginning to get back on your feet. He knows he's losing his hold on you. That's why he's come back grovelling.'

'I wouldn't exactly say he was grovelling—'

'What do you want to do?' Veronica asked.

Shona sank down on a chair.

'You're going to hate me for this,' she replied, watching Fee. 'But I can't help myself. I want him home. I'm not the type who can operate well when there's only me to think about . . . the idea is too terrifying.' Shona shook her head. 'And there's the boys . . . they need a father around—'

'But is Edward likely to be around?' Jean asked quietly.

'Yes, he most certainly is,' Shona replied firmly. 'If he comes back, he comes back on my terms. I know I've got something he needs . . . I know I have a bargaining counter now.'

Veronica smiled and gave Shona a quick hug. 'Go back in there, state your terms clearly and don't let him bully you.'

'I wouldn't dream of it,' she said.

Ten minutes later, she was back again, white-faced.

'He says that he won't come home unless I . . . we . . . drop the whole Spannier's project. He says it's an unsuitable enterprise and will cause nothing but trouble. He says he's prepared to buy us out. He says he's prepared to be generous. He doesn't want his name associated with this – and he doesn't want me to work for you—'

Jean Stoker had been sitting on the kitchen floor, packing brochures into boxes. She stopped and stood up slowly.

'Hold on a minute. Let me get this right. Your husband has said he won't come back to you unless we ditch our business?'

Shona nodded.

'How much is he offering?' Veronica asked, ever the accountant.

'£160,000.'

'He's mad,' Jean pronounced.

'No, he's not,' Veronica corrected her. 'He's got the money to give. And it's worth it to him to avoid the risk of future embarrassment . . . But that's hardly the point, is it? Are we in this for the money – or because we want to do something for ourselves too?'

'We're in this for the money,' Jean answered crisply. 'Although, I can't pretend I haven't become very fond of Spannier's already—'

'Jean's right,' Fee said. 'It is about cash. She started this whole thing because she needs to clear her debts. If she accepts Edward's offer, she can go a long way towards that . . . and still start another business. Isn't that right, Jean?'

'But?' Veronica asked.

'But', Fee answered, 'you'll have to give up on what could be a highly successful idea. Presumably, Edward wants you home alone, again.'

Shona nodded. 'The truth is, I've got no real say. I've only put in a couple of thousand, so it's for the three of you to decide.'

'But what would you prefer us to do?' Veronica asked, expecting no surprises. The three women waited.

Shona took a deep breath. 'What I'd like you to do,' she hesitated, and the rest came out in a rush. 'What I'd like you to do – is turn him down flat. I'm sorry I even considered what Teddy has to say. I *know* Spannier's will work—'

Shona looked at each of the women around her.

'What do you say, Jean, Veronica, Fee? The money – or the business?'

'The business,' the women chorused as one.

'What if Edward leaves you?' Jean ventured.

421

Shona gave a wan smile. 'Perhaps Fee is right, perhaps it's time he did.'

Edward Spannier banged the front door of his flat so hard the milk bottles on the window-sill in the kitchen performed a brief impromptu jig.

'There goes a happy man,' said Fee. The women walked into the sitting room expecting to see a distraught Shona. Instead, she was composed.

'I told him we didn't want his money. He said he'd sue me for using his name. I pointed out it was my name too. Then I said that we also intended to accept his former mistress's kind offer to appear on television—'

'And he marched out?' said Jean.

'Yes,' Shona replied. 'But we made progress.'

Jean looked puzzled. 'You did?'

'Edward never raised his hand, not once.'

'Do you think he'll be back?' Jean asked, bemused by the terms on which Shona was prepared to accept a relationship.

'He'll be back,' she replied. 'Imogen's made Edward realize that – no matter what his fantasies – he needs a wife, a certain type of wife. So, yes, he'll be back. But whether I continue to be the kind of wife he wants—' She shrugged. 'Who knows?'

Fee returned to her flat shortly after and discovered that Clem had called in her absence. His message was tentative and simple, as if uncertain of her response or who might hear the message.

'Fee? It's Clem. My father's not so good so I won't be home until the day after tomorrow. I'll be on the 9.15 a.m. from Chester, if you can meet the train? If not, I'll understand. I've got so much to say. I'll try again. I . . . I . . . miss you.'

The word, 'home' made Fee experience an unexpected flash of jealously. Did he mean Claire's flat? Was that still home? Perhaps, now that Clem knew that Claire was pregnant, his feelings towards her might change again?

She gave herself a small shake. This anticipation of disappointment proved her to be, if nothing else, her mother's child.

'Don't question his motives,' Fee told herself firmly. 'Consider your own.'

Chapter Forty-One

NUPTIA EUROPA was not at its best. A couple of dummies stood in one corner of the window, naked except for battered floral head-dresses; the Muzak had been terminated; the muskrose-perfumed air had been replaced by a slight smell of damp.

Fee had telephoned earlier that morning to say that she would be picking up Claire Harper's bridal dress. A voice unknown to her had told her to ring the doorbell since the business was no longer open to the public.

Fee had arrived punctually with her mood much improved. Before leaving the flat she had briefly looked at her mail and discovered three offers for jobs. None interested her in the slightest but at least she had been asked. There was also an invitation to her own farewell party, arranged by friends and colleagues at F. P. & D. for the following weekend.

'If you can't come,' read the handwritten note on the card, 'we'll mourn in your absence. PS, Did you know that Gerry has moved in with Diana Woods?'

If Fee had harboured any regrets for walking out of F. P. & D., they were banished now. Gerry in love and presumably sexually active for the first time in years was a challenge too far.

Fee rang the doorbell again. Michele Canning appeared at the top of the stairs, recognized her, and came down to let her in.

'You've heard?' she said unnecessarily. 'Do you know what's going to happen to the place?'

Fee shook her head, following the woman back the way she had come.

'It's going to be a bookshop dealing exclusively in romantic fiction. Can you imagine it? The new owner says there's more money in fiction than in marriage these days. Customers want a happy ever after they can believe in—' Michele Canning gave a hollow laugh.

She cheered up considerably when Fee recounted the rise and fall of Claire's marriage plans.

'So she's given him the push?' she mused, carefully packing Claire's mercifully frill-free bridal gown into a large cardboard box. 'I didn't like to say so at the time. But from the first five minutes in that cubicle, I could see it coming. Never been wrong yet.'

As Fee turned to leave, she accidentally dropped her car keys which appeared to sink without trace into the deep-pile carpet. As she was down on her hands and knees, her eyes were caught by a pair of shoes in the curtained cubicle to her left.

They were ridiculously high, absurd bright blue and suede. 'Now isn't that strange?' said a voice Fee recognized.

'Rita.' Fee didn't even need to look up. 'Where the bloody hell have you been? And what are you doing here?'

Rita Mason, a well-worn Sandra Dee, smiled. 'I'm buying my wedding dress. What do you think I'm doing here, silly?'

Twenty minutes later, Rita and Fee were in the wine bar next door to Nuptia Europa, drinking coffee. Fee hammered Rita with a series of questions. Why had she run off with Gwynfor Pryce's money? Why had she stolen Fee's belongings? Why had she disappeared without telling anyone where she was going? Why had she lied about her name, her mother's death, her job, her life? Why hadn't she phoned?

Fee found herself growing more irate. The anger came not just from the inadequacies of Rita's replies – but also because of the casualness of her approach.

'Didn't you realize how much trouble you put so many people

through?' she asked. She knew she sounded like the mother of a teenage runaway.

Rita Mason in turn, affected an almost infantile bewilderment that anyone should have been so bothered. She had *told* people where she had gone – was it her fault they hadn't listened? She was under the impression that Fee hadn't wanted to see her again anyway. So what was the problem?

'God, Rita, I could shake you,' Fee replied, exasperated. 'What about the bedsit and all your things? I had to give your stuff to Will to stick in his spare room.'

Rita looked blank. 'Why did you need to move my stuff? I sent the landlord a cheque with my rent in advance . . . I'm popping round there now—'

Fee explained that if Rita had sent a cheque, it had failed to arrive. She had been evicted. Why hadn't she informed her employers at Tendon Hospital how long she would be away?

Rita pouted. 'I worked really hard at that place and when I asked for my fortnight's holiday plus an extra week unpaid, they said it wasn't possible, so I thought, stuff 'em, why should I care?'

'All right, why did you stand me up when you arranged to meet me for a drink?' Fee asked.

'I rang in the afternoon,' Rita answered sulkily. 'That woman Gill answered. Nearly bit my head off. She said she'd tell you. I also tried your office but they said you were unavailable . . . they said you were on a blind date or something—'

Fee shook her head in mock-despair. 'So where *have* you been Rita?'

She beamed. 'My fiancé Roger came over from Saudi Arabia. I told Walt and Jim – you must have met them at the house – I told them Roger was coming. Perhaps they forgot. Or perhaps they thought it was another one of my—' Rita stirred her coffee noisily. It was the nearest she had come to admitting that reality might not be her strong suit.

'Are you telling me that Roger actually exists?' Fee asked bluntly.

'Of course, he does,' Rita replied indignantly. It was all right to label herself a liar – it was a liberty for anybody else to suggest it.

'Why did you have my photos in your room then?' Fee asked. 'Why did you tell Walt and Jim that my old boyfriend was your fiancé?'

Rita shrugged. 'It's a bit of fun. Why not? Nobody's harmed. Sometimes it does a bit of good. Besides, you wouldn't have known if you hadn't gone into my room . . . And, to be honest, Roger's a lovely man but he does not take a good photo.'

'But why all the lies, Rita?' Fee pressed. 'You're not a radiographer, you haven't got a cottage in Sussex, your mother's not dead and you sure as hell owe Gwynfor Pryce a lot of money.'

Rita took a sip of her coffee. 'He's a crook. I only gave him a bit of what he dishes out to others. I've got his money, I'll send it back when I'm ready. I wanted to teach him a lesson, show him he's not the only one who can take people for a ride. I bet he was furious, wasn't he?' Rita giggled.

Fee could see now that Rita Mason's whole life was an exercise in escapism. She didn't consider the impact of her lies on others – perhaps because, for too many years, there had been so few people around who might be affected.

'You're looking a bit lost, Fee, if you don't mind me saying so,' Rita commented chattily, as if the matter of all the unanswered questions had been more than adequately dealt with and it was time to move on.

'I told Roger, from the minute we met, I could tell you were a bit . . . rudderless . . . You needed someone to look after you. That's why I followed you and your friend to the place next door,' Rita smiled, pleased with her own act of generosity.

'Who? Claire?'

'Yes, there was something about her I didn't like – and I had a bit of time on my hands, so it was no trouble. Anyway, when Roger and I decided to bring the wedding forward, I thought of next door right away. Got a lovely dress and dead cheap.'

Fee was about to speak again but she stopped. Rita was away in another place, her face was wreathed in one of her dazzling smiles, her eyes shining.

'There's someone I want you to meet,' she said. Fee turned. She saw a man at least twenty years younger than Rita. He was flashily dressed in black slacks, yellow cardigan and a black and yellow dogtooth-check tie. He wore a Rolex watch and ostentatiously carried a mobile phone.

'Roger?' Fee asked.

'Terry,' Rita replied. 'Fee, I want you to meet my baby, Terry.'

'Terry?' Fee repeated weakly.

'Yes,' Rita smiled even more radiantly. 'Terry Waters. Terry, my son. You found the place all right, sweetie? And this', she added, with a little flourish of her hand, 'is Roger Buxton, my fiancé.'

Roger Buxton looked far more suited to the role of Rita's baby than Terry. He had a smooth, pink face and a fuzz of downy hair. His smile revealed a number of gaps in two rows of tiny white teeth. If Roger had offered Fee a rattle, instead of his hand in introduction, she wouldn't have been surprised.

'Sit down, boys,' Rita ordered maternally. 'Fee can't wait to hear how we all got together. Can you believe it, she thinks you're all figments of my imagination? Terry, my son, you tell her your bit of the story.'

Terry duly obliged.

Terry Waters, Rita's son, had been adopted thirty-four years earlier by a couple in Bristol. He had had a happy childhood. His adopted parents had run a small hotel until they retired. They were both still alive. Terry had also moved into catering, and now ran a successful pub and restaurant. He had been married for six years and had two girls, aged four and nine months.

It was when his first child had been born that Terry decided to trace his natural mother. Rita's continual changes of names and addresses hadn't helped. Temporarily he had given up the hunt.

428

Roger Buxton then took up the story.

Eighteen months ago, in Saudi Arabia, he had replied to an ad. for a pen pal. The woman had been Rita. They corresponded for six months, during which time Rita, according to Roger, 'told a few porkies' but also recounted a great deal of the truth about her life.

Roger too had been in trouble in the past. He had been brought up in care and had no family that he knew. He understood Rita's desire to invent what had, as yet, failed to materialize in her life. Roger came home on leave. They met. He retreated, surprised by how much older Rita was. Then he missed her letters. They resumed writing. On the second leave, several months ago, he had proposed. 'I've known her personally, one to one, about ten weeks in all,' he announced to Fee with some pride. 'It mostly rests on the written word.'

It was Roger who had decided to find Rita's son. He inserted an ad. in several newspapers. Terry Waters took his wallet from his breast pocket and pulled out a cutting, handing it to Fee.

The ad. read: 'Rita Mason, also known as Rose Sutton, also known as Mary Hastings . . . would like knowledge of her son, born Terry Hastings. Last heard of in Bristol.'

'That's where the mother and baby home was,' Rita explained. 'That was the address on the birth certificate.'

'I came home three weeks ago because I managed to swap leave with a mate,' Roger Buxton added, eager to claim ownership of the most dramatic part of the saga. 'And, by then, I'd already written a few times to our Terry here. As soon as I met him, I knew.'

Mother and son smiled at each other shyly. Roger Buxton reached for his fiancée's hand. 'I thought to myself, "Roger lad, best strike while the iron's hot, in case one of these geezers changes their mind." So I came to London, told Rita that it was now or never. She had to see her son.

'We all met in Bristol and stayed down there for a week, so these two could get to know each slow like—' Roger put an arm around Terry and Rita.

'Everyone was nervous, but it went well. Now I'm a granddad at thirty-seven, and very pleased about it 'n' all . . . Course, we may face a few hurdles ahead but, right now, it feels nice, it does really. Happy ever after?' He winked. 'I'll have a bit of that—'

The three sat opposite Fee, an unlikely trio – but one that she found very touching. Roger Buxton, in Rita, had found a wife and mother; Terry Waters had discovered why he'd been given away and Rita finally had both son and lover.

Later, as they left the wine bar, Rita put her hand on Fee's arm proprietorially.

'That flat,' she said. 'The one opposite you. They're moving out soon, aren't they?'

'The Spanniers?' Fee answered nervously.

'That's it,' Rita smiled. 'Well, we thought rather than rush into buying a house, we'll wait until Roger's back from Saudi for good—'

'And in the meantime, you'll rent the flat opposite me?' Fee finished for her.

'That's it. I'm really looking forward to it, aren't you?'

Word of mouth took Jean and Veronica by surprise. At the same time as Rita Mason was re-creating her family tree for Fee, Spannier's three telephone lines, temporarily housed in Shona's flat, began to ring.

Spannier's had received twelve calls by the time Fee returned with Claire's dress in the early afternoon. Some of the women who were calling as potential clients were bold, some were extremely nervous, others were honest about their lack of expertise as first-timers.

In Shona's sitting room, Veronica handed Fee the growing list of women who had asked to be sent a brochure. Amy, Veronica's next-door neighbour, had informed several of her friends. A woman called Sheila Scott, going through a divorce, had been told about Spannier's by Hilly Byrne. And Imogen herself appeared to have told everybody who was female, over thirty-five and with sufficient cash flow.

'But then she would,' Veronica said drily. 'She starts filming tomorrow when we move into the new offices.'

Fee made her way to the kitchen to make a cup of tea and witnessed a sight she never imagined that she would see. Her mother was sitting at Shona's large kitchen table on the phone. Helen had Spannier's fat album of 'associates' in front of her and was confidently nipping backwards and forwards through its pages.

'I've got a really lovely man here. I've met him myself so I know,' she was telling someone at the other end of the line. 'He's forty-nine, a widower and, sadly, he's bankrupt. His two garages recently went bust and he works as a mechanic now. Hence his shortage of cash, otherwise I'm sure he'd be paying his way. Anyway, he comes thoroughly recommended. I know you won't be disappointed—'

Later, Fee lay in her bath, and attempted to bring her thoughts into some kind of order. For the past twenty-four hours, her emotions had yo-yoed through excitement, guilt, anticipation, confusion, doubt, pleasure, but what had failed to emerge was any kind of certainty.

If she and Clem decided to – what? Move in together, try a relationship, make a commitment? Would that be a mistake on her part, or a vindication of the past few weeks when she had tried to distinguish between her own desires and what for years others had told her she ought to yearn for?

Falling in love at thirty-eight is different from falling in love at twenty-eight or eighteen, she reminded herself. At thirty-eight, as Imogen had once told her, love can't afford to be blind. Time's too short.

'If it's Clem's c.v. you want, you've got it,' Fee reminded herself drily. It had what might charitably be called inconsistencies but then her own record wasn't perfect by any means. And Clem had planned to behave honourably towards Claire. He had intended to tell her the truth, at the appropriate time, not go behind her back.

'And what does that tell me?' Fee asked herself wryly. 'That if he rats on me, I'll be the first to know? How reassuring.'

She pulled the plug out with her toe and watched as the water subsided. The years were beginning to make her body soften and spread. Sometimes she minded; sometimes she didn't. This evening, she did. Her thoughts were interrupted by someone banging on her door. She grabbed a towel and let Veronica into the flat.

'I'm off home,' Veronica explained. 'Les is cooking supper and he hates it when I'm late. I've been meaning to give you this. As a sort of thank you . . . for helping me out.'

Fee stood dripping in the hall. She took a small package from her sister and followed her into the kitchen. As she walked, Fee unwrapped the parcel. It was one of her father's old westerns, carefully covered.

'I know you've already got a lot of his books,' Veronica shrugged, slightly embarrassed, 'but this was the very first our dad bought when he began to collect them after he and Mum married. See—'

She showed Fee the book, *Gene Autry and the Thief River Outlaws*, published in 1944. Neatly printed on a label, in her father's hand, were the details of the secondhand bookshop from which he'd bought it and the date: The Avalon Book Shop, Leicester, 1948.

Veronica drew up a chair to the kitchen table and gently, carefully, began to turn the pages. 'He was a funny old boy, our dad,' she said softly. 'Out of his time. I used to think he was living in a dream world . . . Listen to this, it's about Gene Autry and his horse—'

She began to read, growing more sentimental by the second, '"Each recognized certain friendships and duties from time to time but neither man nor beast felt any need to depend on any other creature. They had learned to trust in no help but their own strength, courage, speed, wits and fighting hearts—"'

Veronica glanced at her sister and abruptly stopped reading. 'Fee? Are you listening? Only you seem miles away—'

Fee smiled broadly and flung her arms around her sister, giving her an enthusiastic kiss on the cheek.

'Veronica,' she said, 'you're a gem.'

Chapter Forty-Two

FEE'S FAREWELL party was in a private room above a wine bar five minutes from F. P. & D. The drinking had begun illicitly in the office in the middle of the afternoon. So by the time Fee arrived, Trish Castle was making herself comfortable on Will Evans's knee and several of Fee's former team were telling each other *frankly* what they thought. About what, was unclear.

It wouldn't be long, Fee judged, before the tears and vomit would be flowing in equal proportions. Her arrival was greeted with cheers and catcalls and applause. Will, ahead of schedule, presented Fee with a large glass vase and gave an impromptu speech. He proclaimed Fee as the greatest woman ever to turn her hand to business.

To her surprise, Fee saw Gerry Radcliffe and his wife, Marie-Jeanne, holding hands and being very attentive to each other by the bar.

Oriel Ashcroft came over and, following Fee's gaze, smiled. 'Gerry couldn't stand it without Marie-Jeanne,' she explained. 'He went back five days after he left to live with Diana. The atmosphere in the office has improved no end.'

'How is Diana?' Fee asked casually. Oriel's smile widened.

'You haven't heard?' she said. Fee shook her head.

'She's resigned – and she's in love. I've taken over her old job – but no seat on the board as yet,' she added wryly.

Fee gave her a congratulatory hug. 'Well done,' she said. 'But make it easier on the others who come up behind you – don't work all the hours that God sends. It makes you do strange things. Believe me, I know—'

Oriel nodded with her head towards the door. 'Diana said she'd look in, to wish you well. But I thought she was going to come later to avoid Gerry's wife—'

Fee turned. Framed in the entrance was Diana Woods, and, by her side, in denim and *diamanté*, was Serena Alwyn, Harry Macklin's managing director.

Oriel whispered in Fee's ear, 'They worked together on the account and love blossomed. Now, Diana's employed full-time with Macklin. Isn't that sweet?'

The following morning, Fee was awake at five. She left for the station much too early at eight. Half the time she was convinced she wouldn't know how to react until she set eyes on Clem; the rest of the time, she knew exactly what she was going to say. He had called again three times and each time, she had been out. She fretted that he hadn't left a number so that she could ring him back.

She was ridiculously excited, not just because she would be seeing him again, but because the unexpected, the unforeseen, a small taste of danger, had returned to her life.

The train was late. It was five minutes, then ten minutes, then twelve and a half minutes late. Finally, just before nine thirty, when the station was jammed with commuters, Fee spotted the top of Clem's head by the ticket barrier. Instinctively, she began to run towards him, then stopped, apprehensively.

He had no such qualms. Fee watched as he searched the faces, then a smile of recognition appeared. He put his holdall down and both arms out. She went to him, and let him hold her close and kiss her. And kiss her again.

It was only then that Fee Travers became certain what it was that she wanted to do, what it was that she *really* wanted to do.

*

The coffee shop on the station was busy with demands for takeaway drinks and food, but Fee and Clem were only two of a handful of customers sitting at tables. They could talk in relative privacy.

Clem had wanted to drive to Fee's flat; Fee had preferred to have this conversation on neutral ground. It was fairer – to her at least. She didn't want to be tempted into changing her mind.

'Are you asking me if I'll wait for you for six months?' Clem repeated the question, his face puzzled and bewildered. Fee shook her head.

'No, of course not.'

'Are you telling me that you don't feel as strongly for me as you thought?' Clem asked.

'No, of course not,' she repeated.

'Are you saying that you're frightened that I might realize that I've made the wrong choice and go back to Claire and her . . . our . . . baby?'

Fee shook her head again. Clem banged his hand down on the wrought-iron table.

'Well, Fee, what the bloody hell are you trying to say? What makes you so *contrary?* This isn't a game, you know. It's about grown-up people with grown-up feelings.'

Fee realized that Clem had understood her all too well – but he was reluctant to accept the implication of what she had said. She regretted that she was causing him pain, but she was also aware, with increasing clarity, that she had made the right choice.

'I know I have strong feelings for you, Clem,' Fee explained gently. 'But I also know that there's still a lot I want to do that will only make sense if I'm on my own.

'I want to break away from the rat race; I want to learn to trust myself more . . . I want to develop a fighting heart, Clem, to replace the weak and malleable one that trips me up too often now.'

'Isn't any of that possible with me?' Clem asked quietly.

'Of course it is.' She reached out impulsively for his hand. 'But however good, it would be a totally different experience. If I don't take this chance now, on my own, I'll never be in this frame of mind to try again. And I know I'll regret it always.'

Clem gently touched her cheek. 'If you love a person,' he said, almost as if talking to himself, 'you want her to be free . . . If I'm still here when you come back from wherever it is you're going . . . who knows?'

He attempted a smile. Fee almost changed her mind. No man had ever valued her freedom before – except in his own self-interest.

'You're very special to me, Clem.' Fee knew that she was crying, but there was nothing to be done to stop the tears.

'We'll see,' he replied. Then, he kissed her cheek and was gone.

Fee waited for the familiar, cold sense of abandonment. Instead, while there was some sorrow and a scattering of doubts, she experienced a sudden surge of optimism. Why not work with Lea in India? Why not take up Walt's offer to travel to the now not so Wild West? Why not spend time on her newfound friendships with Anna and Alan and Shona and Jean? She had Claire's baby to welcome, Rita Mason to evade and Percy and the twins to enjoy.

She had finally come to understand that it was time to be her own woman – after that, anything might be possible – even love that didn't harm.

It might not add up to a conventional happy ever after, Fee told herself, smiling, but it wasn't bad for a new beginning.